The MYSTERY OF THE STRANGE PIPER

PRAISE FOR *THE GHOST OF HELEN ADDISON*

'A great talent is announced. A fascinating, original and beguiling detective is born.'

Hugh MacDonald, *The Herald*

'A hugely enjoyable murder mystery with a sprinkling of the supernatural, *Helen Addison* is Tartan Noir with a difference.'

Daily Record

'Charles McGarry has opted for the road less travelled. His central character, Leo Moran, is a private detective with a passion for fine food and wine ... I enjoyed meeting him after a slew of novels featuring jaded cops and hard-bitten private investigators.'

The Scotsman

'McGarry explores evil, faith and human nature by telling a gripping murder mystery concerned with gender politics, class and misogyny. This debut features richly drawn characters and a potent atmosphere of dread, marking McGarry out as one to watch.'

Real Crime Magazine

'Leo Moran is a Glaswegian private eye who is unlike any you'll have met before, which is in itself a reason for cheer. Charles E. McGarry has presented a new voice to Scottish crime fiction, and a memorable character to match.'

Alistair Braidwood

'My pick of the year for sheer entertainment value and spectacular leftfieldness, Charles E. McGarry's *The Ghost of Helen Addison* combines three of my ruling passions: Scotland, the supernatural and Golden Age crime fiction. Leo Moran is refreshingly different from the usual crop of hardboiled, hardbitten detectives operating in an urban Scottish environment. The style is distinct, harking back to the past, with a strain of otherworldliness which is very Scots, strangely familiar and comforting.'

Donna Heddle, *The Bottle Imp*

PRAISE FOR *THE SHADOW OF THE BLACK EARL*

'Moran is a new and unique addition to the Scots crime fiction heroes roster. Like its predecessor, this is very well written and always thrilling.'

Daily Record

'A riveting, gothic-esque novel that delights in grabbing you by the hand and pulling you along all its twists and turns.'

Dundee Courier

'[An] enchanting novel ... The fast-paced moments of realisation and revelation are mixed with peaceful walks through the landscape and personal encounters with characters in their natural habitats. Although it can be unnerving, this balance gives the book a stillness not often seen in the world of Scottish crime fiction.'

Róise Nic an Bheatha, *The Bottle Imp*

'To say this is a Glaswegian gumshoe with a difference is ridiculous understatement writ large. Quite simply, you will never have met a character like Leo Moran. A character as ineffaceable and distinct as him deserves a long literary life, and that goes doubly for Charles E. McGarry.'

Alistair Braidwood

'Charles E. McGarry has sent his Leo Moran, private detective and seer of visions, deep into the glorious Galloway countryside in his brilliantly quirky new novel. Both Galloway and the book deserve a wider audience.'

Daily Mail

'The author manages to create characters that are refreshingly different while effortlessly weaving Scottish history into this book, making for an intriguing narrative.'

Scottish Field

'Tartan Noir lover or not, you'll enjoy this book.'

Westender

A NOTE ON THE AUTHOR

Charles E. McGarry studied History and Politics at the University of Glasgow, graduating in 1994. He has lived in London and Edinburgh, and in 2012 he co-wrote *The Road to Lisbon* with Martin Greig. He lives in Glasgow where he was born and bred, and works in the media industry. He has written three Leo Moran murder mysteries: *The Ghost of Helen Addison*, *The Shadow of the Black Earl* and *The Mystery of the Strange Piper.*

The MYSTERY OF THE STRANGE PIPER

THE THIRD LEO MORAN MURDER MYSTERY

CHARLES E. MCGARRY

BACKPAGE

First published in Great Britain in 2021.
This edition published 2021 by
BACKPAGE

www.backpagepress.co.uk/press
@BackPagePress

ISBN: 9781909430464
eBook ISBN: 9781909430471

www.charlesemcgarry.com

A catalogue record for this book is available on request from the British Library.

Typeset by BackPage
Cover design by Lídia Puccetti (www.lidiapuccetti.com)
Printed in Great Britain by Clays Limited

To Robert, Mark, Catherine, Julie and Bill

I will pour out of my Spirit on all flesh
And your sons and your daughters shall prophesy
And your young men shall see visions
And your old men shall dream dreams.

ACTS 2:17

Prologue: 1973

THE Mark VI 1956 Humber Hawk traverses the north of the broiling city. It is the Moran family's pride and joy, its waxed two-tone paint job still glorious in turquoise and cream. It has been solemnly serviced by Leo's father in honour of the trip, in spite of the modest distance to the ferry terminal. It was quite a posh saloon in its day, but its age hints to the Morans' straitened finances. And anyway, it was originally gifted to them, second-hand, as was the forthcoming use of the holiday room-and-kitchen in Kilmichael on the Isle of Sonna. It has been three years since they have enjoyed a proper vacation.

They pass a derelict Art Deco cinema, then a white roughcast garage, Valvoline flags hanging limply in the still air. As they enter the tunnel, Leo observes a ritual that has sprung up among Glasgow children to hold your breath until you reach the other end. Then the new motorway. He gazes at the Luma Lightbulb Factory, a masterpiece of Streamline Moderne. Pylons shimmer molten silver, the concrete overpasses are blindingly white, a petrol haze hovers over the scalding asphalt. A mechanical mastodon truffles the garbage at a huge refuse plant. It is some kind of tractor, oversized yet dwarfed by the ever-burgeoning mountain of trash it vainly endeavours to harvest. The place exhales a sour halitosis which marries the sewage stink the Clyde dredger has thrown up, the cloying fusion doubly putrefied by the evil heat. Lorries – Blue Circle Cement, Burmah Oil, 7-Up, National Freight Corporation – grumpily eruct black diesel fumes from the inside lane. In the middle distance, a shiny freighter screams as it cruises towards the Abbotsinch runway in gleaming slow-mo. A glimpse of the control tower of the old airport which is abandoned and grassy now, the modernist terminal with its elegant parabola too small to cope with the 1960s airline boom.

Leo looks at the occupants of other vehicles and guesses their stories. The M8's pleasure-seekers all long for that first glimpse of the Firth of Clyde. They long for the open sky and the salt air, and to leave behind the gigantic structures: the granary, warehouses and whisky bonds, the shipyard cranes and tower blocks. They long for the seaboard, for that one resort with its evocative name to which a past generation of their family laid claim. The optimism of the Beatles decade has fast dimmed, and they want to briefly replace the decimalised uncertainty of these new times with seaside traditions and quaint pursuits. They long for Dunoon, Gourock, Brodick, Kilmichael or Millport. For Largs, Fairlie, Saltcoats, Ardrossan, Troon or Girvan. The decaying grandeur of these Victorian retreats, where Somme veterans in smart blazers sit by manicured lawns. They saw hell upon this earth, these men, demons coming up from the stinking ground. Lest we forget – if only they could forget. Their backdrop is buildings peeling seashell pink or baby blue. They stare beyond the white railings at the perpetual, cathartic waves, trying not to let the sinister black submarines spoil the view. Boy racers, handsome guys in Ford Escorts and Capris, vie for the fast lane as they will later vie for the fast girls at seaside milk bars and discotheques, institutions Leo by now feared he would not graduate to. Already he could tell that females didn't fancy him and he simply didn't *get* the pop music that blared at the candy floss stands and amusement arcades whenever the Morans went on a day trip. Johnny Thunder rides the highway on his Bonneville T120. RAF goggles, a vertical tricolour stripe on black leather, straggly hair swirling in the sunlight – the last gunslinger before the helmet law kicks in. He seeks only the next horizon and the prayer of a broken-hearted girl who lives in some crippled town. He coasts alongside for a moment, magnificent on his two-wheel stallion, the manifold barking and crackling. Then he flips the transmission and opens up the throttle, leaning gracefully to bank and weave his machine through the growling traffic as the twin pistons rip and sing.

A horseshoe-moustachioed dad in a Mexico Brown Rover P6 aims to rekindle the passion on Sonna. The mum snaps at the three needling offspring in the back. The dad winds down the window to swap fag fug with the pollution, sweat pooling his nylon shirt. An era of faith in these abrasive synthetics: Terylene and Orlon, polychloroprene and polytetrafluoroethylene, dichlorodiphenyltrichloroethane and benzoyl peroxide, methamphetamine and phenobarbital. Later that summer, a hundred miles to the south, fifty other holidaymakers will be incinerated when a building clad in Galbestos and polymethyl methacrylate catches fire.

Another car hauls itself abreast with the Humber. It contains no passengers. The male driver's jaw is set in stone as he observes the road ahead. Something about him particularly piques Leo's interest. Suddenly the man, as though sensing he is being watched, turns and regards Leo. His closed face betrays no emotion, his eyes are obscured by dark sunglasses; he is like a fly. And as Leo's gaze is drawn into those two black plastic pools, a sense of horror swells within his viscera, then rises like bile. Then the man looks ahead again and breaks the spell. He plunges the clutch and throws the stick into a lower gear, then accelerates away. Leo is left with the vestige of the feeling, as though he has tuned into the man's cold appetite for mayhem and evil. But the feeling – the towering significance of which he had not guessed – and the memory of it, would soon fade into the ether.

Arrival

THE Humber Hawk rolled onto the ferry, the soft double thump as the ramp took the weight unmooring within Leo some nebulous sensation from four decades ago. The motor car was still going strong, its cherished paint job still in good trim. Leo considered his ugly, burnt hands which gripped the wheel. After his accident he had initially worn gloves to conceal them, but at university he had grown weary of the jibes ('The Undertaker', 'The Boston Strangler', 'Alvin Stardust', etcetera) invented by one of his contemporaries, Marcus Troughton. Therefore, one evening in the students' union bar, when Troughton was being particularly pitiless, Leo, to sicken the fellow, had with great theatricality peeled off and then literally thrown down the gauntlets, and from thenceforth displayed his hands in all their grisly glory. It was extraordinary to think that he was about to meet Troughton again after all these years.

Leo disembarked from his car and climbed the narrow metal stairways to the top deck. The crossing took approximately half an hour, and he wanted to enjoy the prospect of the island as the vessel neared it. Troughton was a native of Sonna, Leo recalled, and he remembered him as coming from a moneyed background, with a boarding-school education and a posh anglicised accent. According to his first communication, he was, like Leo, unmarried, and now proprietor and editor of some monthly magazine, *The Belmartine Repository*. Leo pulled the letter from a jacket pocket and re-read it for the twelfth time. Apparently, Troughton was probing several mysterious deaths which had occurred on and off the south of the island over the last twenty or so years. Remembering his fellow alumnus' alleged crime-solving talents, not least the visions he experienced which helped him to solve cases, Troughton had resolved to part the curtain of the decades and get in touch, requesting that Leo take up the role of lead investigative journalist. He would put him up at his house and give him a fair cut of the resultant editions' profits. Leo wasn't interested in, and indeed didn't require, any remuneration; the simple fact was that duty called, albeit from the unlikeliest of sources. Also, he was curious to meet Troughton after all this time, and, lacking any amusement of late, was heartened by the promise of some new work to get his teeth into.

The craft's name *MV Venus* and her home port of Glasgow were proudly displayed on the life belts. Boats, including the ferry's counterpart, *MV Mercury*, coming in the opposite direction looked majestic with their masthead flags and splendid liveries. Leo listened to the rapid throb of the diesel engines and the churn as the bow cut the waves, and felt the thrill that comes with crossing a body of water, the anticipation of stepping onto a different, confined, insular world. He could see the fine buildings of Kilmichael, splayed around the entire bay, now heave into view, with the jagged profile of the distant Isle of Erran above. A seabird flew low as it scanned the sun-kissed surface. He looked to starboard, and recalled an evocative line from a traditional song: *The great black hills, like sleeping kings, sit grand round Kilmichael Bay*. Leo and Troughton had been part of the same gang at the University of Glasgow, both studying Arts. They had lost touch after the former's mental breakdown immediately after their final examinations. Leo always suspected that Troughton's peevishness stemmed from the fact that they had both romanced the same girl, Maddi. She had become Leo's Juliet, yet sadly their relationship had not survived his descent into madness. The agony still resounded to the extent that when Leo had written back to Troughton assenting to his proposal, it was on the strict proviso that the subject of Maddi never be broached.

Upon his arrival at Kilmichael, Leo parked the Humber near to the war memorial, an august cenotaph topped with a bronze angel defiantly holding a cross aloft, where he had arranged to meet Troughton. He got out of the car and admired the esplanade, which was reminiscent of resorts on the English South Coast and which he vaguely remembered from the summer of 1973. Neatly shorn lawns and putting greens were lined with palm trees and bordered by floral beds and rockeries. The benches and railings were of decorative ironwork, as were the drooping lamp standards, between which were draped strings of different-coloured fairy lights. Holidaymaking families strolled by the winter gardens, an impressive fountain, quaint wooden rain shelters and painted kiosks selling ice cream or seafood. Leo inhaled contentedly as he felt the sun on his face, listened to the call of the gulls and detected the genial scent of candy floss ingratiating itself with the salt air. However, time wore on and there was no sighting of Troughton, so his mood soured. Could his prospective host already have passed Leo by, the two men not recognising the middle-aged versions of each other? No, Troughton would surely have enquired with him to make certain, regardless of the ravages of the years. Leo then endured a moment of panic as he wondered if he had got the wrong day, but when he produced Troughton's final communication it confirmed that he was indeed standing at the right place at the right time. He withdrew his phone and entered the mobile number on the letterhead, but when he pressed CALL the line was dead. As a man who abhorred tardiness, he was now feeling distinctly displeased, as well as perturbed.

'Damn and blast!' he exclaimed.

'Everything all right, sir?'

Leo turned to see a police sergeant, who was carrying a stack of traffic cones towards a cruiser which was parked nose to tail with the Humber. A bored-looking, blonde-haired female officer sat in the passenger seat.

'Forgive me, Sergeant; I'm supposed to be meeting someone here and following him to his house, where I am to be residing for a while. But there's no sign of him and his phone is dead. Could you please direct me to the Palmery, Belmartine?'

'Belmartine is really just a continuation of Kilmichael town,' said the man, placing the cones on the ground and gesturing towards one extremity of the bay. 'You follow the shore road and once you round the headland at Battery it's about a mile and a half to the south. The Palmery is on your right just after Belmartine Bay.'

'Thank you, Sergeant. Permit me to introduce myself – Leo Moran.'

'Ronnie MacKellar,' said the copper, accepting Leo's proffered hand. MacKellar was aged in his middle thirties, a lean man with an open, handsome face and cropped, receding brown hair. He had an easy manner and amusement twinkled in his small hazel eyes. 'So, you'll be staying with Marcus Troughton?'

'Indeed.'

'Lucky you! That fella keeps me in a job.'

'I don't know him at all well.'

'Just last week he chased off a TV Licensing officer with a pike. Denied it, of course. All the best to you!' said MacKellar with a wink as he bent down to pick up the cones.

Leo climbed back into the Humber, his sense of foreboding increased by the police sergeant's tale. He wondered what, exactly, he was getting himself into.

Leo motored around the grand bay, its tall nineteenth-century apartment buildings and hotels giving way to fine stone-built villas with pretty painted metal lacework. Past the headland, towards Belmartine, the shore was furnished with red rock and the abodes became even more magnificent, many set within leafy grounds garnished with the odd profusion of palm trees or mountain of rhododendron or flowering hydrangea. He came to Belmartine Bay, a stately, sedate little inlet with a red GPO telephone box and a honey-stone church perched on a wooded promontory. The quay there was a relic of when paddle steamers would convey wealthy Victorian commuters to their offices in Glasgow. Leo decelerated, and, just as Sergeant MacKellar had described, found the entrance to the Palmery not far beyond this bay, the name carved into the stone gateposts. Leo swung the Humber up the drive, which was bordered by broad-leafed trees and masses of rhododendron. The bitumen ellipsed at the top to circumnavigate a giant maple. Leo parked in front of the house, a grey mid-nineteenth century building in the Scottish Baronial style. The edifice had a faintly jaunty air, replete with decorative flourishes such as corbelled pointed turrets and parapets. He climbed out of the car and looked towards the gardens to his left. Beyond the lawns, on which were palm trees, a Korean fir and a towering monkey puzzle, was an expanse of lush shrubbery, much of it ablaze with a richly varied riot of blossom. The glass roof of a Victorian hothouse protruded from amid this vegetation, and the entire grounds were enclosed by a tall perimeter of mature sycamore and lime and a high stone wall, to the rear of which the terrain rose to pastures and woodlands.

Despite the pleasant surroundings, Leo's sense of trepidation was about to become full blown. He heard a descending sizzling sound accompanied by a voice from above shouting: 'Look out!' He instinctively leapt back, and avoided a firecracker which landed and erupted on the ground not two yards from him.

'Great Scott!' exclaimed Leo. Outraged, he looked upwards to see a figure at an ashlar-bracketed balcony beneath a second-floor window. It was wearing a fencing mask – an alarming sight – and motorcycle leathers.

'Sorry – I thought you were Troughton,' it said.

After taking a moment to compose himself, Leo stepped towards the front door and pushed the bell button, which was set within an ornate brass rendering of a glum toad's face. He waited, pushed it again, and then peered through the bay window to his left, but this side of the house was in shadow and he couldn't discern any life within. He tried the door and found that it opened heavily, and called up the vestibule – a dingy corridor that had seen better days – but no one responded. He entered, passing doors to different rooms, and reached a hall with an iron-balustraded staircase on its far side which led to a mezzanine above. The chamber was furnished with substantial antiques, including a superb grandfather clock by John Craig of Glasgow. Leo took a moment to admire two large paintings near the foot of the stairs: *Eurydice Recumbent with Lilies* and *Psyche in the Grove* by Arthur Hughes, one of the pre-Raphaelite Brotherhood. He was struck by the grandeur of the place, but also by an ambience of clutter and decay; it looked as though it needed cleaned and redecorated. Suddenly, a firework arced through the space and glanced off the top of the finely carved newel post. It fizzed angrily by an urn filled with ferns before the inevitable bang. The thrower – a different one, a rangy figure dressed in a leather gabardine, a First World War German coal scuttle helmet and a gas mask – appeared at the mezzanine, backlit by multi-coloured rays which flowed through an exquisite stained-glass window depicting Christ Resplendent. He took off his helmet, unpeeled his mask and began descending the stairs. Leo recognised him as Marcus Troughton.

'Moran! Good to see you,' he said. 'Do forgive the banger – I thought you were Nicky. He's here to join us for dinner.'

He approached Leo and made to shake his hand when a bottle rocket screeched down from above, narrowly missing Hughes' *Psyche*, scoring the faded William Morris wallpaper and then expending its remaining gunpowder in a spasmodic fit by a hat stand.

'Nicky you oaf! I am unmasked – obey the rules of the game,' yelled Troughton. 'Never fire upon an unmasked man!'

'Hello, Troughton. I thought you were supposed to meet me off the ferry?' said Leo, his voice betraying his irritation. 'You weren't there so I rang you, but the phone was dead.'

'Sorry old fellow, but the car's broken down and my mobile's out of credit, so I just switched it off. Must top it up. If only the thing wasn't so damnably confounding.'

'But you can still receive calls even if you don't have any credit.'

'There's a thought. Anyway, I knew a clever detective such as yourself would find your way here with ease. And behold: here you stand! You have passed your first test.' Leo didn't return Troughton's amicable grin. 'Don't be grumpy, old chap. After all, you could have rung the landline.'

'You didn't put your landline number in your letterhead.'

'Haven't you heard of Directory Enquiries? Oh dear, perhaps your problem-solving skills aren't all that remarkable after all.'

Nicky, who had also taken off his mask came down the stairs to join them. He was aged around forty, of unimpressive stature and rather overweight. He had thick dark hair and a large flat face, with moon eyes and womanly ruby lips.

Leo noticed that Nicky was appraising him, brazenly inspecting him from head to foot.

'How do you do? Leo Moran.'

'Nicky Barrett. How was your crossing?'

'My crossing was smooth; my landfall has been somewhat choppier,' replied Leo, perceiving the indifferent tone in which the man had asked his question. He also noted that, at variance with the limp handshake, thin voice and overall soft-boiled impression, Nicky's palm was unexpectedly rough – that of a sailor, perhaps.

Troughton was busying himself with a decanter at a console table and brought filled glasses for his guests, then fetched one for himself.

'Your comradely arrival is as good an excuse as any for sherry, Moran. Here's to you,' he said, raising his glass and emptying it in a single draught.

After Troughton had downed another two sherries, he helped Leo carry in his considerable luggage from the Humber. Nicky had muttered something about catching the horse racing and skulked off to wherever the television set was located, speaking rudely to his turf accountant on his mobile.

'It's been a long time, Moran,' observed Troughton as they climbed the stairs.

'Indeed.'

'Have you been to the island before?'

'Once, during the summer of 1973. We borrowed a flat in Kilmichael, which belonged to a relative. Here's a blast from the past for you, Troughton: do you remember Stephanie – Stephanie Mitchell? She was one of our gang at university.'

'Why, of course I remember her!'

'Well, she and I are still very much in touch,' said Leo. 'Purely platonically, I can assure you,' he added in response to Troughton's ribald wink. 'Anyway, I telephoned her after you wrote to me. She was intrigued that you had been in communication after all these years, and insisted that I inform you that she was enquiring as to your good health.'

Troughton seemed slightly thrilled by this information. 'Stephanie Mitchell indeed!'

'She's a fiscal now.'

'A fiscal, eh! What a clever wee thing ... and a fetching little filly, I seem to recall. Do pass on my regards to her.'

Troughton showed Leo to his quarters on the first floor and left him to unpack and freshen up. It was a threadbare room, with a forsaken-looking leather sofa beside a pile of jumble, but it was pleasant enough and passably clean, and had a good view south over the grounds. The quaint brass terminal of a speaking tube was positioned on the wall by the bed. The masculine bedchamber was counterpoised by its feminine en suite, which contained a clunky pull-chain cistern, and a Victorian sink and bath painted with wildflowers.

Once he was ready, Leo went downstairs, following the odour of cooking. In the hall, he browsed Troughton's record collection – which consisted of numerous recordings of Johannes Brahms, to the exclusion of every other composer who had ever drawn breath. He took a basement corridor towards the rear of the house, noticing the preponderance of worn patterned linoleum and various framed botanical and zoological colour plates, and also display cases containing the little corpses of exotic insects, chiefly butterflies and moths. Leo liked the aesthetic of the Palmery, yet couldn't help but disapprove of its jadedness and chaos – which he now feared reflected the personality of its sole inhabitant – and contrast it with the harmonious order of his own abode in Glasgow.

The kitchen had a sloping ceiling from which hung ancient copperware. The evening sun slanted in through windows on the far wall which were above hobs and deep sinks, the light alchemised lime-yellow by the lush tree leafage outside. Troughton was busy chopping amid a hubbub of gushing taps, bubbling pots and sizzling pans. A confusion of ingredients and utensils were splayed across work surfaces as the chef got rapidly sozzled, having evidently already demolished half a bottle of Château La Clare.

'I see you are a devotee of Brahms,' said Leo. 'And, it would seem, only Brahms.'

'When a man has Brahms, what more does he need? I keep my records and gramophone in the hall, as the acoustics there are first-class.'

'The food smells marvellous, Troughton. May I be of any assistance?'

'Merely top me up, old boy,' said the host, gesturing to the bottle before casting some scallops into a pan of hot butter with a flourish. 'I always drink claret while cooking as it stimulates one's artistic juices. And do help yourself; that was a top year for the Médoc. Or perhaps you would prefer a more conventional apéritif to unlock your palate.'

Troughton still possessed the same manic energy Leo remembered from their student days. His features were also little changed: laughing eyes set beneath the slightly pronounced ridge of his brow. A longish face with a high forehead, but still enough hair – blondish although darker than it had been, with its familiar red tinge – to be swept into his trademark side parting. His voice was commanding but, Leo recalled, its authority could be exploited within an instant to convey withering rage, sarcasm or melodrama.

'Your letter provided scant detail,' said Leo, after refreshing Troughton's glass and fixing himself a Campari and soda.

'Precisely why Nicky is here, to help me fill you in over dinner. He is my sometime drinking partner and has a keen interest in the mysterious deaths ... or rather one of them.'

'Tell me a little about your magazine enterprise.'

'I publish it more to satisfy a sense of duty to the island than anything else. And anyway, I have a private income,' replied Troughton loftily. 'It has been running for two or three years now. I revived the title; *The Belmartine Repository* was an Edwardian journal in these parts. It comes out every month, and I own, edit and write for it; all the other content is submitted. I have created an office space upstairs which you shall have the run of during your time here. As for the mysterious deaths, I haven't published anything about them yet although I have undertaken preliminary investigations. They started with a spate during the summer of 1989; I should mention that I wasn't resident on the island at that time and have little personal recollection of those ones. I haven't found any records of incidents of note prior to then. The police aren't interested; they are satisfied with the original recordings of accidental death or suicide.'

'And where do I fit in?'

'I wish you to take the lead role, as a kind of roving investigator. You possess this second sight thingy and perhaps studying the case will evoke some of your celebrated visions. Also, as editor I am kept far too busy here at base. And, to be perfectly frank, if you do the probing it has the added advantage of my not alienating the locals; good relationships are crucial to the long-term success of *The Repository*. Now, be a good chap and carry this tureen through to the dining room. I shall bang the gong and rouse old Nicholas.'

The Boy Who Fell

THE dining room possessed several tall windows, and the walls were clad in varnished wood panelling; higher up, emerald lining paper peeled in places. The dining table, which sat upon a worn Wilton carpet, was constructed of solid mahogany, standing on finely turned and carved inverted tulip legs with companion chairs. Troughton had lit candles that were ensconced in silver candlesticks which, along with the elegant cutlery, Leo guessed were by James Ker, the eighteenth-century Edinburgh silversmith. He was a little dismayed that Troughton omitted to say Grace, but reflected inwardly that it was his house in which to follow or omit whichever customs he so pleased. Leo was also irked that Nicky hadn't dressed for dinner; it would become apparent as he peppered the meal with vulgar allusions to his prosperity that certainly he could afford the proper duds. At least Troughton had made some effort, although his red velvet jacket was a touch shabby and clashed with his denim jeans, and also, he had foregone a necktie, content to let his chest hair pour over his opened shirt collar. The meal was of admirable quality, considering the chef's keen commitment to drunkenness. There was an appetiser of seared scallops, then homemade cock-a-leekie soup, locally caught poached turbot, game pie – the filling was Sonna hare, marinated in port – served with waxy new potatoes, and then '*pêches melba*' announced by Troughton in a sotto

French accent. He kept leaping to his feet and disappearing to the kitchen to check on or fetch the next course, or to the cellar to bring up more wine.

'So, this second sight you possess, how does it manifest itself?' enquired Nicky during the hors d'œuvre, evidently keen to get down to business.

'I see visions, when my mind is in an unconscious or semi-conscious state: when I am dreaming, or even just daydreaming or during contemplation. Occasionally they visit when I am entirely alert. The vision can be of a past event or of one happening in the now, or even in the future. Often the same one recurs, perhaps with different elements or from a different perspective. They can be oblique or symbolic.'

'And with our cases?'

'Nothing, so far. Troughton said you would help fill me in on the detail.'

'First, I shall provide you with the high level,' declared the host as he refilled the gentlemen's fine crystal goblets with an excellent Montrachet. 'There is a considerable peninsula which projects from the bottom of Sonna, which is known simply as "the south end". A stretch of its inner coast is populated by a village called Ardcaden Bay. I should state at the outset that many folk, myself included, perceive a peculiar atmosphere to the south end, as though the very land emits a strange energy. Anyway, this is the scene for all our dramas, which began during the summer of 1989. First, a scuba diver from Aberdeen did not return from his exploration over the ridge – the ridge is where the shallow tidal bay of Ardcaden falls away into the depths of the firth. This man was an expert, with many hours including deep-water commercial diving in the North Sea behind him. He was super-fit, safety-first and the conditions were perfect. When his drowned body was located his equipment was found to be functional, and the post-mortem examination couldn't detect anything of note – no jellyfish sting or coronary arrest. A couple of weeks later, an experienced motorcyclist, an Italian fellow doing a solo tour of Scotland, was killed when his machine smashed into a metal barrier at the bend in the road just prior to where it enters Ardcaden Bay village. It was broad daylight and he was not drunk.'

'Perhaps there was diesel or a pothole on the road,' suggested Leo.

'There was not,' replied Troughton. 'And here's the thing: he *accelerated* as he went into the bend.'

'Perhaps it was a mechanical fault. Or perhaps he turned the throttle accidentally.'

'All highly unlikely.'

'Perhaps he had a death wish.'

'That was looked into; apparently he was an easy-going, happy and thoroughly sensible man. Later that tragic summer came the death of Andy Lamb, an eighteen-year-old who one night fell from a height in the hills which dominate the peninsula.'

'More on him soon,' chimed in Nicky.

'In the intervening years we have endured the deaths of two Ayrshire men who had gone sea fishing; their boat plunged to the bottom of the drink off the south of the island in fair weather on a calm sea. Some blamed a surfacing submarine capsizing them – the men were within the submarine training area, but both the Royal Navy and the US Navy strenuously denied having a vessel in these waters at that time.'

'Could a large marine creature have struck the boat and caused it to sink?' interjected Leo.

'It is just possible, but such events are extremely rare,' responded Nicky.

'Then there was poor Miss Green, a woman from

Glasgow in her forties found hanged from a tree in the woods behind Ardcaden Bay,' continued Troughton. 'The pathologist found death had been caused by asphyxiation, corresponding with hanging. The police ruled out foul play and a verdict of suicide was recorded. However, Miss Green was reputedly a very level-headed person who had no record of mental illness, and there was no recent tragedy or upset in her personal life. Then there came the end of Farmer McGrouther's twenty-year-old son, found impaled on agricultural machinery; their farm was the first one you come to on the Lagg Road, which is a single tracker that accesses parts of the south end. It was deemed to be a freak accident, but to my mind the police struggled to provide a reasonable explanation as to how it had occurred. The McGrouther family were heartbroken so gave up their tenancy and left for a new life somewhere in Canada. I haven't been able to trace them there, I'm afraid. Lastly, three years ago a lone English rambler by the name of Geoffrey Willett dropped dead near the lighthouse at the island's southern tip. He was aged thirty-five with no history of heart problems or any other illness. The pathologist found no apparent reason for his demise, and ruled it "Sudden Adult Death Syndrome".'

'But Troughton, these deaths don't sound at all connected. I'm not even sure that they sound all that mysterious.'

'Perhaps. Perhaps not. Nonetheless a legend grew about the south end being cursed, and any investigative journalism we publish about the deaths will be of wide interest.'

Nicky took over, adopting a pompous tone: 'Initially, you are to focus mainly on the Lamb case. And let me make my position clear: I believe it to be unconnected to the other deaths, which unlike Troughton I have no interest in. I believe that Andy Lamb was murdered and I know who the murderer is. Troughton isn't convinced by my claims, however neither does he dismiss them and furthermore I have agreed to bankroll the cost of publication of the issues of *The Repository* which deal with *all* of the deaths on the proviso that you investigate Andy's first, and promise to do so while being mindful of my theories.'

Leo was a little taken aback by this turn in proceedings, but simply remarked: 'All right. I suppose I've got to start somewhere, so it might as well be with that fatality.'

'Like Troughton, I am an islander, originally a native of Ardcaden Bay,' continued Nicky. 'My best friend during every childhood summer was Andy, whose family, like several others, would come down to the village from Glasgow. There was a whole gang of us teenagers who used to pal about every holiday. A half mile north-east of the village is a prehistoric henge, standing stones set within woodland, and on the fateful night a dozen of us had been sitting around a bonfire there, drinking and passing a few joints. For a bit of a lark and in an effort to scare ourselves we tried out a summoning invocation. You see, there was a daft old legend about a demon piper who dwelled under the hill behind the village, waiting to be called forth. If you encountered him it would spell your doom. Obviously we didn't actually expect anything to happen, but we thought it would be worth a dare whereby after the invocation the loser of a draw, who turned out to be Andy, had to go to the top of the hill, which is called the Cathair, and back. For added spice, he would have to go via the ruins of Saint Caden's Chapel, which was said to be haunted by ghostly monks.'

'Whose idea was all this tomfoolery?' enquired Leo.

'I can't recall precisely,' mumbled Nicky, examining the Spode china dish on the table in front of him. 'I suspect it was a joint idea, really. Anyway, three of the gang could drive and had cars parked on the Lagg Road near to the stone circle. So we headed up that narrow road to where it ends. We all got out and watched Andy make his way up the path towards the chapel. He would have to go some way beyond that over some rough terrain before he arrived at the back of the Cathair. But for some reason he fell from a height before he even reached the hill and bashed his head open on a boulder. After waiting for what seemed like an age, a girl called Janey Gribben followed Andy up as she had become worried about him. But she couldn't find him.'

'Did everyone else stay at the cars?' asked Leo.

'Yes. When Janey came back, she seemed out of sorts, but everyone assumed Andy had got fed up and gone home, over the Cathair. The next day it became clear he hadn't returned home. The police were called and organised a search. They found Andy's body late that very morning. The investigation concluded that the death was a tragic accident.'

Nicky stopped speaking and tried to compose himself.

'My dear fellow, please, do take your time,' said Leo gently.

'I'm all right now,' said Nicky, after taking a long draught of wine. 'Everyone felt Andy's loss acutely, myself more than most. We were the same age and he was a great guy and in some ways my life would never be the same after he died; I'd give a million quid to have my mucker back. But of course, *everyone* loved him. Apart from one person – one Vincent Comiskey. You must understand: it never made sense that Andy was at the top of that height – it was a detour from what should have been his trajectory of travel towards the Cathair. Comiskey must have barred his path, frightening him into running that way. I believe he cast Andy over the edge. Comiskey was a wild and cruel fellow. He belonged to a heavy Glasgow family, and caused all sorts of bother whenever he came to Ardcaden. That summer, his behaviour was so wayward that we all eventually ostracised him. Almost a year ago he moved to the island, having set up a microbrewery business. He lives alone, and his solitary, frugal lifestyle seems that of someone with a guilty conscience. Also, I saw him where Andy's body was found – I think he was at prayer. I believe he has come to live near to the scene of his greatest crime, in order to come to terms with it. After I saw him there I tried to trace others who were present that night. I managed to contact Janey after she joined social media – she has a married surname now so she wasn't easy to track down. Anyway, I visited her in Glasgow – just zoomed right the hell up the Clyde in my powerboat – and asked her a few questions. She told me that she had been keeping a secret all these years: that when we were at the standing stones, she saw Comiskey in the firelight, spying on us from the trees. He would have heard us discussing the dare and drawing lots. I mean, what on earth was he doing there *but* to create harm, which is what he had been doing all that summer?'

Leo swilled his wine for a spell, studying the way the candlelight played upon it. Then he said, 'But to commit murder ... it seems extreme.'

'Well, now we come to another protagonist in this sorry tale: the *femme fatale*. The beautiful Amy Agumanu. She was mixed race – which back then seemed exotic to everyone – and really artistic and all the lads idolised her. She was a regular holidaymaker from the mainland and she too has now moved to Sonna – a couple of years ago. She's a talented painter and I hire her services quite often to do work on my yacht and my other boats. In the summer of '89 Andy was involved in a holiday romance with her. And, what's more, Comiskey was a rival for Amy's affections and was obviously jealous. She admitted to me recently what everyone had always guessed: that back in the day she would meet Comiskey in secret, which would have intensified his jealousy and sense of entitlement when he saw her with Andy.'

'You said you had all been drinking and smoking pot at the henge,' said Leo. 'So presumably Andy Lamb was inebriated. Couldn't he simply have become disorientated and fallen by accident?'

'Andy could handle his intakes. He was as sure-footed as a mountain goat, and he wouldn't have lost his way.'

'But it was night-time. Did he have a torch?'

'No.'

'What were the light conditions like?'

'It was a northern summer's short night – it doesn't get quite fully dark. Also, the sky was clear and there was bright moonlight.'

'What was the date and time?'

'August the tenth. It was a Thursday. We headed up the Lagg Road at some time after eleven.'

'Therefore, his anniversary is in a few days,' observed Leo.

'And therefore, the perfect juncture at which to request your assistance,' interjected Troughton.

'Indeed,' said Leo, 'as it often helps to investigate a cold case at the same time of year as the incident occurred. Helps jog people's memories and whatnot.'

'Janey confessing that she saw Comiskey spying on us confirmed what I have always suspected,' said Nicky. 'Even back then I told the cops I would bet my life that he was responsible.'

'Did the police speak with Vincent Comiskey in 1989?'

'Yes, and he convinced them that he was at home all evening, which is now proven as a lie by Janey's new testimony. After overhearing our plans, he could have made his way on foot overland while we looped round in the cars, and lain in wait for Andy.'

'Have you informed the police of Janey's recent revelation?'

'Yes. I approached one Sergeant Ronnie MacKellar in Kilmichael, but he's not interested. Now, there is another dark chapter to all of this. After Comiskey returned to Glasgow following Andy's death, it emerged that the sick bastard had raped a half-witted village lassie called Elizabeth Meiklejohn that summer. She was a bit younger than us; nowadays she lives in Kilmichael with her parents. Comiskey was aged eighteen back then, and legally fully responsible for his actions. Of course, he never came back to Sonna, the coward. Until now. Perhaps he thought that after all this time folk would have forgotten what he did, but we haven't. Andy had a kid brother, Johnathon, who moved from the mainland to Ardcaden Bay a number of years back – he's much younger than us, so he wasn't there that night, but I reckon he buys my theory and he is keen to see justice done. Not to mention Norris Meiklejohn, Elizabeth's father.'

'I have photocopies of numerous local newspaper reports relating to all these deaths, and other files and photographs for you to peruse at your convenience,' said Troughton.

'Capital,' said Leo. 'As for tonight, I'd like to obtain a map, one I can carry around with me. I want to have marked where all these deaths occurred, and also where the people you have mentioned presently live on the island.'

'Then, when we are finished our repast, we shall repair to the drawing room and prepare one,' declared Troughton.

At dinner's conclusion, Troughton used a brass snuffer to extinguish the candles, slurring his words slightly as he declared that the clearing and washing of the dishes could wait until morning. He led his guests across the vestibule and into the drawing room, which was the chamber Leo had tried to peer into through the bay window upon his arrival. Troughton switched on some table lamps to illuminate the surroundings. It was a fine room with good, if flaking, cornice work and an elaborate art nouveau embroidery behind glass above an imposing fireplace of carved dark wood. A work by Sir James Guthrie, one of the Glasgow Boys, adorned a wall, while a dusty taxidermy cabinet, containing stuffed exotic birds which Leo found rather ghastly, filled another.

Troughton busied himself at a drinks tantalus; all three men opted for the cognac decanter and then lit some fine Cuban cigars which Nicky had brought. Nicky slumped in a bergère chair and Leo and Troughton perched themselves on a leather couch, examining an Ordinance Survey map of the island which the host had produced and spread upon a Queen Anne walnut table. Troughton commentated as he used a pencil to plot the map with the loci of where all the mysterious deaths had occurred. Then Nicky leaned over and marked the current abodes of the protagonists in the Lamb case, annotating their addresses in the margin. Once they had finished, Nicky promised to take Leo out on his yacht in the near future, and the pair exchanged mobile numbers. Nicky then made a call, requesting that his driver collect him. After he had hung up and the conversation had resumed, the party was disturbed by the shrill summons of the doorbell.

Troughton crept up to the window and looked outside. His drunken expression dissolved. 'Shit – it's the fuzz!' he hissed urgently. 'Be a top fellow and answer it, Moran. Tell him I'm not here. Tell him I've nipped out for a bit of owl spotting or something.'

With that, he evaporated behind an Edwardian screen decorated with colourful tropical flora, where a quivering

Nicky had already concealed himself. Leo was about to express his indignation, but instead decided to seize the opportunity to engage with the local law again. He marched down the vestibule, the insistent bell ringing now accompanied by loud knocking, and opened the door.

Sergeant Ronnie MacKellar stood outside.

'Good evening, Sergeant.'

'Hello again, Mr Moran. Could I speak with Mr Troughton, please?'

'I'm afraid he is indisposed.'

The policeman squinted over Leo's shoulder down the corridor. 'I've had another complaint from his neighbours. About a firework landing in their garden earlier, while they were sitting out. It nearly hit the lady of the house. Her husband reckons it was deliberately aimed at her.'

Leo recalled the impressive white building next door, which, judging by the legend on its gateposts was once a convalescent home. 'Look, Sergeant, it is true they were letting off pyrotechnics, but I'm sure they weren't aiming at people – not the neighbours, anyway. A rogue rocket must have gone through the trees.'

'Who's "they"?'

Leo was silent.

'Tell him I'll need to speak with him tomorrow.'

'Naturally. Sergeant, I wonder if I might pick your brains for a moment. I am enlisted to research a series of unexplained deaths at the south of the island for *The Belmartine Repository*, starting with the drowning of a scuba diver in 1989. Then apparently a motorcyclist died –'

'Let me stop you right there, sir. I am already well-versed with Mr Troughton's list of woe, in fact I've been pestered relentlessly about it. And let me assure you, Mr Moran, that these deaths are not "unexplained"; sometimes pathologists just don't get perfect answers. I'd advise you to give Mr

Troughton's hare-brained notions a wide berth. And his pal Mr Barrett should watch his step, casting accusations about Vincent Comiskey. I heard he's now getting Johnathon Lamb worked up about the matter.'

'Which of the deaths did you personally investigate?'

'The ones from Miss Green's suicide onwards,' replied the copper with a sigh.

'As for one of the cases preceding that – that of Andy Lamb – I believe you are aware of new information pertaining to it?'

'Yes, assuming that you're referring to that women having now said she saw Vincent Comiskey on the night in question at the druid stones. But it doesn't make any difference. It was an accident. They were all accidents or suicide.'

'Who was the investigating officer for the earlier deaths?'

'A good man by the name of Archie Kerr. He retired not long after the fishermen drowned.'

'How would I get in touch with Mr Kerr?'

'He lives in Saint Madden's, on the west coast of the island. But you'll be wasting your time as well as his. I'll say goodnight, Mr Moran.'

'Goodnight, Sergeant.'

The Lady of Sorrows

Leo awoke feeling hungover, but his usual seltzer remedy restored his resolve to attend early Mass at Our Lady of the Isles in Kilmichael where he would pray for success in his investigations. Troughton had informed him that the only other still-consecrated Catholic church on the island belonged to the Baronet of Sonna. It was apparently a sumptuous affair of Italianate splendour and Carrera marble set within the nobleman's grand house, which was tucked away in his private policies near Kilkenny, a settlement of Tudor houses with a maypole not far south of the Palmery. The morning was anointed with sunshine and a pleasant breeze, although clouds which processed across the sky occasionally subdued the light. Leo parked, disembarked from the Humber and took a moment to behold the church's Byzantine exterior. He then stepped inside, into a realm of pink sandstone (even the tabernacle was constructed from the stuff) interspersed with dark wood, and arches: a large arch spanning the altar, arched windows and arches supported by the aisle columns. There were a few vivid splashes: The Stations of the Cross and several depictions of saints on the breast of the choir loft. There was also some good ironwork at the Lady chapel, in which was located a reproduction of the Black Madonna and Child, and a beautiful caramel and gold statue of Our Lady. It was here, at the end of Mass, that Leo noticed a prepossessing woman lighting a votive candle. She was wearing a mantilla, yet he could discern the expression written on her countenance and deduced that she was burdened by some great sorrow. Her striking appearance and the fact that she was of mixed race made him think of Nicky's description of Amy Agumanu. Certainly, she fitted the age profile.

When Leo returned to the Palmery he wheeled last night's dirty dishes to the kitchen on a serving trolley, filled a sink and began washing up. Through the window he could see the upper half of Marcus Troughton rhythmically appearing and disappearing over the roof of a wooden outbuilding as he took his exercise on some unseen piece of apparatus. After a while, Troughton came in through the kitchen door, drenched in perspiration. He was wearing a tracksuit and had a towel draped around his neck.

'Trampolining, Moran – nothing quite like it for stirring the blood! Works wonders for a hangover. My regime is: trampolining to clear the mind, syrup of figs to clear the system. On that note, should I have to dash off abruptly, I'm sure you will understand.'

'Perfectly.'

'Jolly decent of you to attend to the dishes.'

'It's the least I can do, after all the effort you went to for dinner.'

'Need a hand?'

'No, thank you. In fact, I am finished,' said Leo as he unpeeled the rubber gloves.

'In that case, shall I show you the office now?'

'No time like the present.'

Leo took his jacket from the chair upon which he had hung it, and the men climbed the stairs to the first floor, and proceeded to a large, sunny chamber which was located immediately above the dining room.

'I've always loved this room,' said Troughton, 'the way the light dresses it on a morning such as this. So, when I decided to revive *The Repository* I thought, "This must and shall become my office."'

'It is delightful,' agreed Leo, surveying his surroundings. The bare floorboards were noisy and the ceiling and woodwork needed a lick of paint, but the room indeed claimed a certain charm, with its odour of old wood and its bookcases crammed with library sets and dusty files. A heavy mahogany desk was positioned at the window, which had fine views over the firth and the mainland beyond. Leo noticed with some surprise that an Olivetti typewriter sat on the desk, and indeed apart from an antiquated mobile phone he couldn't see any electronic equipment at all. He withdrew his own phone and noted with dismay that it registered no Wi-Fi signal, and indeed that the regular signal was weak and intermittent.

'Troughton, in the interests of keeping in touch, would you permit me to top up your mobile telephone? I think you intimated that you found the task a touch fiddly.'

'I'd be delighted, old boy.'

Leo, hardly a technophile himself, spent a few minutes using his bank card to add credit to the thing.

'Let me reimburse you,' said Troughton.

'No. Think of it as a small thank-you for last night's superb repast.'

'Most grateful. Now, I'll let you get on with devouring the case files,' said Troughton, gesturing towards a shelf on a nearby bookcase. 'You'll also note the wall map ...' His attention had been diverted by something outside, and Leo looked through the window to see a Royal Mail van come to a halt at the top of the driveway. A postman got out and began unloading transit crates from its rear. 'Oh, happy day – it has arrived!'

'What has arrived?' enquired Leo.

'A new plaything for Troughton! I wonder, Moran, if I could delay your research for a few minutes and impose upon you to help me bring these parcels into my workshop?'

Leo followed his host downstairs and to the front door, where he took possession of the crates from the postman. The two men then carried the heavy items to the outbuilding at the back of the house. Leo was charmed to discover that its rear wall had been skilfully decorated to resemble the façade of a grand mansion, with two miniature urns at the false doorway, a tiny replica of a 1904 Humberette motor car and a sign saying 'Toad Hall'. During his stay at the Palmery, he would be beguiled to discover at the buttress of a larch tree a small door – with the nameplate 'Mr Mole' – and a diminutive, beer-ringed garden table, 'The Residence of Mr Badger' at a knowe amid the perimeter trees, and on the bank of a little burn 'Ratty's House' with a scale model rowing boat alongside.

With a token word of thanks for Leo's assistance, Troughton disappeared into the outbuilding to be alone with his mysterious boxes, where he would remain for the rest of the morning.

Leo returned to the office. He began by examining the large-scale map of Sonna which hung on the wall and into which Troughton had inserted different coloured pins to mark the location of each fatality. Alongside the map were brief colour-coded notes giving each decedent's full name, date of birth and date of death. There was also a photograph of each individual. Leo then began wading through the box files on the bookshelf. Some of the filing was shoddy, but there was plenty of interesting material, not least photocopies of coverage of the deaths in the island's newspaper *The Sonnaman*. There were also original reporters' notes and even the odd police witness statement and a couple of PM medical summaries; Leo dreaded to think how Troughton had come to possess these items. After studying steadily for a couple of hours, and diligently jotting any highlights in his crocodile leather-bound notebook, he decided to take a break.

He noticed a pile of past editions of *The Belmartine Repository* on the floor and nosed through a few of them with a burgeoning sense of horror. Not only were the production values poor, but the content was a fudge, with pretentious arts and highbrow pieces clashing with begrudged staples such as agricultural and society news (Rotarians, Masons, Soroptimists, Philatelics, Young Farmers, NFU, RMT, Churches, Boys' Brigade, Girls' Brigade). Leo skimmed some of the outlandish editorials and a few columns by 'The Barfly' (above which was featured a silhouette of Troughton wearing a fedora) who made ham-fisted attempts at waggish observation of island life in a faux New York dialect. There was the odd decent article on Sonna's wildlife or history, but Leo noted that these were submitted by local enthusiasts. He suddenly wondered at the viability of the publication, given its general lack of quality and the fact that the island's population, which already sustained the weekly *Sonnaman*, was barely six and a half thousand, albeit swollen during the summer by tourists. Now the proprietor had turned to serious investigative reporting – and enrolled Leo as the mug who was to undertake it – in an effort to increase sales. Nicky Barrett's financial influence made Leo feel queasy, yet the claim about Vincent Comiskey killing Andy Lamb at least felt that it had some coherence to it, and was some reason for ploughing on. But there was every chance all of the deaths were mere accidents – certainly Leo's visions hadn't been invoked following his invitation to Sonna.

Deflated, he walked downstairs to the hall where he

placed the gramophone needle on the final movement of Brahms' First Symphony. The composer had been brilliant from the outset, just like Mozart and Beethoven, but unlike them he didn't really get any better, mused Leo, he didn't evolve much. The other two didn't just reach the gates, they gave us a glimpse into the very halls of Paradise itself. Once the music had ceased, Leo plodded back upstairs, noting on the mezzanine three easels bearing oil landscapes in different stages of completion. More of Troughton's third-rate efforts, no doubt.

Leo studied for another hour or so, noting with particular curiosity some photographs of Andy which, according to a note, had been taken by Nicky during the summer of 1989. It was striking how anachronistic the high street print developer's wallet now seemed. The pictures gave better detail than the passport mugshot on the wall and showed Andy as a handsome boy with cropped brown hair, sharp, quick features, white teeth, an easy tan and youthful vigour glinting in his eyes. Two of the snaps also featured Nicky, and in one of them he was gazing up with adulation towards Andy. Leo sensed that Nicky wasn't gay, and that this was an entirely platonic devotion.

Leo was keen to know who had found the bodies, but according to the files, none of the discoveries seemed suspicious. The scuba diver was found by the RNLI after his girlfriend in Aberdeen had raised the alarm because he had failed to telephone her as arranged. The Italian motorcyclist's crash was witnessed by a holidaying Irish family who were on Ardcaden Bay beach. They had all glanced up just before the impact because of the dramatic sound of the bike accelerating, which was extraordinary given that it was going into a bend. When the father attended the scene, he found the biker had died instantly. The police located Andy Lamb's broken body during their search. The coastguard found the two missing fishermen from Ayrshire in their boat on the seabed after two days of searching. Miss Green was happened upon by a 'local dog walker'. Farmer McGrouther, poor man, had endured the terrible misfortune of discovering his son's body. And a pair of retired lady walkers from Edinburgh stumbled on Mr Geoffrey Willett lying dead near the lighthouse.

Leo joined Troughton, who had changed out of his tracksuit into corduroy trousers and a paisley-print shirt, for a luncheon of leftover game pie. Leo tried to probe his host about his activities since university, particularly the lost years before he moved back to his native Sonna, but he was fobbed off with a vague response: 'This and that. A few business ventures and such like.' Leo defied Troughton's devilish pestering that he join him in consuming 'a rather fetching little Côtes du Rhône'. He had to explain more than once that his abstinence was due to the fact that he would be driving later that day. Troughton eventually relented, and proposed a postprandial stroll during which he would show his guest around the gardens.

As Leo waited for his tour guide – who had insisted on a further visit to the cellar to liberate another bottle – he admired the castellated south elevation of the house, with its corbelled oriel windows and turrets. A lovely detail on the breast of a balustrade above a large bay window depicted an angelic stonework male and female gazing at each other in devotion.

'My ancestors, from when they were young and in love, rendered as cherubs,' said Troughton as he shambled towards Leo, replenished goblet in one hand, bottle in the other. 'The man is the house's founder. He was a successful nineteenth-century Glasgow merchant. His eccentric brother was a keen botanist, who travelled widely, collecting samples. Many of the specimens here are descendants of those originals. An obscure species of passion flower is named after him. An interest in plant and animal life – particularly plants – came down through the generations, although it rather passed me by; militaria is more my bag. However, I adore the rhododendron blossom. It's a shame you missed it.' They ambled along a pleasant path lined with palms.

'The Gulf Stream warms the island enough to enable these trees to grow, although the palms on Sonna are in fact *Cordyline australis* or cabbage palms – not strictly speaking a palm, as it's not sufficiently mild for bona fide ones. Hence the arboretum.'

They entered the old glasshouse, a sunken, humid place with cast-iron roof girders and the trickle of water from an ornamental stream.

'Moran, I feel that there's an elephant in the room that needs addressing,' said Troughton, his voice stark in the enclosed space. 'After uni, you were taken ill.' Leo nodded and pretended to ponder a Mediterranean dwarf palm. 'Look here, I'm sorry I didn't come and visit you.'

'That's all right.'

'I've had my dark days too, you know, although it's not a competition. Anyway, the more I put off seeing you, the harder it became. Eventually I just felt paralysed with guilt. I was a young man, I was selfish, and, frankly, I was uncomfortable with mental illness. Anyway, I am sorry.'

'There's really no need to apologise. Let's face it – we may have hung around in the same group at university, but you and I were never all that close.'

They stepped out of the hothouse and proceeded to stroll fragrant gravel paths, the hum of pollinators and the song of thrushes providing a soothing backdrop. There were all manner and colour of shrubs and plants and trees from every corner of exotica – Japan, China, the Himalayas, Amazonia – and Leo considered how traversing the gardens was like entering miniature versions of these distant places. Newts and goldfish inhabited a restored Victorian pond and there were lawns with rare orchids and a plethora of native wildflower species. However, the area was somewhat unkempt and overgrown, as though it now lacked proper husbandry.

As though reading his mind, Troughton said that he had been forced to let the gardener go due to 'a temporary cash-flow situation'. 'Had to furlough the housekeeper as well,' he added. 'I spoke to the Baronet about an idea of mine to open the gardens to the public during spring and summer, as a tourist attraction, you know, a money-spinner. I asked if he'd consider investing, to prime the pump, but I haven't heard back from him yet.'

Perhaps vexed by the thought, Troughton abandoned his wine glass on a little wooden bench and began greedily slugging from the bottle.

'Troughton, I'm afraid I shan't be dining with you this evening,' said Leo. 'I'll get something to eat in Kilmichael. I need to get cracking on my investigations, and there are people and places I wish to visit. I hope this does not inconvenience you.'

'Think nothing of it, old boy. *La mia casa è la tua casa.* Come and go as you please.'

'I wonder, Troughton, do you happen to know Amy Agumanu?'

'No, but I've seen her in church.'

'I think I saw her this morning when I attended Mass. And what about this Janey woman who Nicky mentioned?'

'I've never met her. Remember, I wasn't resident on the island for several years, when I was a younger man. Therefore, neither do I know Vincent Comiskey – although I've seen him around, latterly. And I never came across poor Andy Lamb. If you visit or bump into his brother Johnathon, I must warn you that he's something of a prickly character. Nicky's quite thick with him.'

'And Archie Kerr?'

'He was a copper of middling abilities, but he's a decent old bird, if a touch intolerant of my recent probing.'

'What about Norris Meiklejohn?'

'I see him from time to time – he drinks in the Golfers, a pub in town. He's all right is Norris.'

'I shall aim to visit Archie and Amy later today. Norris, I think tomorrow morning; that's a more awkward proposition and I will sleep on it. As for the Comiskey fellow ... I suppose I'll have to get round to seeing him, too. I need to figure out my approach first.'

'If you want to get on Archie's good side, take him a bottle of Speyside.'

Troughton led Leo out of the grounds and over the coast road to the shore. There were curious piles of flat stones assembled there, which Troughton began kicking over.

'What on earth are you doing?' asked Leo.

'Rock stacking – it's just so bloody ... middle class!' Troughton smiled mischievously and took a long draught from his bottle. 'I say, Moran, when you are in Kilmichael, could you be a splendid fellow and pop into the hardware shop on Dougal Street? The harridan behind the counter there had ordered some typewriter ribbons for me, but when I went in to collect them, she said my tick was all used up. I ended up giving her a piece of my mind and was promptly barred.'

West of Eden

ONCE Leo had finished trawling Troughton's files he freshened up and drove to Kilmichael. He parked the Humber by the Co-op and popped inside to select a decent bottle of malt, then strolled down Dougal Street. He was visited by a vivid remembrance of his childhood holiday and was transported back to a different epoch. How the ambience of the quieter, shaded, narrow street had contrasted with the hubbub and sun-exposed tracts of the parallel promenade. The cheerfully painted corner shop – now a beauty salon – which had sold garish child's fishing nets, miniature sailboats and Airfix kits. Having browsed inside too often and being too timid to risk the ire of the shopkeeper, Leo would gaze through the window wistfully, knowing that his meagre pocket money couldn't make the stretch to any of the cherished items.

Leo went to the hardware shop to purchase the typewriter ribbons Troughton had ordered. Contrary to despatches, he found the lady proprietor to be perfectly pleasant, and felt rather embarrassed by his association with his host. He also called at the office of *The Sonnaman*, which was on Albert Street, the town's seaward drag. According to the young female secretary and male reporter on duty (Leo soon discerned that the fellow was more or less in charge of the whole operation, thanks to years of cuts by the newspaper's proprietors), the journalists who had worked on most of the mysterious deaths had themselves gone to meet their Maker (prematurely, in accordance with the dipsomaniacal tradition of British gentlemen of the Press). Upon request, the staff permitted Leo access to their archives, but a superficial rummage through old editions and files revealed nothing novel; Troughton's photostats evidenced that he had already undertaken this task adeptly. Leo quizzed the reporter about the deaths upon which he himself had reported – those of the farmer's son and the English rambler – but extracted nothing of substance. He persisted to further probe the horrible end of Farmer McGrouther's son, who had been found impaled on agricultural machinery and which Troughton had claimed the police had never properly explained, but the newspaperman merely muttered vaguely that, 'The lad must have been mucking about or something.'

The next port of call was the library, a brutalist building that offended Leo's aesthetic sensibilities. He preferred Kilmichael Castle which sat just across the road. Its seasoned stone and trimmed lawns looked bonny in the afternoon sun as mallards cruised the moat, yet this benign picture was at odds with a bloody past; Norsemen had taken the keep in the thirteenth century with great violence and loss of life. Leo was dismayed to find that the account for the card Troughton had lent him had £8.45 in fines owing, and once he had paid the librarian he installed himself at a computer terminal and Googled a series of search criteria which he had jotted down while studying the case files at the Palmery. He exhumed no new information, nor could the librarian or the assistant at the quaint local history museum next door point him to any archives related to the mysterious deaths.

Leo scoped out his next move over a tasty fish tea in a backstreet chippy, glad of the cheerful hubbub of holidaying families. In order to forestall imposing upon the tea of Archie Kerr he then killed an hour with a chess problem and a glass of ginger beer in a dingy pub before heading back to the Humber. He drove westwards towards Saint Madden's in the lovely evening light. The waist of the island was gentle pastureland, downs with smooth ridges and the odd rocky outcrop. As he motored, Leo considered the tourist information he had read about Sonna. The island measured fifteen miles from tip to tail, and its breadth was approximately four miles. Most of the population lived in Kilmichael, which sat about halfway up the eastern, mainland-facing coast. There were other notable settlements on this sprawling shoreline; to the capital's immediate north was Port Penelope, and eight miles to its south was Ardcaden Bay. The western seaboard was only sparsely peppered with an occasional house or farmstead or hamlet. The northernmost third of Sonna was a harsh terrain of bald hills, bogs and deep forestry, with the only decent road traversing its eastern coast. This portion of the island was separated from the mainland by a narrow channel called the Straits of Sonna. The remainder of Sonna, particularly that south of the Loch Anna valley, which was part of the Highland Boundary Fault, was formed of old red sandstone and was softer country than the old metamorphic rock of the north, verdant and fertile but for a stretch of interior moorland. The landscape became rough again at the volcanic peninsula known as the south end. Scholars differed over the etymology of the name 'Sonna', which is pronounced the same as 'sauna'. Most believed it was rooted in the days of Dalriada, and was derived from the Old Irish word 'sona', meaning prosperous or fortunate. Others thought it was a bastardisation of an Old Norse word, from when the Vikings ruled before Somerled's rising and the Lordship of the Isles.

The country was now criss-crossed with mature broadleaved trees, and dotted with grand houses or granges or roadside cottages. Leo was afforded a splendid view down the sloping land and over the large western expanse of water known as the Sound of Sonna, on which a tall ship was conveying sightseers back to her home port. Beyond the sound was Erran, with the prospect of Kintyre in the far distance.

Leo rolled to a halt beneath an ash tree by a field of Friesian cows. A flock of goldfinches took fright, their colours vivid and gorgeous in flight. Leo got out of the Humber and regarded the prepossessing hamlet, a cluster of old houses and cottages in glorious trim and tendriled by ivy and climbing roses, and with all manner of flowers cultivated in their pretty little gardens. He asked a friendly retired Englishwoman who was cutting back her lavender where Archie Kerr lived and was directed down a lane which possessed a ramshackle, homely feel and was hedged by dog rose with fat orange-red hips and bonny pink-white blossoms, and also beech and briar interspersed with cow parsley and meadow cranesbill.

When he had entered the lane, Leo had experienced a peculiar sensation that he was being watched, and three times glanced over fields to his right, towards the road by which he had arrived. He cast the notion from his mind, but his instincts had been attuned because peering over a hedgerow there through a pair of binoculars was a powerful man, clad entirely in black. A man intensely interested in the personage of renowned detective Leomaris Peregrine Moran. A man who could barely recall a time when anger did not grip his heart.

Archie's was the last abode, a pleasing dormered house constructed from stone which had been mellowed by the passage of time. Leo knocked the dark-blue painted door to summon a portly, jolly-looking man with a ruddy face, a bulbous nose and a double chin. He wore thick plastic-rimmed spectacles and unruly fragments of grey hair were pulled across his large skull.

'Good evening, sir. Mr Kerr, I presume?'

'You presume correctly.'

'I am sorry to disturb you. My name is Leo Moran. I am doing some investigative reporting for *The Belmartine Repository.*'

Amusement seemed to inhabit in the ex-copper's features. 'Doubtless regarding the deaths at the south end which seem to so vex the gruesome twosome of Troughton and Barrett?'

'Let me assure you, sir, that I approach these matters truly with an open mind. I just need to get a feel for the background data. And I come bearing a gift,' added Leo with a smile as he held up the bottle he had bought in the Co-op.

'You've brought the good stuff! In which case, you can come away in. And do call me Archie.'

Leo was led into a shabby living room, and Archie apologised for its untidiness before sighing, 'My wife passed away nine years ago, she would be ashamed of how I keep the place. Would you care for a dram?'

'Thank you but no – I'm driving.'

'You don't mind if I ...' said Archie, rapidly filling and draining a patterned tumbler. 'I'd offer you some tea, but as a matter of fact I was just about to take my evening air – doctor's orders – if you'd care to join me.'

'Delighted.'

The two men strolled down the lane to the shore, which here, at the northern reach of Saint Madden's Bay, was of grey-dun sand with a belt of shingle and browed by masses of sea radish bearing small yellow flowers. To the left, the bay became flint, then at its midpoint grey rocks oranged with lichen. Seaward, beyond a stinking salt marsh, was a little peninsula, which, incongruously, was inhabited by Jersey cattle and farm buildings, and at its tip was a ruined Celtic chapel. Beyond, sitting just outside the mouth of the bight was Inchmadden, Sonna's calf isle, where apparently a seal colony bred. A curtain of rain had drifted into the sound and fell within the great gullies of Erran. The men sat on a metal bench, an object which Leo politely admired after being shown its dedication to Archie's late spouse. Gulls called plaintively above the *pseep* and trill of rock pipits.

'The Barrett lad always had a bee in his bonnet about the Comiskey lad being responsible for the Lamb lad's demise,' began Archie as he swept a recalcitrant strand of hair back across his scalp. 'Even at the time he tried to blame him. Of late, he's been ramping it up.'

'Was foul play investigated in 1989?'

'Aye, surely. The Comiskey lad was a troublemaker, and it was well known that he and the Lamb lad disliked each other, that they had once come to blows. But there was just no evidence for the Comiskey lad or anyone else being involved in the death. He simply said he was at home on the evening in question, and his father corroborated this. We know the time when the Lamb lad set off for the hill, because Davie Heron, the farmer at Inkpot to this day, remembered hearing the youngsters' car engines and seeing light from the headlamps and checking the time. It was half past eleven. You'll know about their daft ceremony by the standing stones?'

'Indeed. Whose idea was all that japery and ballyhoo?'

'The Barrett lad's. I imagine he has had to live with that fact. But it was just teenage high jinks that got out of hand.

I didn't want to nail him to the wall.'

'Troughton's files said that the police found Andy's body. Who was it who actually made the discovery?'

'Myself. It was bloody awkward to move it from its position and then get it to the road; it took four strong men: myself, my colleague Jackie Aitken and a couple of firemen from Kilmichael. Myself and Jackie, God rest him, were the only polis stationed on the island at that time. The lad had taken a tumble over a steep slope and was brained by a boulder on his way down. As I said, there was no evidence that an offence had been committed. The post-mortem found that the contours of the boulder matched the head wound, plus there was some of the lad's tissue on the boulder. Which is to say that the injury wasn't from being bashed over the head *before* he fell. Neither were there any other injuries sustained – puncture wounds or throttling abrasions for example – which were inconsistent with the fall. And there were no witnesses to another party being present, and take my word for it, we carefully questioned all of those kids, including the Jane Gribben lass, who you may know went up to look for the Lamb lad after she became concerned. It was misadventure, pure and simple.'

'But it was a light night of the northern summer – visibility isn't that bad. Why would the boy have marched off that drop?'

'The sky might have been brightish compared with autumn or winter, but this was fifty days after the longest one, and on the ground, it would have been shadowy, especially among the complex land. Plus, the lad was doped up and drunk, and probably scared witless by that daft occult game they had been playing. The post-mortem report stated that he had alcohol and THC in his bloodstream, quite high levels of the latter. THC being Tetrahydrocannabinol, the psychoactive element in marijuana, and the report said that marijuana was found in the Lamb lad's stomach contents. We tried to find the dealer, but those kids kept schtum. And, to be honest, we didn't want to come down too heavy on them because they were so upset. If one of them had supplied the Lamb lad with a bit of wacky baccy we reckoned they would be feeling bad enough about what had happened. And who knows, maybe the lad ate something beforehand entirely unbeknownst to the others. It was all just a tragic accident.'

'You mentioned Janey Gribben. Nicky Barrett recently traced her in Glasgow and visited her. She now claims that she saw Vincent Comiskey spying on the kids as they conducted their ceremony at the standing stones. Yet he informed you that he had been at home all evening.'

'So what? Even if the woman was willing to testify, what would it prove after all these years? Comiskey could just say he and his father lied about being at home in case he got into trouble, what with him being from the criminal classes. And anyway, his being at the henge doesn't prove he was capable of committing murder.'

'Was he capable of committing rape? Elizabeth Meiklejohn accused him.'

'Indeed, she did. But we couldn't make an arrest because it was her word against his, and there was no physical evidence available to us by the time she made the complaint.'

'What about the other deaths from during your era: the scuba diver, the motorcyclist, the fishermen?'

'I'll tell you the same thing that I told you about the Lamb lad's demise: that there was no evidence whatsoever to suggest anything irregular.'

'I know it was after your time, but the files said that Miss Green's body was found by a local dog walker. Do you know who that was?'

'Tam Logan. These days he's the owner of the Saint Caden's Hotel in Ardcaden. A decent man, straight as a die. Just like all the people who discovered the other poor folk – not a single one of them suspicious. Look, what happened was this: during the summer of 1989 three unusual deaths occurred in or off the south end, and a legend grew up on the island about that area being cursed. Afterwards, any death down there that was slightly out of the ordinary became part of that legend. It's all just local bunkum. Now, this fresh air is making me feel a wee bit seasick. I'm heading back to the house to get another tot of that nice medicine you kindly brought me.'

Leo bid Archie farewell and set off again in the Humber, driving past gently sloping fields until he glimpsed Herrick Bay, the next bay to the north, the amber light so rich as to seem tangible. The breeze had picked up and a procession of whitecaps were breaking on the golden beach, the brine a vivid blue against the deep green of the headland. He paused beside a deserted tearoom to admire the majestic fells of upper Erran, which slanted gracefully down to the sea across the sound. A flock of shelducks flew above the perfect sands, which to the bay's flanks became striped with tidelines and marred by angular rocks and jetsam and seaweed. Leo consulted the map which Nicky had marked with the precise location of Amy Agumanu's place, and then coaxed the Humber along a narrow strip of tarmac which was bordered by a grassy foreshore with gorse and hawthorn and sea radish and the big daisy-like heads of sea mayweed, and the yellow of tansy and flag iris and sow thistle and hawkbit flowers, and the purple of knapweed. The border soon widened to a soggy merse on which sheep grazed. Amy's residence, Fagr Vágr, was the last of a cluster of cottages and little houses on the south-facing shore, a brown Scandinavian-style structure with a red corrugated roof and a lean-to sunroom. It was set apart from the other homes and back from the road, and was partially screened by a vanguard of sycamores which stood amid rank grasses. After Leo had parked the Humber on the verge, he entered Amy's fragrant garden via a rusted kissing gate and walked up a wide gravel path, which was banked by a neatly trimmed lawn.

Leo now saw her, kneeling as she attended to some roses. He called out a friendly 'Good evening,' hoping not to startle her. She stood up and smiled at him, her teeth brilliant in the pre-crepuscular light. This was indeed the woman he had seen in church.

'Forgive my intrusion upon your evening. My name is Leo Moran, I am a private detective,' he said with a slight bow. 'I am an associate of Marcus Troughton and Nicky Barrett. I am currently staying with the former, investigating various fatalities at the south end of Sonna for *The Belmartine Repository*.'

'And you want to discuss poor Andy Lamb's death all those sad years ago,' said Amy as she walked down the lawn towards him. Leo nodded gravely.

She was barefoot, her mass of curly brown hair tied back, and was wearing blue jeans and a navy sweatshirt. She was carrying a pair of secateurs and a single white rose, and jangled with bohemian bracelets as she moved gracefully across the turf. As she neared it became evident that her face was prematurely lined and tired, that much vitality had been washed from her countenance and that a pain seemed to reside deep within her cerulean-blue eyes. Yet these were appealingly exotic against her caramel skin, and she possessed what one might term a good jaw, full lips and exquisite cheekbones, and her features were in perfect harmony. Amy Agumanu was, Leo considered, beautiful.

'Forgive the gardening togs,' she said in her rich voice, perhaps recognising the stark contrast with Leo's smart Harris Tweed sports jacket and polished shoes. 'Gosh, I just love your car. Talk about retro!' she added, admiring the Humber while Leo tried not to obviously admire her figure.

'Thank you.'

'So, you're a private detective. I expect that involves lots of fingerprinting and analysing the types of soil on a suspect's Wellington boots?'

'To be honest, I find that simply speaking with people gets the majority of my results.'

'You mean you're a nosey parker?'

'Correct.' He smiled. 'And while we're on the subject, I must confess that I noted your presence at holy Mass this morning.'

'Yes. My car is kaput until I can afford an expensive repair, but I managed to cadge a lift to Kilmichael. Listen, the midgies are starting to bite. Would you like to come into the sunroom for a refreshment?'

'Most kind.'

Leo entered the room directly from the garden, a pleasant space with white-painted floorboards, wicker furniture and little nautical curios. There was also a representation of the Mother of Sorrows partly constructed from sea glass, driftwood and shells, with seven daggers piercing the heart of Mary. Leo was sitting admiring it when Amy arrived carrying two virgin strawberry daiquiris.

'Did you make this work of art?' he enquired after he had thanked her for the drink.

'Yes,' she said, taking a seat on the chair facing him.

'It is superb, and highly unusual. Perhaps you know the origin of the daggers from Simeon's prophesy in the Gospel of Luke, as he addressed Our Lady in the temple?

Yea, a sword shall pierce through thy own soul also, that the thoughts of many hearts may be revealed.'

'I'm impressed!' said Amy, making her guest feel a little embarrassed that he had flaunted his knowledge of Scripture.

'I have to say this is a perfectly charming room. It's wonderful the way the light fills it, and what a splendid view you have of the bay through the trees.'

'It is the result of a divorce settlement, but we weren't super-rich. So I paint boats, when I get the business. Sometimes I paint them artistically, more often it's just a good coating or sealing. Sometimes I do jobs at the yard outside Port Penelope, even if it's just cleaning vessels. But mostly my work is folk bringing a dinghy on a trailer to my shed out back or sailing a yacht to my mooring out there,' she said, motioning towards the sea.

'Nicky Barrett complimented the quality of your work.'

'He's my most regular customer,' said Amy, suppressing a smile at the way the daiquiri made Leo look as though he had applied lipstick. 'Although he can be a pest. Not least his constant allegations about Andy Lamb's death. You will know that he believes Andy was murdered, and by Vincent Comiskey?'

'Indeed. And what do you think?'

'I don't buy it. No way. Andy's death was just a terrible accident. A banal accident, really. It is my opinion that the more banal a tragedy, the more people have to invent conspiracy theories, in an effort to give meaning to it.'

Leo considered the sadness which inhabited Amy's beautiful eyes, and he recalled the sorrow that seemed to burden her in the church that very morning, and what Nicky had said about her going out with Andy yet meeting Vincent for secret trysts during the summer of 1989. Could her anguish not only be for the boy who fell, but guilt for how her duplicity had stoked up jealousy and resentment between Andy and Vincent, resulting in the latter killing the former? Perhaps even her religious devotion and her decision to move to Sonna were subliminal efforts to somehow come to terms with what she had catalysed. And perhaps the firmness with which she asserted that Andy's death was accidental was to suppress the dreadful truth to a lower stratum of her consciousness.

'Did Nicky tell you about his speaking with Janey Gribben?'

'He hasn't stopped banging on about it. But even if Janey *did* see Vincent spying on us at the standing stones, it doesn't amount to a hill of beans. Nicky keeps trying to badger me into admitting that I believe that Vincent was capable of murder. But I don't.'

'Forgive my bluntness, but I'll wager neither did you think he was capable of violating Elizabeth Meiklejohn.'

Amy sighed. 'That part of the story is just too wretched. It has always troubled me. I guess that, deep down, that's why I have never sought Vincent out since he moved to the island. I've seen him at Mass and driving his brewery van around, but I've never felt the urge to have a chinwag.'

Leo sipped his virgin daiquiri, suddenly wishing it contained rum as courage for the awkward topic he had to broach next.

'Nicky claimed that you had been seeing ... *both* Andy and Vincent that summer. His contention is that Vincent, as your ... paramour, had become possessed by jealousy over you and Andy.'

'They were rivals, all right, and I don't doubt that my behaviour intensified that. They even had a punch-up one day, on the seafront at Ardcaden Bay. My father, may God rest his soul, happened by and split them up. He was a wise man, my dad, and he read the situation and gave me a talking to in private, sensing that I was leading both boys on, playing them off against each other. I'm not proud of that. But the idea that I drove Vincent so crazy that he committed *murder* – it's too fantastic.'

'I am told that while you were all waiting for Andy to return from his dare, Janey became worried and went to look for him. Did everyone else stay at the cars?'

'Yes. Eventually Janey arrived back and said she couldn't find him. We all just figured he'd had enough of the nonsense and gone home. Ever since, I've always felt guilty that I didn't feel more concern on the night itself, like Janey did. At the time I just thought she was being a panic merchant, and I was quite happy to continue swigging Thunderbird and toking on a joint. The next morning, I went to see if Andy was at our meeting place in the woods just north of Ardcaden Bay towards the Lagg Road. Have you been there?'

'No.'

'It is a perfect place, like somewhere elves would live. The trees are so tall that they kiss the sky, and the ground is covered in long grass and huge fallen mossy branches. Pools of sunlight get through but then the woods get thicker and thicker as the Cathair starts to rise and I don't think any light gets in up there at all. Anyway, that's where we would go to be together. Andy to the north, Vincent to the south; that way I could separate out the experiences in my mind, not feel so shameful and selfish. But he wasn't there. I remember it like it was yesterday.' Amy gazed outside. The sunset was spun across the west in a vast golden gossamer, its nucleus an intense lambency of infinite depth and gorgeousness. 'Then the police started searching for him. Found him. Andy was a beautiful soul, wasted in the glory of his youth. It was just a dare that went wrong. Just a stupid, tragic accident. But I doubt if any of us who were part of that night will ever be free of it. We felt a sense of collective guilt for being involved in a stunt that ended so appallingly. Myself more than most. After all, he was my boyfriend.'

'So why did you make your home on Sonna?'

'Because I still adore it. Because when the sun sets over Erran with Inchmadden in the foreground, and I hear the lonely call of the curlew and the rhythm of the sea, it is like peace itself. But when I decided to move here, I opted for the north of the island. There are just too many sad memories down at the Bay – I mean Ardcaden Bay; folk who love it just refer to it as "the Bay" as though it is the only such geographical feature in the world worth mentioning, or sometimes we call it "AB". Plus the south end resonates with some weird energy which I've never quite come to terms with, although I often feel it elsewhere on the island to a lesser extent. I also think the south end just looms too large in my imagination, because it was where I had so many formative experiences, and I mean nicer ones as well, childhood ones, before all that awfulness unfolded.'

Amy then acceded to Leo's request that she relate her version of that terrible night in 1989. When she had finished, he said: 'Andy was, as the Americans would say, loaded?'

'Yeah, he was pretty gassed. I remember that Nicky seemed to take great amusement in the fact.'

'Whose idea was the night's festivities?'

'Nicky's. He was in his element.'

'How did Nicky and Andy get along?'

'Nicky idolised Andy, but I believe he also envied him.'

An idea occurred to Leo: that Nicky had been infatuated with Amy and therefore jealous of Andy. Perhaps even to this day he only employed her to paint his boats in order that he could spend time with her. However, he kept his counsel on the suspicion.

'Earlier I spoke to Archie Kerr, the retired policeman. He believes that Andy's intoxicated state would have contributed to his fall.'

'Absolutely, especially as Andy could get very drunk on just a little alcohol. He would then have these nightmare hangovers. I would tell him not to drink, or to take it easy, but he would still do it, even though he didn't really like it. I reckon he didn't want to seem unmanly.'

'What about marijuana?'

'He had an aversion to it. It made him really sick.'

'But the post-mortem report said marijuana had been found in his system.'

'Yes, and I recall being a bit surprised when I heard that at the time. I remember we supposed that he must have taken a few puffs in some moment of drunken bravado.'

'But the autopsy found that Andy had ingested the drug. Would he have eaten something with marijuana in it?'

'I doubt he'd have knowingly done that. I remember the cops saying that Andy had eaten it, but I think we all just reckoned that they were wrong, you know, country squares who didn't understand dope. None of us had been eating hash brownies or anything. We just believed that Andy must have taken a few tokes or that maybe he ate a bit of hash by accident or something.'

'Did other people know about his allergy to drink and drugs?'

'Yes. Although they wouldn't have teased him about it – Andy was quite proud in his way.'

'Who provided the marijuana?'

'Nicky. He was always showing off like that, coming the big shot.'

'Was Andy with you earlier that day, before you all headed to the henge for the ceremony?'

'No, he was round at Nicky's. They met the rest of us at the stones. There's something you won't have heard about, not that it signifies anything of great importance: Andy confided in me that someone had been trying to frighten him that summer. Terrorise him.'

'Do go on.'

'He felt as though something malign was tracking him. He pretended not to care, but I could tell he was scared. It started one night when Mr and Mrs Lamb had gone to the Saint Caden's Hotel for a drink and left Andy at home to look after his kid brother. He saw this strange light shining in the woods on the hillside behind their flat. On another two or three occasions on his way home at twilight he felt sure he was being followed. He had this wee car his parents had bought him, a Vauxhall Nova, and one day he found a dead crow placed under one of the windscreen wipers. Then one night it escalated. Andy's parents had gone to the mainland with his brother for a few days. He was sitting in alone watching television and there was a knock on the door. When he went to answer it, there was nobody there. This happened again: a knock on the door, but nobody there. Then, after he heard a knock for the third time, he opened the door and there was a creepy figure standing on the landing with its face completely covered by a dark mask. It turned on its heels and took off. I think Andy felt embarrassed that he didn't run after it. I think it shook him up. But I would have been terrified, too. After all, the south end is a place that abounds with supernatural legends, not least that of the demon piper.'

'Did you tell the police about all of this, after Andy died?'

'No. Why should I have? It had nothing to do with his accident.'

'Could Vincent Comiskey have been pranking Andy?'

'I suppose it's possible. Mind you, all sorts of

strangeness descended that summer.'

'I take it you mean the deaths of the scuba diver and the motorcyclist?'

'Yeah, but a whole lot of other weird stuff went down. I mentioned how the south end resonates with some peculiar energy, but that summer I reckon the astral channels were *really* humming, as though someone had invoked something to give them a shake. There was a crazy atmosphere that seemed to have taken over the place. A building in Melford caught fire. Two cows in a farmer's field were mutilated; one of them was so hurt she had to be sent for slaughter. There was a night storm and several boats in the Bay were unmoored and sunk. The Lambs' dog went mad; it was amusing at first but it kept yelping and yelping and running around in circles. The next morning it was dead, the poor wee thing. One of the gang nearly got some of us killed when he took us out driving in the dark after he'd drunk a gallon of cider. One night when we were all skinny dipping in the Bay, Andy swum really far out and a shark brushed against him. In these waters it must have been a basking shark, but it really freaked us out because back then none of us realised that they don't eat anything big. Then there was ... Andy dying.'

'So, you mean that this astral disturbance could directly or indirectly have caused Andy's death?'

Amy sighed. 'I don't know what I mean. If that were so then it would still, to all intents and purposes, constitute an accident. But probably I just think that one night a drunken teenager on a dare lost his bearings and fell from a high place to his death. And broke everyone's hearts.'

'Where are all the other kids who were there that summer?'

'Scattered to the four winds, Leo. Scattered to the winds.'

Leo drove back to the Palmery through the thickening darkness and upon his arrival strode to the billiard room, summoned by Troughton's concise text-message invitation 'snooker?' It was an impressive chamber, dominated by the full-size table. There was also a diorama of a section of the Battle of Borodino, with 1½-inch painted metal combatants, in which hussars and dragoons repelled General Compans' forces from one of Prince Bagration's earthworks. Beside the door frame was a series of miniatures detailing infantrymen in Napoleonic-era uniform: French, Polish Legion, British, Prussian, Austrian and Russian. From the high ceiling, which was painted sky blue and had wonderful gilded cornice work, dangled the steeds of a later defensive battle: 1:72-scale Hurricanes hurling themselves at a formation of Heinkel bombers, Me 109s peeling off to engage the RAF fighters.

Leo updated Troughton, who was already drunk on Ferreira ruby port, on his day's adventures but kept certain nascent theories within his breast. 'Suffice to say, I'm keeping an open mind,' he concluded, 'but I am yet to be convinced that Andy Lamb's death was the result of foul play.'

'Are you still planning on visiting Norris Meiklejohn tomorrow morning?' asked Troughton.

'Yes. After that I think I shall head to the south end. Tramp about a bit, get a feel for the place.'

'The farmers at the last two farms on the Lagg Road have been up there for years. Why not have a chat with them, see what they remember? I can fill you in on their backgrounds.'

'Good idea,' said Leo as he chalked his cue and then broke, considering how curious it was that snooker was popular really only at either end of the social spectrum, among working-class chaps like himself and toffs such as Troughton. 'What about the farm where the McGrouthers lived?'

'The folk there now are the second lot of tenants since the tragedy, so I shouldn't think that they will be of any use.'

As the frame unfolded Leo realised that on two occasions his opponent had distracted his attention by pointing out items of interest in the room – once a cabinet of vintage firearms and a few wall-mounted early-modern Scottish pikes and broadswords, once the paintings *Wellington's Entrance at the Duchess of Richmond's Ball* by Lady Elizabeth Butler and *Ensign Ewart seizes the Regimental Standard* by James Howe – in order to move the balls to a more advantageous position. The wicked strategy worked, and Troughton soon forced Leo to concede the frame.

Then he announced Micawberishly: 'I must say, Moran, I'm in an excellent disposition of mind. You see, I came up with an idea earlier: I'm considering increasing the scope of *The Repository* to include Great Cunrae. There are another fourteen hundred souls on that island in need of enlightenment, and by my calculations the increased revenues would tip the magazine into profitability. Mind you, old boy, there probably isn't any need for expansion, because with the sizzle these investigations into the mysterious deaths will create on Sonna alone, we'll not only be in the black – we'll be in the pink. In the meantime, we'll muddle through. As you know, Nicky has promised to invest in whichever issues deal with the deaths, as long as we make the Lamb case our main initial focus.'

'Nicky seems to be a man of means.'

'Indeed. He set up his own company and made his fortune during the information technology boom. Quite something for a plain tobacconist's son.'

'He's a singular fellow,' said Leo obliquely.

'I have no delusions about Nicky. He is a vulgar, craven little pipsqueak with a mail-order wife, and not the sort of fellow you'd want in a trench beside you. But as a financier, he is a useful ally.'

Leo took a sip from a glass of port he had poured for himself, then said: 'I hope you are not dancing to your patron's tune too much.'

'I had already begun probing Andy Lamb's demise as one of the series of mysterious deaths,' replied Troughton stiffly. 'Nicky's offer to help financially came quite unprompted – albeit because he had never let go of the theory that Vincent Comiskey murdered Lamb and his interest in proving it had been rekindled.'

'Do you believe that the deaths at the south end are anything other than a sequence of tragic accidents? Are you sure you are not just fuelling the myth of a curse in an effort to sell more magazines?'

'I am indeed trying to sell more magazines, but I do not believe that the deaths were all accidental.'

'Be frank with me, what do you make of Nicky's theory about Comiskey killing Lamb?'

'I am truly open minded about that particular death. I don't think that our giving it our full attention first, as Nicky requires, particularly matters, because I believe that you will uncover the truth about it. Perhaps it was a complete accident, perhaps Comiskey was responsible in some way ... or perhaps it was an entirely different killer altogether.'

'Do go on.'

'My belief is that there have simply been too many unusual deaths for them all to be freak accidents. It is just too coincidental, statistically speaking. However, that does not mean that *one* or *some* of them were not accidental. What I do know is that UFOs were not responsible, and neither was a demon piper or an ancient curse on the south end or lunar effect or radiation from the nuclear power station on the mainland or military intelligence bumping off people who had been prying at the comms station on the shoulder of the Cathair – all theories I've heard expounded in the public houses of Sonna. I believe that most of the deaths, and very possibly Andy Lamb's, were the work of a serial killer. Someone who lives in the Ardcaden Bay area.'

'A serial killer! I doubt it, Troughton. Fishermen perishing when their vessel was sunk, a scuba diver drowning?'

'Perhaps it was someone with a boat. And as I said – I'm not necessarily saying that one or some of the deaths were not accidental. Regarding the fishermen's deaths for example, the Royal Navy or the US Navy might have lied about there not being one of their submarines in the area at the time, or there might have been a Russian or other foreign sub in our waters. However, overall, I consider my serial killer proposition sound.'

'What about the English rambler dropping dead or the motorcyclist's crash – how on earth could those fatalities be the work of a murderer? And anyway, serial killers tend to use the same modus operandi, and their victims tend to fit a particular profile.'

'As for victim profile, perhaps these unfortunates offended our killer, even just looked at him the wrong way.'

'No, Troughton – this is a horse that won't run.'

The Loving Father

LEO's pleasant dream, which was of a mildly erotic nature, was spoiled by the arrival in it of Troughton, who was wearing lipstick and rouge and a snow-white periwig, and calling on him insistently.

Leo awoke, yet the calling persisted, disembodied now. He initially thought it was coming from downstairs, but as the fuzz of slumber abated, he realised that it was, in fact, emitting from the speaking tube at the bedside.

'Troughton?' Leo croaked into the brass mouthpiece. A glance at his travel alarm clock told that it was only a quarter past eight and he was surprised to realise that his host had risen before him, given the quantity of port wine he had consumed the previous night.

'Moran you indolent bastard. You must come out to the grounds at once. I have assembled my delivery. I wish you to witness the grand switch-on.'

'But I'm not dressed yet. Troughton? Troughton?'

Leo grumpily pulled on trousers, shoes and a jacket, and after a brief visit to the lavatory proceeded in a daze downstairs and out into the grounds, peering through the morning sunshine to locate the big event. He stepped onto the lawn, then paused as he became aware of a figure wearing some sort of headgear hunched behind a piece of apparatus, partly concealed by vast leaves of Chilean giant rhubarb, *Gunnera manicata*. Now Leo recognised the personage as Troughton, and suddenly the apparatus – which at the penultimate moment he realised was a World War One Vickers machine gun – burst into life in an opus of rapid-fire percussion, more monstrous even than the modern classical compositions regularly inflicted on him as preludes to performances of Mozart and Beethoven at Glasgow's City Halls. Leo spun round and fled, crying out 'Sweet mother of God – he's trying to kill me!' as through his mind flashed a theory that this was all a trap, all of it: his being invited to the Palmery, the deaths at the south end not mysterious at all, just a lure, a pretext for his assassination. Troughton was perhaps deranged, or worse given over wholly to malevolence after solitary years spent brooding upon some ancient offence from their university days. Leo made for the cover of the terrace wall, hopelessly, expecting the bullets to bite at any moment. But by some miracle, or due to Troughton's dearth of marksmanship, he made it.

He lay on the gravel hyperventilating as the gunfire ceased and was replaced with hysterical laughter. Leo dared to peer over the balustrade to see Troughton, who was wearing a tin bowler and a trench coat with his grandfather's Pip, Squeak and Wilfred pinned to it, staggering across the lawn towards him, seized by throes of untrammelled hilarity.

'They are blank rounds, you fool! The look on your face! Haven't soiled yourself, have you Moran?'

It took Leo a long time to be calmed by Troughton's hollow apologies, yet he couldn't resist his antagonist's invitation that he take a look at the gun. Leo touched it, admiring the clever water-cooling system. Troughton's voice sounded softly from behind. 'That's it, fondle him. Stroke his barrel. That is original 1916 merchandise. Why don't you have a look through the sights? Tease the trigger. In fact, why don't you let him rip?' Troughton then peeled open a carton and fed in a fresh belt of ammunition. 'Make as though you are shooting up the house.'

Leo took aim at an upper window and squeezed the trigger. He became aware of how at close quarters the report was less a series of little explosions than something mechanical, a clipped sound as the ammo was drawn in, the metallic clicking of an aperture opening and closing, moving components interacting with machine precision, the smell of cordite and oil sharp and clean. He thought of 1916 – this was the industrial ingenuity brought onto the battlefield, death automated, mass manufactured.

He had been firing for about twelve seconds before they realised that the rounds were live, and that in fact Leo *was* shooting up the house, masonry sparking, glass fracturing, slates ejecting. Leo released the trigger and the men looked at each other, horrified.

'Christ Almighty Moran – the ammo was supposed to be all blanks!' gasped Troughton. 'My fault for purchasing from a dodgy South African arms dealer. I see now that these rounds have different-shaped tips to the ones which I fired.'

'What if you had fired *this* belt at me, you bloody madman!' exclaimed Leo.

Troughton at least had the decency to look apologetic. 'But the main thing is that I didn't, old man,' he said. 'Let's thank God for that.'

'What a stupendous act of stupidity,' remarked Leo.

'Bloody funny though!' observed Troughton, contrition now giving way to mirth. 'And who cares, I'm fairly sure the house is insured anyway.'

'Against heavy machine gun fire? I very much doubt it,' replied Leo, before storming off.

Leo showered and prepared for the day. As he ate a scrounged breakfast of toast and marmalade in the kitchen, he received a text message from Nicky honouring his promise to take him out on his yacht, with a detailed proposal that they proceed tomorrow and circumnavigate Sonna. Leo replied, accepting the invitation.

He took a back road to Kilmichael, hoping that the novel scenery would cure him of his high dudgeon caused by Troughton's antics, which had been the last thing he needed as preparation for the awkward visit to the Meiklejohns. The tarmac rose through mixed woodland and past some farm buildings, and then traversed sun-bathed agricultural land lined with hedges of hawthorn studded with the occasional ash tree. Leo descended into a fertile valley with livestock on its slopes, passing a waterworks at the tip of a lake called Loch Belmartine, then a yellow house which sat starkly on the glen's brow. He drove past a golf course and a beautiful mature beech wood enclosed by stane dykes and in which he fancied he glimpsed a red deer, then approached the rear of Kilmichael, descending a steep road of hairpin bends called The Serpentine, this being the lower reaches of Mount Pleasant, the woody hill which overlooked the town. This quiet quarter of Kilmichael was evidently affluent, as it was graced by numerous magnificent stone-built abodes. Leo paused to consult his map, then swung the Humber along a narrow side road called Mitre Terrace, located the Meiklejohn residence and parked outside, behind a ghastly maroon Land Rover. After rehearsing his opening gambit for a final time, he removed his summer spectacles, got out of the Humber and climbed the steps to the handsome house, which was solidly constructed of gold sandstone with a curlicued wrought-iron canopy at the front door. He rang the bell and took in the view over the harbour and pier, where the ferry had just docked.

After a few moments a man wearing a canary golf shirt

and powder-blue slacks opened the door. He was past middle age but retained a good complexion and a full head of salt-and-pepper hair. He had a small mouth and his grey eyes were alert behind his rimless glasses.

'Good day to you, sir. Might I enquire, are you Norris Meiklejohn?'

'I am.'

'Permit me to introduce myself. My name is Leo Moran, I am a private detective. I am undertaking some investigative reporting for *The Belmartine Repository*, on behalf of its proprietor Marcus Troughton.'

'I am acquainted with Mr Troughton,' said Norris.

'I am currently residing with him. My task is to probe certain deaths which have occurred at the south end of the island. To be frank, sir, this matter is somewhat delicate. Mr Troughton's associate Nicky Barrett is convinced that one of the deaths, that of the teenager Andy Lamb in 1989, was not accidental. He believes that the same man who attacked your daughter back then was also responsible for his demise.'

'You'd better come in.'

Norris led Leo through a sedate hall with heavy, perfectly polished furniture and a Scottish longcase clock which ticked solemnly. They entered a large, sunny kitchen.

'Marie, there's a gentlemen here to see us. Leo, meet my good lady wife Marie.'

Leo exchanged pleasantries with Marie, a kindly, powdered lady with a nest of pure-white hair who was in the midst of a scone bake. He politely declined her offer of tea. At the table sat a younger woman, who didn't look up from her task of creating a childish drawing using wax crayons.

'Elizabeth, say hello to Leo,' said Norris.

'Hello,' she said, glancing up from beneath her

dark-brown fringe. She had a broad freckled face and deep green eyes.

'Hello, Elizabeth,' said Leo as she returned her attention to the crayons.

'Leo, why don't we go to the parlour,' said Norris.

Leo followed his host into the main chamber at the front of the house. For politeness' sake he complimented the décor, but the grey textured wallpaper and beige tartan suite weren't to his taste, although decent watercolours of Loch Striven and Loch Riddon hung on a wall. Leo refused Norris' offer of a dram and sat down as he waited for his host to pour himself a formidable measure, in spite of the hour, at a sideboard.

'You've probably realised that Elizabeth is of low intelligence. We don't have any other close family, and I worry about her for when my wife and I are gone,' said Norris after he had seated himself in an armchair facing Leo.

'You have years left in you, sir. I wish I knew your secret for keeping so healthy-looking.'

'Hillwalking and plenty of it. The more rugged, the better. The island's got plenty of obscure corners to explore. I also play golf but that doesn't get the heart pumping so.'

'I appreciate your letting me meet your daughter.'

'I was happy to. I'm not one to boast, but I am blessed with a certain insightfulness: I know a good man when I see one.'

'You are most kind, Mr Meiklejohn.'

'Call me Norris, please. I introduced you to Elizabeth because I wanted you to realise how heinous a crime it was, for a man to force himself on an innocent like that. She was fifteen years of age. I can tell you about what happened, but only for your own private context. I don't want anything about my daughter going to print.'

'You have my word, Norris.'

'Comiskey had caused havoc all that summer, he got up to all sorts of nonsense. He was a really nasty young man. The other kids his age had sent him to Coventry, so he used to roam the hills and the back woods alone. That was where it happened, in the woods on the side of the Cathair behind Ardcaden. Elizabeth never told us anything, at least not right away. She became withdrawn and moody. Andy Lamb died, so we assumed she was mourning for him – he had always been kind to her. Then we recalled that her moodiness had in fact started *before* that tragedy. Then Marie noticed faded bruising on her lower neck and her inner thigh. She asked what had happened and Elizabeth said that she had fallen. We were worried and had a doctor examine her, which confirmed our fears. Eventually she told her mother in her childlike way about what had been done to her. She hadn't had a clue what was going on, but she suggested that Comiskey was quite forceful. He had returned to the mainland by the time we found out all of this, but we reported the matter to the police. They spoke with him in Glasgow, however they said they couldn't arrest him because he flatly denied the allegation and it was too late to get any forensic evidence.'

'How dreadful for you all.'

'Dreadful for her, mostly. We moved to here in Kilmichael from Ardcaden, hoping that leaving the scene behind us would help her recover, but it took a long time and it ruined her trust in people. The whole sorry tale leaked out and the news spread, and so did Comiskey's notoriety. I considered hunting him down, taking the law into my own hands, but I decided against it. Sometimes I wish I had. I find it sickening that he has moved to the island, the *arrogance* of it. I worry about Elizabeth recognising him, that it will reignite the whole trauma for her.'

The Watchful Father

LEO bid Norris goodbye and drove the short distance to Dougal Street where he bought a savoury cheese sandwich and a pork pie from a long-established bakery, and two bars of Fry's Orange Cream from a sweet shop. These he stowed in his knapsack; he would require sustenance during his epic next task of exploring the south end. He intended on arriving via a scenic route because of a photograph he had seen in a guide book of the splendid view from above Scallop Bay on the west of the island down towards the three highest peaks of the south end: Cathair Caden, Tor Mòr and Hangman's Hill. He drove westwards past hedgerows of briar, hawthorn, fern, thistle and flowering fuchsia, and hung a left well before reaching Saint Madden's, and was soon held up by a shepherdess on a quadbike who was herding a flock of sheep along the road towards a fresh pasture. Leo stopped the Humber and switched off the engine. He relaxed in his seat contentedly, glad that the dreaded interview with Norris was over and had gone smoothly. He popped a segment of Orange Cream into his mouth and observed the pleasant scenery: the gently rolling countryside, then Inchmadden, Erran and Kintyre over the shimmering sea. He considered how an island is a singular entity. Its own kingdom within its sea-lapped confines with its particular history and politics and class divides and tragedies and rivalries. A country in miniature with its uniquely varied topography, its capital city merely a small town, every parish like a county, every farm like a parish. Its highlands loom as large in the circumscribed imagination as the Cairngorms, its freshwaters as mightily as Loch Lomond.

Leo watched a charming Border Collie obey the shepherdess' commands with precision, finally scuttling towards her and leaping onto the back of the quad. He was only vaguely aware of the powerful green car behind which had followed him from Kilmichael, its engine idling in a menacing low growl.

The sheep had been neatly corralled into their new pasture and Leo returned the friendly wave from the shepherdess as he passed her. The road climbed and then ploughed past farmsteads and rugged fields towards Scallop Bay. Soon the green car, a coupé, was tailgating Leo, and he was annoyed with himself that he unconsciously relented to the pressure by increasing his speed. At one point the road veered leftwards, yet it was at this perilous juncture that the coupé's driver decided to overtake. Leo recognised the Jaguar emblem on the vehicle's rear and then realised that a cloth had been bound to its number plate. Then, bizarrely, it slowed, causing Leo to press the brake pedal. Then it drifted into the right-hand lane, decelerating even more such that Leo was again in the lead. As they passed, Leo glanced towards the motorist but his face was obscured by an old-fashioned leather driving helmet and goggles. Suddenly the reality of the situation dawned on him – he was being deliberately targeted by this person. When the Jaguar swung in behind, Leo realised that the front number plate had also been obscured. He decided to pull in at the next opportunity but there was no verge here and it was not safe to do so. The road climbed further and then Scallop Bay came into view and a sign warned him of the sharp left bend ahead. Leo tried to slow down but the Jag was now almost touching the rear of the Humber, and then he felt a slight jolt as his car was nudged.

'Come on old girl, hold the road, hold the road,' he muttered as he gripped the wheel tightly.

The highway broadened now and Leo cursed himself for not hugging the left. The Jaguar powered into the space and made to cut him off from following the abrupt curve and force him through the hedge ahead and, Leo suspected, over a drop. At the last moment he noticed an opened gate to a farm track to his front right and steered the Humber towards it, praying that there wasn't an oncoming vehicle, plunging the clutch but taking care not to depress the brake pedal too heavily to avoid losing control. After sixty yards of rumbling down the track, which shot off at an angle, the car came to a halt amid a cloud of dust. Leo took a long breath and looked to his left. The drop wasn't as steep or as high as he had feared, but might have been enough to have injured him or even ignited his petrol tank and incinerated him. Probably the Jaguar driver had obscured his plates and worn his helmet and goggles lest he be identified in the eventuality which had, in fact, unfolded – Leo's survival. He looked ahead and only now noticed the stunning view of the three highest peaks of the south end. Not exactly under the circumstances he'd had in mind.

Leo, who realised his emerald polo shirt was drenched in sweat beneath his tweed jacket, backed the Humber up the track, and once he reached the road paused and looked in his rear-view mirror. The Jag must have turned, because it crawled by, before steaming off northwards. Leo was suddenly seized by rage and incautiously reversed his car into the highway, deciding to give chase to his antagonist even though he knew it was unlikely that he would catch up.

He drove his elderly motor car as hard as it would tolerate, but his progress was hampered by a tractor which pulled out ahead of him. He struck the steering wheel in exasperation and impatiently overtook the lumbering machine on the next straight stretch. Soon the road descended into the valley where Leo had encountered the shepherdess and her flock. He glimpsed a car below him which was the same colour as the coupé. It was heading westwards on the Saint Madden's route, and it disappeared from view where the road became obscured by a wood.

Leo slowed at the junction at the foot of the slope, hung a left and accelerated in pursuit, the Humber engine roaring dramatically as he ascended the gears. The bitumen undulated and skirted the broadleaved wood, sunlight flashing on the windscreen. He noticed the entrance to a drive which penetrated the wood, where a man wearing a flat cap was closing a gate; evidently a vehicle had just entered, most likely Leo's quarry. He drove round a bend, crested a brae, and then turned the Humber and slowly coasted back down towards the wood. He passed the drive entrance and rolled the car onto a grassy area to his right, just beyond a quaint white milestone. He got out, peeled off his sunglasses and jacket and cast them onto the passenger seat, and took in his surroundings, enjoying the cool, shaded, herby air after the rigours of the highway. A bower elliptically framed a beautiful view of a large house with the sea and Erran in the distance. Leo crept across the ferny, soily floor. Woodland apparently bordered the quite extensive grounds of the residence on all four sides, as well as a new wire fence with two layers of barbs. Leo fetched one of the car mats from the Humber and also his World War II Barr & Stroud binoculars. He used the binoculars to scan the house, which was finished with pink painted harling dressed with grey stone, and which nestled by a grove of tall trees. Suddenly he noticed a guard patrolling the park's perimeter, a surly-looking tough with a five o'clock shadow whose suit needed a press. Leo hid behind a mass of rhododendron as he waited for him to pass. Then he draped the car mat over the barbed wire and with a complete lack of aplomb scaled the fence. He removed the mat and threw it over the fence where it nestled in the understory of the woods. He looked from left to right, then made a dash across a large expanse of open greensward. Leo had almost reached the trees which hugged the house when he heard gunfire, two shots nearby. Seized by mortal terror he sprinted the final few yards and threw himself to the ground behind a towering horse chestnut. A few seconds later he heard two more shots, but this time he realised that they had been preceded by the command 'Pull!' and had issued from the other side of the building. He breathed a sigh of relief but wondered how much more his nerves could take – already today he had believed he was being shot at on two occasions and had been run off the road by a maniac, and it wasn't even lunchtime yet. He peered at the rear of the residence, which Leo, ever the aesthete, couldn't help but note was a mid-eighteenth-century Palladian construction with flanking pavilions, very possibly designed by one of the Adam family.

He stole across a neat lawn and peered through a window, unsure of what he was looking for, and was met by a dining room, empty but for its sumptuous furniture. He crept round the eastern pavilion and spied the front of the house, admiring the pedimented entrance and Venetian windows. The clay pigeon party were on the terrace, three older men and an attractive woman in her late thirties who was fixing herself a cocktail at a table with a parasol. Leo needed to locate the coupé to confirm that this was indeed the abode of his road warrior antagonist. Perhaps the other pavilion, which was approximately where the drive terminated, was converted to a garage. He doubled back and made his approach. He cursed himself for not having brought his detective's kit with its skeleton keys, but when he tried a side door he found it to be unlocked. Inside were five vehicles: a Porsche SUV, a BWM 7 Series, a lovely Daimler Majestic Major, an old Wolseley 6/80 and, at the far end, a modern green coupé. Leo walked towards it and noted that it had recently been driven because its engine was ticking as it cooled. However, his heart sank when he realised that it was not the car that had persecuted him – it had the marque of Aston Martin, not Jaguar. Leo then heard a sinister growling sound and spun round to see a German Shepherd at the doorway through which he had entered. The beast regarded him evilly, its muscular body poised to attack.

Suddenly a voice ordered: 'Sultan – heel!' and the figure of one of the shooters filled the doorframe. The dog stood down. The man was well over six feet tall, aged in his late fifties and had a bald pate, saggy jowls and lips like a trout's. He was wearing a tattersall shirt and holding a shotgun, not exactly pointing it at Leo, but not exactly not.

'Who are you? What are you doing on my property?' he barked as he stepped into the garage.

'Sir, I know this looks bad, but I can assure you I can explain my presence here. My name is Leo Moran, I am a private detective. A vehicle similar to this one just ran me off the highway by Scallop Bay. I wanted to confirm if it was your car, which I saw on the road several minutes ago. As it transpires, it is not. I can only humbly beg your pardon.'

'Tell it to the police – they have already been called and are on their way,' said the man in his stentorian, upper-crust voice.

Behind the irate man, the guards now arrived: the one with the flat cap who Leo had seen closing the drive gate, and the rough-looking one he had seen patrolling the perimeter.

'You are supposed to be protecting my family,' their employer admonished. 'All that money I spent on security systems. I could weep, I really could.'

Leo spent an awkward ten minutes sitting on the concrete garage floor being watched by the two goons before Ronnie MacKellar arrived. The landowner sent the guards back to their posts and listened as Leo explained to Ronnie everything that had occurred on the road to Scallop Bay, and how he had been shaken by the experience and had then mistaken the identity of the coupé on the Saint Madden's road.

'What you saw was my wife returning from shopping in Kilmichael in the Aston,' remarked the man.

'You can understand how he could have made such an error, sir,' said Ronnie reasonably.

'It doesn't give him the right to march into other people's private property. I want him charged with housebreaking.'

'How about trespassing?' tried Ronnie.

'That is not a criminal offence in Scotland. Do your duty, Sergeant, or I'll call my lawyer.'

Defeated, Ronnie led Leo towards the police cruiser.

'I'm terribly sorry for all this bother, Sergeant,' said Leo as they drove towards Kilmichael after pausing at the Humber to allow the accused to collect his jacket. 'Mind you, you must admit it's a bit suspicious that fellow being so security-sensitive. Guards and dogs and barbed wire and all.'

'He has a right to be,' snapped Ronnie. 'Mr Ashby is a wealthy man who, when he lived in Dumfriesshire, almost had a child kidnapped for ransom. Which is precisely why he moved to the island, to be more private and secure. The point is, Leo: nobody has bothered him over here. Until today.'

'Oh dear, I feel dreadful. I must apologise to him.'

'You will just leave it, Leo. I'll try my best to smooth things over. Mr Ashby just wants a quiet life, and he's not the only one. And here's you and Nicky Barrett and your pal Marcus Troughton digging up the past, trying to uncover dire deeds which never took place.'

'Then why did someone just run me off the road?'

'Maybe it was a boy racer at the wind-up.'

'A boy racer with his number plates covered? With his features obscured?'

'I'm sure there was no murderous intent. By the way, there was a report of machine gun fire coming from your esteemed host's place earlier. You wouldn't happen to know anything about it, would you?'

'I'm sure there was no murderous intent,' replied Leo.

The police station was an ugly grey roughcast building constructed during the 1970s and situated around the corner from the library and the museum. Leo sat on a plastic chair beneath a collage of crime prevention posters as he waited to be booked. He picked over what had unfolded. First of all, he estimated that the height and posture of the Jaguar coupé driver was that of a man. It was odd, he considered, that the driver had doubled back as though he wanted to check on his fate, yet had not molested him further when he saw that the Humber had come safely back up the track. Leo gazed at a roadmap of Sonna mounted on the wall facing him. Unless he had a bolthole nearby, the Jaguar driver would then have proceeded to the junction and either headed east for Kilmichael – although he could have gone there more directly by not making his U-turn and picking up a road to the capital just below Scallop Bay, or west towards Saint Madden's and Herrick Bay. His eventual destination could have been anywhere in the north of the island. Had Leo perished, the incident would have looked like an accident, assuming there hadn't been any witnesses. The question was, who would have wanted to harm him? Could Norris Meiklejohn have followed him after their conversation? But surely there was no possible motive. He imagined that Troughton and Nicky were loose-lipped sorts, especially after a few drinks, so potentially anyone on the island could have known about Leo becoming involved in investigating the mysterious deaths. A person with something to hide might have researched Leo, learned of his psychic powers and possessed the perspicacity to fear him. And Vincent Comiskey, who would know he was the prime suspect in the Andy Lamb case, fitted the bill. However, Leo reminded himself that he needed to keep an open mind and consider everyone he met on Sonna. The Jaguar driver could have been connected to one or more of the *other* deaths, or be entangled in these matters in a way as yet unimagined. Whatever was the case, Leo was now sure that there was meat on the bones of his investigations, despite the fact that he had not experienced any visions as yet. Because if someone wanted him out of the way, then at least one of the deaths had not been a mere accident.

Ronnie called Leo into the station office and asked him to view the manufacturer's profile of a car which he had pulled up on his computer screen. It was a Jaguar F-Type coupé in British racing green, and Leo confirmed that this was indeed the correct model and colour.

'Funny,' said Ronnie.

'What?' asked Leo.

'To my knowledge the only person on the Isle of Sonna to own such a motor is Nicky Barrett – he's got several cars.

And guess what: it's racing green. I would be extremely interested if he was behind the wheel because he's currently serving a ban after being convicted of driving under the influence. I'll pay him a visit.'

'I must confess I'd feel rather awkward if you did that, Sergeant. Nicky is an ally, so it would be absurd for him to try and do me a mischief. Also, I reckon the driver was a taller man.'

'Well, I'm sorry, but I need to find out if he or anybody else was driving his car so aggressively.'

'Just out of interest, Sergeant: what type of vehicle does Norris Meiklejohn own?'

'A maroon Land Rover Discovery, with grey and white action flashes on its flanks. It is one ugly set of wheels.'

'Oh yes, I recall seeing it parked outside his home. What about Vincent Comiskey?'

'He doesn't have a car. Just his brewery van.'

A desk phone rang and after a two-minute conversation Ronnie replaced the receiver and spun round in his chair to face Leo.

'I should stick a few quid on a horse, if I were you,' he said mysteriously, his eyes twinkling.

'I beg your pardon?'

'You should back a horse, because your luck seems to be in today. That was Mr Ashby. He doesn't want to press charges after all. Apparently, your name rang a bell with him. After we left him, he recalled that a Leo Moran was in some way associated with his friend, one Baron Greatorix. He phoned the baron, and heard how you have become best pals with his younger brother Fordyce, who apparently greatly admires your detective work and super-heroic commitment to justice, not least when you helped solve murder cases at Loch Dhonn and Biggnarbriggs.'

'It's not what you know, it's who you know,' said Leo

despondently, feeling squalid for having benefited from the influence of the rich and powerful.

'Not only that, Mr Ashby came across your Humber Hawk. Reckons that a chap who drives a classic like that can't be all bad. Cheer up,' he added, 'it's better than spending a night in the cells. Come on, I'll drive you back to your museum piece.'

Soon they were motoring towards Mr Ashby's property, and Ronnie struck up conversation.

'So, Leo. That case at Biggnarbriggs Hall last summer – it was something of a sensation. You were involved?'

'It is true I did my bit in helping the police with their inquiries. You won't have read about me in the newspapers, though, because I was subject to a Witness Anonymity Order.'

'You can count on my discretion.'

'Sergeant, regarding this Comiskey fellow: I wonder, does he have a police record?'

'Plenty, but nothing evil or kinky – and he's been as good as gold for years.'

Ronnie coasted the cruiser onto the grassy area where the Humber had been abandoned. Leo was granted permission to nip back through the woods to retrieve his car mat. Upon his return, Ronnie lowered his window, removed his Polaroid sunglasses, fixed Leo in the eye and said: 'Now, Monsieur Poirot: I want you to drive off and stay well away from here from now on.'

Leo obeyed.

The Farmers' Tales

LEO drove the dreaded stretch of highway again, more than a little anxious after the morning's trauma. He kept glancing in his rear-view mirror for a sinister green car, but his journey passed uneventfully and this time he was able to properly enjoy the view from above Scallop Bay before joining the secondary route between Kilmichael and the south end known as the west road or the country road. The rich land was cultivated or good grazing, with copses and farm buildings nestling in its folds. Leo passed a rugged nine-hole golf course and at a cemetery on the edge of a village called Melford he took the single-track Lagg Road instead of continuing to Ardcaden Bay. His first port of call was the stone circle where the youths had held their drunken rites all those years ago. It was well signposted, and Leo parked the Humber and walked the short distance towards it through a plantation of Norway spruce, Sitka spruce and lodgepole pine. A similar plantation mantled the slopes of this side of the Cathair – which was a pudding-shaped hill which dominated the area. The Bronze Age henge was a curious place with four stones, one of which was pink and shaped like a lollipop, but it bequeathed nothing remarkable; one of Leo's objectives for the day was to discover if any of the key sites from the dramas of 1989 and onwards might stimulate instinctive insights or visions. He then consulted the OS map which Troughton had marked with the key loci and worked out an approximate route for the afternoon's odyssey.

The fertile isthmus at the south-west of the island where the standing stones were located connected with the south end. The peninsula was igneous, the lava having coursed across the sandstone to create a strange ossified landscape of cliffs and crags and ridges and rocky hillocks and outcrops. Ardcaden Bay was on the eastern coast, while the Lagg Road penetrated part of its interior and had a spectacular outlook over the weird basalt formations by the western shoreline, then the glittering sound, then Erran.

The old McGrouther place, which was named Manach Farm after the bay it overlooked, was a cluster of whitewashed buildings at the top of the south end. Leo halted the Humber at the gate, got out and picked his way through the dirt, which was cloven by the tracks of heavy tyres. He knocked on the farmhouse door and then strolled into the yard and called out, but there didn't seem to be anybody around. He entered a large outbuilding where the farm machinery was kept and where presumably the McGrouthers' son had met his dreadful end, but he reckoned whichever beastly apparatus had impaled the poor lad was long banished. He murmured a prayer for him and his loved ones. He went back outside and rounded the outbuilding, and saw two farm workers toiling in a distant field. He returned to the Humber and drove further down the Lagg Road, past rough cattle pasture festooned with hawthorn and yellow-flowering gorse. At one point, Leo noticed two roe deer bounding joyfully across an open expanse. He passed a drumlin and then a broad-leafed wood to his left, beyond which was Inkpot Farm, the home of Mr and Mrs Heron, whom Troughton had explained were a childless couple who had taken up their feu during the 1980s, rearing chiefly sheep on the rugged terrain behind and across the road from their steading.

The Humber Hawk's engine complained as Leo gunned the accelerator in low gear to overcome the steep gradient that led to the farmyard. Heron was loading green plastic trays of white eggs into a 4x4 vehicle. Leo got out of the car and remarked upon the gorgeous red-orange vividness of the new berries on Heron's two rowans, which were planted at each side of the yard entrance.

'I dug those trees in myself, years ago,' said the farmer.

The sun was hot but a breeze had picked up and there was a queer quality to the moment. Leo noticed that from the rowan branches were hung brass triquetra wind chimes, tinkling faintly above the background clucking of hens.

'My wife's idea, for prettiness,' said Heron, reading Leo's inquisitive expression. He was pale-skinned, and had watery green eyes and a thin reddish-blond beard, and Leo thought he looked more like an artist than a farmer.

Leo introduced himself and explained the nature of his visit, then said: 'Archie Kerr told me that you were aware of cars passing on the night of Andy Lamb's death, as the kids made their way from the stone circle to the end of the Lagg Road.'

'That is correct,' said Heron. Leo found his tone a little testy, but simply waited for the man to elaborate. 'My wife and I were in bed. I looked at the clock and saw it was half past eleven. It was highly unusual, having vehicles coming by at that time of night. The next day we found out that the Lamb boy had died after taking that fall. A terrible waste.'

'Whose land was the body found on?'

'The Baronet owns most of the land on Sonna.'

'What I mean is: whose tenancy does that land fall under?'

'Mine.'

Mrs Heron appeared at the front door of the cheerful

farmhouse, closing it behind her. She approached the men, greeting Leo pleasantly. She was a bony, rather bedraggled woman, with lifeless hair but keen hazel eyes.

'There have been several other mysterious deaths at the south end over recent years,' said Leo after explaining his purpose to Mrs Heron. 'I wonder if there is anything either of you could tell me about them?'

'There was the poor McGrouthers' son,' said Mrs Heron. 'It cast a real pall over the farms round here. But it was just a horrid accident.'

'If you don't mind, we need to get these eggs to Kilmichael,' said Mr Heron.

'Where are you off to now?' enquired his wife politely.

'I'm going to retrace Andy Lamb's steps. I'm looking forward to seeing Saint Caden's Chapel.'

'Often the early medieval Christians would build churches and monasteries on or near pagan shrines and alcoves, to sanctify them,' said Mr Heron. 'There's a well up there, and the ancient Celts believed that water had sacred properties. They might associate a well with a water goddess. I bet that's why they built the monastery there.'

The 4x4 was better positioned to negotiate the exit from the yard, so Leo politely signalled to the Herons to proceed first. Unfortunately, when Leo descended, he misjudged where the narrow track was in relation to his tyres and took the turn back onto the road too sharply, beaching the Humber on the steep verge such that the rear wheels hadn't enough traction on the turf. He turned off the ignition and got out to assess the situation, feeling horrified that he had inflicted something heinous upon the beloved motor car, and embarrassed and unmanly at his panicked state. He beseeched Our Lady for her intercession, and at the next instant the miracle arrived in the shape of a dented tractor travelling southwards. However, it puttered on as though it would pass by and thus mock the subsequent prayer of thanksgiving Leo had just sent up. He inwardly cursed the driver's heartlessness. However, the man, suddenly realising the situation, then slowed, pulled in at the side of the road and dismounted.

He was a cloth-capped farmer, unshaven, handsome and aged in his early sixties. He was broad-faced, had receded brown hair and laughing chestnut eyes, and a good deal of strength seemed to still dwell within his trunk and limbs. Leo explained his predicament to the man, who told him that he would return presently in his Land Rover with a chain to try and pull the Humber off the bank. He possessed that sunny, uncomplicated mien often found among country folk which sometimes shames urban visitors who bring with them the cynicism and street-wise mistrustfulness of the city. Within barely fifteen minutes the farmer indeed reappeared, accompanied by a lanky, blond-haired teenager. They attached the chain, and Leo climbed into the car and checked that the transmission was in neutral and that the handbrake was off. The 4x4 then took the strain and Leo steered his vehicle down the slope and onto the tarmac. He was mightily relieved that its underside seemed undamaged by the mishap, and expressed his profound gratitude to the farmer, who subjected him to a gentle ribbing.

Momentarily Leo envied the farmer his decent, simple, family life, lived connected to land. He regretted thinking ill of the man when he had thought the tractor was going to pass by, and wished he was better disposed towards looking for the best in people. The farmer's kindness had humbled him, and he had to remind himself that he, too, would have stopped to help in similar circumstances.

Leo's beatification of rural types was suddenly revoked when a metallic-blue Audi 100 C1 sedan burst into view, causing him to leap to safety. The driver had an aged, severe, cadaverous face, thinned jet-black hair and hard, deep-set green eyes behind round-lensed spectacles. He sounded his horn furiously as he used a passing place to avoid the stationary vehicles, barely slowing as he did so.

Leo took a breath and then introduced himself and his current investigative capacity to his rescuer. The man accepted his handshake and identified himself as Rab Haddow, the farmer at Lagg Farm at the end of the road. The teenage lad was introduced as his grandson.

'I wonder, might I impose upon another few minutes of your doubtless precious time?' asked Leo.

'All right, but we'd better get these motors out of the way. There's a bit of hardstanding to the side down there, where the road finishes.'

Leo noticed that the angry Audi driver had hung a right at this dead end – which was six hundred yards or more away, down a private track that disappeared into a copse which cloaked the lower reaches of an impressive hill.

'That's the second time I have almost been killed by an automobile today,' said Leo after he and the farmer had disembarked from their vehicles at the hardstanding and Haddow's grandson had mumbled a goodbye and begun to walk home. Leo noted mentally that he was standing where the teenagers had waited in vain for Andy Lamb to return from his dare on that fateful night in 1989. He also realised that someone looking out from either Inkpot farmstead or the upper floor of the house at Lagg Farm, which was two furlongs down a track from where the road terminated and on the other side of a slight rise, would have had a view of Andy heading up a sloping, signposted path towards Saint Caden's Chapel. Perhaps such a watcher, with mischief in mind, could have intercepted him on his way back from his dare by taking a circuitous route.

'That road hog was Dr Morgenthaler, the misanthropic old bugger. He lives by himself in a lonely old place called Crochadh House, down there,' said Haddow, motioning towards the west coast, 'tucked round the side of Hangman's Hill.' This hill indeed provided a dramatic backcloth, its eastern flank steep, its north face a perfect arrowhead, verdant but for a fringe of naked rock.

'Has he lived there long?'

Haddow thought for a moment. 'Since the early 1980s, I'd say. He used to bide abroad, but I don't know where exactly. On the rare occasions when I've spoken to him I've noticed a foreign twang that I can never place. Our old postman, now retired, used to say he would receive letters and parcels from South America. If he's a medical doctor, he's never practised since he's been on Sonna.'

'He couldn't have seen anything from his house on the night Andy Lamb perished, because it is out of sight of this road,' observed Leo.

'Aye. Anyway, he probably wouldn't answer the door if you were to go down there to ask him about it. He's excessively private. Secretive, even.'

'What do you remember about that night?'

'Nothing – we were sound asleep as farming folk ought to be. The first I knew about anything being wrong was when the polis came by the next day, asking if we'd seen the Lamb boy.'

'He seems to have been a well-regarded lad,' stated Leo. He perceived Haddow raise an eyebrow. 'What's up?' he enquired.

'Just that one day he came by out of the blue to flatter my daughter. Even though he was supposed to be stepping out with that half-caste lassie at the time. But I must have brung her up well, because she saw right through him. Dirty wee bugger, God rest him.'

The men chatted in the sunshine for a while: about the island, about nature's beauty, about animals, about the soil, about family. Haddow had a deep tan, the result of constant outdoor living, yet his neighbour Heron had somehow avoided this seasoned complexion. Leo liked Haddow's wry good humour but also detected a shrewdness to him, that he was eminently wise and sensible. Leo had a sense of unspoken dimensions to the man, of depths and countries he would not divulge unless required to. He was a person quietly sure of himself and his right to be on this earth and tend his little portion of it, to raise his daughter and grandchildren there in peace.

Leo steered the conversation onto the other mysterious deaths at the south end, emphasising that of Farmer McGrouther's son but a mile north along this very road.

'Things don't really change down here,' said Haddow, 'and there isn't really any crime. That's why folk love Sonna, why folk who move away return, why folk who holidayed here as children bring their children to holiday here or even end up retiring here. These deaths you speak of – they are all just separate rural tragedies.'

Haddow departed and Leo prepared for his hike, which would be favoured by lovely weather, anointing himself in high-factor sun cream and opting to leave his tweed jacket in the Humber. He placed his bushman hat upon his balding crown, hauled his knapsack over his shoulders and set off.

A stone dyke flanked one side of the path up to Saint Caden's Church. This wall was taller than Leo had first realised, but he noted that someone looking out from Inkpot would still be able to see the head and shoulders of anyone of six foot or more; judging by the photographs he had seen, Andy Lamb fitted this height profile.

According to two heritage interpretation panels, Saint Caden's had originally been a monastery, its eponymous founder establishing it in the late sixth century. It was believed to have been destroyed by bloodthirsty Norse raiders. The chapel, which was the best-preserved item, was built later and operated as a parish church until the Reformation, after which it fell into ruin. The entire monastery precinct was on raised ground, perimetered by a wall known as a vallum. It nestled within mixed woodland of sycamore, beech, Scots pine, tall ash and elm, and was sheltered from the north by higher ground above little crags. Songbirds sang merrily to atone for the occasional grumpy caw from a murder of crows who sunned themselves on the high branches of a tree just beyond the vallum. Leo sat upon a shaded bench with a superb view down the hillside and over to Erran, the perfect spot at which to consume his packed luncheon. He reflected on the numinous beauty of this place. He had felt a little on edge after he had left the Humber in case the driver of the green Jaguar came for him on foot, but as he shared crumbs with the finches he found peace amid the prayer-soaked stones of Saint Caden's, the vibes of ancient Masses still humming through the centuries. He considered how so many of Scotland's western islands or places on those islands were named for some intrepid Dark Ages Irish saint or hermit who had crossed the sea. They had lived in a warrior culture that legitimised and promoted violence as redemptive, therefore these monks were undertaking a true revolution of consciousness by adopting a life of peace, silence and humility. Yet by some miracle the warriors swore themselves to protect them and sought their blessing. Then the Vikings arrived.

Leo had two segments of half-melted Fry's Orange Cream as dessert and began hiking again, at one point cresting a sloping greensward which was studded with tumescent outcrops of calcified lava, and enjoying a spectacular view down to a faraway sandy bay. He ascended further to an area of humpy, multi-levelled geology where he examined the OS map. It was of a highly detailed 1:25,000 scale and therefore Leo was able to easily locate the grassy shelf from which Andy had fallen. As Nicky had stated, to get there indeed required a short detour from the path which should have taken him through a bridle gate before hanging a right down an easy decline into the valley of Glen Colm and from there up the rear of the Cathair to complete his dare. Instead, he had veered off to the right too early, in the direction of the steep drop. He might have done this accidentally, considered Leo. He was inebriated and may simply have lost his bearings in the poor light and turned right too soon, forgetting that he still had to come through the bridle gate. Then he might not have seen the edge clearly or had seen it but drunkenly tripped over and plummeted to his death. Or if Andy was moving quickly and an intimidating person was coming towards him, this might have caused him to change course abruptly. Perhaps that person gave chase with murderous intent, and drove or threw Andy off the edge. Or perhaps that party simply wanted to frighten Andy or fight with him. Perhaps he then fell during such a fight or perhaps in the panic of a chase he forgot about the danger of the terrain he was traversing and didn't see the edge clearly, or was looking over his shoulder at the crucial moment, or ran along the edge and tripped and fell over. Anyway, Leo decided that he would like to see what this topography looked like on a similar moonlit night.

He gazed down Glen Colm. It was a bleak place. He realised he was standing on a mighty terraced spine of land which rose to Torr Mòr, a desolate, wind-blasted peak at the bottom of the south end. The high land on the other side of the glen was bland in comparison to the crags and scree slopes of this side. The north presented a far pleasanter prospect, a fir grove and pastures and then the fertile isthmus and the azure sea beyond.

Leo located the bridle gate and strode down onto the floor of Glen Colm. There, upon an area of thick turf dotted with meadow buttercups, he came across a curious thing: burnt bones amid ashes. He couldn't determine the bones' species because he couldn't locate the creature's skull. He withdrew his detective's kit from his knapsack and pulled out an evidence bag. He placed two smaller bones into this; he would post them to his clever friend Fordyce Greatorix for identification. Leo then circumnavigated a large moss and walked to the foot of the drop down which Andy Lamb had plunged. He took out his rosary and kissed its little crucifix as he thought about what had happened here. He looked up and estimated he was about seventy feet from the grassy shelf. It wasn't really a sheer cliff, rather a very steep slope – a scarp would be the best definition. Leo estimated that it wouldn't necessarily be fatal to fall from it, but one's chances of dying by being brained or snapping one's neck would be fairly high. A boulder someway up looked the likely candidate for rupturing poor Andy's skull.

Leo poured his rosary into his trouser pocket and began the haul up the back of the Cathair. He was glad of his hat and the slight breeze as he toiled beneath the relentless sun through grazing meadows buzzing with insects and ornamented with field marigolds. There was an abundance of painted lady butterflies and larks spilled their song from the flawless sky. Eventually he saw the cairn that marked the hill's summit. The Cathair was a volcanic plug, its official Gaelic title being Cathair Caden, meaning the seat of Saint Caden, and Leo enjoyed the incredible 360-degree vista from its top, with Great Cunrae, Little Cunrae and then the mainland to the east, some of the embayments of Sonna's west coast visible to the north, and the mystic mountains of Erran to the west with Kintyre in the far distance.

Leo located a thin path which was cut into the heathery hillside and began his descent towards Ardcaden Bay, which was splayed out gloriously below. He passed the occasional spreading sycamore and then encountered a fly-ridden sea of primeval ferns which were difficult to wade through and made him dread what putrescence they might conceal. He entered the Cathair woods, a realm of oak and ash and alder and elder and hazel and rowan, much of it quite immature and jungly, with the odd interloping pine. To Leo's left this sylvan tract became thick commercial conifer forestry. He cut a walking stick of hazel to mitigate the gradient, and caught glimpses down through the lovely leafage of the village's slate roofs and chimneypots and the grey rear stone of its tall tenements. He came across a swing, a hawser bound to an impossibly high branch which would oscillate over a steep drop that was clad in abundant, extravagantly fragrant vegetation. Into the trunk of the swing tree was carved love hearts containing faded initials, relics of bygone holiday romances. One bore 'AL + AA' – surely Andy Lamb and Amy Agumanu. Leo found a precarious way down to a narrow earthen track, taking care to avoid menacing thickets of towering nettles, which ran behind the back gardens and allotments of the properties, then followed a little lane to the road.

The Villagers' Tales

LEO found it peculiar finally arriving at Ardcaden Bay, the nexus of his investigations. He somehow felt as though he was trespassing on other people's sa territory, stepping onto the stage on which the teenage dramas of years ago which he had heard so much of had been played out. He popped into the local shop on the pretext of purchasing a roll of peppermints. It combined the functions of a post office, a tearoom and a grocer's, and was stocked as though it was still the 1950s with canned goods, sacks of coal, bars of plain chocolate and tins of tobacco. He chatted with the proprietor, a friendly, rotund woman beyond retirement age who recalled the Andy Lamb tragedy but was unable to offer any new insights into this or the other mysterious deaths.

'Some say the south end is cursed,' she concluded.

'This island seems to have quite a pull,' said Leo as he made to take his leave.

'It gets into your blood, this place,' said the woman. 'Especially the Bay. Folk always return.'

Leo walked to the approximate site of the fatal motorcycle crash just outside the village. He looked along the arrow-straight road which led to the so-called Wee Bay, which referred to those homes between the settlements of Ardcaden Bay and Melford. He pictured the doomed Italian motorcyclist powering along this stretch at a terrific rate.

Then he gazed out to sea and thought about the Aberdonian scuba diver who had drowned alone, out beyond the ridge. He felt a pang of melancholy and said a little prayer for both men.

Leo headed back to the woods which loomed high behind the village, walking past the rear gardens of the properties which were a ménage of allotments, drying greens, the metalwork of exterior stone stairs, cabbage palms, greenhouses, upturned boats, coal bunkers, potting sheds, washhouses and disused lavatories. He located the hanging tree where Miss Green had expired, which was easy to identify because someone had tied a bunch of flowers to it in remembrance. It was situated amid a sloping carpet of wild garlic and Leo imagined that when it flowered during May it must seem like a sea of miniature lilies, as though planted in Miss Green's honour. He placed his palm gently against the tree, which was a mature ash, and made the Sign of the Cross.

He strolled the front of Ardcaden, breathing deeply of the marvellous salty, seaweedy air and admiring the cottages and the tenements, which were quainter and more idiosyncratic than their urban Glasgow counterparts. He approached an old stone pier off which a boy with a pail of cockles was bait fishing, and looked to his right for a drive. He walked up this and located Johnathon Lamb's residence, a narrow, yellow cottage, but nobody apart from a barking dog seemed to be at home.

Leo's next destination was the grandest building in the village, a nearby white-painted, nineteenth-century, three-storeyed hotel, its prominent feature a central French-pavilion roofed square tower. The only vehicle parked outside was a powerful motorcycle. Leo walked up the steps, opened a heavy plate-glass door and walked through a lobby which had a singular, comforting odour somehow evocative of his childhood. There was only the bored-looking hotelier and one other patron in the public bar.

Leo ordered a glass of ginger beer and requested a refill for his Swiss-made aluminium water flask. The hotelier, Tam Logan, who Archie Kerr had stated had found Miss Green's body, was an overweight, jowly man in his late fifties with a moustache. Apparently, he had owned the Saint Caden's for more than a decade and had lived in the Bay all his life. As they chatted, Leo became increasingly aware of the eyes of the other customer, who was sitting by the window, drilling into him. He glanced over and noticed the fellow regarding him quite insolently from over his pint of lager, a slight smirk on his countenance. Fortunately, background pop music was playing, just loud enough to drown out Leo's conversation. He brought up the subject of his investigating the mysterious deaths.

'I found one of them,' Tam volunteered. 'The poor Green woman. It was morning, I always take the dog out early. We went up the back lane and I let him off the leash. Suddenly he bolted up into the woods and started barking like crazy. I went to get him and got the shock of my life when I saw her just ... dangling there.'

'That must have been dreadful.'

'The worst thing was the look branded on her face. It was beyond describing. It was of sheer and utter horror. As for the other deaths, I can't tell you anything you won't already know, but I can tell you one thing: that is Andy Lamb's brother sitting over there.'

Leo nodded to Tam and walked with his glass past a pool table and over to where Johnathon Lamb was. He had a buzz cut and was wearing black leather motorcycle trousers and a Wild Turkey T-shirt which stretched over his impressively muscular torso. One bulging bicep bore a tattoo of a military emblem and the words: *Black Watch Basra Beano,*

2003. Leo noticed a similarity in Johnathon's face with Andy's, despite it now having years on his dead brother's, although his features were arranged less sympathetically.

'Mr Lamb? Leo Moran,' he said, offering his hand. Johnathon issued a crushing grip to establish the physical hierarchy. 'I say, that's quite a handshake you have there. I'm here to investigate –'

'I know who you are and what you're here for,' interrupted Johnathon rudely. 'Already seen you, already got you all figured out. I had you under surveillance yesterday.'

'Oh really?'

'Aye, when you were at Saint Madden's. You were visiting Archie Kerr. I had clocked you in Kilmichael earlier getting into your car. Nicky Barrett had told me about your arrival, and mentioned that you drive a vintage Humber Hawk, so I knew it was you and I decided to follow you on my bike.'

The obnoxious manner in which Johnathon had boasted about spying on him meant that Leo couldn't help but wonder if he was the driver of the green Jaguar, bullying him off the road in some bizarre power play.

'Why, may I ask?'

'Let's just say I'm a nosey fucker,' he replied gruffly. Anger seemed to emanate from him like a halo. 'Especially when it comes to anything to do with my beloved brother's death, which you are investigating. So, I wanted to size you up.'

'You seem like a man who likes to be in control.'

'You got that right. In fact, I even hung around and followed you again. Saw you visit that Amy slut.'

'I must demand that you do not speak of her in such ungentlemanly terms.'

'Sounds like she's got your prick well teased. Find out anything juicy?'

'No. But I can assure you I will do everything within my means to get to the root of what happened to your poor brother. Mind if I sit down?'

Johnathon nodded and spent the next few minutes telling Leo his backstory. He had moved to Ardcaden Bay from the mainland, and was not 'burdened' by a wife or children. He had a good job as a technician at the nuclear power station on the Ayrshire coast, to where he commuted using his speedboat. This week he was off, using up some annual leave, just messing around on his bike. He had been eight years Andy's junior, and he told how he had worshipped his brother, who had been a kindly, heroic young man. He explained that Andy was interred in the cemetery by Melford because he had loved the area, and also because it had been his parents' intention to retire down here so they had wanted him buried where they would be. As it happened, his mother and father had both died before they were able to realise their plan, because, Johnathon believed, of their broken hearts. Part of the reason that Johnathon himself had decided to move to the island was that he liked being near to his brother's mortal remains. 'Not that I go up to the grave. Too depressing,' he added.

Leo felt sorry for Johnathon, but he couldn't bring himself to like him. He spoke ill of people and had a particular over-confidence which was probably grounded in a spoiled upbringing. When probed, Johnathon said he had no opinion about the other mysterious deaths at the south end.

'What do you think of Nicky's theory that Vincent Comiskey was responsible for your brother's death?' asked Leo.

'I don't know for sure yet, but we'll find out for sure. And if that Fenian bastard killed my brother, then I'll put him in a wooden overcoat. What I do know for certain is that he is a rapist. It really pisses me off that these Papes can just go into a wee box, state their crimes and be done with it.'

'It doesn't work like that. A person must feel real remorse deep down in his soul if he wants absolution, truly repent and make a firm desire of amendment. And anyway, if a man confessed to murder, the priest would urge him to come clean to the police in order to ensure full remittance.'

'Oh. I didn't realise I was talking to one.'

'I thought you already had me all figured out?'

'I'm hitting the road,' muttered Johnathon before draining his lager, pulling on his biker's jacket and leaving without a goodbye.

Leo decided to roll out the Columbo routine, and caught up with Johnathon in the lobby where he was fiddling with his motorcycle helmet. 'Just one more thing, Mr Lamb. Do you ever drive a green Jaguar?' Leo carefully watched for the reaction on his interlocutor's face.

'Eh? No, I don't have a Jag. And if I did, it wouldn't be fucking green. Nicky's got a green Jag. An F-Type coupé, the flash wee bastard.'

'Do you mind my enquiring: where were you at around 10.30 this morning?'

'I do mind, but as it happens I was busy with a dirty wee bird in Kilmichael. I'd stayed the night. Why do you ask?'

'Forgive me. It's only that someone was driving such a vehicle aggressively at me by Scallop Bay.'

'Well what the fuck are you asking me about it for?' growled Johnathon as he leaned in belligerently.

Leo didn't doubt that this man would quickly use violence to get his way or to square an offence. He swallowed, and then said: 'To be frank, because I found it so downright odd that you were spying on me yesterday, and that you so breezily admitted to it.'

Johnathon backed off. 'You could try Nicky, but he's currently banned from driving. And why would he do that anyway? He's on the same side as us. Just fucking investigate my brother's death, don't start investigating us.'

Leo believed Johnathon. He returned to the bar and looked out of the window and watched the man mount his steel and chrome steed, kick-start it and accelerate away.

Leo now wanted to scope out the southernmost portion of the peninsula, and visit where Geoffrey Willett, the English rambler, had dropped dead. He left the hotel and strode to the end of the village, then past a wood of birch, willow and alder filled with chirruping birds to where the road terminated at a bus turning place. He went through a wooden gate and followed a marked walking route with steep slopes and cliffs to his right, and ridges of black and then grey volcanic rock jutting into the sea to his left. The hike became progressively more difficult, first over boards bound in chicken wire, then an earthen trail through ferns, then a pebbly path, then a precarious clamber over mighty stones beneath a near-vertical incline of sheer rock, at which point Leo abandoned his walking staff. He came across a raised beach adorned with tormentil, cat's-ear, eyebright, bird's-foot trefoil and thrift, then encountered a rocky landmark clasped by ash and elder known as Merlin's Neb, and a cave littered with rusted lager tins. The landscape became more dramatic as spilled boulders clotted the scarp. It was like standing in some prog rock album cover from the 1970s and Leo had a peculiar sensation as though he was the only person alive in the world. An unearthly silver-gold radiance came to rest on the water, into which a cormorant plunged. The path – shingle now, and shining – climbed towards a cleft which cradled the light like a portal to heaven, and when Leo reached this crest, he saw the lighthouse. He walked across a boulder field past the red sandstone headland and approached the gigantic slabs upon which the manmade structure sat. To the south-west a schooner with black sails had rounded Grog Head, which is the very extremity of Sonna; to the south east were the monstrous cliffs on the elbow of Little Cunrae. Leo reached the proximity of the lighthouse and said a prayer for the two Ayrshire fishermen who had perished off the coast here and for Mr Willett, the doomed hiker, and for all the people who loved them. He sat down and rested for a few minutes, listening to seawater coughing in a cistern deep below as a languorous seal surfaced nearby and regarded him with curiosity. Suddenly it occurred to him that something other than the morning's brush with the green Jaguar had been affecting his emotions. That the very fabric of the south end of the Isle of Sonna indeed vibrated with a sonorous energy as had been suggested to him. That this was a place rich with magic.

The bay here was called Glencolm Bay, and Leo got to his feet, shouldered his knapsack and began to negotiate it. He picked his way through large stones that looked like marble because of the white veins of dead lichen which clung to them. Silty waves lapped the black volcanic sand, and the beach and foreshore was a stony waste littered with inky seaweed, above which towered Torr Mòr, craggy and scabrous and barren compared with its more verdant neighbours. This was a moonscape, a chillingly bleak territory even in the perfect weather. Leo rounded the bay and endured an undulating hike above a series of ragged little coves. He cut inland through a gap in a ridge to find a strange, enclosed, treeless valley. The land was fretted with rock but essentially pastoral, the grass on which sheep nibbled an unnatural, near-lime green. To his right was a lochan choked with bulrushes and home to teal and tufted ducks, and to his left the steep inner side of Hangman's Hill which was banded by two high tiers of cliffs. The path rose through bracken, tall grasses and gorse, and the promise of the soft woodland which cloaked Saint Caden's Chapel was visible to the north, before which nestled Lagg Farm. It occurred to Leo that there were three enclosed glens at the neglected bottom of the south end: the desolate, lengthy Glen Colm to the east, this greener central one in which Rab Haddow farmed, and, according to the map, a smaller western one below Crochadh House where Dr Morgenthaler lived.

The Cats' House

LEO was glad to complete his walking circuit. He felt sun-tired and his limbs ached, and as he drove the Lagg Road he had to unwind the Humber window to expel the overheated air. It had been a long day and he hoped Troughton had something in for dinner.

He hung a right at the cemetery for the shore road, but as he passed the Melford Hotel, a white-painted country inn at a junction with craw-stepped gables, he paused, quite seduced by the view of the gentle land which stretched towards the coast and the way the genial evening light rested upon it. It was intersected by a single-track road, and Leo pulled in to consult his map. It informed him that this route would wind round and join the shore road further up, and only constitute a modest detour. Leo indicated and proceeded down the byway at a sedate pace, the fulsome, sun-washed trees looking grand in the summer eventide, a flock of sparrows rising from a field. After just a third of a mile, his enchanted mood was broken when the Humber's engine spluttered and then cut out; Leo hadn't noticed that the needle had been trembling in the red zone of the temperature gauge. Now there was only the low rumble of the tyres on the macadam as little pirouettes of steam issued from beneath the bonnet.

He coasted the Humber to a halt on a grassy verge to his right, in front of an old house which was in the lee of a rank of mature trees, their high canopies slanted as though to optimally shade the residence. Its features were plain but of pleasing proportions, its exterior finished with polished grey sandstone. Several added wings projected from the original eighteenth-century construction. Leo noticed a man, presumably the householder, regarding him from over the drystone wall which encircled his property. He was a big, black-bearded fellow aged around fifty, with dark eyes and a hearty demeanour. He wore canvas trousers and a collared T-shirt which commemorated Scotland's 1983 victory at Twickenham.

'Engine trouble?' he called out.

'I'm afraid so,' replied Leo through his opened window.

'Shall we take a look?' suggested the stranger.

Leo disembarked, popped the bonnet and pretended to examine the inner workings of his car meaningfully. The stranger, however, seemed to genuinely know what he was looking at, questioning Leo about precise details of the breakdown as his massive back hunched over the engine.

'I can't check the water level until it cools,' said the man in his bass voice. 'Why don't you come inside for a while? Take a refreshment while we wait.'

'I don't wish to impose upon you, sir.'

'It would be nice to have the company – I live alone, you see. Gus Blessing's the name.'

'Leo Moran. I am much obliged to you,' said Leo as he shook Blessing's massive paw.

Leo grabbed his jacket from the car and followed Blessing up a gravel path lined with attractive shrubs and into the house. They walked through a hallway ornamented in an old-fashioned order with a waxed sideboard, a grandmother clock and a barometer, and then into a drawing room which overlooked fields and then a wood, through which the water in outer Ardcaden Bay twinkled. This room was also an anachronism. A Persian carpet covered most of the heart-pine floorboards, which were stained in the same dark varnish as the wainscoting. There was elegant ball and claw foot furniture, an antique upright piano and a carved hardwood fireplace which was set within an inglenook and surrounded by beautiful Art Nouveau tiling. There was no television, only an outmoded radio cassette player.

'What a charming home you have.'

'Thank you. Folk round here refer to it as the "Cats' House". I've lived here an age, but I've never discovered why.'

Blessing seemed rather baffled by Leo's demurral of an alcoholic beverage lest he still be required to drive the Humber, and provided him with a glass of dandelion and burdock. Leo relaxed in the queer but pleasant atmosphere of the space, enjoying the view. Without divulging many details, he explained to Blessing his purpose on the island and found him to be an attentive listener, a solid fellow with a kindly nature. After a while, Blessing went out to the Humber. He returned ten minutes later, wiping grease from his hands with a rag.

'I've checked the radiator, the coolant level is fine. I reckon the head gasket has gone, I'm afraid. That's a big job. Perhaps fatal.' Leo sighed, barely able to contemplate the prospect of losing his cherished vehicle. 'I'd ring the mechanic, Harry Taylor, in Kilmichael for you,' added Blessing, 'but the nearest telephone is at Melford.'

'That's all right, I can use my mobile,' said Leo, producing his phone.

'The marvels of modern technology,' said Blessing, staring at the device in wonderment.

Blessing consulted a little notebook and read out the non-business-hours number of the mechanic. Leo dialled, slightly anxious about the lack of reception displayed on his phone, but was connected and explained his predicament. The elderly female voice on the other end of the line informed him that her husband Harry was long retired. However, her son Iain, who now ran the business, happened to be round, and she put him on. Leo spoke to the man who said that he would attend within the hour. He thanked him and hung up.

'The silver lining is that you won't be driving tonight,' said Blessing with a wink as he enticingly rocked a curiously shaped bottle in one of his giant hands.

'There is that,' smiled Leo, noticing that the liquid seemed to change colour as it swirled, at one moment amber and resembling merely whisky or brandy, but then blushing viridescent, then damson, then jasper.

'I call this the "Concoction". Let's just say it's an old family recipe,' said the host as he poured measures into two engraved sherry glasses. 'Be sure to sip it gently!'

The mysterious fluid, which had the viscosity of a liqueur, had a not unfamiliar, elegant base and was sweet and honeyed and high in alcohol content. Yet it also possessed novel upper complexities suggesting unknown roots which had been truffled out from the black humus of a shadowy Sonna forest alcove, myriad floral infusions bequeathed by laborious hunts and prickly pickings and careful pressings, and high-quality spices from far-flung lands which had been subjected to arcane processes. Its effect was instant, and was comforting yet extraordinarily enlivening to the senses. Leo didn't exactly feel drunk, more drugged, and was content to listen to Blessing's monologues, which were peppered with references to everything from Sonna's ancient history and folklore to poetry to Shakespeare. The draught bequeathed a profound mellowness and Leo felt as though he was half present, half elsewhere in some magical realm or dreamlike state. The patterns and aspects of the room became intricately fascinating, and the vividness of colour seemed to intensify in the glassy yellow evening light – particularly purples and greens. Smoke from a pipe which Blessing had lit smelled marvellously rich as it rose to the ceiling in an elegant, textured visual ballet. Leo felt a surging array of emotional sensations, each evoking a lost moment from his past all the way back to early childhood. Time became elongated or perhaps stopped altogether, and he forgot entirely about the pending arrival of the mechanic.

At one point, Leo remarked upon the eerie energy which seemed to inhabit the south end and Blessing concurred with his observation, stating that it vibrated across the isthmus into his locality too, and to a lesser extent beyond and into the rest of the island. He then mentioned 'the demon in the hill' feeding off such vibes 'to my fateful detriment'.

'Isn't that just a local legend?' said Leo.

'Put it this way: you wouldn't catch me anywhere near that dark road at night. Or anywhere near Glen Colm, the crucible of evil.'

Blessing then related something about an archaeologist who had suddenly given up a dig in Glen Colm in 1982. He stood up and gazed out of a side pane of the bay window in the general direction of the Cathair. 'He'll walk forth again soon,' he muttered obliquely.

At that, Blessing said that he believed he had heard a truck on the road, and Leo was snapped out of his reverie. He hauled himself to his feet and walked with his host out into the garden, where Blessing halted.

'I've enjoyed your company, Leo,' said Blessing. 'I'm usually dead to the world tucked away here. Will you promise to come again soon?'

'You have my word, Gus,' said Leo as he shook a shovel-like hand. 'I thank you kindly for your assistance and good hospitality.'

Leo introduced himself to Iain Taylor, a taciturn, stocky man aged in his late fifties, and his apprentice Gary, a wiry young fellow with a chirpy disposition.

'A creepy old place to break down of an evening,' remarked Iain, before Leo explained what had befallen the Humber.

'The engine is as dead as a doornail,' he concluded.

Iain opened the bonnet and inspected the dipstick, using a torch because the daylight was diminishing. Gary then got into the car and tried the ignition. And, miracle of miracles, the engine turned over at the first attempt. Gary laughed good-naturedly and gunned the accelerator to get the revs up. Leo felt a mixture of relief and embarrassment at this development and turned to tease Blessing about his mechanical misdiagnosis, but he had already gone. Only tiny insects now inhabited the garden, flickering in the winnowed light.

'Looks all correct to me,' said Iain as he scanned the vibrating components using his torch. He then turned his attention to the colour of the exhaust fumes and checked below the exhaust manifold for any tell-tale leakage on the bitumen. 'Cars as old as this girl tend to overheat, sometimes quite inexplicably. Keep your eye on the temperature gauge and if she plays up again, bring her to the garage and I'll take a proper look.'

Leo apologised to Iain for his wasted journey and requested that one of the mechanics drive him to the Palmery in the Humber, because he had taken a drink. Gary therefore remained at the wheel, evidently thrilled by the opportunity to pilot such an antique.

Leo was happy simply relaxing in the passenger seat enjoying the pleasant afterglow of the Concoction and listening to the young man's cheerful chatter as he drove. His mobile rang and he begged Gary's pardon as he took the call. It was Ronnie MacKellar, to whom Leo had given his number after his arrest earlier that day. He was perfectly amiable despite the offence at the wealthy Mr Ashby's house, and Leo wondered if the easy-going copper could remain cross with anyone for long. Ronnie, considered Leo, wasn't adroit at professional inhumanity. He was, in the usual run of things, the perfect fit for a rural bobby – reasonable, equanimous, practical, wise – but they would eat him alive in the mean streets of Glasgow.

'I did a computer check: Nicky is the only registered owner of a Jaguar coupé on Sonna,' said the sergeant. 'I finally got hold of him this evening at his house and he strenuously denied being anywhere near Scallop Bay this morning or lending his car to anyone. He has a cast-iron alibi: he was schmoozing with several bigwigs on his yacht, including the Baronet's brother and a Justice of the Peace, both of whom have just corroborated the fact. Nicky and I went to his lock-up garage which was secure and the green Jag was inside. The number plates weren't covered. Nicky is the only keyholder for the lock-up so it is highly unlikely that the car was borrowed for an unauthorised joyride. I reckon your road-rager was a visitor from the mainland. We *could* go through CCTV footage at the ferry terminal.' By his tone, Leo doubted that Ronnie was going to divert police time to this endeavour, especially as the crime itself was unprovable because there hadn't been any witnesses. 'Anyway Leo, I just thought I'd update you.'

Leo thanked Ronnie and hung up, then saved the police sergeant's mobile number to his phone's contacts – a potentially useful resource for later. The Humber pulled up the driveway of the Palmery while Iain hovered at the gate in his truck, waiting to convey his underling home. He paid

Gary the call-out fee, thanked him and bid him goodnight, then paused before entering the house. He drank in the exotic evening perfumes of the grounds which hung heavy in the air and gazed at the stunning sunset, which was a red ember draped by cloud which was bruised charcoal and wisteria and plum.

Leo heard a television sounding from a room at the rear of the house. Unfortunately, when he made to enter the door handle came off in his hand.

'Sorry Troughton,' he said, holding the thing up as he stepped inside.

'That's all right. It tends to do that.'

Leo noted that no counter-apology was issued for the morning's machine gunning, surely the more heinous offence. There was a kind of shabby luxury to the room, and Troughton was sprawled on a worn sofa regarding Celtic's Champions League away-leg qualifier as he languidly smoked a cigarette. An empty wine bottle and a half-empty one sat on a table alongside a glass.

'Come away the Bhoys!' Leo called out when he saw that his team was winning.

'We are playing rather well,' remarked Troughton. 'I say – have you eaten?'

'I haven't, as it happens. A spot of car trouble held me up. I could ring the chippy in Kilmichael to see if it delivers.'

'Nothing of the kind. I have prepared a quite superb beef Stroganoff. I will serve you up a portion at full-time.'

The television picture went wonky and Troughton leapt to his feet and issued a few strategic blows to the top of the veteran set which more or less realigned things. Leo wondered if Troughton's mood was somewhat sullen, perhaps due to a torn betting slip for a race at Chepstow which was lying discarded on the table.

'What have you been doing today, Troughton?'

'Other than polishing the Vickers, I began rereading Antony Beevor's *D-Day*, which inspired a humdinger of an idea for an article for *The Repository*. It's about how during World War II Inchmadden was evacuated and used as a commando training area in preparation for the Normandy landings. I intend on typing some more of it before I retire tonight. How did your latest investigations go?'

Leo gave Troughton an abridged version of his day, the places he had visited and the characters he had met. He didn't have the energy nor the inclination to reveal every nuanced observation he had made and for some reason he didn't care to mention the fellowship or Concoction he had enjoyed with Gus Blessing. He also didn't appreciate the cruel mirth which was evoked in Troughton by his tale of being run off the road by the green Jaguar and then being arrested at Mr Ashby's property.

'Still no visions?' enquired Troughton after Leo had concluded.

'No.'

The two men cheered as Celtic scored a late second goal to seal the victory.

'Go through to the dining room and I shall serve supper,' directed Troughton.

Leo took his place at the table and as he waited for Troughton to attend he admired some features of the room. Two large china vases flanked a green marble hearth, above which hung an early William Dyce painting, *The Greene Knight reveals his Identity to Sir Gawain*. With a theatrical solemnity, Troughton entered carrying a tray and placed down a steaming bowl, a basket of bread and a butter dish, and then filled a goblet with a very drinkable claret. Leo detected the odd mood again and ventured to break the silence.

'Nicky is taking me out on his yacht tomorrow. I am hoping it will be a blessed relief after my morning's task: I intend on visiting with Vincent Comiskey.'

'How in God's holy name could socialising with that gnome be a blessed relief from anything?' snarled Troughton.

Leo ate quietly for a few moments as Troughton filled up his own wine glass.

'This is splendid, thank you Troughton.'

His host ignored him and seated himself on the next but one dining chair. For a while he merely slouched and drank and watched Leo hungrily consume his Stroganoff at a rate just restrained enough to maintain decorum. Then Troughton lit a cigarette, exhaled a stream of blue smoke and said: 'Look at us, Moran, the two rejects. Pathetic and lonely and feeling sorry for ourselves.'

'That's not very nice.'

'Solitude is why men like us drink. Primarily to deaden the fundamental urge, although not only that, not only that,' said Troughton mournfully. 'We are gone to whisky and ruin, which is why neither of us will see three score and ten.'

'Speak for yourself,' said Leo before polishing off another mouthful.

'I mean to say, consider the subject which shall not be broached.'

Leo placed his cutlery down heavily. Then, in a low, intense voice he said: 'For the love of Christ, Troughton, I appeal to you: *do not utter her name.* I shall not revisit the sorrowful countries of the past.'

'You really *are* a sensitive soul.'

'Why this vicious ambush? I informed you of my strict terms of engagement in my letter. Damn it, man – I will hold thee to thy oath!'

'Do you know, that to still mourn a youthful romance defines you as a *beta male?*'

'Just the contrary, I am a Catholic gentleman,' said Leo without conviction as he slumped back in his chair.

'Ha – I've struck a nerve!'

'So what if you are right? So what if I am what you say I am? It is too late for me anyway – hound me if you must, I no longer care.' Suddenly Leo recalled dark moments which had passed between them during their university days and rage bloomed within his breast as he aimed a glare at his antagonist. 'Same old Troughton. Vituperative as ever.'

'Same old Moran. Holier than bloody thou.'

'I was hoping that age might have mellowed you.'

'It has.'

'In that case, may Christ's Holy Mother and His beloved saints fly to thy aid.'

With that, Leo drained his wine glass, stood up and stormed towards the door. He paused before taking his leave, a rare echo of raw Glaswegian drawling in his accent as he added: 'By the way, Troughton, if you ever point that bloody machine gun at me again, I will ram it up your hoop – guaranteed.'

After he had prepared for bed, Leo walked along the corridor to the office to close its door in order to soften the clatter of Troughton's drunken typing. Before he did so he peered inside to watch the man at work on his article. Evidently the prodigious amount of wine he had consumed had provided him with a second wind. He was chain-smoking and making a mess as he absent-mindedly flicked his cigarette at where he imagined the ashtray to be. He paused only to take another draught of Château Gazin. At that moment, Leo tried not to despise his host.

Leo had trouble nodding off, despite sneaking downstairs

to help himself to a large brandy. He was still smarting from Troughton's sly and treacherous attempt to bring up the subject of Maddi, his long-lost love. When he had made his decision to embark for the Palmery he had naively assumed that he would find Troughton altered, that his reaching out in his letter implied maturity and humility, earned by the latitude of years. That petty youthful rivalries wouldn't be worthy of mention let alone prolongation. That was the way things were meant to evolve, Leo had supposed. To pick up where they left off would be dishonourable, and surely the indecency of it alone would shame one towards civilised behaviour. The other matter that was keeping Leo awake was his impending task of probing Vincent Comiskey. He dreaded it, because he himself knew what it felt like to be falsely accused of something and he honestly didn't know whether Comiskey was innocent or guilty of Andy Lamb's death. He listened to the faint clamour of the Olivetti along the corridor and recalled Troughton's initial satisfaction when, many years ago, the slander against Leo had come home to roost.

Objectively, a person can realise that you shouldn't let bullies' barbs catch. But they still do.

During the long hot summer of 1976 Leo, following the influence of a vision, rescued a nine-year-old local boy who had been snatched by a paedophile. The police came to suspect that Leo might have been an accomplice to the kidnapper. They eventually dropped their interest in him but rumours about him persisted at his school and in his Glasgow neighbourhood, and he was roundly abused and ostracised. A year later, Leo failed to intervene effectively after he experienced a vision about another crime, fearing the consequences if he again demonstrated special knowledge. As an indirect consequence of his inaction, a teenage girl was gang-raped and later died, probably by her own hand, in the house fire in which Leo's hands were burned.

The experiences left Leo traumatised, embittered and cynical. He even cultivated an Edwardian idiolect to augment his eccentricity in order to cock a snoot towards the working-class community which had borne him and then rejected him. By the time he attended university he had learned to repress his feelings of self-loathing, guilt and resentment, and if they ever surfaced he would pass them off to himself and others as merely symptoms of his saturnine nature. Like many melancholics, it never even occurred to him that something was wrong that needed fixing, let alone that it could actually be fixed, or at least soothed; his state seemed nothing other than inevitable and utterly deserved. His childhood religious faith was of scant consolation, but the academic life and meeting a wide variety of new people – debating with them, sharing ideas with them, socialising with them – was a tonic, as was meeting Maddi, who by some miracle reciprocated his affection. Booze also seemed to help. In the early days he wondered if he actually had an allergy to alcohol, such was the sickness it induced, but he was dedicated to his cause and eventually punished his body and psyche into submission. He would have liked nothing more than to have left the city behind, but he had snubbed his Cambridge offer for the University of Glasgow. His father was dying and a sense of duty meant that he stayed. He needed his mother, too. However, there was always a danger that someone from his past in the north of the city would drift into the West End and into his life. And, one day, that is precisely what happened.

It was in one of those shops which sold cheap pints, which meant that it was where two worlds collided, or at best coexisted in mutual mistrust. The two worlds being those who laboured hard to pay their taxes, and those who studied while living off those taxes, simultaneously seeking out causes via which they could telegram their virtuousness to the world. With hindsight, it was the type of establishment that Leo should have avoided, lest he risk exposure.

He was standing at the bar with his beloved Maddi and five of their gang, four of whom could have been classified as good friends, while the remainder, one Marcus Troughton, he was tolerably averse to. He felt a painfully jocular jab in the ribs and froze with dread, at some level knowing instantly that everything was about to unravel. He could tell from the exaggerated pitch and slur of the greeting that the rib-jabber was inebriated. He felt the blood drain from his face and noticed a smirk form on Troughton's features in gleeful anticipation. He turned to see the face of a former pupil from his alma mater Saint Joseph's Secondary grinning like a lantern.

Through gritted teeth Leo made the introductions, the interloper enjoying his obvious discomfort. Apparently the young man had made good in the world, was happily married with a child on the way and was making real money repairing commercial refrigerators, hence the fact that he had moved to this better neighbourhood. It was his day off, just a few harmless pints planned and a browse of the *Racing Post*, until lookie-here, if it isn't old Leo from the Joe, out for a jar with his pals from the college of knowledge.

The fellow spun a self-mythology that he was a boy from the wrong side of the tracks come good, but the reality was that he had been a cruel bully and remained one, and no amount of overbearing effusiveness could mask it. He seemed affronted by Leo's newfound pretence of equality, his insolence at claiming his place in the world, and attempted to revive the pecking order of the playground. Therefore, he dominated the conversation, shutting his ex-classmate out apart from the odd jibe, and giving the rest of the company almost all of the eye contact while ceding Leo the minimum required to maintain basic civility. He recounted some bygone occasion on which Leo had made a fool of himself ostensibly as humour, but really to re-establish the previous power dynamic between them, not least because to recount one old story meant he could easily recount another. He viewed Leo with a wry smile, as though daring him to react lest he raise the accusations that had once swirled around him. Yet as the man hurled draught after draught of heavy down his throat, like a runaway train the conversation hurtled excruciatingly and inevitably to that precise destination. And when the secrets began being uttered aloud, loudly, Leo didn't even try to intervene because a dreamlike quality had descended, a sense of unreality. This was not really happening, because if it was, the outcomes would be truly seminal. The extent of the truths was unabridged. It included how suspicion still stuck to Leo for the nine-year-old boy's abduction due to his leftfield claims regarding magical visions. It included how the local villains, the Harrington mob, had taken it upon themselves to interrogate Leo under threat of torture. It included how Leo had sustained his burns, thus debunking the disinformation he had fed Maddi and his university peers. It included how Leo had blamed himself for not protecting the girl who had died in the fire from being attacked (how the hell did this bastard *know* such subtleties?). The litany was so horrific and came from a world so alien to Leo's chums that it even wiped the smile from the face of Troughton. When describing the fire victim, the interloper kept using the words 'rape' and 'raped' again and again, as though to hammer every last nail into Leo's reputation. He couldn't look Maddi in the face.

Leo completed his remaining two final examinations the next week, trapped within a strange daze, as though madness had the good grace to pause, before unleashing its awesome power.

At Last We Meet Vincent

It was a sultry night, and after finally getting over Leo only slept fitfully, his slumber racked by unpleasant dreams. He was awoken very early by the strains of *Denn alles Fleisch ist wie Gras* from Brahms' German Requiem emitting from the gramophone speakers in the hall, the amplifier turned to full volume. Leo stumbled out of bed, walked to the mezzanine bannister and looked down. Troughton was standing in the haggard light conducting his imaginary orchestra using an unsheathed World War II US Marine Raider stiletto as a baton, a manic, demonic energy in his sleepless eyes as he grinned up at Leo, the chorus swelling to its powerful crescendo, a cognac bottle nearby. Leo, despairing, turned on his heel and returned to bed, clasping a pillow over his head.

Leo's travel alarm roused him at 8 a.m. and the sunny morning found him in a fraught temper which was alleviated by a shower – its briskness enhanced by the fact that the water temperature kept plummeting, and two strong cups of coffee which he drank in lieu of breakfast.

The night's humidity had abated and a slight wind had picked up, and Leo was encouraged when the Humber engine started without any histrionics. His first port of call was the post office in Kilmichael, where he bought a padded envelope into which he inserted the burnt bones he had found in Glen Colm. He posted it to his friend Fordyce in Kirkcudbrightshire whom he had primed with a text message informing him about his investigations and about his wish to have the items analysed. He also purchased a quarter pound of orange creams for sharing on the yacht trip.

Leo then drove northwards, through the upper reaches of Kilmichael Bay which was a pleasant residential area known as Fairfax, and then into the next bay where Port Penelope was located. He continued northwards, passing a boat builders' yard and entering a die-straight stretch of road that hugged the coastline and which eventually led to a place called Cladach Buidhe, from where a small secondary ferry crossed the quite narrow strait which divided this part of the isle from the mainland. The countryside was spiked with violet spires of rosebay willowherb. To the left were hills, some of them forested and on the other side of which was the rugged, sparsely populated hinterland of the upper third of Sonna. Leo kept checking his rear-view mirror to see if the dreaded green Jaguar was in pursuit. He soon arrived outside Vincent Comiskey's residence, a simple white roadside cottage in fine trim with two roughcast outbuildings to the rear. Leo parked on the verge, and as he walked up Vincent's path he steeled himself for the forthcoming exchange. He crept round the side of the house to peer through the window of the first outbuilding to see if by any chance it contained the green Jaguar. Instead, there was only Vincent's delivery van with *Sonna Mash Co.* emblazoned on it. Leo heard sounds coming from the next outbuilding. Its large doors were wide open and as he approached he saw that the space served as Vincent's microbrewery. A man was there, sitting on a stool and busying himself with an adze and an old wooden barrel.

'Excuse me, you're Vincent Comiskey, aren't you?'

'Whatever I did, I beg your forgiveness,' said the man, without so much as looking up from his task.

'Did you do such a whole lot of bad things?'

Vincent put down his tool and regarded Leo. 'More than my share, perhaps, although fewer than I've been accused of.'

He had intense features and dark good looks, although he was aged by flecks of white in his sleek hair and had a smoker's wan complexion. He had hirsute arms and was wearing work dungarees under which a white T-shirt clung to his sinewy upper body. Leo asked him about his utilisation of an old-fashioned barrel.

'If you want to make a living nowadays, all you need to know is this: there is no amount of gimmickry the middle classes of this country will not lap up, especially when it comes to food and drink. They're all so desperate to outdo each other, to try out the next fad that's in the lifestyle pages of the Sunday papers and then post it on social media. So, I'm fixing up some old whisky barrels so that I can age some of my ale in them in order to create a special edition. However, I sense that you didn't drop by to discuss traditional coopering techniques.'

Leo introduced himself and explained the purpose of his presence on the island, concluding: 'I would like to speak with you regarding the demise of Andy Lamb on this very day in 1989. But let me first establish that I have a personal allergy to throwing around unsubstantiated allegations. So I am not here to accuse you, Mr Comiskey.'

'Has that pain in the prick Nicky Barrett been spreading conspiracy theories again? One day, not long after I moved to Sonna, he was shouting accusations through the open window of his motor. I approached him but he told his driver to take off. I'm a bit of a recluse, but by chance a wee while later I got wind that he had been putting his shite about. So I decided to pay him a home visit. Just to talk things through, not to hurt him or anything, but you should have seen the way he cowered behind his wife. We discussed the matter but I didn't get anywhere – he's just fixated on the idea that I killed Andy Lamb.'

'It must vex you.'

Vincent shrugged, then said: 'I could give you a whole lecture on Nicky Barrett.'

'Go on then.'

'I've studied the Nazis quite a bit. I'm fascinated by the horror of the whole thing: their rise to power, the psychology behind their ideology. I play this wee game sometimes. I imagine we're living in 1940 and the Germans win the Battle of Britain and then cross the Channel. Some heroic types take to the hills to resist, while most folk just get on with their lives as best they can, maybe collaborating to some degree in order to survive. But there are certain others who actively, enthusiastically take up with the enemy. In my game I try to identify people I meet who would fall into that last category: the spiteful, the ineffective, the self-loathing. People who now, unrestrained by the standards and laws of our civilisation, show their true colours. And I see Nicky among them. It starts off that he attends a few meetings, returning home to lecture his uneasy family about the need for order, and about how the Jews – against whom he previously held no grudge – have held the whip hand for too long. He reads. He establishes his blood line and nurtures a reputation for being a dependable, efficient sort with just enough of a streak of cruelty which could be drawn out and passed off as zeal. Soon he gets a uniform, although because he's a small man – and not just in soul – they can never quite get a tunic or overcoat neat enough for him and he's always drowning slightly in the peaked cap. Then he gets a promotion which he, a man previously unappreciated by our decadent society, feels worthy of as he steps forth to stake his place in the coming age.'

Vincent's articulate speech was delivered in a slick, wise-guy urban accent which put Leo in mind of the Glaswegians he was brought up alongside. 'I have to admire your courage, returning to the island and setting up your business,' he said.

'Courage? I'm not letting a false accusation restrict my life. Some folk in the south end have long memories and won't buy my beer, but fuck them. I'm entitled to love this island too. Listen, I was not a nice young man. I pulled a lot of bad shit and I have to live with that. I had this rage inside me – I've come to realise it came from my mammy dying when I was wee. Cry me a river. But I'm not that person any more. And I never killed Andy Lamb, or anyone else for that matter. And I never raped anyone – oh, I'm sure you've already heard all about Elizabeth Meiklejohn, but I never laid a finger on the lassie. No doubt her father would still like to see me strung up from the Tarzan swing behind Ardcaden.'

'What makes you say that?'

'I passed him on an aisle in the Co-op in Kilmichael one day. If looks could kill I'd have dropped dead right there and then, beside the tinned veg.'

'However, Elizabeth *was* attacked.'

'I know she was attacked, but by someone else.'

'By who?'

'Mr Moran, even if I had a theory, my life has been blighted by a false rape allegation, so I'm not about to start slandering another guy.'

'I believe the police spoke with you after Andy's death?'

'Aye. I told them I was at home all evening.' Vincent read the look of dubiety on Leo's face. 'It was a long time ago, Mr Moran. A lad died and, believe it or not, I found that very sad. But it had precisely fuck all to do with me.'

'People think that you might have been jealous of Andy's relationship with Amy Agumanu.'

'They can think what they want.'

'Do you know that Amy lives on the island?'

'I see her in church, but she tends to sit at the front on the far side and lingers after Mass is finished. Other than that, I saw her one time, standing outside the boatyard near Port Penelope.'

'You didn't feel like stopping to say hello?'

'I just prefer to keep myself to myself these days.'

'It is alleged that you were seen at the foot of the escarpment where Andy died, at prayer. Is this true?'

'So what? I felt like sending one up for the boy.'

'Did you ever try to frighten Andy that summer?'

'What do you mean?'

'Someone was terrorising him. They shone a light from the hillside behind the Lambs' flat at night, followed him, left a dead crow on his car and paid him a creepy nocturnal visit while wearing a mask.'

'I honestly have no idea what you are talking about.'

Leo believed him. 'Do you mind my enquiring: where were you at around 10.30 yesterday morning?'

'Why do you ask?'

'Someone ran me off the road.'

'I was here, working hard. And no, there aren't any witnesses to the fact.'

'Do you happen to know anyone who drives a British racing green Jaguar F-Type coupé?'

'I think Nicky Barrett has one, but I'm not sure – I'm not into cars.'

Leo gazed around the room, impressed by the complex brewing apparatus. His eye glanced upon a cask on a rack with a label attached to it bearing the name 'Morgenthaler'.

'I see Dr Morgenthaler is one of your customers.'

'One of my best. I deliver him a fresh firkin of pils first thing every Thursday.'

'Quite the drinker,' remarked Leo. 'He nearly ran me over yesterday. Seems a strange egg.'

'A man of few words, is Dr Morgenthaler. I seldom see him, I just drop the barrel by his front porch and he leaves out a cheque for me. He is a very private person – not that there's anything wrong with the pursuit of privacy,' said Vincent pointedly.

'As a matter of fact, I am myself somewhat predisposed towards private, quiet living,' said Leo.

'I can't say I'm partial to him, or that I like going near his house – it gives me the creeps. But, as I say, he's a good customer, and anyway, I don't like going *anywhere* in the south end for deliveries.'

'Because of all the personal strife you associate with the area?'

'Not only that.'

'What else?'

Vincent hauled the barrel he had been working on across the concrete floor. 'Let's just say I don't like the ... psychic energy of the place. Now, if you'll excuse me, I've got work to do.'

'One last thing, Mr Comiskey. Do you happen to know Johnathon Lamb, Andy's younger brother?'

'I've seen him around. A couple of times I've noticed him glaring at me, thinking about coming the hard man.'

'I should watch out for him if I were you.'

'Duly noted,' said Vincent, but Leo didn't think he was in the least bit concerned.

The Kraken Wakes

LEO drove back to Belmartine, noting that he had plenty of time left in which to prepare for his sailing excursion. Nicky had stated in his text that he would send his driver to pick him up. Leo parked in front of the Palmery, and when he entered the hall he heard Troughton shouting from above: 'Christ Almighty, I am entirely out of Askit powders!'

Troughton began descending the stairs. He was wearing a silk dressing gown and had a hand clasped melodramatically to his brow.

'Behold: The Kraken wakes,' jibed Leo. '*In roaring he shall rise.* No trampolining today, Troughton?'

A while later Leo found his host languishing on the chaise in the drawing room in a state of acedia, awaiting an excuse for a first drink. Nearby was a huge globe, freestanding in its cradle. He reached out and spun it disconsolately.

'What am I, Moran?'

'I beg your pardon?'

'What am I? I shall tell you what I am: I am the last of my line, the end of my house. A dead end, a terminal. And when, finally, I wither away, perhaps this stately, crumbling pile, instead of being sold off to some parvenu to mend my debts, will collapse in upon me for my sarcophagus. Look here, Moran, if I teased you last night, then I am sorry.'

'That's all right.'

'I feel as though I have lost all of my zest and zeal.'

'Can I get you something?' asked Leo, feeling a little sorry for the man. 'A nice cup of sweet tea, a seltzer – I have some in my bathroom, or a cordial perhaps?'

'Yes, Moran, I think I do require something to pep me up. In fact, there's an opened bottle of Pomerol in the kitchen, and it would be a sin to waste it. Furthermore, it's only an hour or two until luncheon. Moreover, it's my late Uncle Conrad's birthday, and I always toast his beloved memory with a glass or two of claret.'

Leo fetched the wine and served it.

'Thank you, Moran, you make a good nursemaid. How did things go with Vincent Comiskey?'

'He denied everything.'

'Did your psychic instincts tell you if he was being truthful?'

'It doesn't really work like that. I can't read people's minds. He was certainly plausible.'

'I get the feeling that you believe him.'

'Let's just say I'm maintaining an open mind.'

The telephone rang and Troughton said: 'Moran, answer that if you would. If it's the printers, tell them I'm not here.'

Leo picked up and enquired as to who was speaking, then held the receiver to his breast as he explained that it was the manager of the Albert Hotel in Kilmichael. Troughton signalled that he would take the call and spent a minute in a terse dialogue with the woman, then concluded abruptly and slammed the receiver down.

'Another *Repository* advertiser bites the dust!' he exclaimed. 'That's the thanks you get for trying to enhance the cultural life of this bloody shithouse of an island!'

Leo changed into a tennis shirt, grey flannels, a boating blazer and espadrilles, and was picked up by Nicky's driver, a diminutive, smiling Indian man with limited English, in a waxed silver Lexus at the arranged time.

Nicky was waiting for Leo in the garden of his house, a fine villa with a sea view on the posh Marine Drive in Fairfax. Leo was shown inside and complimented the abode, although privately he was offended by the ultra-modernity of its interior which while doubtlessly rendered at great expense he found to be frigid and clinical.

'Thank you, but it's too within my means. I'm waiting for something grander to pop up in Mount Pleasant or Battery,' said Nicky, who was dressed in white knee-length shorts and a white polo shirt. 'In the meantime, I enjoy the fact that I'm near my moorings in Port Penelope.'

In the kitchen, Leo introduced himself to the lady of the house, Vera, a looker with an east-European accent who was at least fifteen years younger than Nicky and a few inches taller. She fussed over the two sailors, ensuring they had applied sunblock and putting the finishing touches to their extravagant luncheon. Nicky was quite offhand with her, and when he disappeared to fetch something Leo insisted on helping her to pack a hamper and a cool box. There were two loaves of French bread, oatcakes, an entire ham, goose liver pâté, cold chicken in aspic, langoustines on ice, truffles, red-black grapes, Shropshire honey, figs, glacé fruits, champagne and ruby grapefruit juice. It was all very magnanimous of Nicky, thought Leo, but his proletarian sensibility and memories of his hard-up childhood meant he abhorred wastefulness and he knew that there was no way two men could do justice to such a banquet.

The yachtsmen and their provisions were deposited by the Lexus, which now had a trailer bearing a rubber dinghy harnessed to it, in Port Penelope, which was only a short distance away. It was a harbour village with a marina, a functional but by no means unappealing settlement of cheerful tenements and little hotels. They launched the dinghy and Nicky rowed them out to his sleek yacht *Agnus*, declaring that it was the most impressive of the numerous craft moored in the bay. Nicky nimbly climbed aboard and Leo passed the hamper, cool box and a boat bag up to him. Then he clambered inexpertly over the gunwale and the men hauled the dinghy up and lashed it to its berth at the stern. They thudded around the blond decks of the well-appointed vessel, Leo obeying Nicky's nautical commands. Then the yacht threw off her moorings and they motored out of the bay.

'We'll put her under sail once we get around to the sound,' said Nicky.

'She's a beauty,' said Leo. 'Fifty foot?'

'Yep. That's thirty-six grand a foot, but worth every penny. But I always say: if you've got it, spend it,' said Nicky with a charmless wink.

Poor Nicky, thought Leo. Such people never comprehend that what is classy, what impresses people is precisely *not* to flaunt one's riches. Serendipitously, Leo realised by its maker's logo that a luxury yacht which had been approaching Port Penelope from their starboard was built in the same yard as Nicky's. As she glided past them, Leo couldn't resist remarking: 'What a grand lady – she must be nigh on seventy foot.'

Nicky didn't respond, and merely glowered over the wheel. That's the trouble with the rat race, mused Leo inwardly. You'll always be vulnerable to angst because no matter how much wealth you accumulate, there will always be someone richer, someone with a bigger boat, someone with a bigger whatever.

Nicky swung the *Agnus* northwards and after a while he eased off the throttle and requested that Leo briefly take the helm. Leo felt an adolescent thrill at steering the graceful craft as she cut through the salt, and noticed that Nicky was engrossed in peering through a telescope which he had fastened to a mounting bracket. Leo realised that they had come abreast with Vincent Comiskey's place, which explained his skipper's distraction.

'As it happens, I visited there this morning,' said Leo.

'And?'

'And I found him to be a credible denier.'

'He's a scumbag from a scumbag family of Glasgow mobsters.'

'A man can't choose his family.'

'No, but I'll bet his family brought him up well-versed in the art of credible denial.'

'Nicky, there's something I want to clear up,' said Leo, changing the subject. 'Yesterday I was run off the road by a racing green Jaguar F-Type coupé. After getting into a spot of bother I reported the matter to the police, and Sergeant Ronnie MacKellar told me that he spoke to you about it, because he knows that you own such a vehicle. I just want you to understand that I never suspected or accused you.'

'Understood.'

'I wonder if the incident could be something to do with the case.'

'Who knows,' said Nicky, taking the wheel.

The mainland clamped this portion of the island between the jaws of two gigantic peninsulas, and only the channel known as the Straits of Sonna divided the facing shores. They passed the little ferry terminal at Cladach Buidhe, then dodged a cluster of little islands known as the Maidens of Sonna, then carefully rounded the top of the isle.

As they voyaged, Leo provided Nicky with a high-level and selective update on his investigations so far, concluding: 'Hopefully I shall continue to make good progress, permitting Troughton doesn't drive me bonkers.'

Leo had meant the remark jocularly, but Nicky seized the opportunity and proceeded to spoil the idyllic scenery by excoriating Troughton. For all Troughton's iniquities, Leo as a rule objected to backbiting and character assassination, and therefore listened in silence, regarding the water coldly.

'The man is a sponger and a deadbeat and a barely functioning alcoholic,' opened Nicky. 'Wait and see – before the weekend is out, he'll be tapping you up for a few bob, or requesting that you bring groceries home, promising "I'll pay you later". He tries to suck up to the Baronet, but you can tell his Lairdship has no time for him. As an only child he was sole heir, but he managed to squander his late parents' fortune on some whim or other, not least his ridiculous magazine. Do you know what folk on the island call *The Repository*? *The Suppository*, because its best use is shoving it up your arse to save on lavatory paper. It is supposed to come out monthly but it barely ever hits its deadlines what with Troughton's drinking and hare-brained schemes. He is a complete technophobe and has no idea how to transfer anything to digital. I believe the magazine's existence is just a desperate attempt to bring some meaning to his sad, lonely life. What really annoys me is that he has delusions of grandeur as to the lousy rag's value to the culture of Sonna, and he acts as if he is performing some heroic act of duty in producing it. Advertisers keep pulling out and it's haemorrhaging money. Which is why he's now leeching off me for funding – I have no illusions about his motives in seeking my friendship. However, I am happy to exploit the situation to further my own interests: to get Andy's death properly investigated and publicised.'

They approached the mouth of the strait, where it merged with the Sound of Sonna, the expanse of water between Sonna and Erran. Nicky went dead slow in reverse towards a white buoy. At the last minute he instructed Leo to take the helm, while he leapt to the aft deck and adroitly used a boat hook to grab the mooring line. Leo was ordered to kill the gurgling engine.

'This is Amy's mooring,' said Nicky as he tied up, 'she won't mind my using it, not least because of the amount of business I throw her way.'

Leo realised that they were adjacent to Amy's property at Herrick Bay. It was interesting to enjoy such a different perspective on a place on the island which he had visited. He noticed Nicky gazing in the direction of Fagr Vágr and mused upon his theory that he was in love with the woman who lived there, and wondered if this was the reason he had chosen this spot to stop for luncheon, just to be near her.

Nicky's diatribe against Troughton hadn't been the ideal appetiser, but the mariners turned their attention to the magnificent picnic which Vera had prepared. As they chomped and quaffed, Leo said: 'You never told me you had spoken with Vincent since he moved to the island.'

'I guess it was an unpleasant experience with an unpleasant man which I didn't really wish to revisit. And anyway, he didn't say anything enlightening. Just denied all charges.'

To underscore how unpleasant an individual Vincent apparently was, Nicky related some of the mischief he had pulled during the summer of 1989. He had set a shed at Ardcaden Bay harbour on fire. He had graffitied 'FTQ' (which in the tribal West of Scotland is an abbreviation broadly understood as an insult to the incumbent monarch) on the Lambs' boat. He had shoplifted from the post office on half a dozen occasions. He had beaten up a guy from Kilmichael who had come to the Bay for the evening and passed a remark. He had brawled with Andy Lamb. He had thrown a jellyfish at someone. He had surreptitiously urinated into an empty lager can and given it to someone to drink. He had defecated inside a scrap-wood den the gang had built on the beach. He had ruined a disco in the church hall by chucking a live wasp nest inside. Then, there were the more heinous allegations of crimes against Elizabeth Meiklejohn and, of course, Andy.

'The theory that Andy's death was accidental doesn't hold any water,' expatiated Nicky. 'It just doesn't make sense that he was at the top of that drop. Comiskey must have barred his path, frightening him into running that way, and I would speculate by wielding a weapon. Andy wouldn't have dodged a square go – he hadn't bottled out of his fight with Comiskey on the seafront at Ardcaden Bay. He was a brave lad, physically strong and fearless. He once swam across the Bay at night, he performed insane feats on the Tarzan swing – that's a big rope swing in the woods behind Ardcaden which is there to this day – not least when he was playing knifie.'

'Pardon me, what's knifie?' interrupted Leo.

'It's a game played on a rope swing. The first competitor sticks a knife into a hard-to-reach place on the ground or in a tree. The next competitor then gets on the swing and has to withdraw the knife and then stick it in a different difficult place. Andy was brilliant at it. Anyway, Comiskey used to carry a knife in a sheath attached to his belt. I bet he chased Andy with it, then pushed or wrestled him over the edge. It's just possible that Comiskey didn't have a knife, and that he just wrestled Andy all the way down to the drop, but I doubt it.'

'Andy had ingested marijuana. Do you know how?'

Nicky shrugged his shoulders.

'Who provided the substance?'

'I don't remember.'

'Regarding the ceremony that was conducted at the henge, presumably some sort of spell was procured?'

'There was this guy Roderick McCaskill who used to holiday in the Bay. He was from the West End of Glasgow and was the same age as us but he was kind of peripheral to the gang. His parents were quite strict and he wasn't allowed to stay out late – so he wasn't with us that night. Anyway, he had this interest in the occult and he lent us one of his weird books.'

'That's a singular hobby for a teenaged boy. I wonder how he even accessed such literature in the pre-internet age.'

'Roderick was cool, a nice guy actually. But he was a bit offbeat.'

'Who specifically procured the book from him?' asked Leo, before adding pointedly: 'And please don't tell me you don't recall that either.'

Nicky cleared his throat, then said: 'I don't remember exactly why, but it was me who ended up borrowing it.'

'Why on earth did you undertake the rite?'

'I told you at the Palmery: it was just for a daft lark, a laugh, for something to do.' Leo was silent and gazed out over the water. 'Surely you realise there's no harm to it?' said Nicky.

'I just think that some things are best left well alone. For example, if someone comes to you with a Ouija board wanting to play, my advice is to take it from them, break it over your knee and destroy it by fire. Do you have contact details for this Roderick fellow?'

'No. I haven't heard anything about him in years, and he's not on social media.'

'I think I will pay a visit to this Janey woman in Glasgow.'

'Go for it; if you can get past her prick of a husband.'

'Do you have her contact details?'

'I'll text you them when I get home.'

After luncheon was finished, Nicky set sail while Leo

cleared the leftovers – which to his dismay were enough to feed the five thousand. However, he then managed to enjoy the sheer pleasure of sailing, champagne heightening his contentment. The yacht handled beautifully, nudging seven knots, and to complete the moment Nicky supplied them each with a Cohiba cigar, bragging: 'I bet this is the only vessel on the Firth of Clyde with its own humidor.'

They came abreast with the south end and Leo used the telescope to examine its spectacular coastline. He noted Crochadh House beneath Hangman's Hill.

'That's Dr Morgenthaler's abode,' he said, peering at the gaunt chimneys and dark upper windows. 'Do you happen to know him?'

'Can't say as I do,' replied Nicky uninterestedly, before suddenly shouting: 'Bloody hell – come and see this!'

Leo dashed to the starboard side of the yacht while the skipper urgently slacked the mainsheet. 'Shite, it's submerged again,' said Nicky. 'Wait – it's coming back up!'

At that, a huge sea creature broke the waves like a monstrous apparition, foam pouring from its mottled, slimy grey-brown skin. Leo was drawn into the mournful gaze of the primeval brute's left eye, a small dark orb witness to countless aquatic atrocities, an opaque window to strange transcendent dreams dreamed in sunless abysms.

'What a specimen – it must be nearly thirty foot from tip to tail!' said Nicky.

The leviathan dipped just beneath the surface, its mouth gaping horribly, its gill slits fanning out like alien appendages. It cruised alongside the *Agnus* for a while, before sliding down and down into the murky depths.

'Wait until they hear about this at the yachting club!' said Nicky, but Leo had been disturbed by the encounter with the basking shark, as though it augured something evil, something ugly and foreboding for his time on Sonna.

Nicky trimmed the mainsail and steered round Grog Head and along the bottom of the south end, turning northwards at the lighthouse.

'I've an idea: let's go for a pint at the Saint Caden's Hotel,' he said. 'I've a mooring in Ardcaden Bay.' Leo hesitated. 'Come on, it's the anniversary of Andy's death. Raise a glass to him with me.'

The public bar was quite busy. Nicky got in pints of draught heavy and whisky chasers for himself and Leo, then pompously announced that he would stand everyone in the joint a drink. Leo felt embarrassed by this vulgar display, and he guessed that Nicky was flashing the cash specifically because this was his home village. It had already struck Leo that Nicky's many fancy turns of phrase and his bourgeoise twang didn't match his simple Ardcaden roots.

Haddow was in, sitting on a barstool alongside a dour companion wearing fisherman's garb who declined proudly: 'You're all right, pal. I'll buy my own.'

However, Haddow merely said: 'I'll take a large malt from you, since you offer,' and winked at Leo. Leo liked Rab Haddow.

'I think I'll get my driver to pick us up from here,' said Nicky once the sailors had established themselves at a pressed-copper table beside a wall ornamented with maritime paraphernalia. Leo suspected that he was on a mission to become inebriated. 'I can't be bothered sailing the *Agnus* back to Port Penelope.'

Nicky kept ordering more drinks, offending Leo's working-class honour which demanded that rounds are bought alternately. He began slurring his words as he described what it had been like being brought up in the Bay, condemning the pettiness of small rural communities and fantasising about spite which his financial success had stirred in local breasts. He proposed the umpteenth toast in memoriam of Andy Lamb, and refocused his monologue onto his pet subject.

'He had this ... charisma, and he was the finest fellow I have ever known,' he eulogised, 'but he was denied his flourish into manhood. He was my best friend in the world, even though I only saw him at holidays.'

Leo couldn't help but wonder if the adulation had been reciprocated. A team of young men descended and soon enamelled balls were clacking on the felt of the pool table as they competed. Nicky watched them for a while and then mentioned how Andy had been the most skilful pool player in their gang. Apparently, he was so superior that sometimes he would remain at the table all night, undefeated.

Nicky's intoxicated narrative then bizarrely lurched towards contradiction, as hero worship became resentment: 'You see, Leo, during the summer this village and the countryside around it was the stage for young men's rites of passage. Winning at pool, at knifie, at football, at swimming, at stone skimming, in scraps. Winning with the girls. When the holidays ended, most of the other young men went back to their lives on the mainland galvanised, their status in the world affirmed. But for some of us, the losers, we had just had confirmed what we already suspected about our place in the food chain. Do you remember those charmers from your youth – you know, the good-looking, effortlessly cool bastards who were confident around females? Well even as a grown man I've never actually stopped looking back and hating them, envying them. They never knew what it felt like to long and long after a girl, and for her never to so much as notice you.'

Leo pictured Nicky gazing from the yacht towards Amy's property, when they had tied up at her mooring to take luncheon.

'The world tells us that if you work hard and develop yourself as a person you will be attractive to the opposite sex, but it is a lie,' continued Nicky. 'Physically attractive people attract other physically attractive people, period. They have a colossally better life than everyone else. When their heart gets broken, there is always another beautiful person waiting in the wings.'

Any empathy Leo might have had with Nicky's observations was poisoned by the disgust he felt towards him for relating them in such self-pitying and bitter terms. He was glad when the silver Lexus arrived to convey them home. They drunkenly loaded the dinghy onto the trailer, their backdrop the old stone pier and then the firth and then the Cunraes and then the mainland, which was marred somewhat by the austere towers of its nuclear power station.

Leo Again Sups of the Concoction

LEO enjoyed the view as they left the village, noting the sandy beach of the inner bay, which was browed with marram grass and bracken. To the north the land was gently rolling swatches of fields beneath a big sky, like an English idyll, and as they passed through the Wee Bay and entered Melford he noticed an old-fashioned red GPO telephone box and a quaint country schoolhouse that was like something out of a Thomas Hardy novel.

A sudden notion took possession of Leo, and he requested that he be deposited outside the Melford Hotel rather than at the Palmery, stating that he wished to drop in on an acquaintance. He needed a dose of Blessing's placid company and indeed another dose of the Concoction, both of which would provide antidote to spending so long in Nicky's spiky presence. He expressed his gratitude to Nicky for the yachting trip and for his all-round generosity, thanked the driver, disembarked and watched the Lexus pull away, noting with amusement a fingerpost at the junction which pointed to Kilmichael in both directions (one being the shore road, one being the country road). He then ambled up the byway on which Blessing's residence was located, swatting biting midges as he proceeded. He was greeted warmly and ushered into the drawing room.

'How's the car behaving itself?' enquired Blessing.

'As good as new, although I don't have it with me,'

smiled Leo. Blessing motioned for his guest to be seated and without standing on ceremony proceeded to serve the Concoction. The little sherry glasses looked absurdly dainty pinched between Blessing's unwieldy digits. The potion again worked its soporific charm and Leo, thus disarmed, was unusually forthcoming, giving a detailed if rambling account of his investigations since arriving on Sonna. Blessing listened attentively as he puffed on his pipe, tobacco crackling cheerfully as it burned in the bowl. Unlike the previous evening he was largely silent but for the odd interjection. For example, when Leo related how Norris Meiklejohn had described Andy Lamb's kindness towards his daughter, Blessing remarked: 'He was kind to her all right, he certainly won her trust.' And when Leo mentioned that today was Andy's anniversary, unwittingly referring to his death as his 'accident', Blessing stated: 'It wasn't an accident, purely speaking. Evil was behind it.'

Leo would later regret that he hadn't probed Blessing on his comments, but his mind had been a fug due to the effects of the Concoction. Perhaps Blessing had been referring to the 'evil' of jealousy which had somehow led someone to cause or indirectly precipitate Andy's demise, or perhaps that evil was something entirely different. He took his leave and strolled serenely in the perfect evening light back to Melford, where he stopped off at the hotel and ordered a plate of soup, which was all he had the appetite for after his lunchtime feast. The flavours exploded in his mouth, the Concoction seemingly having accentuated his sense of taste. He then telephoned for a taxi, and enjoyed a J&B and soda as he waited for it to arrive from Kilmichael. He noted that Vincent Comiskey's ales were not stocked here, and neither had they been available in the south end's other licensed establishment, the Saint Caden's Hotel, although they had been on draught in the pub he had visited in Kilmichael.

Leo disgorged himself from the cab at the Palmery, wobbling slightly after his day's intake. As he opened the front door, he wondered what kind of temper he would find Troughton in; still listless mooning, hopefully – at least that was inoffensive. He walked along the vestibule and into the hall, the floor of which was a shambles of fallen plaster. He started as his host's voice called out brightly from above.

'Good evening, Moran! How was the sailing?'

Leo looked up to see Troughton perched on the mezzanine as he worked on an oil painting, wearing a beret and a stained smock.

'It was fine. What happened here?'

'Some of the ceiling came down, worse luck. Not to worry, I'll sweep it up later. I say – there's an opened bottle of plonk on the console table to your right. Be a splendid fellow and bring it up, so that I may replenish my glass. And do fill one for yourself. Oh, and I beg of you not to sneak a peek at my masterpiece – I never display my paintings until they are finished.'

Leo fetched the bottle and a glass, and ascended the stairway to where Troughton had installed himself. He poured the wine and then took a sip so sublime that it compelled him to examine the label.

'Haut-Brion '59 – a very nice little number. Troughton, I have no wish to be impertinent, but if you have a cash-flow problem you could sell some of the bottles in your cellar for a pretty penny on eBay.'

'E-Pay? Never heard of it. Is that one of those internet things? Don't get me wrong, I'm all for progress – I keep meaning to get hooked up. However, these wines are for drinking – not for selling.'

'Well, what about that bust on the stand behind you. I believe it is an early Bourdelles. It could fetch a right few bob at auction. To say nothing of some of the paintings in this house. It would be advisable to get the optimum price for such things before the bailiffs turn up.'

'As it happens, Moran, I've had a stroke of fortune, financially speaking.'

'That is good news.'

'A well-endowed relative has shuffled off the old mortal coil – may God rest her soul.'

'Oh, I'm terribly sorry.'

'It's quite all right. To be perfectly honest I barely knew her. And she was a hundred and two.' Troughton raised his glass and added: 'Here's to you, Great Aunt Prosperia, aptly named.'

'How are you feeling apart from that?' enquired Leo. 'You were somewhat down earlier.'

'Much better, thanks. Not least because a dear chum of ours is coming to join us on the morrow.'

'Oh really. Who?'

'Stephanie. She's at a bit of a loose end, so I invited her down to stay for a few nights.'

'*Stephanie?* My friend *Stephanie Mitchell?* Coming *here?*'

'There's no need to sound quite so shocked, old man.'

'But you don't know her!'

'Don't be silly, Moran: you are perfectly well aware that we were pals at university,' said Troughton as he regarded his house guest studiously over his easel.

'But that was *years* ago,' said Leo, feeling possessive of his female friend. 'How did you even get in touch with her?'

'I didn't – she telephoned here today. She tends to worry when you're investigating a case and she had been trying to get hold of you on your mobile this afternoon but it must have been out of range of a signal, presumably with you being out on Nicky's tub. So, she looked me up in the book and gave the Palmery a tinkle.'

Leo wondered if Stephanie had truly attempted to contact him on his mobile, or if the tale was a mere subterfuge and in fact nosiness had compelled her to ring Troughton's landline, in the hope that she would chat with the legend himself.

'We had the most marvellous chinwag,' continued Troughton. 'We spoke for over an hour, reminiscing, catching up. I told her how you and I were having the most famous time together, so why not nip down and join us.'

Leo, more than a little discombobulated by this turn of events, said: 'But I was set on going to Glasgow tomorrow, as part of my investigations. I intended to stay overnight at my apartment.'

'Go ahead and do so. I am perfectly capable of making Stephanie welcome by myself. What did you have planned in the city?'

'I was going to attempt to visit one of the protagonists from the summer of 1989, Janey Gribben, and the family home of the late Miss Green. By the way, did you ever meet a chap by the name of Roderick McCaskill who used to holiday at Ardcaden Bay?'

'Never heard of him, old boy.'

Leo finished his wine and bid Troughton goodnight.

And So Leo Visits Janey

LEO rose with his travel alarm at 8 a.m., but his hangover meant that he prepared for the day inefficiently. He packed his monogrammed portmanteau as an overnight bag and carried it downstairs, where he found a remarkably lively Troughton instructing two women who were wearing tabards on certain domestic tasks. A plasterer was preparing to mend the ceiling. Leo said his good mornings and goodbyes, then left the Palmery. He had to squeeze the Humber down the driveway because the women's van, which had *Sparkle and Shine Cleaners Inc.* stencilled on its side, was parked there, as was the plasterer's vehicle and a flatbed truck belonging to two gardeners who had begun taming the grounds. As he turned onto the coast road he noticed a grocer's delivery van indicating to enter the drive.

The day was overcast and muggy with a threat of rain. Leo consumed a brunch of two bacon rolls and a cup of coffee on the ferry, and then proceeded to the top deck from where he telephoned Stephanie. The moment the Humber Hawk had rolled onto the vessel he had been seized by a sense of guilt regarding her impending visit to Troughton's lair. He realised he ought to have postponed his Glasgow trip and chaperoned her with the madman, to ensure that she felt comfortable and that he behaved himself.

Stephanie was busy packing when she picked up. She

said that she had already booked a taxi for that afternoon to take her to Glasgow's Central Station, from where she would catch a train to the ferry terminal. Leo suggested that she defer until tomorrow, when he could give her a lift to Sonna, but she was obstinate. 'Please don't worry about it, Leo,' she reassured him. 'It won't be awkward – Marcus and I were much closer pals at uni than you two ever were.'

The weekend traffic on the Clyde coast was light and Leo made good progress, eventually turning off the motorway and taking a road through the north of Glasgow which passed near to the neighbourhood in which he had been raised. He was revisited by ancient memories and reanimated sensations, not all of them pleasant. Nicky had texted him Janey's address and telephone number and also a photograph of the woman, which by dint of her distracted expression Leo suspected had been taken surreptitiously. Leo had decided to drop in on Janey unannounced. He was concerned that the recent visit of Nicky might have put her off further discussion of the case, and an initiatory text message or phone call would have risked an all-too-easy instant snub. Leo was, however, not looking forward to meeting her allegedly ogreish husband.

He found Janey's peaceful road in Bishopbriggs, which was lined with modest post-war semi-detached family homes, with pebbledash, red brick and wood panelling exteriors. As he crawled along trying to locate the house number, he saw her crossing the road a short distance ahead, accompanying three primary-school aged children, one boy and two girls. Once safely across she let them run ahead of her down a wooded path. Leo parked and felt awkward getting out of the car and addressing her.

'Excuse me, I'm sorry to bother you,' he began, sedulously concentrating on maintaining the least psychotic grin he could muster. 'My name is Leo Moran. I'm an associate of

Nicky Barrett, and I am investigating the death of Andy Lamb on the Isle of Sonna in 1989. I wonder if I could trouble you for a few minutes of your time?'

Janey took a moment to size him up, and then said: 'Come with me to the playpark.'

They walked the few yards to where the path reached a grassy expanse bordered by trees and houses. The children were swarming over the equipment at a play area and Janey shouted at them to be careful before sitting down on a bench beside Leo.

'Are you and Nicky close?' she enquired.

'I barely know him.'

'He made quite an impression when he came to visit. Kept dropping hints about how flush he was. He was also very unfriendly to my husband, who is the nicest guy you could meet.'

'I believe he spoke with you about the summer of 1989, about everything that happened at Ardcaden Bay.'

Janey was of elfin proportions and wore her vibrant red hair in tight glossy locks. Instead of quieting her colouring, she accentuated it in a defiant style with bright clothing and potent cherry lipstick which complemented her self-assured carriage and gallus urban inflection. She withdrew an e-cigarette and began vaping.

'Sometimes I look back and I just can't believe it's such a long time ago. It feels like yesterday. All that youthful energy and excitement, all gone. I remember somebody brought a tape of The Stone Roses with them to the Bay that summer. It was Andy, I think – he was always the coolest. The album had not long been released. The whole gang of us sat in a circle in somebody's flat and listened to it for the first time. We were just blown away. It was like it was *our* thing, that *our* generation had arrived. Like this was the beginning of something wonderful. And then everything turned to shit.'

'Tell me about the night Andy died.'

'Usually if we wanted to do something fun in the evenings we'd just get pissed and maybe pass a joint or two. We'd head to somewhere cool like the cave near Merlin's Neb or the lighthouse, build a fire and play Led Zep and Pink Floyd and Tangerine Dream on somebody's ghetto blaster. Maybe go skinny dipping in the moonlight. But Nicky wanted to push the boundary. There was this legend about a demon piper who lived in the Cathair who you could summon, so we headed to the standing stones and did this spell. We didn't seriously expect anything to happen, just thought it would be a bit of a gas.'

'So, the evening's activities were entirely Nicky's conception?'

'Aye: the ceremony, its location, the dare – everything. After Andy's body was found the next day, the wee shite spent hours desperately trying to hush everybody up as he didn't want to cop the blame. But somebody's mum overheard him doing this and told him to spill to the polis that it was all his idea. To be fair, I have some sympathy for him. He revered Andy and has had to live with the knowledge that his stupid stunt ended up killing him.'

'Do you think Nicky actually believed he would be invoking the demon?'

'I don't think so. To him it was just a carry on. But I reckon that he fixed the draw to decide who would have to climb to the top of the Cathair.'

'Oh really?'

'Do you know those creepy guys who teach men how to seduce women?'

'Pick-up artists?'

'Yeah. They use techniques like reading a girl's palm or impressing her with magic tricks. Well, Nicky was like one of those guys, even though this was before anybody had heard of pick-up artists. He would perform these magic tricks, although it failed to make any of the girls fancy him. But, to be fair, he was brilliant at them. He must have spent hours practising, probably because he had fuck all else to do stuck in the Bay all winter. It would have been easy for him to have fixed that draw with sleight of hand or whatever. At the time I just had this intense feeling that whoever lost the draw would be who Nicky wanted to lose the draw.'

'But why would he pick on Andy, whom he so adored?'

'Maybe he wanted to humiliate him. Andy was in many ways a brilliant guy, but if he had been made of chocolate, he would have eaten himself. It's good to be confident in life, but he was *over*confident. Sometimes I glimpsed this wee edge to him, as though he thought he was a cut above everybody else, kind of entitled. One time he boasted to me that he'd never once been rejected by a female he fancied. And Nicky followed Andy around like a wee pet lamb, he hero-worshipped him. Maybe he felt emasculated by this. I remember one time a few of the boys were playing knifie at the Tarzan swing in the back woods and when it was Nicky's turn, he got into difficulty. He lost his nerve and ended up just dangling on the rope, frozen with panic. Andy had to rescue him and we all tried not to laugh, but we couldn't help ourselves.'

'Could he have been jealous of Andy because he had the hots for Amy Agumanu?'

'Nicky had the hots for everybody.'

'I am told that a boy called Roderick McCaskill provided the grimoire?'

'The what?'

'The book which contained the invocation rite.'

'Yeah. Roderick was a lovely guy but a bit of a strange fish. He had a great music collection and loved late 1960s/ early 1970s rock and folk. He once played *Stairway to*

Heaven backwards for us. He brought an entire ounce of hash with him that summer and was great at rolling joints.'

'Was he the seller of the marijuana that was smoked that night?'

'Yeah.'

'To whom did he sell it?'

'Nicky. He scored a big chunk from him.'

'Do you know how I could get in touch with Roderick?'

'I actually bumped into him four or five years ago, in the city centre. He told me he was living alone in a cottage flat in Blackcrook. He may well be there yet, if he's still alive – he looked fairly unhealthy, like he needed a good feed, with plenty of vegetables.'

'Did Andy to your knowledge eat anything with the drug in it on the night of his death? Baking perhaps?'

'No, Andy hated dope. Apparently, he took a whitey when he tried smoking it in the Bay one time and was in his bed for a day. He once snapped at me for asking him about it.'

'But the pathology report stated he had marijuana in his system.'

'I didn't know that. My family went home soon after he died, and we never returned to the Bay.'

'Nicky said that when he spoke with you recently you told him that when you were all gathered at the standing stones you saw Vincent Comiskey spying from the trees.'

'I told that wee dick to keep that to himself.'

'Why didn't you tell the police this at the time?'

'Because I never believed that Vincent killed Andy, and I didn't want to drop him in it. I felt sorry for Vincent. Yes, he was wild and did some bad stuff, but the way we ostracised him ... it was cruel. Him just roaming the hills by himself with nobody to talk to. I reckoned he'd had a fairly fucked-up upbringing, and I could empathise as I was a bit of a wild child myself, a bit troubled, you know. Funny to think that I've become so conventional, married with kids. Vincent's family were something of a firm on the South Side; whenever any of them came into the bar of the Saint Caden's Hotel in Ardcaden all the other customers would get nervous. Vincent was from the wrong side of the tracks, and I doubted he'd get a fair hearing from the law.'

'Nicky said that Vincent used to carry a knife in a belt sheath.'

'So what? Lots of the boys had knives, although their parents forbade it. It was for country living: fishing, playing knifie, carving and the like.'

'Of course, there was that awful allegation regarding Elizabeth Meiklejohn.'

'Yeah, Roderick told me about that when I bumped into him. He also told me that it was never proven.'

'It's often a notoriously difficult crime *to* prove.'

'True, but that doesn't mean that every man who is ever accused is also guilty. And Elizabeth wasn't the full shilling.'

'I am told that you were the only person who went to look for Andy, after he had disappeared into the hills for his dare?'

'Yeah. I got worried about him when he didn't come back down. Not even Amy went up, even though she was his girlfriend. I didn't want him to go on the dare in the first place because he was pretty wrecked, and I tried to persuade him not to, but he was too full of drunken bravado.'

'Why did you go up?'

'I told you, I was concerned.'

'Why did *you* go up?'

Janey paused, then said: 'I guess I was a bit crazy about him. But he didn't fancy me back and I reckon he just thought I was a wee slag. One day that summer I bumped into him on the shore and he came on all flirtatious and asked if I wanted to go for a walk with him. We went to the woods north of Ardcaden, up towards the Lagg Road. It's a really beautiful place. We sat on a fallen tree trunk and we actually snogged. It was wonderful. Then he got all randy and tried to get his leg over with me. But even though I was dead into him, I wasn't having it, because I realised that he just wanted to fill his boots, I knew that he wasn't interested in me as a person. He only had eyes for bloody Amy Agadoo-doo. All the boys fancied her. Butter wouldn't melt, but she was a narcissistic bitch.'

'Surely we can't judge each other by our teenaged selves. I've recently met Amy and she was perfectly charming. Surely it is the adults that we become that counts?'

'Fair enough. But it was nauseating the way she fancied herself, lapped up all the male attention. One guy admiring her was never enough – she had to have *two* alpha males battling it out over her, and I hated the way everybody was so stoked speculating about this big love triangle melodrama. I hated the way everybody kowtowed to Amy and Andy, worshipped them as the perfect bloody couple. Even their *names* complemented each other. Has Amy got *you* under her spell, too?'

Leo ignored the remark and continued: 'Nicky stated that you had seemed out of sorts when you re-emerged from trying to locate Andy that night. Why was this?'

'Only because I couldn't find him,' mumbled Janey as she rubbed her nose and then stared at the ground.

Leo kept his eyes fixed on the side of her face. After a few moments she turned her head and looked at him nervously.

'Did you see something up there, Janey?'

She gazed across the grass, as though reaching into the past, and said in almost a whisper: 'I've never told a soul about it. Not even my husband.'

'Tell *me* Janey.'

She swallowed, took a long draw on her e-cigarette and then began: 'There is a gate you go through before walking down into Glen Colm. I went through it and looked down the slope. And I saw a ... figure moving across the glen. I'm certain it wasn't Vincent. It was quite far away, but I don't think it was a *person* at all. It was as though it was ... *supernatural.*'

'Could it have been some confederate of Nicky, perhaps? A trick played on Andy, someone dressed up to frighten him?'

'But it had this weird, dirty light to it. And there was this faint sound, like unearthly bagpiping.'

'But you had been drinking alcohol and smoking pot, and were no doubt in a suggestible state after the invocation at the henge.'

'No – *we had raised something up!* We shouldn't have let Nicky do the spell. That *thing* must have thrown Andy off that bloody drop, or sent him running towards it.'

'Is there anything else you can tell me about the appearance of this figure?'

'No. As I said it was quite far away and I lost sight of it after a few moments. I ran back to the others and didn't tell them anything.'

'Why not?'

'When I was a kid I tended to make stuff up, and I had been called out for it a couple of times that summer. I knew that if I described what I had seen, nobody would believe me and everybody would slag me off. But it wasn't only that. What I had seen creeped me out so much that I've just been too *frightened* to ever speak about it, as though by doing so it might somehow summon that entity again. So, I just prayed that Andy had headed for home. I felt bad for not persisting in trying to find him, but I was too scared. Anyway, I soon came to think that Andy was already dead when I saw what I saw. The polis spoke to all of us, especially me because I was the only one who had gone to look for Andy. If I had told them what I had seen, they would never have believed me, a tearaway teenager who was stoned and drunk.'

Leo thanked Janey for her time, stood up and turned to leave.

'*Vanity of vanities, all is vanity.*'

'I beg your pardon?' said Leo, facing her once again.

'I said *vanity of vanities, all is vanity.* I guess it's pathetic for me as a grown woman to still sound bitter about Amy after all these years. But please don't think badly of me, because the truth is I *do* know that in the end none of it matters: all the bling and one-upmanship and beauty contests of life.' Janey motioned towards her children and concluded: 'The wellbeing of my kids – *that* matters. What happened to Andy Lamb matters. And a whole bunch of other stuff matters. All the other bullshit just fades away.'

The Witch and the Wizard

On his way back towards the motorway Leo noticed a public library, and he came off the main road and found a parking space. Inside, he consulted a telephone directory but it did not yield any Roderick McCaskill living in the city, let alone in the riparian district of Blackcrook. Undeterred, he headed to that neighbourhood and traversed a long drag which followed the north bank of the Clyde and was lined with industrial premises and commercial depots. He came abreast with the gables of a few rows of cottages, parked up and disembarked from the Humber. He supposed that these would have been shipbuilders' residences when there had been plentiful work on the nearby river, but several of them were now in a state of disrepair. The daylight was dim for the time of year and a passing gang of youths eyed him insolently.

Leo had devised no strategy but to knock on doors, so he walked up an overgrown lane and tried two abodes, receiving no reply. He rapped on the peeling green paintwork of a third door and after a while a warty crone opened it, the reek of her filthy living quarters arresting Leo's nostrils.

'I'm sorry to disturb you, madam. I'm trying to locate a Roderick McCaskill. I believe he lives hereabouts?'

'Who are ye – polis? A sheriff's officer?' she snarled.

'No madam, I come in peace. I just need some information from him.'

'He's wan up, wan along – and don't tell him that I telt ye; I don't want him to put the hex on me. If he does, I'll put a bloody hex on him!'

With that, she slammed her door shut. Leo felt disconcerted by the hag's aggressively negative energy, and as he stepped towards the next address, he briefly entertained a crazy notion that he was being set up for some ghastly trap. He pushed the exterior door for the upper apartment, ascended a stairway with a shabby carpet and pressed the bell, which buzzed rudely. After a while, the door opened a few inches. Leo could barely discern the features of the creature who peered out from the shadow.

'Sorry to bother you, are you Roderick McCaskill?'

'Maybe,' came a voice.

'My name is Leo Moran. I'm a private detective currently investigating the death of Andy Lamb on the Isle of Sonna in 1989. I wonder if I might impose upon a few minutes of your time?'

Roderick opened the door fully and gestured for Leo to enter, then led him into the living room. Leo had barely guessed that people still lived in such squalor in Britain in the twenty-first century, and tried not to obviously show his distaste for the disorder and gloom of the place; it almost made him feel ill. The rough floorboards were naked, the wallpaper presumably in vogue when Jim Callaghan was Prime Minister, and the windows entirely blacked out. Leo moved a horror movie prop in order to take a seat on a decrepit sofa.

'I'd offer you a cup of tea, but I'm all out,' said the man in a thin treble voice. He was slightly built and dressed entirely in black, with sharp features and keen, intelligent green eyes. He was also entirely bald, and looked underfed and pallid as though in need of direct sunlight.

'That's perfectly all right,' said Leo as he scanned the

occult iconography which ornamented the room.

'It was terrible when Andy died,' said Roderick as he perched himself on a chair opposite Leo. 'He was a beautiful guy. He was kind. For example, I remember how much time he had for that mentally disabled lassie Elizabeth Meiklejohn. She worshipped him.'

'Oh really?'

'Yeah. He used to push her on the swing up in the Cathair woods, buy her Lemonade Sparkles – that was the type of ice lolly she liked.'

'I have no wish to pass judgment, but I am told that you sold the marijuana to Nicky Barrett for his activities at the standing stones?'

'Yeah. If my parents had found out they'd have killed me. But everyone kept quiet after poor Andy died.'

'Did you peddle anything that summer with the drug cooked or baked into it?'

'No. Although I remember that one day Nicky asked me how to bake with dope, so I showed him.'

'Why do you think he asked you that?'

'He was always trying to be the cool guy, the guy who was cutting-edge, in-the-know. He probably just wanted to show off to the others.'

Leo steeled himself for his next, more accusatory line of questioning.

'On the night of the tragedy, had Nicky enlisted you to assume a disguise and give Andy a scare, when he was undertaking his dare?'

'No way man! I was at home all that night. I had this daylight curfew even though I was sixteen years of age. It was mortifying, but my dad was very strict. One time he found a joint in my bedroom and I was grounded for two months.'

'Someone had been terrorising Andy that summer.

They shone a light from the hillside behind the Lambs' apartment at night, left a dead crow on the windscreen of his motor car, followed him and also paid him a nocturnal visit while wearing a mask. Do you have any idea who was responsible?'

'That's the first I've heard of it.'

'You weren't in any way involved?'

'*No* man!'

'Nicky never mentioned it?'

'No man – honest!'

Leo believed him. 'Nicky said you provided the grimoire.'

'Yes.'

'Did he request the one he used specifically?'

'No, he originally asked to borrow my Ouija board, but I told him that a particular rite used to summon hill spirits would be more appropriate for what he had in mind. Then I nearly didn't lend him anything because he was being a total arse.'

'In what way?'

'He clearly didn't believe in any of it, he was just treating it as a parlour game, something to freak people out with. But he persuaded me, slipped me a few bob.'

'What was the text?'

'Something obscure by Aleister Crowley, *Liber Advocabit Oreas*.'

'Do you still happen to possess it?'

Roderick consulted a bookshelf, withdrew a dusty volume and located the text. Leo perused it and began photographing the relevant few pages with his mobile phone. He noted that a bonfire was required for the ritual, and that ideally it should be conducted near to where the entity was thought to emerge from the landmass and in the first darkness after the sun sets.

'I know quite a bit about the demon piper folk tale,' said

Roderick. 'He is said to dwell within the Cathair. Legend has it that there was once a cave which was thought to go deep inside the back of the hill. It was believed even in ancient times to be inhabited by a demon. One day – this would be hundreds of years ago, the local clan chief put up a prize for whoever was brave enough to enter the cave and measure how deep it went. A travelling piper took up the challenge and was never seen again. A party of men was raised to search inside, but as they approached there was a collapse which sealed the piper in the earth's dark womb forevermore. The entrance to the cave would become overgrown and forgotten, but a year after the collapse a shepherd encountered the piper's ghost. He said that the demon had possessed him, and that from now on when invoked he would rise to destroy whoever he happened across. Moreover, he stated that his power could be channelled: he could be instructed to smite the summoner's enemies or indeed create mayhem or carnage further afield.'

'What do you believe happened up in the hills that night?'

'Most folk reckoned it was just an accident. But what if Nicky and the gang conjured something evil and destructive? I've been tortured by that possibility ever since. You know, that maybe lending Nicky that book for a few lousy bob inadvertently led to Andy Lamb's death.'

Leo liked Roderick, who had a gentle, mellow disposition, and felt sorry for him because of his sordid living conditions and was disturbed by his unhealthy interest in magick. As he was shown to the front door, he turned to Roderick and pressed a little Miraculous Medal into his palm.

'I beg of you, pin this to your wall. And give it precedence over all the idols in your home.'

Now Stephanie Joins Our Story

AFTER visiting his mother and finding her in good fettle, Leo enjoyed an evening in the old-fashioned elegance of his West End apartment, glad of the solitude and familiar surroundings. Before departing the next morning, he scooped up a few Beethoven symphonies for the gramophone at the Palmery, feeling a need to vary the Brahms diet. He also slotted a bottle of fourteen-year-old Tomintoul malt whisky into his portmanteau.

It was a dull morning, the sun a mere soft glow behind a grey shroud. Leo attended Mass at a church in North Kelvinside and then drove the short distance to the address of the late Miss Green, who according to Troughton's case files had lived there with her sister and elderly parents.

It was a Victorian townhouse in a beautiful blond sandstone terrace set within a leafy crescent. Leo parked the Humber, climbed a short flight of exterior steps and rang the doorbell. A middle-aged woman answered. She wore thick plastic rimmed spectacles and a plain green frock, her greying hair styled to cling to her head in a rather severe fashion.

'Good morning, madam, I am sorry to disturb you. My name is Leo Moran, I am a private detective.' The woman regarded him coldly. 'I am undertaking some investigative reporting into various deaths at the south end of the Isle of Sonna in recent years. I believe this was the residence of

Miss Green, who sadly passed away by Ardcaden Bay?'

'She was my sister.'

'My condolences. It must have been a dreadful shock to you all. I wonder if I might speak with you about what happened?'

'Why should I permit that?'

'Because I wish to confirm that the given cause of death was valid.'

'It wasn't.'

'I see.'

'I will never stop mourning my sister's passing, and I am now more convinced than ever that she did not take her own life.'

'Why, might I ask?'

'Because she had no reason to. Because it would have been entirely out of character.'

A forlorn female voice called from deep inside the townhouse, and the woman concluded: 'That is Mother coming. I don't wish her to be upset, so I'll say no more on the matter. Good day to you.'

The woman closed the door firmly and Leo returned to the Humber, turned the ignition and began the journey back to Sonna.

When Leo arrived at the Palmery he was greeted by the sight of a gleaming vintage gold Mercedes-Benz 450SL. Troughton was taking down the roof, optimistically because the radio had predicted wet weather although rays of sunshine were currently peering through the cloud cover.

'Good day to you, Moran! Taylor's garage finally released the Benz.' His complexion glowed with cologne, his hair was swept back with Brylcreem and he was wearing an open-necked shirt with a crimson ascot. Leo provided a superficial summary of his Glasgow trip as he maladroitly tried to help fold the soft top, omitting any theories that he had formed. Troughton then said: 'You go inside and say hello to Stephanie while I finish up out here. You're just in time for late luncheon.'

In the hall, one of the cleaning women – Leo wasn't sure if she was *Sparkle* or *Shine* – was finishing up, presumably having been paid double time on account of it being a Sunday. The place smelled of beeswax and floor cleaner, and a visit to the kitchen would reveal that the pantry and cupboards were suddenly well stocked. It was there that he found Stephanie, looking relaxed and happy as she put the finishing touches to a colossal feast. She was wearing slim three-quarter-length cotton trousers and a cropped blouse with a botanical print. Her hair had been straightened and lightened, her teeth whitened, which along with a recent bronzing from the Aegean sun had taken ten years off her.

Leo bent to kiss her pretty cheek. 'Everything all right?' he asked.

'I'm having fun,' she said in her sexy, slightly husky voice. 'Marcus is a brilliant laugh. I told you it would be cool. How are your inquiries going?'

Leo provided a synopsis of the case so far, evoking horror in his friend when he related the drama of his run-in with the green Jaguar.

'Have you had any visions relating to the mysterious deaths?'

'No, and to be honest I find the fact somewhat troubling. Usually, my detective work is initiated by a vision, and on other occasions when I have responded to a request that I investigate a case the visions have always been forthcoming. Therefore, I fear that my involvement in these matters is not providential.'

The highlight of the extravagant luncheon in the dining

room was a massive Loch Anna fish, its googly-eyed entrance on a parsley-garnished platter greeted by the host with the exclamation: 'Bring on the trout! Trout for Troughton!' He then leapt to his feet and set upon the broiled scales with vicious dagger strokes to expose the luxurious pink flesh, like a man making the address at some madcap pescatarian supper, Stephanie trilling with amusement instead of baulking at the grotesqueness of the proceedings.

Leo was irked by how Troughton was suddenly acting like the lord of the manor in the presence of Stephanie, as though his penury had been a mere blip. More chagrining was the manner in which Troughton and Stephanie brazenly flirted with each other, her beautiful green eyes sparkling at his every witticism – most of which were at Leo's expense. Troughton had adopted a remarkably charming demeanour, and managed to pass his jibes off as playful. Leo resisted the mean-spirited temptation to recount the man's recent disasters and outrages. Certainly, Stephanie's presence had invigorated Troughton, who appeared to have got his act together – not least in curbing his alcohol consumption, having been lately so prone to despondency.

After luncheon Leo found the pair in the hall, attired for motoring.

'See you later Leo – Marcus is taking me on a tour of the island,' said Stephanie, who was wearing cat-eyed sunglasses, a pink silk headscarf and a matching lambswool cardigan.

'Only room for two in the Benz, I'm afraid Moran,' said Troughton, who was sporting a herringbone jacket, a flat cap and string back driving gloves. 'I need to check that she's purring like a kitten again. Hopefully the weather will hold.'

Stephanie, reading Leo's slightly crushed expression, added: 'Sorry Leo. We had planned this earlier, and we didn't know when you'd be back from the mainland.'

'That's perfectly all right. Anyway, I've got casework to do,' said Leo, pretending not to feel left out.

Leo had a visit planned for that evening and he set about killing the next few hours, first going for a meditative stroll around the newly cropped Palmery gardens, and then heading to the office where he typed up notes, tried to diagram his theories and stared at the wall map fruitlessly. Eventually he descended to the kitchen and opened a tin of soup and consumed it with some French bread and leftover trout. He noticed that the rain had come on and he gazed out at it, feeling lonesome and wondering where Troughton and Stephanie had got to. He picked up his mobile phone and rang for a taxi.

The Brewer's Tale

At the south of the island the lighthouse sat perched on its bleak promontory, its beam ripping through the dreichness as its companion on Little Cunrae blinked in sad empathy. The plangent note of a ship's fog horn drifted in from the sound. At the north of the island, the narrow straits presented a dreary prospect, the little ferry ploughing the heaving water at Cladach Buidhe beneath blackening hills, her lanterns dirty yellow in the murk.

Leo walked up the path to Vincent Comiskey's cottage, the rain drumming on his umbrella. He drank in the aroma of salt air, wet soil and wet vegetation, undergirded by a yeasty smell from the microbrewery. He rang the bell and waited for Vincent to open the door.

'It's real fugitive's weather, so I thought I might seek shelter. I've brought something cheering for us,' said Leo, holding up the bottle of Tomintoul he had liberated from his Glasgow apartment. 'I took a taxi here, and shall take one home. *Ergo*, we can raise a glass together. Who knows, you might even let me sample your fine ales as an accompaniment.'

'You might as well come in then,' said Vincent. 'Excuse the mess, I don't get many visitors. In fact, I don't get any visitors.'

Leo shook the rain from the silk canopy of his cane crook handled umbrella and stepped inside.

After Vincent had pulled on a pair of shoes and a cagoule, the men exited the rear of the cottage and dashed across the back yard to the microbrewery. Once inside, Vincent stoked the boiler stove and they ensconced themselves in a small lean-to room which contained a couple of comfortable chairs and a refrigerator stocked with various ales for tasting.

Vincent explained that his beers were named after the three greatest embayments of the island's west coast: Herrick Pils, Saint Madden's 70/- and Scallop Pale Ale. Leo also sampled a prototype milk stout, and was intrigued to learn that Vincent brewed his pils to concord with the *Reinheitsgebot*, the German Beer Purity Law.

'I now supply several of the island's pubs and hotels, one off licence and a few private residences. Plus I'm in talks to have my bottles sold on the ferries.'

'They are all fine fluids,' said Leo, genuinely impressed by the products as the alcohol warmed the conversation. 'You are a fellow bachelor?' he enquired.

'Aye. I had so much to unravel, so much to process that by the time I was done I was too old to be a husband or a dad.'

'It's not too late.'

'Yes it is, but to be honest with you, Leo, I don't really care about all that now.'

Leo took a sip of pale ale and then said: 'What happened to you, Vincent?'

'I saw the face of Christ.'

'In a vision?'

'No. In another human being. After the delinquency of my teenage years, the perfect alibi awaited me. You see, the whole ecstasy thing was underway, and I could join in the claim of my spoiled, selfish generation to be in some way "fucked up", to claim some vague sense of victimhood rather than actually take responsibility for the way I thought and the way I acted. We pretended the whole drug thing was us striking out against the Man, but really it was just pure hedonism, and after a while hedonism will corrode the soul. The truth is we were vain, dishonourable little bastards. Anyway, one night a crowd of us were piling out of this hip bar in Glasgow, on our way to some cool club. And then I saw this young woman walk by, about our age. Her face was unremarkable – I reckon nobody else would have given her a second glance – unbonny, but appealing in a kindly way. She seemed meek and vulnerable and I could kind of tell that she was lonely. She glanced at us, the in crowd, the beautiful, confident people coming up on pills, and then she quickly looked away, staring downwards, and rushed off. And I hated the very idea that *she* should feel inferior to *us*, awed by *us*. Because in her face was purely simplicity and goodness. That moment of grace was my glimpsing the sacredness of the human race in one personage. It was like a lightning bolt, it completely arrested me, stopped me in the street.'

'What did you do then?'

'I turned on my heel and fucked off, my pals all confused, calling after me. When I got home I wept and drowned myself in Scotch. I went into a depression as I faced up to what I had been, but I never despaired – I knew something beautiful and meaningful had happened, I knew I was through walking on the wild side. It was both the most painful and the most glorious time in my life.' Vincent chased a sip of whisky with some lager, then continued: 'On the subject of simple, beautiful souls, I've decided I'm going to visit Elizabeth Meiklejohn, to ask her to clear my name. I want to get this crap cleared up once and for all. Don't worry, I'll go gently.'

'Someone who was at the stone circle on the night Andy

Lamb died saw you watching from the trees. I have spoken with this witness.'

'So, at last we get to the nub of your visit.'

'Do you deny it?'

Vincent lit a cigarette from a silver Zippo as the rain pinged on the asbestos roof, then said, 'No, I don't deny it. I was spying on them, wishing I could be part of the fun.'

'But you stated you were home that night.'

'That's what I told the polis when they spoke with me. My old man, God rest him, backed me up, but the truth is he'd been drinking in his pal's flat all evening. In our family, in the neighbourhood where I was brought up, you always backed someone's alibi.'

'Did you go elsewhere that night, after the standing stones?'

'Aye. I overheard the dare they were planning because Nicky was shouting in this grandiose way, loving being the centre of attention. For most of that summer I'd been completely alone, an outcast. I amused myself by roaming the hills and coast of the south end. I loved the lie of the land and it became like my territory, my private world. The *energy* of the countryside down there kind of gripped me, although nowadays I don't like it so much. And I thought it might be fun to do some roaming at night, to spy on Andy. So I cut across country and went to this grove of fir trees I knew, from where I could have a view of him passing. It's a right beautiful place, that grove, the way the sunlight on a summer's day shines in wee pools on the long grass and the plants on its floor. I waited for a while, but Andy never came by. I was cold, so I just headed for home.'

'Was it your intention to frighten or attack Andy?'

'Honestly, it wasn't. Giving him a fright is exactly the kind of thing I'd have pulled back then, and I admit I couldn't stand the fella. But it just didn't enter my head that night. Do you hear how vague and unconvincing this would have sounded to the polis? Do you understand why I had to lie?'

'Why did you dislike Andy so?'

'At first I hung out with the gang, and Amy would play me and Andy off against each other. Even after I was cast out, she'd meet me down by the lighthouse or by the cave near Merlin's Neb or at the reservoir below the village. What's that Latin phrase, about not speaking ill of the dead?'

'*De mortuis nil nisi bonum.*'

'Well, I'm afraid I am going to have to speak ill of Andy Lamb. Because even before Amy had stoked up jealousy between us I thought he was an arrogant prick. He treated Nicky like his slave, and bullied and manipulated him and a couple of others in the gang. He could be snidey and he was cruel to a dog his family had, used to kick the wee thing in order to get it to fuck off. He'd tell lies and he was competitive something chronic. For example, I remember he taped my Stone Roses album and later I heard that he had played it to the rest of the gang, making out that it was *he* who had discovered them. Yet everyone, especially Nicky, acted like the sun shone out of his jacksie. One time, he and I had a square go, on the seafront at Ardcaden Bay. I was getting the better of him, but Mr Agumanu happened by and broke it up. However, Andy put it around that *he* had been winning the fight and had been about to batter *me*, even though he knew it was a lie. But he was just a young lad, barely shaving, and I was horrified when I heard that he'd died. And more than a wee bit scared that I'd be put in the frame.'

'Did you see anyone else up there?'

Vincent cleared his throat. 'I saw no other human being up there.'

'Did you see anything out of the ordinary –'

'The cross-examination is over,' interrupted Vincent firmly. 'Now, I need to ask: do you believe me when I swear to Almighty God that I did not kill Andy Lamb or, for that matter, sexually assault Elizabeth Meiklejohn?'

'Yes,' replied Leo. 'I believe you.'

The men continued drinking and talked about matters other than the case, enjoying each other's company. After a while, Leo looked out of a window and observed: 'My goodness, it's dreich tonight.'

'The rain sings to my soul,' said Vincent.

'You enjoy its melancholy?'

'Maybe. But also, I'm a Celt, not designed for constant sunshine, which is why Scotland suits me fine. You know, once I had figured out all the chaos and shite that had gone down in my life I asked myself: what will reality be like if I stop making demands of it? That's a hell of a proposition, because we humans seem programmed to always be yearning for greener grass, we're never at peace. Yet I stopped living for some unattainable future and instead just accepted things as they are. So, I live privately and quietly and try to enjoy the little things – even the drizzle over the East Strait. And do you know what, Leo: life's not so bad. And when my death comes, this week or thirty years from now, I'll be ready for it.'

'But don't you get lonely up here, out of the way all by yourself?'

'Sometimes. I speak to at least one of my big brothers on the blower every night, but they live in Glasgow, and apart from them I've not a friend in the world. I've come to accept that lonesomeness is my cross to bear. But if I've used life's suffering to reform myself, to get to heaven, then *so what* if I have to while out my remaining time here alone?'

The Knave's Tale

LEO awoke to loud hammering from below, a bass drum to accompany the post-alcohol snare beating inside his skull. His room was stuffy and filled with filtered sunlight, and his mouth felt as fat and dry as a piece of leather. He had overslept. He stumbled to the en suite and urinated tumultuously, rinsed his mouth and then prepared a seltzer. He took this to the bedroom window, opened the curtains and hauled up the sash, and sipped as he watched the two gardeners labouring below.

After he had prayed and prepared for the day, Leo descended to find a joiner fixing some skirting in the hall and two decorators at work in the dining room. Stephanie and Troughton were nowhere to be seen, and outside a master builder, who was assessing the house's exterior, informed him that they had gone for a drive to take advantage of the splendid weather, and hadn't said when they would return. Leo felt a little annoyed that they hadn't informed him of their plans and spent the remainder of the morning slumped in a shaded steamer chair trying to come to terms with his dismal hangover and the weighty task which awaited him. The day was very hot and last night's rainfall was being scorched from the land's memory. Leo had missed breakfast, but he managed to eat a boiled egg with a slice of toast dismembered into soldiers for a meagre luncheon. Then he got into the Humber and set off for Fairfax.

Nicky was on the lawn of his Marine Drive villa when Leo pulled up. He glanced up from his solo game of croquet, then put down his mallet and guiltily watched his visitor approach, as though divining the coming showdown. Leo requested that they speak in private, and was shown into a study lined with library sets and wooden panelling. Nicky yelled out for Vera not to disturb them and the men sat down on a pair of oxblood Chesterfield chairs.

'On that tragic night in 1989, after you made the invocation at the standing stones, did anything strange happen or did you feel anything weird?' opened Leo.

'You can't be serious – the demon piper is just a daft old story,' said Nicky, a nervous catch in his voice.

'Speaking of daft stories, you've been spinning me quite a few of those lately. And I propose that you've been hoping that certain witnesses had become hazy on certain details about that night, or that I wouldn't ask them about or stumble upon those details. Or, you were banking that we'd all be so fixated on your new piece of witness testimony – that Janey had seen Vincent spying at the standing stones – that we would disregard those details. Perhaps you are the type of arrogant person who thinks everybody else is stupid. Perhaps when Troughton suggested hiring a psychic detective, you envisaged some feeble mystic with his head in the clouds who wouldn't ask any difficult questions.' Nicky shifted uneasily in his chair, and Leo continued: 'First off, you lied to me about not remembering who had conceived of the whole evening's nonsense: the ceremony and the dare. The entire caper was planned by you.' Nicky looked at the floor. 'Furthermore, you fixed the draw so that Andy Lamb would lose it, didn't you?' Nicky was silent. 'I asked you a question!' snapped Leo, and Nicky at last made eye contact and nodded slightly. 'Moreover, you lied to me about Andy being able to handle alcohol and marijuana. You knew full well that he was virtually allergic to both. You lied when you told me that you didn't remember who had provided the dope that evening – which was you, and you lied when you told me that you didn't know how Andy had come to ingest it. You spiked him, didn't you?'

'Yes, I spiked him,' mumbled Nicky.

'Speak up man!' barked Leo.

Nicky stood and poured himself a malt whisky from a crystal decanter which was sat on an ebony desk. He took a sip, resumed his seat and said: 'Earlier that evening, Andy was round at mine. I had invited him, set it all up. I knew that my parents would be out for a golfing medal and dinner in Kilmichael. I cooked us a meal, and for dessert I served him some cookies I had made earlier. Of course, I didn't tell him that they were *hash* cookies. It had all been months in the planning. I wanted someone other than me to act like a dick for once, to say and do all the wrong things. And you should have heard him at that bonfire up at the stones, babbling every shade of shite. Meanwhile I was cool as Clint Eastwood. Andy was all anxious and jumping at shadows – it was *beautiful*, someone else being the coward instead of me. You know what I really liked about that night? The feeling of having *control*. For once *I* was just like one of the popular guys, the handsome guys to whom power just flowed. I was like a puppeteer. All I had to do was yank a string and Andy responded. Then everything just spun into chaos.'

'It was you who had been terrorising Andy that summer, wasn't it?'

'One evening Andy and I had a few cans of lager together and he blurted out that on the previous night someone had spooked him by shining a light from the woods on the hillside. Fuck knows who had done it, but he felt sure it was meant for him. The next day I realised he had evidently forgotten that he had confided in me about it, on account of him being such a One Can Dan. So I decided to start my own campaign: following him, putting a dead crow on his car, visiting him at night while I was wearing a mask. He told me about the masked caller and to freak him out even more I made up some bullshit about there being a part of the demon-in-the-hill legend which stated that before striking, the piper would visit his next victim during the night.'

'The poor guy must have been pretty on edge by the time he met his destiny. On the night of Andy's death, did you have a confederate waiting for him in the hills, someone dressed up to give him a scare?'

'I swear to you, I didn't.'

Leo found Nicky convincing on this point, and continued: 'I put it to you that ever since that terrible night you have regretted sending Andy off on his dare in such a state, placing him in a position of danger. Therefore, you *wanted* to believe that Vincent killed Andy at that scarp, because it would assuage your guilt. And if you convinced yourself that Vincent had murderous intent that summer *anyway*, then you would be entirely self-exculpated, because Andy's demise was only a matter of time. But the reality is that Vincent is wholly innocent, and now you have poisoned Johnathon Lamb's mind against him with your theorising. I believe you loved Andy Lamb but also envied him. And you couldn't abide him being with Amy Agumanu, because you idolised him and were besotted with her. So, you wanted him to look bad that night, perhaps to make yourself feel better about your lowly status, perhaps even in some desperate hope of making Amy repelled enough by Andy that she would break up with him. Who knows, maybe then you'd be able to sweep her up in your arms. I don't think you're free of that summer, and I don't believe you ever will be until you stop blaming Vincent Comiskey and take responsibility yourself.'

Nicky took another sip of whisky, then said: 'Are you certain that Comiskey didn't kill Andy?'

'Quite certain.'

Nicky wept. After a minute or two he dried his eyes and began: 'Andy could have been anything he wanted to be, a real addition to humanity. Everything you say is right. Apart from one key detail: it wasn't Amy I loved, it was Janey. Everyone fancied Amy, but Janey ... she had *mystique!* She was so full of wit and vitality, and had this kind of crazy, wayward energy. And as for her red hair! When I visited her recently, I saw that it had lost none of its lustre, and neither had she. But she was nuts about Andy, you could tell. It was all so *frustrating* – she and I were both always single during the holidays, and he never even gave her so much as a second glance. So, I figured if only I could burst Andy's aura then she might notice me. Which is why I humiliated him that night. My love for Janey reached right back into my childhood, since I was maybe eight years old. Every summer of the 1980s I'd gaze for hours at the road, praying that every car that emerged from the Wee Bay was her family's. And every holiday turned out the same: me following her around like a puppy, desperately trying to impress her, and she following Andy around like a puppy, hanging on his every word. I'd try it on with other girls to make her jealous, but they weren't interested in me either. And then, one day, she'd leave. Go back to her big city life where she doubtless never gave me a moment's thought. And I'd feel awful because I knew I'd have to wait a whole year before I saw her again, and when you're a kid a year is like a life sentence – it might as well be forever. The holidaymakers would come to Ardcaden for a few weeks during the glorious summers, and then I would be left there with the rains and the winter as the Cathair darkened. I remember one summer her family didn't appear. Her cousins – they used to holiday in the Bay, too – told me that Janey's lot were going to Spain that year instead. It was like being kicked in the stomach, except the feeling lasted for *weeks*. I went around pretending like nothing had happened, but inside I honestly didn't care if I lived or died. After Andy's death, Janey's family stopped coming to Ardcaden and I guess I just buried the whole issue. Then, one day, do you know what occurred to me? That I had amassed all my wealth for her, to impress her, to win her, without ever consciously realising it. Then, out of the blue, Vincent set up his business on the island which reinvigorated my interest in Andy's death and it felt like the perfect excuse to approach Janey. I managed to trace her. I found out that she was married with kids but I still went after her, visited her, and do you know what – she didn't even remember my name. I mean she did, after a minute or two, but then she kept overusing it, as though to cover the fact that it had slipped her mind.'

'So, let me get this straight – your strategy was to break up Janey's family and then presumably dispose of your own marriage?' enquired Leo.

'My marriage is empty, a sham. I picked Vera up on the internet like you would buy a new yacht. I figured that maybe I'd find that Janey was in an unhappy relationship too, and even if I couldn't have made her love me I could still have enticed her with the high life. Maybe that would have been enough for me.'

'I believe you are wrong about one thing,' opined Leo. 'I think Vera cares about you.'

'The truth is that she offends me just by *being* there, because she is kindness right through.'

'And why should her goodness shame you? Don't you like yourself?'

After a pause, Nicky said: 'Perhaps not.'

'Therefore, you fill the hole in your self-worth with status symbols, with the prestige of wealth.'

Nicky rose from his Chesterfield and refilled his glass. He sat down again and took a sip, and his eyes became unfocused as though he was gazing inwardly at his very soul. Then he said: 'If I dislike myself now, then it's nothing as compared to when I was a teenager.'

'You were barely more than a child, and you made a terrible error.'

'I was an egomaniac with low self-esteem. That's some combination – that's how war crimes get committed, that's how real evil is done.' Nicky laughed hollowly, then continued: 'Do you know I would adopt dialects and alter egos and any cloak I could, just to be *anything* that wasn't me? I still haven't gotten over what an arsehole I was back then. How idiotic and self-centred and vain I was. But that's a vanity too, isn't it – not releasing yourself from the past? It's funny, Leo, but I don't believe you much like yourself either. I have a sixth sense for noticing it in others.'

Leo considered this, then said: 'Yes, there is that. But I accepted myself a bit more the day I realised I couldn't ever be one of the cool guys, that I just wasn't constructed of the same fibre as them. The novelist William McIlvanney wrote of greatness being not taking the bad stuff out on other folk. I suppose, in the end, it's about the choices you make, rather than what you feel or think about yourself or how attractive other people find you. I hope that, sinner as I am, most of the time, for most of my adult life, I didn't hide from my conscience.'

He stood up and made to leave, but Nicky clutched his sleeve. 'Leo, when you went to see Janey, did she at any point ... ask after me?'

'Yes,' lied Leo. 'As a matter of fact, she did enquire as to your health. But she's happily married, so it's best just to leave it now. You have been musing upon this infatuation for so long that you think it forever has its grip of you. But you can let go of this, Nicky. In fact, you must.'

Poor bastard, thought Leo as he strode towards the door.

Back at the Palmery, Leo found Troughton and Stephanie relaxing on the terrace, sitting beneath a parasol at a white-painted metal table, a pitcher and glasses between them. Stephanie looked lovely in a summer dress and sunhat.

'Moran! Do help yourself to a gin sling,' greeted Troughton, a Panama pulled lazily over his brow.

'No, thank you,' replied Leo, before drawing up a chair and updating his host on his investigations.

Troughton listened with fascination, yet he seemed uneasy at hearing of Leo's denunciation of Nicky, presumably fearing that *The Belmartine Repository's* benefactor had been alienated. He might then have remembered his recent financial windfall, because he suddenly brightened, saying: 'Anyway, Moran, I've been patiently awaiting your arrival for the big event.'

'What big event would that be, Marcus?' asked Stephanie.

'Why, the grand unveiling, my dear. Of my latest masterpiece.'

With that, Troughton led Leo and Stephanie into the house, up the vestibule and into the hall. Troughton had set up an easel near the foot of the stairs, a cloth covering the canvas. With stately gravity he approached it, took hold of the cloth and disrobed the painting in a single swift movement. He then bowed in humble acceptance of Stephanie's sole applause.

It took a few moments for Leo to realise that he was

looking at an uncommissioned portrait of himself, and a few more moments to realise that it was a shoddy rush-job which was unflattering. Extremely unflattering. At first, he wondered if the rendering was so ghastly merely because of the artist's lack of talent, and held his tongue lest he offend his feelings.

'I am only a gentleman amateur,' said Troughton, 'but I do believe I have captured a certain essence of you, Moran. I propose that it hangs in an honoured place in this great hall forevermore.'

Leo stepped forward and examined the travesty more closely. The worst of his features had been grossly caricatured. His head was massive, the extent of his baldness exaggerated, his noble eyes depicted as piggy and cruel, his nose drooping and booze-crimsoned, his jowls saggy. Moreover, the creature looking back at him wore a brooding scowl.

'So, Moran ... what do you think?'

'It's, it's ... m ... m ... m ... *monstrous!*' ejaculated Leo finally.

Troughton maintained his deadpan facial expression for a few seconds longer, then collapsed to the parquetry where he writhed in a paroxysm of laughter. Leo noticed that Stephanie was giggling quietly. He regarded her gravely and uttered: '*Et tu*, Stephanie?'

Troughton remained convulsing in delicious agony until eventually Stephanie admonished him half-heartedly, saying: 'Marcus, don't be cruel.'

Leo stormed off huffily.

The Eternal Mother

Leo sulked in his room for a while reading *The Tablet* before freshening up and changing his shirt. He gazed in the dressing table mirror for a few moments, hoping that his visage wasn't as unappealing as Troughton had conveyed. He then set off in the Humber.

He drove the coast road through Kilmichael, and as he slowed to swing westwards just after Port Penelope he noticed Vincent Comiskey coming from the direction of his cottage in his van. His eyes were fixed determinedly on the highway and a gasper was clamped between his lips like a defiant sacrilege to his mortality. Leo traversed a pleasant pastoral neck of land below the bulging, rugged upper reaches of Sonna. The road passed a lovely ruined church and was edged with hawthorn hedges which teemed with chaffinches and wrens. He reached Herrick Bay and parked beneath the sycamores at Fagr Vágr. He walked through the kissing gate and up the gravel path, but when he knocked on the front door Amy didn't seem to be at home and neither was she in her workshop shed. On some instinct he decided to head further up the single-tracker on foot, quite expecting to find her.

Leo walked the tarmacadam, which was lined with gorse, fern, nettle, seeding grasses, dock, sea aster, hawkbit, sow thistle, buttercups and foxglove. The hills soon crouched nearer to the road, which was now avenued by grey willow, and also scrub of oak, ash and hawthorn. A lone bat, disorientated and incongruous in the daylight, fluttered above his head. The mellifluous song of birds was infused with the low drone of crickets and flying insects. Prior to a large bank of bracken Leo turned left through the squat woods, towards the sparkling water.

She was there on the baking antediluvian shore, resolutely beautiful, her sad eyes blue like the sea. She was crouched amid bleached rocks, which were angular and jagged and some of them marbled, working with a sanding block on a sun-blistered rowboat which was sat upon a bed of flint. She was wearing denim shorts and a cut-off T-shirt, and her hair was tied up in a headscarf.

'Leo, what a nice surprise! You have found my secret cove,' she said as she stood up from her task.

'It is impressive to see the master craftswoman at work. Is the boat one of Nicky's?'

'No. I found her washed up and wrecked here. Restoring this wee girl is my labour of love.'

Her backdrop was the West Strait, on which was dotted several crafts with pretty sails, some of them at rest at their moorings.

'I wanted to tell you that Vincent did not kill Andy,' said Leo as he sat upon a rock. 'I believe that neither did he molest Elizabeth, and all I need to do now is prove it.'

Amy perched herself alongside him. She seemed unsurprised by this news. 'I *told* you he didn't kill Andy. Back in the day I used to lead Vincent on, snogging him a few times – daft teenage stuff. But I *did* care for him. I wanted to protect him from himself because he was so self-destructive. I liked his bad-boy image, but he never acted in an aggressive way with me, you know, sexually. I was shocked when I heard the rumour that he had attacked Elizabeth. I never really believed he was capable of something like that.'

'I sat drinking with him last night and I must confess I rather like him. I believe him to be a good man.'

'Look Leo, I've had enough of boat-sanding for one day. Why don't you stay for dinner? I'll open a bottle of wine and you could take a taxi home, and pick your car up tomorrow?'

Leo was glad to accept the invitation, not least because it would absent him from Troughton's company for an evening. They cut directly along the rocky shore, then across the sandy flank of the bay, which was bearded with sand sedge, saltbushes, sandwort and sea purslane. They chatted merrily, blackened seaweed pustules pop-popping underfoot as they avoided stranded jellyfish, a desiccated seabird and ocean-worn glass. Martins, crows and gulls were manically busy, and a ringed plover nodded its head in greeting as it pranced across the heaped shingle. A shag stood perfectly motionless on an outer rock, waiting to strike.

Leo admired the sunny little rooms of Fagr Vágr, which were painted in cheerful colours and furnished in a whimsical style. Some local landscapes, skilfully painted by Amy, hung on the walls. She busied herself in the kitchen, declining Leo's offer of assistance as she prepared a dish quite alien to his experience involving squashes and hazelnuts and kale and polenta. He picked up a framed photograph from the upper shelf of a Welsh dresser. It was of a small, curly-haired girl, her eyes not quite focusing, her smile crooked, her features slightly askew.

'My daughter,' said Amy.

'I beg your pardon – I'm being nosey.'

'That's all right. She died when she was three.'

'I'm terribly sorry, Amy.'

'She had a congenital disorder. That's the thing about

islands, Leo: they are places where people come to hide, or to escape their past.'

'What was her name?'

'Olivia.'

Now Amy's sorrow at the side altar in the church in Kilmichael when Leo had first seen her made sense. *This* was what her sadness was for. Now the religious sculpture she had constructed also made sense. The attitude of the Madonna expressing the endurance through and sanctification of all maternal anguish and loss, and indeed of all loss, all agony, all longing, throughout all ages.

'I saw you last week, at the Marian altar,' he blurted.

'I sense her presence there, in that church.'

'Your daughter's?'

'No, silly – Our Lady's. When the obstetrician told us that something was wrong, he said that I had another option, but I couldn't. Do you ever think that loving people can make you feel sad? I don't only mean after they are gone, I mean when they are here, I mean when you are actually in the moment of loving a person. You feel sad because they are vulnerable and mortal, because they are prone to suffering. From Olivia I learned about life, about its preciousness ... about what it means to love unconditionally, unselfishly. To me, she was the most gorgeous thing in the whole world. She taught me what true beauty is, and I realised how the pursuit of glamour and popularity and fame – I used to dream of being famous – is so much baloney. It's not a dynamic that is fashionable to speak about, but when I was young, I had power over boys and men because I was physically attractive. And I abused that power, and attractive women sometimes do abuse it because they're immature and insecure. Boys liked me, and I loved the adulation. I fed off it. And you keep feeding off it and although the buzz diminishes you are hooked, so you chase it more and more.

And then gravity takes its toll and your beauty fades and so does the adulation. And the new beautiful girls on the block arrive. I was swapped for a younger model – karma paying me back for my vanity when I had my looks. But, to be fair to my ex, things had never been the same between us after Olivia died. It was tragic, really.'

'You are still beautiful, Amy. Shakespeare wrote that *Beauty doth varnish age, as if new-born.*'

'Flattery will get you everywhere, no matter how insincere,' smiled Amy. 'The truth is, Leo, that I don't care about all of that nowadays. I'm stripped down, I'm free. What was it that other poet, Bob Dylan, said, *When you ain't got nothing, you got nothing to lose.*'

Leo cleared his throat, then said, 'You mentioned the power you had over males. How did Andy respond to that?'

'Andy was a nice guy, although on one occasion he did get a bit rough. He wanted to, you know, take things further, but I said no and eventually I managed to get him to back off. He was quite a randy guy, even for a teenager. We fell out, but a couple of days later he apologised and we were back in love. You know how young hearts are.'

'Boys used to be taught how to be gentlemen, to respect women. Ever since the cultural revolution of the 1960s it has just become more and more of a free for all. Everybody gets hurt in the name of individual liberty.'

After dinner they migrated with their glasses and a bottle to the sunroom, where Amy lit candles and proposed in a mellow voice that people ought to smell the flowers and drink the wine while they can. At one point Leo noticed her staring absent-mindedly at his burnt hands as though she hadn't noticed them before, in a not entirely dissimilar way to which he had just been entranced by her lovely long brown legs. She turned her thoughts to Ardcaden Bay.

'The thing about it was that *everybody* got it, *everybody* understood how special it was. Our schoolmates might have gone to some Spanish resort at summertime, but we all knew we had it better. And if such mutual love for a place can exist, then there's something communal about the human experience after all. And wherever you go in the world and whatever happens you know that this peaceful spot is still there, unchanging, and that you can visit it in your imagination at any time.'

She then slipped into hazy reminiscence about the Bay, describing what it had been like back in those prelapsarian days. Leo listened, hypnotised by her voice and the wine, and gazed through the window. In the garden an apple tree caught the gentle light, its gnarled trunk so aged and crooked that it rested directly on the earth. The sweet fragrances of the summer evening had descended. In the surrounding countryside, hardwoods and clumps of flowering whin cast long shadows in the lateralising rays. The sun on the island's hills and across the strait was a thin yellow, and a different, silvery luminance had descended in pools upon the low-lying fields and meadows, every object there about to turn to silhouette. Rabbits safely grazed the sloping lawn which led from Amy's house to the dense verdant summer border, and martins wheeled and screeched for pure joy in the air above. To the west, above the ocean, the sunset was a swirling lambent fresco of Tyrian purple and jasper.

Amy's monologue turned to Sonna's gloomier side. Everything from the simple inconveniences of country life to the frightening electricity ironman in the back woods, the steep, thickly timbered Cathair darkening at night and the unnerving ambience which seemed to encompass that hill.

'And when Andy died, it was like that darker side of the island had won out,' she explained. 'It was the end of Eden.

Not just for me, but for everyone. All those childhood and teenage innocent days just vanished overnight. After I didn't find Andy at our meeting place I went back to the village. All the other kids were just huddled around the bench where we used to sit. I remember the sky was ominous – just a solid white, not a summer sky – and the police pulled up outside the Lambs' house. A few of us walked along and all we could hear was this wailing as Andy's mum heard the news that they'd found her son's body. You've never heard a person in such despair. We all grew up that day, became adults. The holidays were nearly over and folk started packing their cars and drifting off. Many never returned, my family included. The '90s were before us and soon it would be time to move on ...'

Amy noticed that Leo had fallen fast asleep in his wicker chair. She tried unsuccessfully to rouse him, and so tucked a blanket around him and regarded him tenderly for a few moments before retiring to bed.

The Legend of the Strange Piper

LEO awoke in the night and sat perfectly still for fully half a minute before he could work out where he was. He went to the kitchen where he drank a glass of water, and when he happened to glance out of the window, he thought he glimpsed a satanic horned face regarding him evilly, its eyes of a terrible brightness.

In the morning he was roused by a rhapsody of birdsong as sunlight flooded through the windows and glittered on the sound beneath the granite mountains of Erran. Amy breezed in, fresh from a shower and wearing a towelling robe. She greeted her guest merrily.

'I must beg your pardon for falling asleep here last night,' said Leo. 'I hope I haven't been of too much inconvenience to you.'

'That's all right, Leo, I was glad of the company.'

'Blimey, I got something of a start during the night. I arose to take a glass of water and my vision must have deceived me for I fancied I saw the ghastliest thing outside. A horned head like the devil himself, staring right at me with its black and gold eyes. I only managed to get back to sleep by clasping the crucifix on my rosary to my breast.'

'You must have seen one of the feral goats. A herd is said to inhabit the north of the island, although I've never seen them.'

Leo texted Stephanie lest she be concerned by the fact

that his bed at the Palmery hadn't been slept in. He then freshened up, relieved that Amy was able to furnish him with a toothbrush. They enjoyed a light al fresco breakfast of orange juice, coffee, Dutch crispbakes, Jarlsberg cheese, Greek yoghurt and sliced mango. As they cleared the garden table, Amy mentioned that she planned to take the bus to Kilmichael to do a big shop and Leo insisted that he drive her there and back.

'Anything to oblige a lady,' he added with a smile.

The road across Sonna was washed in sunshine and a pied wagtail rose from the tarmac at the sound of the approaching Humber Hawk, and then undulated through the air ahead joyously. The sky was perfect and it promised to be a hot, dry day. There was a festive feel in Kilmichael as the ferry disgorged its passengers. When they got out of the car outside a pharmacy on Albert Street, which was Amy's first port of call, Leo heard a familiar voice calling him from across the road. He looked over to see Stephanie beckoning him, with Troughton alongside her. Leo, with some reluctance, suggested to Amy that they cross over. After Leo had made the introductions the foursome strolled the esplanade for a little while. Leo and Troughton fell behind, enduring a desultory conversation, the former still frosty from the previous day's portrait prank, the latter typically unrepentant. Meanwhile the women chatted quite eagerly. After a while, Amy left to visit the pharmacy and then the Co-op, from where Leo would pick her up. First, they exchanged mobile numbers lest some delay should occur. Troughton disappeared to the post office to collect a parcel, agreeing to also buy Leo a quarter pound of orange creams there, which he remarked he hoped would 'sweeten him up'.

'So, Leo, someone didn't come home last night!' said

Stephanie suggestively as the friends sat down on a bench.

'I can assure you that my absence was entirely innocent. As I explained to you in my text message, I merely fell asleep in Amy's armchair.'

'I think she fancies you.'

'Don't be ridiculous! Stop teasing ... really?'

'I can tell. She kept asking questions about you. I think you're in there,' said Stephanie with a ribald nudge to Leo's ribs.

'My dear Stephanie, we have been comrades for so long – but sometimes I wonder if you don't comprehend me at all. For although the modern world makes mockery of it and is confounded by it, I remain a man of strict Catholic principle. Even if, for the sake of argument, I admired Amy in that way, and even if, for the sake of the same argument, Amy reciprocated said feelings, there is no question that we could ever actually *be* together.'

'Why not?'

'Because she is a married woman.'

'But Marcus told me that she is divorced?'

'Yet, in the eyes of God, Amy remains a married woman.'

'You cannot be serious? Because your church says so?'

'Because our Saviour said so. Amy might be apart from her husband – they felt it necessary to separate and for that they have my sympathy, not my judgment, and he might have taken up with someone else, which is entirely his concern. As far as *I* am concerned, Amy remains wedded. And even if, again hypothetically speaking, I was attracted to her, I could not in all conscience breach the sanctity of marriage.'

'You mean you'd forgo the chance of happiness for some antiquated rule? The world has moved on, Leo.'

'But you see I don't give a damn for what the world thinks, particularly when I observe how disordered the world has become. What people have forgotten is that this life on earth is only ephemeral. Compared with eternity it is but the duration of a struck match. Respecting a vow made before God isn't really such a great sacrifice when measured against the forever.'

'Well, that's a shame,' said Stephanie with a sigh as she gazed across the formal lawns towards the sea. 'I had kind of hoped that romance might blossom for both of us down here.'

'I'm not sure I follow you.'

'I'd forgotten how appealing Marcus was.'

'Troughton!' exclaimed Leo, quite scandalised. 'The man is a complete arse!'

'He's dishy.' Leo was somewhat shocked by this claim. It had never occurred to him that Troughton was good-looking, but now that he came to consider it, he realised that Stephanie was right and he detected within himself a vague ember of jealousy. 'And he's kind of edgy.'

'Edgy – he's a perfect inebriate!'

'Look who's talking!'

'I'll have you know that I've moderated my consumption in recent times. In fact, I'm doing better in many ways.'

'Marcus has a sensitive, vulnerable side. Can't you see it? I think he's lonely.'

'Oh, balderdash!'

'I always had a crush on him at uni,' continued Stephanie dreamily. 'But he only ever had eyes for the sainted Maddi. Sorry Leo ... I know I'm not to mention her.'

'But he has no sense of duty beyond his own indulgence ... he is frivolous, he has no *depth* to him,' beseeched Leo exasperatedly.

'On the contrary, I think his resolve to figure out these unexplained deaths stems from a real sense of duty.'

'Or from a desperate need to resuscitate his failing

pamphlet. And anyway, he enlisted muggins here to do the actual spadework.'

'Leo, I think the real reason you won't try your luck with Amy is simply that you have become scared of intimacy. I think you are using theology as an excuse to hide behind.'

'Then you are wrong.'

They sat in grumpy silence for a while, but both parties knew that their friendship was composed of stuff supple enough to tolerate regular such contretemps. However, Leo soon began to feel guilty for his lack of tact – Stephanie herself was a divorcee. He also felt bad for having undermined Troughton behind his back. Defamation, no matter how justified, offended his code of honour.

Their attention was arrested by a male voice raised in anger, coming from behind them, and they instinctively turned around. Across the road, an apoplectic Norris Meiklejohn was yelling at Vincent Comiskey. Troughton, on his way back from the post office, had found himself near to the action. Leo rose from the bench, intending on intervening before the situation turned uglier, but a quick burst from a siren announced the arrival of a police cruiser, from which Ronnie MacKellar and his female colleague disembarked. After the sergeant's intercession Norris got into his Land Rover Discovery and drove off. Vincent stood speaking with Ronnie for a few further moments and then took his leave, wheeling a beer barrel towards a nearby hotel.

'Just as well that MacKellar was passing – I thought Norris was going to start swinging punches,' said Troughton when he arrived at the bench.

'What did you earwig?' enquired Leo.

'Apparently Vincent tried to speak with Elizabeth Meiklejohn at her home yesterday, with the intention of asking her to attest to his innocence as to his ravishing her.' Leo recalled seeing Vincent driving determinedly towards Kilmichael the day before. 'Vincent didn't get to talk directly with Elizabeth as her mother forbade it, but it sounds as though he stood pleading at the front door for quite a while. Norris was outraged when he heard about it.'

Leo parted with Stephanie and Troughton, and drove the Humber the short distance to the Co-op to collect Amy. He conveyed her to Fagr Vágr, helped her carry the groceries into the kitchen and then motored back to Kilmichael. He had become increasingly intrigued by the legend of the demon piper and wished to see if he could add to that which Roderick had imparted on the subject. However, his research in the library proved fruitless apart from a brief paragraph in a history book and a couple of cursory mentions online. Neither did the little museum next door provide any illumination. Only one of the volunteer staff on duty, a retired gentleman, had heard of the legend, which he dismissed as mere folklore.

Leo visited the bakery and bought a sliced ham and pork sandwich, a packet of plain crisps and a little bottle of limeade which he consumed while sitting on a shaded bench that overlooked the castle, and then drove to the Palmery in order to perform an overdue shower and shave. Nobody was home, and when Leo lay on his bed to rest, he soon drifted off, having not slept well at Amy's the previous night. When he awoke, the old house was still deserted, and he resolved to visit Ardcaden Bay in order to enquire there about the legend. He opted to catch the bus from a stop just across the road from the entrance to the Palmery, reckoning that a few pints with the locals might loosen lips.

The day was still ferociously hot as the little bus climbed inland above Kilkenny. The late-afternoon sun bled through the canopy, the highway a glorious lime-green tunnel of ash, elm and sycamore flanked by beech hedgerow. Soon Leo saw the distant prospect of Ardcaden Bay framed by a bower of branches. The bus entered the village, a 'Twenty's Plenty' speed limit sign subtitled with the legend *Please drive carefully in the Bay* officially embodying Amy's observation about the affectionate nickname for the settlement.

Leo made the post office before it closed, and after paying for a roll of peppermints he steered the conversation with the rotund woman behind the counter to the piper. She mumbled something in reply about the legend being just a daft local story made up to scare kids, but Leo wondered if the subject had unnerved her a little. After he left, he noticed a postcard in the shop window advertising a holiday flat for let in the village and he jotted down the landlady's telephone number.

Leo then consumed a couple of leisurely pints in the Saint Caden's Hotel, where the proprietor Tam Logan and a couple of barflies cast scorn upon the old tale of the demon in the hill. Leo then headed out of the village and began walking the mile towards the hotel at Melford where he intended to eat, having declined a text message invitation from Stephanie that he join Troughton and her for dinner at the Palmery. The thought of witnessing more of the two lovebirds' fledgling flirtations was decidedly unappetising. Leo strolled the Wee Bay in his beer-mellowed state, noting pretty speedwell, lesser yellow trefoil, rosebay willowherb and clumps of ragwort as gulls glided in the lazy evening air. At one point he was startled by a cartridge erupting, imagining that some draconian farmer was shooting at him for picking an hors d'œuvre ear of corn from a golden field before he realised that the report had, in fact, emitted from an automatic crow scarer. As he neared Melford, he decided on a whim to first walk beyond the hotel to visit Andy

Lamb's grave. He entered the grey-walled cemetery and ambled the rows of headstones. Upon one was epitaphed: 'Elizabeth Meiklejohn 1919-1987'; Norris' mother, most likely. The grave was well-tended and stocked with fresh flowers. He also happened to notice a stone bearing the inscription: 'Angus Blessing, 1932-1984. *His mercy endureth forever.*' Probably Gus' father. Leo located Andy's resting place through a dividing brick partition. It was unkempt, and as he read the graven words something caught his eye. He knelt down to examine the stone more closely, and with his finger traced angry scribbles, faded by the weather.

The Falcon Cannot Hear the Falconer

As Leo passed through the vestibule of the Melford Hotel he noticed a collage of photographs mounted on the wall beneath the lettering 'Melford Golf Club Annual Championship: Last Place Hall of Fame' in which various men downed ale from a yard glass, their humiliation for their failures on the fairways. One of the pictures was of a chap who was the exact physical likeness and approximately the same age as Blessing, and indeed the script beneath it read: 'Angus Blessing, 1982.' The fellow must be Gus' late father, Leo decided.

He enjoyed a fine repast of garlic mussels, roast breast of duck, and jam roly-poly and custard, washed down with two more pints. He then perched himself at the bar, toying with the idea of visiting Blessing to round the day off nicely; his malt whisky digestif was more than decent, but paled in comparison with the Concoction. Also, he wanted to probe the man more efficiently about some of the opaque comments he had made about the south end and the strange goings-on there.

Leo struck up conversation with the landlady, a knowing red-headed woman in her middle-fifties, and two regulars of a similar age to her who occupied the stools immediately to his right. There was also a group of pleasant younger locals – three females and two males – who were installed at a nearby table and who occasionally pitched some exuberance into the general chat. Leo was met with by-now familiar raised eyebrows when he mentioned the demon piper and resolved to give the line of questioning a rest. But he made a mental note to speak with farmers Haddow and Heron about the legend; he especially wanted to discuss it with the latter, whose tenancy incorporated the extremity of Glen Colm where the drama in 1989 had unfolded.

One of the regulars, a thin, balding man who was apparently a factor for the Baronet, changed the subject to the Cats' House, and how he had recommended to his employer that it should now either be renovated or demolished.

'It's become an eyesore right enough,' opined his neighbour, a scruffy, barrel-shaped fellow who oversaw a nearby farm.

'By the Cats' House, you mean the first property on your right as you go along the minor road from here?' enquired Leo bewilderedly.

'Yes,' confirmed the farmer.

'But surely that is Gus Blessing's place?'

'That's right. It's been left to rot ever since he passed away. It quickly became infested with a colony of feral cats, hence its nickname.'

Leo's mood curdled, and he tried to read the faces of the other interlocutors in case some strange and mean hoax was being played, but their expressions betrayed nothing.

'When did he die?'

''84 it was,' said the landlady. 'I remember because a few of us were sat in here watching Seve winning the Open at Saint Andrews when Archie Kerr – he was one of the island's coppers back then – came in and told us he'd found the body. He reckoned Gus had been lying dead up there for weeks.'

'Aye,' said the farmer. 'We all felt hellish guilty for not

looking in on him, but he was quite a private person and could be given to periods of wanting to be left by himself. He would drink heavily alone – I think he was prone to depressions.'

Leo gulped down his Scotch and gestured for a refill. Once it had been served, he asked: 'Did Gus have a son, by the same name?'

'No, he never married,' said the factor.

'But I've been chatting to one Gus Blessing in that very house – I was there just Friday last. It is not a wreck – it is beautifully appointed and in good order.'

A dreadful hush descended on the little assembly and Leo perceived that the patrons were regarding him curiously.

'You must be mistaken,' said the factor quietly as he gazed intently into his pint. 'You must have been in a different house.'

'No!' cried Leo, a horrible realisation creeping over him. 'It was the first house on the back road. I sat and conversed with Gus for a good while ... we *drank* together, for Christ's sake – twice!'

The landlady, sensing the extent of Leo's distress, took pity on him and said: 'You said you were biding out Belmartine way. How about I fetch my hubby and get him to drive you home?'

'No thank you dear. I need some ... fresh air,' gasped Leo.

He necked his whisky and made for his wallet, but the landlady placed her hand gently on his and said: 'That one's on the house, my love.'

Leo stumbled out of the public bar and into the vestibule, glancing at the photo of Blessing with the yard of ale as he passed it. He lurched through the glassy gloaming light like a blind man, knowing in the pit of his being what he would find, but he needed to see it with his own eyes, he needed to confirm it.

The garden was overgrown, rampant with weeds, midge-infested. A lizard basking in a late lozenge of sun skittered away in fright at his approach. The windows of the looming house were dismally dark, gaping like the eye-sockets of a skull.

He pushed the front door and found that it gave, then entered the hallway, which had turned to shadow. He crunched his way through silt and fallen plaster and unspeakable debris, aware of movements in the corners and paws padding across the floor above. There was a cloying animal stench, a feline hiss and snarl. Leo wasn't particularly fond of cats, even at the best of times.

He approached the doorless drawing room and stepped into its desolation. The piano and the lovely furniture were all gone, in their place only a dilapidated kitchen chair. The wainscoting was warped and faded, and the tiles in the fireplace were cracked and filthy. Leafage had breached the decayed ceiling and damp had invaded the walls. Leo speculated for a fevered moment if a Gus Blessing lookalike – a wanton nephew, perhaps – had been enlisted by some hooded puppeteer or black cohort to confound him. And that the evil party had gleefully wrought the cruel mummery upon a lavish set, then restored the building's dereliction, perhaps all to mock the futility of his efforts to unravel the truth of the mysterious deaths at the south end of Sonna. But he cast the notion from his mind. He knew what had truly occurred within this eerie house.

In a daze, Leo walked outside and up to the junction. Beneath the darkling sky he began the long haul towards Belmartine along the shore road, gathering his thoughts as he proceeded. In an adventure two and a half years ago, Leo had enjoined in communications with the ghost of a murder victim, a young woman by the name of Helen Addison. Afterwards he had estimated that he had been experiencing a hitherto unprecedented mode of his second sight, a sort of animate dream in which he was able to dialogue with a metaphysical imprint of the girl. Leo now mused upon his encounters with Blessing. He recalled how just before they had first met, he had been possessed by a peculiar longing to make the detour down the minor road, and he now guessed that this, and the Humber breaking down precisely outside the Cats' House, was ordained. He considered the dreamy, trippy atmosphere of the place, augmented by the nectar his host called the Concoction, which had intoxicated him like some strange opiate. He thought about Blessing's choice of clothing and décor, and his outmoded cultural references – all apparently anachronisms from his later years on this earth. He remembered how sometimes Blessing would speak over him, not rudely, just obliviously, as though he possessed an idiosyncrasy whereby he zoned out, his consciousness consumed by whichever reminiscence he was relating. Except it was clear now that this was not what had been occurring. Instead, those were spells during which Blessing wasn't hearing Leo at all, because he had drifted back towards his own dimension or because static on the astral plane had distorted the clarity of the signal. Since taking up the case, Leo had been vexed by the fact that he had not experienced any visions pertaining to it. Now he understood that this was not so; his intercourse with the deceased Blessing's visitant in the Cats' House had been a form of waking, conscious vision, as with Helen Addison, if more oblique. And while the realisation that he had been conversing with a revenant was disquieting, surely the purpose was providential. The clues that Blessing had hinted at now took on greater weightiness.

The night was pleasantly balmy but the journey on the road was hazardous, and on a couple of occasions Leo had to climb onto a precarious verge to avoid an oncoming vehicle. He was glad when Ronnie MacKellar pulled up alongside him in his police cruiser and offered him a lift home.

The copper had a distant air as he drove, and after a few moments of silence he said: 'I'm relieved to have found you – I was worried about you. You see, I'm just after stopping off at the Melford Hotel. The landlady told me what happened.'

'You're probably wondering if I'm right in the head, claiming to have engaged in tête-à-têtes with a dead man.'

'Last week, when I brought you into the station for your trespassing escapade on Mr Ashby's property, you will remember how that gentleman got you off the hook because he spoke to the brother of a friend of yours who vouched for you as a great sleuth.'

'What about it?'

'Well, during that telephone call with Mr Ashby he stated that his friend had told him something else about you. That you experience visions, which help you solve crimes. That's quite something, Leo.'

'I can tell you are unconvinced. Probably you now wonder if my rub with that green Jaguar was all in my imagination.'

'There's still no sign of that mysterious motor, by the way.'

Ronnie deposited Leo at the front door of the Palmery. Suddenly dog-tired, he headed directly for the drawing room where he poured himself a deep brandy. After a couple of sips, he heard the dinner gong sounding urgently, except it wasn't emitting from its usual berth in the hall but from somewhere upstairs. He sighed as he walked towards the din, dreading what new humiliation his host had in store; he was indeed in no mood for tomfoolery.

Once in the hall, Leo heard his name being called from the mezzanine. He looked up to see Troughton and Stephanie begin to slowly descend the grand staircase, both dressed in colourful gowns which lent them a medieval air. They were evidently indulging in some roleplay. Troughton had adopted an aristocratic bearing and was wearing a species of feathery cloth hat and a sword in a scabbard. Stephanie had a conical hennin perched on her pretty head which made her look like a fairy-tale princess. With both hands she held a silver stirrup cup brimming with liquid. The pair exchanged a conspiratorial smirk and then paused. Troughton unsheathed his sword magnificently and pointed it at Leo, announcing loudly, 'Now hear this, Moran: we are the new masters of this palace and its realms, and you are our underling! So you'd better get in line, my boy ... *you'd better get in line!*'

Stephanie added: 'With this wine we doth declare and bless our sovereignty. May we rule justly and with kindliness,' at which she and then Troughton took a draught from the cup.

'Great Scott – have you both been smoking hookah?' cried Leo.

'Dare not address thy royal lieges so saucily,' said Troughton as he waved the sword menacingly. 'King Marcus and Queen Stephanie of Belmartine – it has a nice ring to it, don't you think?'

Leo did not respond, and simply strode up the stairs past them and retired to his bedchamber.

Assumption

THAT night he dreamt he met Amy again at her secret cove.

They head cross-country for Fagr Vágr, toiling in the torrid heat, but then the rain comes on, marvellously refreshing. They take shelter beneath a giant spreading horse chestnut, laughing. Leo enjoys the drama of the downpour, the drops drumming on the fecund land, slaking its thirst and releasing the rich scent of petrichor. He can hear the distant report of thunder from the Argyll hills, but their shower passes, leaving a world sparkling in the new sunlight. An almost imperceptible breeze is enough to unmoor the weight of water from the foliage and it teems down, causing Amy to squeal playfully. They enter the dripping world. They can hear a burn chattering noisily in its spate and birds tentatively restarting their song. The heat has returned but it is gentled by the rising moisture. They come upon a meadow, enclosed by broadleaved trees and dotted with thorns and young hazel, their steaming leaves bladed at an optimal horizontal. A tragic sycamore reclines on the greensward, dislodged by a freak gust during a recent storm. Spontaneously, they collapse to the wet grass, peel off their clothes and make love in the lee of its exposed roots. They roll and are blooded by the newly raw earth. Cool rain, a gentle sequel to the deluge, now falls lightly upon them in slow-motion, as water cascades from holly leafage and sodden roadside hedgerows, beyond which snails, like tiny painted galleons, trail their wakes across the bitumen ocean.

Leo awoke, and basked for a while in the pleasant afterglow of the dream. He was cheered further by the remembrance that he was to see Amy that very morning. For it was the Feast of the Assumption, and he had arranged to convey her to holy Mass.

The day was dry and sunny, and as Leo motored, he enjoyed the view of sailboats gliding across the firth. Beyond Port Penelope he hung a left and traversed the isthmus towards Herrick Bay, where he happened to notice Norris Meiklejohn's distinctive Land Rover in the tearoom car park. Amy was waiting for him under the sycamores at the bottom of her garden, dappled by the morning light.

The Scottish school holidays had finished and the fore of the church was crammed with numerous children in uniform, and only Leo and a smattering of English visitors now augmented the native congregation. The schoolchildren's presence meant that Amy couldn't take her usual berth at the front right of the church, and Leo realised that Vincent Comiskey happened to be sitting in the next pew to where they had installed themselves. His hair was combed and he smelled of aftershave and was wearing a three-button suit and a chocolate Fred Perry polo shirt. There was an excruciating moment at the Sign of Peace when the brewer, hitherto oblivious to Amy's presence, turned and shook her hand.

As Leo sat in a state of grace after Communion, he noticed Troughton kneeling before the altar with dramatic unworthiness to receive the blissful sacrament. Leo considered Vincent, who was praying intently directly in front of him, and pondered for a moment this reformed character and the miracle of redemption. Leo's gaze then shifted to Amy, who had lingered at the Marian altar in order to deposit a little posy of wildflowers she had brought with her. He admired her for a moment, her mantilla failing to obscure her enduring grace and beauty as a shaft of pure light poured onto her from a high window. Leo had been sincere when he had delivered his dogmatic homily to Stephanie on the Kilmichael esplanade the previous day, but he couldn't deny to himself that he felt a thrill when Amy Agumanu was around.

Suddenly Vincent rose, turned to Leo and whispered enigmatically: 'We need to talk ... about what I saw up there that night.'

With that, he shuffled to the end of his pew, genuflected and walked towards the door.

After the service, there was no sign of Vincent outside. Leo supposed he would wish to speak with him alone, and therefore resolved to drop by his cottage later. Leo and Amy visited the baker's shop to pick up some provisions for elevenses, then drove back to Herrick Bay. They spread a picnic blanket in the shade of the sycamores and ate a repast so fulsome it would suffice as their luncheon: sandwiches, pastries and scones served with tea. They then lazed around for a long while, chatting occasionally but mostly just listening to the birdsong and the whirring of the insects, and enjoying the heady fragrances of late summer. However, Leo was beginning to tire of the persistent heat and eventually he rose to take his leave. He wasn't sure if it was his imagination but Amy seemed a little disappointed at his going.

He drove to Kilmichael where he had previously noticed a barbershop on a side street. He parked and stepped inside, hoping that a proper shave – earlier he had felt ashamed that he hadn't the time to perform this ablution before attending Mass – and a trim of the wiry, dark-brown stuff would revive him. Every haircut divested another alarming increment of ageing: the jowls slightly fuller, the forehead more prominent, the eyes a little more porcine, and, worst of all, the scalp more exposed. Leo had to suppress the little surges of envy he felt whenever he regarded men of his age who were still in possession of a full crown of hair. He was glad to recline and close his eyes while the proprietor, a foreign man with an easy manner by the name of Daryan, worked on him with hot towels and shaving oil. Daryan then whipped up a cumulus of impossibly soft lather, applied it to Leo's face and went to work, engrossed in the task like a Renaissance sculptor. Leo felt drowsy lying back in the chair, the fragrance of the oils soporific. A recording of music traditional to the barber's home country played in the background, the second zurna's drone hypnotic. Leo noted the similarity between the instrument's melancholy song and a Border pipes lament, and as he pondered this cultural parallelism he slipped into a sudden, brief vision, set within the drawing room of the Cats' House and which consisted merely of Gus Blessing addressing him with the words: 'Add me to your list.'

Leo came to with a flinch, causing the razor to nick his neck. Daryan apologised unnecessarily as crimson ran in the virgin-white soap. He applied some astringent to the cut and then shaved the back of Leo's neck and used eucalyptus balm, cologne and a lit taper to finish the job. Leo paid, tipping generously and dreading that Daryan thought him rude for not returning his farewell banter, but the unexpected vision had discomposed him.

Once outside, he telephoned Archie Kerr, whose number he had taken when he had visited him. The retired copper sounded hungover, but greeted Leo pleasantly.

'Do you remember a fellow called Gus Blessing?' enquired Leo. 'He used to live in an old house on the minor road down by Melford?'

'Aye, I mind him well.'

'I was told that it was you who found his body. How did he die?'

'The pathologist stated it was probably a stroke, but it was difficult to determine for certain due to the level of decomposition. You see, it wasn't until weeks after he had passed away that I looked in on him. It was a fair grisly discovery, I can tell you.'

Leo thanked Archie for his time, then hung up. He strolled the esplanade for a few minutes in rumination. Blessing's death in 1984 had occurred several years before the ones listed by Troughton as suspicious, but Leo realised that a middle-aged pipe smoker who drank heavily succumbing to a suspected stroke wouldn't have raised a red flag to his host.

Leo filled up the Humber at a primitive little backstreet petrol station. He then drove to Vincent Comiskey's abode in the north east of the island, anticipating excitedly what the brewer wanted to impart about the fateful night in 1989. However, at the cottage he found nobody home apart from a fierce dog roaming the sun-baked back yard.

Leo dreaded his next duty, but the causes of justice and peace demanded that he fulfil it. He telephoned Stephanie to ascertain that she was at the Palmery, and requested a conference. He arrived to find her awaiting him under the parasol at the terrace table, a pitcher of orange crush and two glasses set forth. Stephanie was wearing sunglasses and looked a touch hungover, and she said that Troughton was dozing in his bedroom. Leo got directly down to business, reciting the mounting evidence which pointed to Vincent

Comiskey's innocence in the rape of Elizabeth Meiklejohn in the summer of 1989. He then enunciated who he believed to be responsible and why. Stephanie listened carefully, only interrupting to ask pertinent questions for the purposes of clarification. Leo announced his intention to interview Elizabeth forthwith in order to test his theory, and then persuaded Stephanie to accompany him. As an experienced lawyer, her skills at interrogating a vulnerable party and discerning truth from falsehood could be precious, and furthermore her sex might help gain access to Elizabeth and put her at ease.

As Leo drove them into Kilmichael in the Humber, Stephanie brought up the subject of the previous night's fancy-dress high jinks.

'I hope you didn't take it the wrong way, Leo. I didn't mean to tease you. I was tipsy, we were just fooling around.'

'I was worried you had been drawn into Troughton's web of cruelty.'

'I know that Marcus acts up, but it occurred to me that he only does it because he is self-destructive.'

'Oh, come on Stephanie, spare me the amateur psychology! Troughton tries to get at me because he dislikes me. He has always disliked me.'

'Wrong. He *does* like you. Marcus dislikes *himself*, so he doesn't think he is worthy of having friends, therefore at some unconscious level he tries to ruin his chances of friendship, which is what he is trying to do with you.'

Leo merely sighed in response as he pulled up in front of the Meiklejohns' handsome villa.

Elizabeth happened to be amusing herself alone on the front lawn, making a daisy chain. She was wearing blue jeans embroidered with floral stitch-work and a red and white hooped T-shirt.

'We should approach her parents first,' said Stephanie.

'They will go nuts if they find out that we spoke with her without their permission.'

'No,' said Leo firmly. 'Her unsupervised presence here is providential. Let us take our chances.'

They got out of the car and Leo greeted Elizabeth, who regarded them vaguely. Leo reminded her that he had visited her home the previous week, and this seemed to stir a remembrance within her mind. He introduced Stephanie as his friend, and then asked: 'Do you remember Andy Lamb?' Elizabeth tensed up and stared at the ground. 'I am told that he was kind to you.'

'Yes, very kind,' she said quietly, glancing up. 'He used to buy me Lemonade Sparkles. That was my favourite ice lolly. Now I prefer Funny Foots.'

'Was he always kind to you?'

She stared silently at the lawn again. A cat slunk from around the house to be in the shade, regarding the strangers warily.

Stephanie took over. 'Most of the time, people are kind because they are goodhearted. But sometimes, not often, people are just pretending to be kind, when really, they want to get their own way. And when we find that out it can be very upsetting.'

Elizabeth's face coloured and she fidgeted nervously with her fringe. Stephanie sighed slightly, an expression of her unease at this unsolicited interview, but Leo was intent on persevering.

'Yesterday we saw your father get very angry with Vincent Comiskey,' he said. 'I'm worried that he might hurt him, and that would be bad for Vincent and also bad for your father. If you tell us what really happened, you won't get into trouble. It wasn't Vincent who hurt you, was it?'

Elizabeth remained sullenly silent, and Stephanie took up the baton again: 'It was Andy who hurt you, wasn't it?

That's why, one day when you visited your grandmother's grave with your family, you scribbled on his headstone with one of your crayons. Because part of you has been cross with him all this time, part of you still wants to know why he was so nice to you and then did what he did to you. I think you were trying to protect Andy's mum and dad when you accused Vincent, because they were so sad after he died. I think that was a kind thing for you to do.'

Elizabeth began hastening towards the house.

'Promise me you'll think about telling your parents,' called Stephanie after her. 'I'm sure they'll be understanding.'

The Crucible

On the way back to the Palmery, the friends agreed that Elizabeth's behaviour had suggested that indeed Andy, and not Vincent, had perpetrated the attack upon her. Stephanie then informed Leo a little guiltily that she and Troughton had booked a table for two at a bistro in Kilmichael for dinner that evening. Leo magnanimously offered to drop them off; he would then pick up a fish supper for his tea. He also divulged his plan to visit the south end that very night.

'I would like to inspect the area where Andy Lamb perished in similar conditions to that night in 1989. Tonight looks like a reasonable match: a near-full moon and clear conditions.'

'Promise me you'll be careful.'

'I will. But don't wait up.'

Later, Leo sat alone at the kitchen table eating his haddock and chips with tinned peas, two slices of bread and butter, and a pot of tea. A good concert of Bruckner and Wagner, broadcast live from Glasgow on BBC Radio 3, was his soundtrack. He pondered Stephanie. It was odd witnessing a normally level-headed person being so enamoured of such a man as Troughton. He had again been beguiling towards her when Leo had driven them to the bistro. Evidently Troughton really could cast a spell.

After he had cleared up, Leo prepared for his night-time research trip, looking out his stout walking shoes, his tweed jacket and his deerstalker. He packed his knapsack with his Stanley torch, his detective's kit, his aluminium water flask, his notebook and a paper bag of orange creams for sustenance.

Leo drove towards the south end, heading up the Lagg Road as the light began to fall away. He spotted a pair of hares tearing across a field as songbirds performed their coda to the day. He wanted to speak with Heron and Haddow, to ask them what they knew about the demon-in-the-hill legend, but his knocking evoked no reply at the former's farmstead. At the latter's, all that happened was that an upper window was hauled open and Haddow, dense hair pouring over his white vest, poked out his head to state simply: 'It's an early night for us, Leo. Unless my barn's on fire, leave your business till the morn.'

Leo drove to Ardcaden Bay in order to kill some time at the Saint Caden's Hotel; he wished to avoid The Melford after the indignities suffered in its public bar the previous night. He span out a couple of lonely ginger beers until closing time, then drove back towards the Lagg Road.

He felt uneasy at being in the deserted south end after nightfall. He parked on the hardstanding where the road terminated, waiting inside the Humber until approximately the time when Andy Lamb had set off on his final journey. He then grabbed his knapsack, got out of the car and began walking.

The moon hung like a gigantic Chinese lantern and clouds rimmed the stratosphere in creamy undulating mountains. Leo passed the gaunt outline of the ruined chapel. The air was steeped in the heady nocturnal summer scents of sweet nectar and fresh herbage. He climbed further up, beyond the trees, passing through a bridle gate into a high pasture where shadowy bovine forms lumbered and groaned unnervingly close. He raked the benighted surroundings with his powerful torch and considered the timeless landscape, fancying that he could connect to the people who had sojourned here in days gone by. The kids in the 1980s who had holidayed in the nearby settlement of Ardcaden, which had been founded by fishermen and expanded by lime quarriers. The Norsemen and the Dalriadans who quelled the soil with sword and sickle. And before them the painted ancients of the Iron Age and the Bronze Age and the Neolithic period. The way the flow of the land betrayed its formation made Leo think of the original, cataclysmic outpouring of spirit and matter, the primordial sacrament of creation, the first incarnation, the one fourteen billion years before the carpenter's wife gave birth.

Leo reached the grassy shelf from which Andy had fallen, with Glen Colm in front of him and the hump of the Cathair in the middle distance. He switched off his torch and realised that he could still discern the dim outline of the shelf's edge against the faint light of the sky. However, an inebriated man, especially if running and if his wits were deranged by the terror of a pursuit, could have mistaken it for the crest of a gentler gradient, or in his distraction even have missed it altogether as he approached, because its profile was duller when it became set against the background of the raised land on the other side of the glen.

Leo stood a couple of feet from the edge of the scarp, and happened to peer downwards into the belly of the valley. There he noticed a curious spectacle: a bonfire, at approximately the spot where he had found the burnt bones during his hike around the south end the previous week. Two figures stood solemnly nearby. Leo crouched down and withdrew his mobile phone. He engaged the video function and zoomed in on the unnerving proceedings, no easy task for his damaged hands. In the poor light and at this considerable distance he couldn't make out who the people were. The figures now seemed to be undertaking some sort of ordinance involving the sacrificing of an animal – a sheep or a goat, hammering and hacking quite viciously at the poor beast. Then its corpse was cast into the flames. One of the individuals then carried something out of the pool of firelight and returned a few minutes later. They then performed some concluding rites, before proceeding up the slope, carrying electric lanterns. Leo dashed up to the path, hid behind a gorse thicket, primed his phone and waited, praying that the inverted light from the screen wouldn't give him away. Soon, the pair approached; they were wearing strange robes and crowns of rowan leaves and berries. As they passed by, Leo aimed the lens at their faces. It was the Herons.

After a little while, Leo went down into the glen to where the holocaust was still blazing brightly, the air carbon-rank. The animal had an iron spike driven through its heart and had been decapitated. Its hide popped and peeled to curlicued cinders, and molten fat coursed angrily down its flank in fizzing rivulets.

Leo began hurrying back to where the Humber was parked, his torch still switched off, speculating as he progressed. He recalled the strange figure Janey had stated she had seen walking across the glen. He wondered if he had just witnessed a summoning ceremony and glanced around the landscape, a horrible prickling sensation creeping up his back as he expected to see the demon piper lurching towards him. Perhaps that was the 'evil' Gus Blessing had referred to as being behind Andy Lamb's death, and certainly Leo had previous experience of evil made manifest. Or perhaps the 'evil' meant something less outlandish. Perhaps Heron had lied about being aware of the teenagers' cars passing that night in 1989, and instead was up in the hills performing his weird rites. Perhaps Andy stumbled across his doings and Heron chased him lest he tell, and he was the strange figure whom Janey had seen. But Janey had stated that she had heard bagpiping – maybe she had imagined this component. Or, perhaps Heron had indeed heard the cars and seen their headlights, then looked out to see Andy set off on his dare, quickly dressed up as the demon piper and rushed out to terrify the lad as part of some bizarre theatre. Whatever had unfolded, Leo felt sure that Vincent had been a witness to it. He resolved to speak with him tomorrow about what he had been referring to in church.

Leo was relieved to climb into the Humber. He closed the door quietly, locked it and then gently turned the ignition. He swung the vehicle round and drove away, going easy on the gas and with his headlamps off lest he rouse the Herons at Inkpot Farm to some terrible deed. He was struck by just how frightened he felt as he passed the place, then turned his lights on at full beam and accelerated down the lonely road.

Leo was glad to reach the Palmery. He found the place darkened and quiet – presumably Troughton and Stephanie were abed. He was weary and disturbed by the Herons' ritual, and performed a perfunctory version of his night-time routine of ablutions and prayers. He then pulled on his pyjamas and dived beneath the sheets. He hadn't even bothered to close the curtains, and moonlight bathed the room, but he fell asleep almost immediately.

Soon he was dreaming, inhabiting that strange hinterland between a nightmare and a vision. The climax was when Leo glimpsed the silhouette of a crooked figure on the brow of a hill and he woke with a start, sweating profusely. As he lay breathing rapidly, he realised that he was not alone in the chamber. A ghastly form stood at the foot of the bed.

It was a tall personage, clad in a shapeless black shroud which veiled even the face. One of the creature's arms was extended, the unseen hand reaching in Leo's direction.

Leo was terrified, his mouth as dry as a cinder.

'What do you want with me?' he croaked, his voice barely audible.

The dark figure was silent, and merely continued to stretch forth its right arm.

'Spectre, what do you want with me?' begged Leo desperately.

After a few moments the thing spoke in a terrible, low voice: 'Mark me.'

'I will,' gulped Leo.

'I am Angus Blessing's spirit, doomed for a certain term to walk the night. And for the day confined to fast in fires, until the foul crimes done in my days of nature are burnt and purged away ...'

As the speech progressed, Leo began to experience a series of realisations. First, that he was listening to lines which had been adapted from Shakespeare. Then that the voice delivering them was familiar, if operating at a lower octave. Then that the voice kept becoming throttled as though affected by some ailment. Then that this was no ailment, but an attempt to suppress laughter.

'Troughton, you rotter!' roared Leo before his host slumped to the floor, seized by a fit of hysterical mirth. 'You could have given me heart failure!'

Leo clicked on a bedside lamp and Troughton peeled back the shroud from his face in order to wipe away tears, eventually composing himself as the hilarity subsided.

'You're the one who invited me to the island on account

of my second sight,' raged Leo. 'Now you make mockery of me!'

'But drinks parties with the deceased – that's a bit much, old man!' said Troughton as he got to his feet and made to leave the room.

Leo rose from his bed and followed him into the hallway. 'How the hell did you find out about my encounter with Gus Blessing?'

'Word travels fast on Sonna.'

At that moment Stephanie, roused by the commotion, arrived on the scene wearing a silk dressing gown. She switched on a light and Leo related what had just occurred. She chided Troughton, saying: 'Marcus, that's a bit much.'

'Are you quite certain that I am real, Moran?' teased Troughton after he had divested himself of the black cerement; he was wearing maroon satin pyjamas underneath. 'Feel me, I am flesh and bone.'

'Sod off, Troughton. Where the hell did you get such a macabre garb anyway?'

'Just some oddment from the dressing-up box,' said Troughton as he opened a large steamer trunk and deposited the garment inside. Leo happened to glance in the trunk and as he did so something caught his eye. He stooped down and withdrew an old-fashioned leather driving helmet and goggles.

'It was *you!*' hissed Leo. 'It was you who was behind the wheel of that bloody green Jaguar that day. It was you who ran me off the road!'

Troughton was silent and stared at the floor, but Stephanie demanded in her best courtroom voice, 'Marcus, tell me truthfully right now: was it you who was driving that car?'

A guilty grin spread across Troughton's features and Leo exploded: 'I was arrested because of you, you bloody *bastard* of a man!'

Stephanie, too, was horrified. 'Marcus, what the hell were you thinking – you could have *killed* Leo!'

'Please know that there was method in my madness,' began Troughton, chastened by Stephanie's tone. 'I was concerned that Moran wouldn't buy my theory about the deaths at the south end being suspicious. So, when he came down to the island, I wanted to energise him, to spur him on, to convince him that something was, indeed, up. I arranged to borrow the Jag from Nicky but swore him to secrecy about it and I didn't tell him my precise purpose. He had it dropped off the evening prior to my little ... road skirmish with Moran. I parked it out of the way, and the next morning I picked up the Humber Hawk's tail outside the Meiklejohns'. I then ... *engaged* with it over on the west coast. Afterwards I returned the Jaguar directly to the lock-up where Nicky stores it.'

'But, you imbecile, you could have got Nicky into serious trouble, if the police had realised – which they did – that he possessed such a model of vehicle!' snapped Leo.

'Not likely. I had covered the number plates. Plus I was aware he'd be hobnobbing on his yacht on the morning upon which I had our little dogfight planned, so I knew he would have a rock-solid alibi. When Ronnie MacKellar came calling Nicky pled ignorance – which I had been banking on, in order to protect me or to protect himself lest he become dragged into things. Look, Moran, why all this fuss? It was just a bit of *sport*, old boy. And considering the speed you were going at you were hardly likely to break your neck. I even doubled back to check that you were okay.'

Leo, quite exasperated, returned to his bedroom, and before slamming the door shut uttered the parting words: 'You are a toad, Troughton. Bloody Toad of Toad Hall!'

Now Cracks a Noble Heart

LEO awoke at 8.00 a.m. His mood was fouled by lack of sleep and the remembrance of his night-time altercation with Troughton, and the day's initial cogitations entrenched him in righteous indignation. The outrageous revelation that his host had been the driver of the dratted green Jaguar was the last straw, and he now resolved to leave the Palmery forever. He would install himself elsewhere for the remainder of his investigations on Sonna.

After he had washed and dressed, he picked up his mobile and went to the office where he knew the local telephone directory was kept. He located the entry for Vincent Comiskey's brewery and rang the number, but it soon diverted to a recording and he hung up without leaving a message; he would try him again later. Leo then phoned the landlady of the flat for let in Ardcaden Bay which he had seen advertised in the window of the post office there – he had jotted down the details in case of the eventuality that Troughton became unbearable – and spent a few minutes arranging with her his imminent arrival.

He ventured down to the kitchen where he prepared himself a breakfast of bacon, eggs, fried bread and tea. As he had sat down at the table, Stephanie appeared. They exchanged brief greetings and Stephanie began poaching an egg while Leo ate in silence.

'Not sulking, are we, Leo?'

'Merely pondering my investigations. Although I have also come to the conclusion that our Mr Troughton is inveterately insufferable, such that I will be quitting these stately halls for a new, humbler residence in Ardcaden Bay today.'

'Running you off the road like that was disgraceful. Marcus goes too far. Which is partly why I've decided to return to Glasgow. I've already packed my cases and booked a taxi to take me to the ferry terminal.'

'I don't blame you. The man is a blighter, a malingerer and a sybarite.'

Stephanie sat down and said gently, 'Leo, I do believe you are jealous of him.'

Leo was initially affronted by his friend's charge – he did not count himself as a green-eyed type, but then he felt shamed as he quickly realised its accuracy. Indeed, he *was* envious of Troughton, and beyond merely his recent appropriation of Stephanie. He envied his spontaneity, his ability to live in the moment, his devil-may-care attitude, his raffish demeanour, his good looks. Both men were flamboyant, but beyond this similarity Troughton was like Leo's alter-ego, the wayward twin he wished he could emulate.

'Perhaps you are right,' he admitted, pushing the breakfast plate away from him as his appetite shrivelled.

'Leo, I know you forbid people from ever mentioning her, but I am going to. As we all remember, at university Maddi first dated Marcus, then later took up with you. And believe me when I tell you that it was blindingly obvious that her affection for him paled in contrast to her adoration for you. So I shouldn't make too skewed comparisons between yourselves.'

After Stephanie had finished breakfasting, Leo carried her luggage downstairs. She asked him to wake Troughton in order that she could say goodbye to him, then went to wait on the terrace for her taxi. Leo happened across Troughton shuffling down the stairs in his dressing gown. The news that Stephanie was leaving sent him scuttling outside wearing a panicked expression.

A few minutes later, Troughton shambled into the kitchen where Leo was washing up the breakfast things.

'There's tea in the pot,' said Leo distantly.

'She has left, Moran. She won't admit it, but I fear last night's revelation about my caper with the Jaguar has mortally offended her.'

'I, too, shall be taking my leave of you today, and for the very same reason.'

'Oh ... everybody leaves me eventually.'

'I am not ready to feel sorry for you quite yet, Troughton.'

'But you can't abandon the case, Moran – if this story doesn't perk things up, *The Belmartine Repository* will go under. I hardly think I can count on Nicky as a benefactor, while Great Aunt Prosperia's legacy won't be enough to sustain it long-term, and anyway, I require that to live off.'

'I didn't say I would cease my investigations. I will merely be based at a flat in Ardcaden Bay from now on. I've written down the address for you,' said Leo, gesturing towards a scrap of paper on the table.

Leo dried his hands and set off to pack. He brought his luggage downstairs and stowed it in the boot of the Humber, then went back inside to find Troughton languishing in the drawing room smoking a cocktail cigarette, a packet of which Leo suspected he had chanced upon, left over from some party of yesteryear. Troughton looked oddly effete as he smoked the brightly coloured fag. He had dressed, somewhat shabbily, but he hadn't shaved.

'Not off to your new digs already, are we, Moran?'

'Indeed I am, although I have a mission to complete en

route. Thank you for the hospitality, such as it was.'

'At least stay for a spot of luncheon. I've got smoked goose breasts in the refrigerator. And I've managed to unearth a couple of cheeky bottles of Château Smith-Lafite.'

'Troughton, I do admire your family's silver, but I am afraid you do not possess a spoon long enough for me to sup with you ever again. By the way, I have paid your electricity bill – you were about to be cut off. Now I will bid you adieu.'

'First, humour me: what is this mission you speak of?'

Leo related his adventure of the previous night, and told how he intended to confront the Herons forthwith about their weird rite. The story greatly animated Troughton, who sat up straight upon the chaise and ejaculated, 'Good God Almighty – it sounds as though you've cracked it! These oddballs could be behind the mysterious deaths at the south end!'

'Well, anyway, I must be off.'

'Not without me. This visit of yours could turn nasty, and it calls for Marcus Troughton – man of action!'

'I have no need or desire of your companionship.'

'Nothing of the kind,' declared Troughton as he leapt to his feet and strode to the fireplace where he withdrew a poker from its berth. 'I shall beat Heron down like a dog should he try any funny business. Come on, Moran, be a sport: one adventure before we part. If you don't let me accompany you, I shall only follow you in the Benz.'

'Very well,' acceded Leo wearily.

They journeyed in the Humber Hawk towards the south end beneath a flawless sky. After they had gone some distance up the Lagg Road Leo's mobile rang, and he pulled into a passing place to answer it. He conversed for a minute or so before hanging up and swinging the Humber into the road again.

'What was all that about?' enquired Troughton.

'It was my dear friend Fordyce Greatorix. I had tasked him with identifying the taxonomy of burnt bones I discovered in Glen Colm, at the same place where the Herons made sacrifice last night. He initially thought they were ovine but they are in fact caprine – goat bones.' Leo's mind glanced to the wild goat herd at the north of the island, a member of which he had seen during the night he had stayed over at Amy's.

'Speaking of ovine – look out, Moran!' exclaimed Troughton.

A sheep was on the road and Leo slammed the brakes, bringing the car to a halt just in time. He then slowly circumvented the animal, which was unusually unperturbed and began nibbling at the grassy verge, and proceeded towards where the road curved slightly around the side of a rocky drumlin, beyond which was a little wood and then Inkpot Farm. However, an obstruction barred the way: an agricultural drinking trough with a figure doubled over one of its ends, behind which was a stationary van. Leo edged towards the odd scene, his curiosity giving way to concern when he noted the inert attitude of the figure. He drew the Humber to within ten yards of the trough, stopped, set the handbrake and switched off the engine. Leo and Troughton disgorged themselves from the car and approached. The person was Vincent Comiskey. Blood and matter seeped from a terrible wound in the back of his skull.

Leo withdrew his rosary and kissed the crucifix, then uttered: '*Requiem aeternam dona eo, Domine.*'

Troughton responded: '*Et lux perpetua luceat eo.*'

Leo said: '*Requiescat in pace.*'

Troughton concluded: '*Amen.*'

'Vincent, I enjoyed lifting a glass with you,' said Leo. 'Upon my oath, I will discover who did this.'

He made a note of the time – 10.19 a.m., then dialled Ronnie MacKellar on his mobile. The signal wasn't strong but he got through and reported the disaster. Troughton, meanwhile, had fetched his poker from the Humber and was scanning the surrounding countryside. 'The fiend might still be abroad,' he said. But the only creatures around were livestock and biting insects which buzzed on tussocks and dung in the rising heat.

Leo observed the crime scene, taking photographs with his phone. To his left, a gate to the land below the drumlin was wide open, through which presumably the sheep had escaped and the killer had wheeled the trough in order to create the obstruction. A strange atmosphere pervaded the area and the brewery van's engine was idling quietly, the driver's door ajar. Vincent must have got out of his vehicle to move the trough, and when he had started to do so been attacked from behind. The severe blow must have been struck by a powerful man. Leo noted that there was quite a deep drainage ditch to the right of the road, encompassed by vegetation: fern, long grasses, hemp nettle, parsleys, briar and dock. It could have been an excellent place for the attacker to have concealed himself. Leo looked for footprints in the ditch and on the ground at both sides of the tarmac but it was either too overgrown or too desiccated to take a decent impression.

Ronnie soon arrived with his female colleague, the police cruiser's klaxon undulating, its blue lights rippling.

'Have you touched anything?' he asked Leo after he had disembarked and cast his eye over the horror.

'I took the liberty of turning off the van's engine. It seemed somehow disrespectful to leave it running.'

'Did you see anyone or any vehicle on your way here?'

'No.'

Ronnie took charge, making a couple of calls on his

shortwave radio and one on his mobile phone. Eventually an ambulance and then two special constables in a police 4x4 arrived, and in the meantime the female officer taped off the scene and began inspecting it, while Ronnie interrogated Leo and Troughton as to what had unfolded. Leo displayed the video of the Herons' ceremony to the sergeant and told him about his earlier find of goat bones, conjecting that it could have something to do with Vincent's death. Ronnie sent the file to his own mobile and admonished Leo not to show the footage to anyone else.

Leo then said: 'Obviously we must maintain an open mind, but perhaps Farmer Heron lied when he said he was aware of the teenagers' cars passing that night in August 1989. Perhaps he was, in fact, up in the hills, and pursued or killed Andy Lamb because he came across him undertaking his occult rites. Or maybe he was telling the truth that he had noticed the cars passing and headed up with evil intent, dressed in some fashion to terrify poor Andy. Yesterday in church, Vincent whispered to me that he wanted to tell me something about what he saw that night. He had previously admitted to me that he was not, as he had originally stated, at home back then but in the hills. I dropped by his cottage yesterday but he wasn't there, and I tried telephoning him earlier this morning but there was no answer – probably he was loading his van.'

'Perhaps Vincent witnessed someone killing Andy Lamb in 1989,' said Ronnie, 'and that person got wind of the fact that he was about to tell you about it.'

'I very much doubt it. Vincent was virtually a recluse – he didn't really talk to anyone about anything.'

'This whole situation pricks my conscience,' said Ronnie. 'Perhaps I should have taken your run-in with the green Jaguar a bit more seriously. Maybe the driver was the same fellow who killed Vincent.'

'No. You can drop that line of inquiry altogether, it's got nothing to do with Vincent's demise,' replied Leo.

'You know who the driver was, don't you?'

'Let's just say it was your average clown on the road. He didn't want me dead, just flapping in the wind.'

Ronnie noticed the unconscious look of disdain Leo cast in Troughton's direction when he spoke, and decided to let the matter rest. He had bigger fish to fry now.

Bibamus, Moriendum Est

RONNIE instructed Leo and Troughton to be on their way, then began walking towards Inkpot Farm accompanied by a burly special constable. The emergency services vehicles occupied the entirety of a nearby passing place, and Leo had to reverse the Humber for two hundred yards before he could find a spot where he could turn, then began driving back to the Palmery to drop off Troughton.

After a mile, Troughton broke their miserable silence: 'Are you still intent on taking up residence at Ardcaden Bay?'

'I must.'

'But there's evil loosed upon the south end, Moran. Stay on at the Palmery why don't you? At least until the killer is apprehended.'

'No, Troughton.'

'Look, to be perfectly honest with you, old man, I'm a touch upset about what we have just witnessed and I could do with some company. I beg of you: at least sojourn one more night.'

'As you wish.'

Upon their arrival at the Palmery, Leo brought his luggage back up to his bedroom and then telephoned the displeased landlady of the rental flat to defer his arrival for a day. Ronnie then rang Leo to advise him that he and Troughton should expect a house call from CID detectives who had been summoned from the mainland. He hung up before Leo could ask what had unfolded when he visited the Herons. Leo and Troughton sat enduring the imbecilic ticking of the drawing room's mantle clock, the rhythm of which seemed to slow as the interminable afternoon dragged on. Leo amused himself by examining some of the room's interesting possessions, such as the globe, a Chinese camphor chest, a brass nautical telescope circa 1800, and a table on which were a collection of items of Russian ruby glass and a number of old family photographs. Leo had to urge Troughton not to imbibe more than two brandies before the police arrived, and neither man possessed the appetite for lunch. At one point, as though under the influence of a brainwave, Troughton sprang into life and returned a while later carrying a bulging oilcloth. He solemnly placed it upon the Queen Anne table, and unwrapped it to reveal two polished handguns.

'I give you two classics,' he announced portentously. 'The Smith and Wesson Model 15 double-action revolver: four-inch barrel, diamond grip. And the Colt M911: semi-automatic, .45 calibre, US Army issue. Both oiled, loaded and ready for battle. Choose your weapon.'

'Are you *insane*, man?' exclaimed Leo.

'Ah – you would prefer something sleeker? A Luger, perhaps? I have one stashed somewhere.'

'No, I don't want a bloody Luger! Troughton, these sidearms are *illegal*, and even if they weren't, I'm not about to start roaming the Sonna countryside tooled up like John Wayne.'

'But Moran, a man is killed – we must protect ourselves.'

'Put them away for God's sake, before the police arrive.'

'Very well. But speaking for myself, I shall be keeping a trusty shooter close to hand until peace is restored on this island.'

Eventually two grey, mistrustful, impassive CID men arrived and interrogated them one after the other about their grisly discovery and their interest in and investigations into the allegedly mysterious deaths at the south end. Leo kept only a few details and theories to himself. His overtures for cooperation were rebuffed, and he got the distinct impression that the coppers wouldn't appreciate his further sleuthing endeavours. They were also immune to his attempts to elicit their suspicions regarding the homicide, merely stating that nobody had been charged as yet.

Leo and Troughton engaged in desultory conversation over an early evening meal, the goose breasts indecently indulgent for the sombreness of the day. Neither man finished his portion, the visceral carnage of the Lagg Road still too fresh an image. They consoled themselves with a roleplay of offbeat domesticity, entering a groove of self-conscious cooperation: Leo washing, Troughton drying, the occasional murmured instruction therapeutically banal. At least the policemen's departure had permitted the drinking to commence in earnest, and after a while Troughton found Leo in the hall, malt whisky in hand, the gramophone blaring out Beethoven's Fourth, the heartrending refrain of the second movement like a noble sailboat riding the open sea.

'Of the nine, the fourth is scandalously neglected,' declared Leo pensively. 'Do you know that Hector Berlioz wrote an essay eulogising Beethoven's symphonies? He said that this *adagio* defied analysis such that it seemed – and I quote – "to have been breathed by the Archangel Michael when, seized with a fit of melancholy, he contemplated the universe, standing on the threshold of the empyrean".'

'Here's another quotation for you, Moran, from Seneca the Elder: "*Bibamus, moriendum est.*"'

'Let us drink, for we must die,' translated Leo.

'Indeed. Therefore, I'm going out to get properly sozzled. Are you coming?'

'Aye.'

A bus happened to be due soon and the men didn't have long to wait at the stop on the coast road outside the Palmery. Kilmichael looked grand in the fine evening sunshine, yet it didn't cheer the drinkers' hearts.

'There are eighteen licensed establishments in Sonna's capital, and I am going to sample a glass in each one,' said Troughton as they alighted across from the harbour and began instinctively walking towards the nearest boozer. 'On second thoughts, Moran, we'd better give this one a miss – my credit's no good in there at present. The shrew behind the bar will have the shirt off my back.'

Thus played out a recurring theme for the pair's bender: Troughton regularly kyboshing Leo's suggestions for their next port of call due to another unpaid tab or 'scandalously unjust' ban. Their choice of pubs was therefore, in fact, rather limited. The chatter among the patrons in every joint exclusively concerned Vincent's murder, and Leo found some of the idle speculation objectionable.

At their fourth stop, a seafront tavern called the Golfers, Troughton got his round in and said to the chargehand: 'Stick these on my slate, there's a good chap.'

'I'm sorry, Mr Troughton. We no longer provide tick.'

'But paying with cash is so *uncouth!*'

Leo had to withdraw his wallet, adding two whisky chasers to the order of a pair of pints of heavy, and realised he was in for an expensive night. Perhaps Troughton intended on jealously guarding that of his inheritance from his Great Aunt Prosperia which he hadn't already squandered. They ensconced themselves at a booth and Leo probed Troughton about the Herons, in the light of his discovery of their weird ceremony. Troughton stated that he barely knew the couple, but that, come to think of it, he had found them to be a touch odd. Troughton then began conjecting wildly about the Herons fitting his serial killer theory.

'As for motive,' he continued, 'they are occultists – perhaps they are sacrificing folk to appease the corn god or the demon piper or the de'il himself.'

'We know that Nicky Barrett, Johnathon Lamb and Norris Meiklejohn all despised Vincent Comiskey,' said Leo. 'The first two because they thought he was responsible for Andy's death, the last because he thought he was responsible for violating his daughter.'

'Nicky might be a consummate vulgarian and a thoroughgoing pain in the arse, but he's no killer. Apart from anything else, he wouldn't have the stomach to brain somebody.'

'I tend to concur,' said Leo. 'And also, I had disabused him of the notion that Vincent had, in fact, done for Andy in 1989. Johnathon, on the other hand, is a different piece of work: as angry a fellow as I've ever met.'

'You know something, Moran, I always wondered that Johnathon doesn't like me because I am a Catholic.'

'I can assure you, that wasn't your imagination. The West of Scotland, I'm afraid to say, still possesses a stratum of such bigots. When I met Johnathon, it was obvious that Vincent's Irish-Catholic provenance intensified his hatred for him. Perhaps his sibling Andy disliked Vincent all the more for the same reason.'

'But for Johnathon to commit *murder* – I'm not sure I buy it. After all, Vincent has lived on the island for almost a year. So why would Johnathon strike *now*, why wait all that time?'

'Indeed. Johnathon is not completely unhinged. He

told me that he would take vengeance on Vincent, but only when he had confirmed for certain that he had killed his brother.'

'As for Norris – Stephanie told me about how you and she visited his daughter. She said that you both came away convinced that Andy, and not Vincent, had been guilty of ravishing her.'

'Just so.'

'Can you imagine if Norris has killed Vincent for absolutely no good reason! Having said that, I just don't believe he is the murdering type.'

'I tend to agree, Troughton, but we must keep an open mind. One shouldn't underestimate what an outraged father is capable of, and we witnessed Norris fulminating at Vincent just two days ago, because he had tried to approach Elizabeth.'

'Could *Elizabeth* have despatched Andy Lamb? For what he did to her?'

'No, it's just too fantastic. A gentle wee thing like that roaming the hills and chasing a strong young man to his death.'

'What if someone else knew the truth of the sexual assault on Elizabeth? What if they witnessed or somehow guessed what happened and resolved to punish Andy?'

'It seems unlikely. Why wouldn't they simply have told Elizabeth's parents or the authorities?'

'What about what Vincent whispered to you in church?'

'As I said today, he had earlier admitted to me that he wasn't at home that night in 1989. He was, in fact, spying on the kids at the standing stones, as Janey had suggested, and then up in the hills being nosey, awaiting Andy passing by. But, clearly, he had held something back about what he saw up there. He subsequently felt ready to share, but now he is dead. I am starting to think that he saw something decidedly weird in those hills that night.'

The chargehand got the karaoke going, warming up the punters with a decent rendition of Roger Whittaker's 'I Don't Believe in "If" Anymore'. At that juncture, a barfly who had been sitting at the neighbouring booth stood up and imposed himself upon proceedings. He was a stocky fellow aged in his sixties with short white hair and a permanent rictus grin. Troughton groaned, but the man didn't seem to hear.

'Good evening, Marcus.'

'Hello, Hen.'

Leo introduced himself, and the interloper's blue eyes twinkled knowingly as they shook hands.

'Henry Gaston's the name. Folk call me Hen.'

'Except everyone thinks you're more of a cock,' Leo heard Troughton mutter under his breath.

Without waiting to be invited, the man drew up a stool, sat down and placed his pint of dry stout on the table. 'I couldn't help but overhear your theorising,' he said. 'If you don't mind my saying, I think you might be overlooking one possibility.'

'What's that?' asked Troughton.

'That some of your suspects acted together to kill Vincent Comiskey. Namely Messrs Barrett, Lamb and Meiklejohn.'

'The notion of collaboration had crossed my mind,' said Leo stiffly.

'Then you should have said it out loud,' said Gaston with a wink.

'I wouldn't have said anything out loud had I known there was an eavesdropper.'

'I have a good reason to believe that the trio conspired,' said Gaston bumptiously before taking two long draughts of stout, slowly, as though to keep the other men on tenterhooks. Something about the fellow made Leo's skin crawl.

'What would that be, Hen?' enquired Troughton.

'I saw them all here together, sitting at this very table.'

'When was this?' asked Leo.

'Lemme see now ... it would be the best part of a fortnight ago. Twelve nights ago, to be precise.' Leo calculated that this was before he had arrived on the island. 'They were talking real quiet like, but deadly serious. As though they were plotting something.'

'Is there anything else you can share with us that you feel might be of importance?' asked Leo.

'No,' said Gaston.

'Where were *you* this morning?' enquired Leo.

'It's a fair cop,' said Gaston, taking the question in jocularity as he held his wrists in front of him as though for handcuffing. 'As it happens, I have the best alibi on Sonna. I had to drop by the polis station about a trifling matter, but it took ages, and I was still there when Ronnie Mac's phone rang with the big news.'

Gaston changed the subject and began to dominate the chat. He exuded sleaziness and thought himself more intelligent than he actually was, and his conversation veered between unctuousness, lame humour and false humility, and self-aggrandisement. After a while, Troughton suddenly cried out as though seized by agony, clutching his right thigh with both hands.

'Troughton – whatever is the matter?' enquired Leo.

'War wound,' gasped Troughton between exclamations of pain. 'Copped a bit of Argie shrapnel in the Falklands. It plays up from time to time.'

'You'll need a large dram to fix that,' said Gaston, rising to go to the bar.

'No ... thank you. The only sure-fire cure is to walk it off. It'll be right after a couple of furlongs. Help me outside, would you Moran. Good to see you, Hen.'

Leo supported Troughton as he hirpled towards the exit. As soon as they stepped into the twilight, Troughton released him and began walking perfectly normally, the grimace of discomfort fleeing his features.

'That's better,' he sighed.

'Explain yourself Troughton – you weren't in the Falklands. In fact, you were never in the armed forces at all.'

'How dare you – I served in the Officer Training Corps while at university, don't you remember? It's not my fault I was never called up to engage. The Falklands shrapnel tale is just a ruse I pull whenever I need to get out of a sticky situation. Or when someone is boring the undergarments orf of me.'

'I must say, Mr Gaston is an unappealing fellow.'

'One thing's for sure: he's not connected to the south end deaths.'

'How do you know?'

'I dug into his background a while back. He didn't move to the island until after most of the fatalities had occurred. In fact, when they started in 1989, he was enjoying full bed and board at Her Majesty's pleasure in Barlinnie, serving a six-year stretch for molesting children.'

Leo shuddered, then said: 'That will be why he was at the police station this morning – likely he has to check in periodically with the local constabulary.'

'You'll find that about islands, Moran: folk move to them to hide and to escape their past. Henry is a creep, but he's not our creep.'

'Do you think he was telling the truth, about seeing Nicky, Johnathon and Norris together?'

'I can't see what reason he would have to lie. And we already know that Nicky and Johnathon are quite thick.'

As they were approaching a hotel with a public bar their attention was arrested by a squeal of brakes. A little Renault reversed and parked next to where the men were stood. Amy Agumanu got out and rushed over to address Leo, a concerned expression on her face.

'Oh my God, Leo, I heard about poor Vincent – it's just awful!'

'There, there,' said Leo as he gently patted her back in an inexpert attempt at consolation.

'I know it's silly, but after I heard the news, I started to worry about you, what with there being a killer on the loose and with you doing your investigations. Anyway, I tried to call you, but it wouldn't connect.' Leo checked his mobile and realised that the battery had run out of charge. 'Then I got the number for the Palmery from the phone book, but when I dialled it rang out. So I borrowed my neighbour's car and drove over there, but you weren't around.'

'He won't be biding there much longer,' chipped in Troughton. 'He's off to sulk at Ardcaden Bay on the morrow.'

'Leo, is this true?' asked Amy, horrified. 'You can't seriously be moving to the south end after what's just happened down there?'

'I need to.'

'But surely it's now time to stop your detective work and leave it to the professionals, for the sake of your own safety?'

'I won't come to any harm. Look, Amy, I appreciate your concern, but a man has been killed. A man who had his reputation serially traduced and didn't live to have it widely cleared. What was it that Teresa of Ávila said: "Truth suffers, but never dies." Well, I intend upon giving truth a gentle nudge.'

'I've got the feeling you won't be dissuaded.'

'I'm afraid not.'

'Then I might as well get back to Fagr Vágr,' said Amy glumly. 'Goodnight, gents.'

They watched Amy get back in the Renault and drive off.

Troughton said: 'She cares about you, Moran. I'd say you're in there, old chap.'

The men visited another four licensed establishments, the final one a pleasant basement bar in Battery, part of the way home. They disgorged at closing time and began shambling the considerable distance back to the Palmery. A rain shower began, blessed relief after the recent drought. 'Is there anything more delicious than summer rain falling at night, the ecstatic chorus of the teeming drops kissing the canopy?' declared Troughton, his arms outstretched, his face tilted to the emptying heavens.

'Thus, in one way at least, we are spirits kindred: fellow aesthetes.'

'Yet this is not the age of beauty, Moran – this is the age of vulgarity. The lower appetites now unashamedly take precedence. And, meanwhile, ugliness abounds.'

'There has always been ugliness, boorishness, banality.'

'Yes, but previously there was something to compare it with, an ideal that was widely exalted. Now the ugliness has won, incivility and coarseness have won, and everyone just surrenders to it, everyone just stares at their phones and their awful television programmes.'

'Truth will reassert itself, it must be so. Did not Dostoyevsky write that beauty will save the world?'

'But what agonies and despondencies must man endure in the meantime! And worse – what if generations have beauty irredeemably weathered out of them? If courtesy and honour and mercy and modesty and genteelness and graciousness and fortitude and diligence become but relics, vestigial echoes from the centuries like the codes of the knights of old?'

Leo was moved, although he almost smiled at Troughton's ode to diligence. Then he said, 'There is still goodness in this world, Marcus. And grace. Always grace.'

Goodbye, Mr Toad

Leo awoke with a ferocious hangover. In recent months, until his arrival on Sonna, he had managed to somewhat tame his demons and curb his alcohol intake, and therefore he had become less used to drinking sessions like that of the previous evening. After he had showered and taken his usual seltzer remedy, he repacked his luggage and carried it out to the Humber. His attention was arrested by a cough from above, and he looked up to see Troughton driving a golf ball from the ashlar-bracketed balcony beneath a second-floor window. He was wearing plus fours and a tweed cap, and paused before his next swing to slug directly from a jug of dry martini.

'Just a curer,' he called down. 'Feeling a tad hungover.'

'You're entitled to – you drank the equivalent of Loch Striven in ale and Scotch last night. What on earth are you doing?'

'It's a pastime of mine. A while back I rigged up a platform, covered it with artificial turf and set a rubber tee in it. I try to hit the sea.'

'You bloody madman – what if there are rock poolers or dog walkers down on the shore?'

'Don't wet your drawers, Moran – if I shank it, I'm always sure to shout "fore!"' Troughton noticed Leo's luggage. 'Don't go, old man.'

'My mind is made up.'

'I promise to be Mr Toad no more.'

'Look, Troughton, as much as anything I want to be nearer to where the deaths occurred, particularly now that Vincent, too, has perished. I want to get a feel for the area, and see if my psychic senses might be stimulated. Also, Johnathon Lamb lives in Ardcaden. You never know what I might stumble across.'

'I'll make sure you get paid in full for your work, once the proceeds pour in.'

'The money is of no interest to me. I'll be seeing you, Troughton.'

The day was overcast, as was the mood of the grey-haired landlady in Ardcaden Bay.

'You'll need to pay me for last night,' she said crabbily after she had opened the door to the ground-floor flat.

'Quite so,' said Leo.

He stepped inside from the tenement's close, which had a comforting odour of old plaster and masonry, and regarded the furnishings and décor, which were largely unchanged since the post-war austerity. He paid the woman a week's rent and after she had provided some perfunctory instructions as to the operation of the elderly water heater and a wonky radio, she departed. He heaved his luggage onto the bed, which was positioned in a recess in the front room, causing the springs to screech in protest, and began unpacking.

The rear of the property possessed a mildewed bathroom that smelled of Wright's Coal Tar soap and Lenium shampoo, and a kitchen with a dripping tap, a scallop shell for an ashtray and a window which hadn't been cleaned in years. Leo peered through it, impressed by the steeply rising woodland at the foot of the Cathair.

After he had settled in, Leo set off for the post office

and bought supplies: tinned pilchards, tinned corned beef, tinned soup, a tin of Spam, tinned Irish stew, tinned peas, tinned carrots, tinned beans, tinned treacle sponge pudding, tinned custard, tinned pears, a tin of carnation milk, a tin of Ovaltine, a half sack of new potatoes, a jar of mustard, a jar of marmalade, a jar of jam, butter, a plain loaf, a malt loaf, a Bakewell tart, tea, milk in a broad-necked bottle, cooking oil, salt, pepper, vinegar, torch batteries, coal, firewood, kindling, firelighters, matches and a tin of little cigars. He then drove to the Saint Caden's Hotel and purchased two bottles of whisky and a crate of brown ale.

News of Vincent's murder had been broadcast on the airwaves and evoked worried telephone calls – which were difficult to field due to the weakness of the mobile signal – from Leo's mother and from Stephanie, who failed to persuade her friend to come home, or at least return to the relative safety of the Palmery. Fordyce Greatorix also called, and was concerned to be informed that the death was associated with the cases Leo was investigating.

'Why not take a break, old stick?' said the dear man. 'Come visit me in Kirkcudbrightshire for a few days – we could dig out the fishing rods.'

'Thank you, Fordyce, but no. Duty calls.'

Leo drove to Kilmichael and parked near to the police station. A few journalists were milling around outside, and Leo went in and approached the front desk, which was manned by Ronnie MacKellar's blonde female colleague.

'Ronnie's not here,' she said. 'He's doing his stint guarding the crime scene. He just texted me, complaining that he's not got any lunch.'

'In that case, I shall bring him sustenance.'

Leo nipped to the bakery and bought the last two sandwiches in the refrigerator, two little bottles of orangeade and two packets of crisps. He then motored back to the south of the island, having to pull in on the Lagg Road to let a television broadcast van pass. He reached Ronnie's police cruiser, brought the Humber to a halt, switched off the engine and got out.

'I hope you like coronation chicken,' said Leo, brandishing the lunch bag at the sergeant. The feeding trough and Vincent's delivery vehicle were still *in situ*.

'Not trying to curry favour with an officer of the law, are we Mr Moran?' smiled Ronnie.

'No need – I assumed my provision of the footage of the Herons' strange ceremony would have restored my credibility with you.'

'Credibility previously compromised by your ghostly soirées with Gus Blessing?'

'I need to speak with you about the case.'

'You should have rung me first if you wanted to chat. These are unusually heavy times for Sonna's wee police force.'

'I would have, but I was afraid you'd only refuse me.'

The two men climbed into the cruiser and began to eat their sandwiches. Leo only managed a few bites, such was the persistence of his hangover.

'I reckon Forensics are finished with the scene, but we are to guard it just in case they want another dekko today,' said Ronnie. 'Myself and my officers are providing support to CID, and they are tapping into our local knowledge. On the subject of CID, Leo, I must inform you that I am obliged to pass on anything you might tell me regarding the case to them.'

'Poor Vincent.'

'I can't help but feel dismay towards your pals, Troughton and Barrett. This might never have happened, had they not dug up the past. Stirred folks' passions.'

Leo considered this for a moment, then said: 'We just don't know if that precipitated Vincent's demise.'

'His body was taken to Greenock this morning, and I've just heard that it has been formally identified by his brothers. The feeding trough had been manoeuvred through the gate in order to block the road. Heron swears he didn't move it. We reckon that after the killer set up the obstruction, he lay in wait for Vincent to get out of his van to shift it. It's the perfect spot for an ambush, not visible from any nearby abodes, which suggests that the perpetrator knew the area or was under instruction from someone who knew the area. Nicky Barrett, Norris Meiklejohn and Johnathon Lamb have been helping us with our inquiries, as they all had the hots for Vincent. The Herons also came in for questioning as the murder took place where the road intersects their farm and, of course, you had filmed them behaving in a decidedly odd manner. Vincent hadn't been robbed. He was driving northwards, having deposited a barrel of beer at the Morgenthaler place. Dr Morgenthaler was in Kilmichael at the time in question. We've spoken to all the local farmers but nobody saw any vehicle or persons, albeit none of them were working near the road. We have combed the entire area, including caves and outbuildings, in case the killer was hiding out. CID are asking around Ardcaden Bay to ascertain if any suspicious characters have been seen, but have drawn a blank so far. Vincent was hit by a heavy, sharp object with great violence. Whoever struck the blow must have been a strong man, making it less likely to have been Nicky or Norris. He'd also need to be fairly powerful to have shifted that trough, if he acted alone.'

'Heron will have a farmer's strength, and Johnathon looks like a gymnasium type,' interjected Leo. 'What about the murder weapon?'

'No sign of it. The pathologist reckons it might have

been a hatchet. We'll keep looking but it could be at the bottom of the sea by now. There was only one wound, and the fact that it was to the rear of the skull and that there were no other injuries suggests that Vincent was taken by surprise from behind and didn't have a chance to struggle. We reckon the killer had been hiding in the roadside ditch. Vincent would have come out of his driver's side door and walked to the end of the trough near the ditch in order to start moving it. He wouldn't have known what hit him. We've lifted a footprint from the bottom of the ditch.'

'But I inspected the ditch and didn't see any prints.'

'The ground is too dry to take a sharp indentation. Even at the bottom of the ditch it's dry, but you'd be surprised at what Forensics can do nowadays. Apparently, they can trace footprints even when they aren't visible to the naked eye. Even the make and age of a shoe can be deducted.'

'What about fingerprints?'

'Forensics have dusted the metal gate and say there are numerous latent prints on it, presumably from walkers opening it or holding it as they hurdled it. However, the only prints on the trough are Heron's – however we would expect his to be on it as he is the farmer, after all – and obviously Vincent's, from when he started to move it. Therefore, the killer must have been wearing gloves, unless it was Heron.'

'If the culprit had gloves with him on a hot summer's day, it would suggest that the decision to act was premeditated rather than spontaneous,' mused Leo.

'The murderer needn't necessarily have touched Vincent, but the blow would have caused blood spatter. Our suspects permitted us to swab them, and to take clothing and footwear for analysis.'

'Have you used bloodhounds to try and trace any scent trail they might have left?'

'There's no point. Heron is the farmer, so his scent will be here legitimately, and the other three claim to have walked hereabouts in recent times such that their scent could be present anyway. Johnathon says he walks his dog all over the south end, Norris says he goes hillwalking everywhere on the island and Nicky says he passes this way, sometimes on foot, when he goes to lay flowers at the scene of Andy Lamb's death. Leo, something happened to Vincent two mornings ago: his brewery was sabotaged. He called the station and I headed over there. He told me he had attended church, bought a packet of fags in the Co-op and then driven straight home. As he put his key in the front door, he heard a sound from behind the cottage. He went round to find that the lock to the outbuilding had been broken and that someone had taken a hammer to some of the equipment – there was fluid gushing all over the floor. He reckoned he had interrupted the intruder. There was no vehicle parked thereabouts, so the saboteur must have fled through the forestry to the rear of his property – presumably they had arrived via that same route.'

'I drove there myself that day, in order to find out what it was he wanted to tell me. The place was deserted but for a dog.'

'Yes, he told me he was going to borrow a guard dog and a padlock from the boatyard near Port Penelope, then catch the ferry to pick up a replacement part on the mainland. Anyway, Forensics are at the brewery now, looking for evidence.'

'Who did Vincent think was responsible for the vandalism?'

'He didn't know for sure so he wouldn't speculate, because he said he knew what it felt like to be falsely accused of something. The perpetrator could have been any one of our suspects, but I think Norris is the most likely candidate, considering how angry he had been with Vincent the previous day. None of our men have corroborated alibis for the time of the sabotage. By the way, Vincent's delivery schedule was on full view in his brewery, so the saboteur could have seen it and plotted his assassination. His first delivery on a Thursday, at 10.00 a.m., was to Dr Morgenthaler's house.'

'But why bother to wreck a man's business if you intend on killing him? The party who committed the sabotage might not have committed the murder.'

'Perhaps their feelings escalated. Yet it's unlikely that Vincent's killer simply acted spontaneously, or was simply following him that morning, because the scene of the crime seems carefully selected, and the idea to drag the drinking trough out onto the road and hide in the ditch seems pre-planned. We reckon the perpetrator knew his routine. It needn't have been someone who had seen the schedule; Farmer Heron would have noticed Vincent passing regularly at the same time every Thursday. By the way, Dr Morgenthaler and a couple of other customers I checked with stated that Vincent was always punctual. Probably you and Mr Troughton came across Vincent's body only minutes after the crime.'

'Dr Morgenthaler knew about Vincent's first Thursday delivery better than anyone. You said he was in Kilmichael at the time of the murder?'

'Yes. He entered an Italian café just after 9 a.m. and had a long breakfast, then went for a stroll along the esplanade, then bought a jumper in a draper's, then dropped by the hardware shop for some light bulbs, then visited the library, then the museum. We have eyewitnesses, electronic transactions and CCTV images to prove it.'

'Could he have been in on it? Could he have tipped someone off as to where Vincent would be?'

'There's just no motive.'

'Let's talk about your suspects.'

'The Herons had no beef with Vincent that we know of, but perhaps he somehow happened across their occult interests and had to be disposed of. Maybe it was the same for Andy Lamb, maybe he stumbled across a ritual that night in 1989. Or, maybe the deaths were some sort of druidic sacrifice.'

'What if the Herons were undertaking some bizarre summoning rite the other night, trying to raise the demon piper which is said to inhabit the Cathair?'

'Who knows? Apparently, they weren't particularly forthcoming on the subject in their interviews with CID. Also, it's suspicious that the homicide took place so near to the Herons' house.'

'But wouldn't Vincent be killed further away from Inkpot in order to throw off suspicion?'

'We are talking about a man who dresses up as Merlin for fun – not the most rational of fellas. It's not beyond reason that his wife was in on it. By the way, he says he was tending sheep on the high ground at the time of the murder, and his wife claims she was at home, doing housework. As for Nicky, his yacht's GPS positions him off Grog Head at the approximate time of Vincent's death. The yacht was stationary, as though it had dropped anchor. Nicky could have rowed ashore and done the deed.'

'That seems too risky a strategy – he could too easily have been seen,' said Leo. 'I think it is unlikely that Nicky is our man. I convinced him that only his silly drunken ceremony at the standing stones in 1989 precipitated Andy's demise, thus removing his motive for harming Vincent. He was quite overcome with contrition.'

'Regarding Johnathon,' continued Ronnie, 'Nicky had stirred him up to suspect that Vincent killed his brother, which obviously gives him motive. We have a witness who said that she saw him walking over the Cathair yesterday morning in this direction, but she was some distance away and can't be a hundred per cent certain it was him. His mobile was pinged by the local mast at the time of the murder, but obviously he lives relatively nearby in Ardcaden Bay, and there is only one mast hereabouts so we can't triangulate to get a more precise idea of his movements.'

'Johnathon is one angry man.'

'Tell me about it. I've had the pleasure of having to arrest him on several occasions, for drunken rages. One time, he chipped one of my beautiful pearly whites.'

'I should tell you, Johnathon told me that he would slay Vincent if he found out for sure that he had killed his brother. I even warned Vincent to look out for him. I believe Vincent was innocent in Andy's death, therefore no irrefutable evidence could have emerged to tip Johnathon over the edge. Unless someone maliciously fed him a fabrication to stoke his fury.'

'Best of all is Norris,' said Ronnie. 'His Land Rover Discovery was seen by a witness yesterday morning, apparently trying to run Vincent's van off the road near his brewery. Norris admits he was there, but says he went home straight afterwards – CCTV in Kilmichael confirms his version of events, and it is backed up by the fact that his mobile phone became static in Mount Pleasant where he lives. However, he could have dropped his phone off at his house – nowadays it is widely known that mobile technology will give away folks' whereabouts – and headed out of the back of the town where there isn't any CCTV and down the west road, and waited for Vincent to come back up the Lagg Road. He'd have been cutting it fine, but it was doable. We've impounded Norris' vehicle – if he used it to transfer the murder weapon, it could have left a forensic trace.'

'If the killer drove, he might have parked on the passing place back there,' said Leo, motioning over his shoulder. 'Are any of Norris' vehicle's tyre tracks there?'

'No, it's well tarmacked, and neither are there tracks on the verges hereabouts which match with Norris' Land Rover.'

'An argument against the theory of Norris being the culprit is that his vehicle is very distinctive. Therefore, had Vincent seen it, he surely would have suspected an ambush before he stepped out of his van to remove the trough. What about Mrs Meiklejohn?'

'She has a rock-solid alibi. She and her daughter were on a morning nature ramble with a church group around Saint Madden's. I spoke with the minister and the walk leader to confirm this. When I intervened during Norris' ding-dong with Vincent in Kilmichael three days ago, he said that he wished he had taken the law into his own hands for what had been done to his daughter.'

'But people say things that they don't mean or only half mean,' said Leo. 'I took the liberty of chatting to Elizabeth Meiklejohn the day after that altercation. I tried to encourage her to tell her parents the truth: that Andy, and not Vincent, had raped her in 1989. I had come to believe that Andy Lamb wasn't such a nice chap after all. That he had groomed Elizabeth in order to win her trust.'

'Did she admit this to you?'

'No, but neither did she deny it.'

'Well, Norris is claiming that Elizabeth had told him precisely that truth the night before Vincent's death. He says that he was only trying to flag Vincent down on the road near the brewery yesterday morning in order to make peace with him. The alternative explanation is that he was simply trying to wreak vengeance, and that Elizabeth only told him the truth *after* she heard that Vincent was dead.

Of course, we can't rule out the possibility that another individual who cared about Andy or Elizabeth was guilty of killing Vincent, or indeed that someone else who had an entirely different grudge against him is the murderer. After all, he must have offended a great deal of folk during his wild days. We also can't rule out the chance that we are being deliberately misdirected by said unknown party.'

'There is also the possibility that Nicky, Johnathon and Norris were in league – for the murder and/or the sabotage of the brewery, albeit that any variance of one or two of them might have done the actual deeds,' said Leo. 'Of course, they or any one or two of them might have hired someone from Glasgow to do the dirty work. Can you confirm that Henry Gaston was with you at the approximate time of Vincent's death?'

'Yes. Why do you mention him?'

'He says he saw Nicky, Johnathon and Norris drinking together in the Golfers a couple of weeks ago. He said they seemed quite conspiratorial.'

Leo drove to Kilmichael and parked outside the library, where he utilised Troughton's membership card to log on at a computer terminal. He entered various criteria regarding Celtic pagan sacrifices into the internet search engine and eventually located a couple of relevant sites. Apparently, there had existed a particular ancient custom which had persisted even into the modern age in parts of Ireland and western Scotland, of sacrificing animals in order to pacify an evil spirit or demon. The oblation was preferably a he-goat, which would be despatched by impalement, then decapitated, then its carcass ritually burned. Certain spells were to be incanted, and the head was to be buried at the place where the power of the entity was considered strongest, or at or near to where it was supposed to emerge from. Notably, considered Leo, there was no mention of human sacrifice on either site, and also this was an appeasing ceremony, an attempt to sate the malevolent spirit, to keep it at bay – *not* to summon it. He considered that this potentially cast a more favourable light upon the Herons' activities of two nights ago. When he was driving to the library, Leo had recalled something that Gus Blessing had mentioned about an archaeologist who had abruptly given up a dig in Glen Colm in 1982. He now visited the Canmore database, which contained multitudinous records of sites of historical interest in Scotland, and entered the search criteria 'Glen Colm + Isle of Sonna'. This brought forth an entry for Iron Age remains halfway down that glen, and the notes section confirmed that a dig had indeed been undertaken there in 1982, by one Professor WG Prichard of the University of Glasgow. It had yielded evidence of a wall, a midden, an axe head and certain items of coarse pottery. The log was brief, and ended with the abrupt statement: 'Excavation Abandoned'. Leo then entered 'WG Prichard + archaeologist' into the internet search engine and located a newspaper obituary to the man himself – first name William, which mentioned that he 'and his beloved wife Edith hosted many a famous dinner party at their beautiful home in Dowanhill, Glasgow'. Leo then visited the British Telecom website to find that only two Prichards were listed in the telephone directory for Glasgow, one of whom, 'E', lived at an address in Dowanhill. Leo found no online death notice or obituary for a Glaswegian Edith Prichard, so perhaps William's widow still resided there.

The Light in the Woods

LEO drove to Ardcaden Bay, parked the Humber and went for a stroll along the front. The cloud cover had begun to break up, and he bought a mackerel from a cheerful adolescent boy who was fishing off the old stone pier. When he returned to the flat, he went for a nap on the creaky bed. When he awoke, his appetite had returned so he gutted the mackerel, sliced and parboiled some potatoes, and scooped them and then the fish into a pan of hot oil. He inundated these items with salt and vinegar, and consumed them with peas, a slice of bread and butter, and a pot of strong tea, followed by a generous slice of Bakewell tart. He then freshened up, went outside and ambled to the Saint Caden's Hotel for a drink. It was the blue hour, and the sun was merging gloriously with the gently rolling terrain above the isthmus. No familiar faces were present in the establishment, apart from Tam Logan, the proprietor. The place was relatively busy on account of it being a Friday night, but the weekend jollity was tempered by the shadow of the latest tragedy to strike the south end. Leo ordered a pint of heavy and fell into conversation with a black-haired roadman, who was seated alongside him at the bar, but was unable to extract any information of worth pertaining to his investigations. The roadman had a poetic streak, and was the type of chap who would obtain a good Arts degree for its own sake, then be satisfied pursuing manual occupations for the extent of his working life. He had moved to the Bay years ago, having fallen in love with the place during childhood holidays, although he wasn't a contemporary of the 1989 gang. Leo enjoyed listening to the roadman wax lyrical about this halcyon world, so secluded and peaceful, yet so within easy striking distance of the big city.

'It has a draw all of its own, the Bay,' he mused. 'There may be more beautiful beaches in the Hebrides, but our idyll was always enough. When I was a kid, every family who came here staked a claim to this land, and appropriated a little portion of the heavens that ceilinged it. Everybody just *understood* it – folk of all stripes and ages. This was one of the last places in Britain where the farmer delivered your milk each morning, pouring it directly into a galvanised churn you would leave at your front door. I can still recall the taste of it on my cornflakes. I am also just old enough to remember the 1960s, when there were still sufficient numbers of holidaymakers to sustain several shops in the village, including a draper's, a baker's and a chippy. There were dances in the church hall every night during the summer, and a gala day and bowling greens and tennis courts. Lots of youngsters met their future spouses here. Many families possessed a boat, maybe just a sailing dinghy or a wee motor vessel, yet a craft still worthy of sentimental name, or even something grander from Greek or Gaelic mythology.'

Leo felt pleasantly inebriated and enjoyed the man's nostalgic ramblings, but at closing time he was content to return to the solitude of his flat, dashing the final hundred yards due to an onslaught of biting midges. He poured himself a generous dram and sat for a while examining the photographs he had taken of the murder scene. At one point he went to the kitchen to fetch a glass of water, and as he glanced out of the window, he happened to notice a light, a queer lambency of indeterminable colour, emitting from amid the darkened trees on the steep hillside. He immediately thought of the strange nocturnal light in the very same woods that Amy had said Andy Lamb had been unnerved by in the summer of 1989.

Leo felt himself rapidly sober up – duty compelled him to investigate. He sighed heavily and muttered, 'Forward, Moran.'

Once he had pulled on his stout walking shoes and tweed jacket, and armed himself with his Stanley torch, Leo left the building by the rear exit and walked up the long, shadowy garden. He looked up to see a helix of bats pouring ominously from the woods, as though spooked by whatever lurked therein. He went through a gate which opened onto the track at the foot of the scarp. He hadn't seen the light since he had stepped outside, but he clambered up through the vegetation to the approximate location of its source. It felt distinctly creepy being in the dense woodland at night, and when Leo recalled poor Miss Green, who was found hanged from a nearby bough, it gave him a fearful chill. He raked the surroundings with his powerful torch, dreading what horror its beam might rest upon as it rendered leafage in a weird beauty of artificial greenness, exposed in savage detail every filament of moss on a branch, and made fantastic crooked shapes of the trees: hags and goblins and grinning ogres. He picked his way northwards for a while, parting branches and taking care not to trip on roots and uneven ground, and then glimpsed the light again, blinking through the foliage. He realised that it had moved off the hill and into the field to the immediate north of the village. Its texture seemed different now, more clinical and less otherworldly, and its beam sharply defined. Leo found a way down the steep leafy slope, inadvertently riding a portion of it on his backside, the torch falling from his grasp and barrelling crazily into some herbage. He was stung by nettles when he retrieved it and after a brief flicker it stopped working. He groped his way up the track along the top of the gardens to where it skirted the field. He had lost sight of the light, but then it reappeared. It was seemingly hovering in the open land, above some indistinguishable physical mass. Leo stared at it for a few moments, as though hypnotised. Then there was a sudden orange-yellow flash alongside it, and an instant later the crack of a shot split the air. Leo turned on his heel, panic seizing his heart as he uttered the words: 'Eternal Mother, Holy Mary, Mother of God, do not abandon me.' Thoughts raced through his mind as he fled blindly. For a moment he wished he had taken up Troughton's offer of a loan of a pistol. Then he thought about Troughton and his pranks and his penchant for firearms – could he be behind this outrage? No – surely even he would by now be too chastened to add such folly to his repertoire. Of course, presuming they hadn't been charged with murder, the suspects whom the police had interviewed would all be free by now – perhaps one of them had fired the shot. At one point, Leo glanced over his shoulder and saw that the light had remained stationary. He calmed as he realised that the shooter wasn't pursuing him, but when he got back to the flat, he double-bolted the door and placed a fire iron next to his bed, just in case.

The Ceremony of Innocence

THE next morning, Leo repaired his torch by replacing the bulb. He drove to Mass, to pray for the repose of Vincent's soul. As he passed the field from which the shot had been fired, he noted that the dark mass that the light had been hovering above was bales of cattle feed wrapped in polythene. The day was dry but grey and threatened to become unsettled. After the service, Leo motored the short distance to the police station in order to report last night's incident, and as he pulled in, he noticed Troughton emerge from the front entrance and light a cocktail cigarette. Leo sounded the horn, and his associate approached. He was unshaven and dishevelled.

'Need a lift?' offered Leo.

Troughton thanked him, cast the pastel-pink fag towards the gutter and climbed into the Humber. He cut a forlorn figure, and his recent eupeptic disposition now seemed a distant memory. Leo set off for the Palmery, any lingering doubt that he may have possessed about Troughton being the previous night's shooter about to be dispelled by the perfect alibi.

'What's up?' asked Leo.

'Yesterday I was still feeling somewhat shaken at finding poor Vincent's body,' said Troughton croakily. 'And what with you and Stephanie abandoning me, I felt lonesome, so I hit the town in the late afternoon. I'm afraid I must have consumed a few too many sherries. Apparently, I was being a tad disorderly in the Golfers, and Ronnie MacKellar insisted that I spend the night at the taxpayers' expense.'

'Oh dear,' said Leo.

'Look here, Moran, as well as contemplating the cosmos from my prison cell, I also gave Vincent's murder some consideration and something occurred to me. It's probably nothing, but it might be of some pertinence. Three days ago, when Vincent made his cryptic comment to you in church, I was also there, on account of it being the Feast of the Assumption. Afterwards, I nipped down to the Co-op to pick up some flowers for Stephanie. As I approached the store, I saw Vincent standing outside it, speaking with a fellow by the name of Dr Morgenthaler, who lives at Crochadh House in the south end.'

'I know of him.'

'Judging by his heaving trolley, this was Morgenthaler's rare shop – he's a man of mystery, seldom seen in town. Anyway, the two parted, Vincent went into the Co-op and Morgenthaler wheeled off his trolley. As I passed him, I nodded politely, but he glowered at me in the most unpleasant manner. This morning I wondered if his foul mood might have been due to something Vincent had said to him. What if he had provoked the man to fiendish rage?'

'Troughton, you have just departed a police station. Why didn't you report this while you were inside?'

'Because to be perfectly honest with you, old man, I don't get on at all well with the local constabulary. They don't take me seriously. I thought it might be better coming via you.'

'I'll mention it to Sergeant MacKellar, I need to speak with him anyway. What do you know about Morgenthaler?'

'Very little. He certainly isn't a native of Sonna. He moved here years ago, during the early 1980s, I should think. He's regarded as something of a hermit.'

'I spoke with Sergeant MacKellar yesterday. Apparently, Vincent arrived home on Assumption morning to find that his brewery had been maliciously damaged.'

'Perhaps Morgenthaler drove directly there to take revenge, if Vincent had offended him.'

Leo considered this for a moment, then said, 'It is unlikely. Sergeant MacKellar said that Vincent had stated there was no sign of a vehicle, suggesting that the saboteur had arrived and departed cross-country on foot, which Morgenthaler wouldn't have had time to do as Vincent drove straight home after buying cigarettes in the Co-op. I wonder why Vincent would wish to provoke the man, who was one of his best customers.'

Leo pulled up outside the front door of the Palmery, but kept the engine running.

'Stephanie said that she'd visit me, but I know she won't,' said Troughton miserably. 'And if she does, she'll find out what I'm really like – if she hasn't already.'

'And what *are* you really like, Troughton?'

'I am faded grandeur, just like my house. Come back and stay with me, Moran.'

'I'm sorry, but the answer has to be no. We are better off apart, you and I, but as I told you previously, my residing at Ardcaden is also so that I am nearer to the loci of the deaths.'

'Well, at least drop by from time to time ... to apprise me of your latest investigations. We could even raise a glass together.'

'I'll update you when my findings are complete,' said Leo.

Troughton got out of the car and walked towards the house. Leo had to admit to feeling a little sorry for him. When he reached the bottom of the drive, he hesitated as he masticated a theory. On the morning of the Assumption, Leo had driven to Herrick Bay to pick up Amy, in order to convey her to church. There he had noticed Norris Meiklejohn's distinctive Land Rover Discovery parked by the tearoom. Leo knew that Norris was an intrepid hillwalker. He withdrew his OS map of Sonna from the Humber's glove compartment and began examining its upper portion. Norris could have left the tearoom car park on foot, hiked a little way up Glen More – the central valley of northern Sonna, then veered off, taking a pass between two peaks, Kilsyth Hill and Windy Standard, the latter being the island's tallest point. Then he could have approached the brewery on the east coast through the forest to its rear. That way, he wouldn't have risked his vehicle being spotted anywhere near Vincent's abode. It was plausible.

Leo drove to the Meiklejohn residence. He rang the doorbell and turned to watch the humpbacked ferry ply her way resolutely across the firth towards the mainland. After a while, Norris nervously half-opened the door, urgently ushered Leo inside and showed him into the front parlour.

'Why are you so anxious?' enquired Leo.

'There are three gorillas parked in a blue Ford Mondeo in the layby up the street. I think they're watching the house. I heard a rumour that the Comiskey brothers have arrived on the island. I'm worried they're out there pondering vengeance for something I didn't do. Would you like a Scotch?'

'No, thank you,' said Leo, as he seated himself on the tartan settee.

As Norris poured himself a stiffener, Leo wondered what state the craven Nicky Barrett's nerves would be in.

'Do you believe that Vincent was innocent of the Lamb boy's death as well as the ... attack upon my daughter?'

asked Norris as he sat down in an armchair.

'Yes, Norris, I do.'

'I happen to agree with you now ... *oh, Christ Almighty!*' he uttered in desperation.

'You told me that sometimes you regretted not having taken the law into your own hands for what you thought Vincent had done to Elizabeth. It's time for answers, Norris.'

'Can we speak in confidence?'

'Within reason. Two weeks ago, you were seen in a tavern with Nicky Barrett and Johnathon Lamb. All three of you had a major grudge against Vincent, who is now dead.'

'That is correct. But if we were planning a man's murder, do you really think we'd have been so daft as to be seen together in a pub?'

'Why were you together?'

'To plot Vincent's downfall. Ideally, we wanted him arrested for the murder of Andy Lamb and the attack on my daughter in 1989. And if not the latter crime, then at least the former, which would carry the heftiest sentence. Nicky knew that you were coming to Sonna in your capacity as a private investigator, and we decided to wait and see if you got results. That first time you knocked on my door, I played dumb as to knowing who you were, as I didn't want to emphasise my relationship with Nicky in case we later decided to do something a bit more drastic together. If we failed to get Vincent arrested, I wanted his business ruined and him exiled from Sonna. I would even have been willing to put his brewery out of action with my own hands. However, Nicky and Johnathon wouldn't stop short of obtaining a conviction. Johnathon even suggested torturing the man to extract a confession, but Nicky baulked at the idea.'

'I'm not sure that Johnathon would have stopped short

of murder, had he believed for sure that Vincent had killed Andy. Did someone stoke him up, tell him a lie to convince him of such?'

'Not to my knowledge.'

'You vandalised Vincent's brewery, didn't you?'

'Yes. I confronted Vincent in Kilmichael the day before because he had tried to approach Elizabeth to get her to recant her accusation against him, but he wouldn't back down. I couldn't sleep with rage, so I took a hammer to his apparatus. But if the police find out that I did this, it will put me further in the frame for Vincent's murder.'

'Where were you when Vincent died?'

'At home, alone. The previous evening, Elizabeth confessed to her mother that it wasn't Vincent who had attacked her, but Andy Lamb. The wee soul had accused Vincent back in 1989 because in her simple mind she thought that there wouldn't be any consequences. Vincent had gone back to "the mainland", which to Elizabeth was a distant place that swallowed people up and put them out of reach forevermore. And Vincent's bitter parting shot to his peers that summer had been something like "Don't worry, you'll not be seeing me again!" and Elizabeth had taken him at his word. Elizabeth accused Vincent, and not the Lamb character, because she felt desperately sorry for a bereaved mother and couldn't bear adding to her woes. Anyway, my wife told me all this straight away. I was consumed by guilt, and it occurred to me that if Vincent hadn't assaulted Elizabeth, he might well also be innocent in the death of the Lamb boy. The next morning, I decided to beg his forgiveness and to tell him I'd put right the damage I'd done to his business and to his reputation. My wife and daughter were signed up to go on a church outing, so I dropped them off, then headed north. As I approached the brewery, Vincent's delivery van was pulling out. I tried flagging him down, but he must have thought I was looking for trouble and went on his way. I pursued him and pulled alongside, and again tried to flag him down, but he just kept going. And then a tractor came towards us and I had to swerve sharply. The Land Rover ended up on the verge. I went home and decided to approach Vincent in a more sensible manner later, maybe by letter.'

'May I speak with Elizabeth, in private?'

Norris called on his daughter. A few moments later she entered, looking downcast and apprehensive. Her father said a few reassuring words and left the room.

'Good morning, Elizabeth. It's nice to see you again. Listen, you aren't in any bother, but I wonder if you could tell me when it was that you told your mother about who had really done the bad thing to you.'

'A few days ago.'

'Can you remember which day?'

'The day you and that lady came to see me.'

'Tell me exactly how you told your mother.'

'I waited until *Coronation Street* had finished because Mummy likes watching it and I didn't want to spoil it for her. She went and told Daddy. Daddy told me that everything was okay and that I wasn't in trouble.'

'Thank you. You have been very brave, Elizabeth.'

'Did Vincent die because I told a lie about him?'

'No, Elizabeth. It was nothing to do with that,' said Leo gently.

Norris showed Leo to the door, and as he opened it, he glanced down the road.

'Looks like the Mondeo is gone. Leo, I know it doesn't look good, but the evidence the CID men are casting at me is all circumstantial. I feel truly terrible about the way I treated Vincent, but you have to understand: I did not kill him.'

'I believe you.'

'Then you won't tell the police about my smashing up Vincent's apparatus?'

'I won't tell.'

'Thank you. Thank you so much. I was wearing gloves, so hopefully there isn't any evidence linking me with the scene.'

Leo called Ronnie MacKellar's mobile but it went to voicemail, so he drove to the police station where he was told by the duty officer that the sergeant was out on official business. He motored to his flat in Ardcaden Bay where he ate a luncheon of vegetable soup and a Spam and mustard sandwich. He washed up, and went for a constitutional along the seafront, musing upon the content of his conversation with Troughton earlier. He then climbed into the Humber, drove to Melford and hung a left up the Lagg Road. The trough and the van had been removed and the road reopened, although a special police constable still stood sentry at the crime scene. Leo drove to the hardstanding, parked and disembarked, and passed through a gate into Lagg Farm. He found Rab Haddow riding a quadbike upon the land which sloped gently down to his homestead. The dullness of the day and the severe backdrop of Hangman's Hill was alleviated by floral purples and yellows in the open ground and its margins: heather, gorse, aster, rattle, hawkbit, foxglove and hedge woundwort. Haddow noticed Leo and steered towards him.

'Afternoon, Sherlock,' he said after he had brought the machine, which had a little trailer filled with wooden posts attached to it, to a halt and switched off its engine. 'Out sleuthing, are we?'

'I wanted to ask you about the death of Vincent Comiskey.'

'A hell of a thing. I didn't know the poor chap, but I'd often see him making his weekly delivery to Dr Morgenthaler, as regular as clockwork.'

'Do you have any views on who could be responsible?'

'None whatsoever.'

'Mr Heron of Inkpot Farm was questioned.'

'Davie Heron is only guilty of having some funny ideas about these parts.'

'What do you think about these parts?'

After a thoughtful pause, Haddow replied, 'I think I don't go into those hills after dark.'

'Why not?'

'Maybe it's the legends playing tricks on the mind, but there are certain secluded corners which give me the creeps.'

'What legends?'

'The demon piper, the ghostly monks. But I suspect you already know about all this, Leo,' said the farmer with a wink. 'Listen, Davie wouldn't hurt a fly, and neither would his wife, in spite of their oddball nocturnal activities. I've known about all that daftness for ages.'

'Does Heron know that you know about his ceremonies?'

'Aye, and indeed I rib him about it from time to time. That and his intentionally awful bagpiping, which he says is to ward off the demon but which only serves to stoke the legend when folk hear it. I never have call to be up in Glen Colm in the dead of night, but one time, years ago, one of my dogs ran away, and I set off to find him and came across this bonfire with some poor beastie burning on it, and the Herons standing alongside all dressed up for Hallowe'en. Davie told me they were appeasing the demon, which might be a touch bonkers, but it doesn't make him a bad person. You'd be surprised, Leo, the extent to which old folk traditions and legends and superstitions live on in rural parts. All perfectly harmless.'

'There was an archaeological survey in Glen Colm in 1982 which was suddenly abandoned. Do you remember anything about that?'

Haddow thought for a few moments. 'No, not specifically. But there have been a few digs hereabouts over the years. The Baronet always requests that we farmers be tolerant of such endeavours.'

'Have you noticed any unusual activity down by Crochadh House of late?'

'Nope. Now, if you'd excuse me, Leo, I've got my impaling to do.'

'I beg your pardon?'

'Fence posts,' said Haddow with a smile as he nodded at his cargo, before firing up the quadbike's engine and trundling away.

Leo walked to Inkpot, not wishing to risk the Humber again on the steep gradient of the track which led from the road to the steading. He heard Heron before he set eyes on him, his dissonant bagpiping scaring off a murder of crows. Leo reached the top of the track and watched the man slowly circle his yard. The farmer ceased when he noticed Leo approaching, the pipes' cacophony abating to a discordant complaint and then dying altogether.

'Driving off evil, are we?'

'Such a hellish skirl is indeed said to have apotropaic properties. You must walk clockwise.'

'I suppose that's also what the rowan trees and the wind chimes are for?' Heron shrugged, which Leo took to be an affirmative, and then sat upon a wicker bench in front of the white-harled farmhouse. 'Where's Mrs Heron?'

'In town. Although she's embarrassed to show her face there – thanks for shopping us to the police. They think we're some sort of human sacrificing cult, or that we killed

Andy Lamb and now Vincent Comiskey because they stumbled across our traditions.'

'Oh, come on, man: I see you and your wife have formed your own druidic grove and are prancing around like a couple of extras from *The Wicker Man*, and before you know it a fellow is murdered a stone's throw from your house – what would you expect me to do?'

'We were merely conducting an ancient ceremony to pacify the demon piper,' replied Heron stiffly. Leo noted inwardly that this chimed with his research in the library. 'It is just folk ritual. White magic. On certain special dates, or when we sense that the demon's power is roused, I catch a goat from the north of the island for sacrificing – there's a wild herd up there and I know where they bide, and we perform the rites. It's all right for Rab Haddow to have a laugh – his farm doesn't take the worst of it. Sit down, would you – you're getting on my nerves, looming over me like that.'

Leo obeyed and sat beside Heron on the bench. Then he asked, 'The worst of what?'

'The demon piper's influence. It's '89 all over again; I think he's struck down Vincent Comiskey just as he did Andy Lamb. He has acted during daytime, which shows how enraged he must have been about something. Evidently our rite didn't work. Anyway, what's the use – you'll be a sceptic, no doubt.'

'I never said I didn't believe you. Although if you are so concerned about evil made manifest, then you would be better served seeking some form of Christian exorcism, rather than indulging in witchery.'

'Now that you mention it, he doesn't roam on the hallowed ground up there. The old monastery is the only oasis of peace. They are kindly ghosts, those monks. And they weren't daft – they built that vallum to designate the holy zone, to keep the darkness at bay.'

'Have you seen this demon?'

'I have glimpsed him at night on a few occasions.'

'What did you see?'

'A large, lumbering figure, with a strange aura.'

'Was there any sound?'

'The skirl of bagpipes.'

'Know of any pipers round here?'

'What are you implying?'

'What happened that night in 1989?'

Heron sighed slightly in exasperation, then said, 'I was aware of the cars passing. When I got out of bed to take a look my wife woke. I told her what was up and we went to the front door. It was a braw bricht moonlicht nicht and the motors had their headlamps on, so we could make out a tall male figure begin to walk up the hillside from where the cars were parked. We could only see his head and shoulders because of the high dyke that flanks the path. The other kids hung around the cars, as though they were waiting for him to return. We were worried about him, on account of what we knew about the demon piper. I said to my wife that I would try to head the fellow off and persuade him to come back down, but she wouldn't let me in case I came to any harm. I've felt bad ever since that I didn't ignore her, but in truth maybe I was too scared to intervene. So, instead we cowered here in our yard, waiting and hoping that we would see the lad return safely. A good while later we walked down the track a wee bit to try and get a different view, and a young woman came along the road, hurrying in the direction of the cars; she seemed feart and she was startled when she saw us. But we never saw the lad again. We would later discover that he was Andy Lamb.'

'You didn't see the girl go up the path earlier?'

'No, but she was only a wee thing, so the dyke

would have concealed her ascent.'

'Archie Kerr never mentioned you seeing the girl on the road. Did you inform the police about it at the time?'

'Aye. Maybe Archie's forgotten about it, the old souse.'

'Why didn't you tell me about it, the first time I spoke with you?'

'You never asked. You aren't the police, you know.'

'Where were you at approximately 12.30 a.m. last night?'

'Abed.'

'Not out shooting?'

'What on earth are you talking about?'

'What did you know of Vincent Comiskey?'

'I'd never so much as met the fellow. Sometimes I'd see him in his van when he was delivering beer to Crochadh House.'

'Have you seen much of Dr Morgenthaler recently?'

'No.'

'There was an archaeological dig by a man, now deceased, in Glen Colm in 1982, which was abandoned for some reason. Do you know anything about it?'

'No. We hadn't taken up our tenancy then. Your archaeologist probably scarpered. He must have seen it. Evil walking.'

Leo now strongly suspected that the Herons were innocent, but he didn't tell the farmer this – he had to be certain. When he got back to the Humber, he rang Janey's number and she picked up. The signal was weak but he was able to relate Heron's version of events.

'Yeah, there's no way the weird figure I saw could have been that man,' stated Janey. 'I didn't think it worth mentioning when I spoke to you, but because I was pretty terrified after seeing what I saw, I took a different route to where the cars were, across some open land. It meant I could avoid the creepy bits near Saint Caden's Chapel. So I ended up reaching the Lagg Road just north of Inkpot Farm, then jogged back to the cars from there. I remember the farmer and his wife standing in their nightwear near the bottom of the track that leads to their house. The woman called out something like, "Are you all right, lassie?" There is no way either of them could have been up in the hills and then returned to the farm in time. Anyway, as I told you before, and I know it sounds nuts, I don't think the figure I saw walking in Glen Colm was really of this world.'

Leo started the engine and set off, noting that the afternoon had become gloomier. His pressing desire to speak with Ronnie was soon sated, because he happened to glimpse the police cruiser parked in a farmyard further up the Lagg Road, where the last slopes of the south end gave way to the flat land of the isthmus. He then saw the sergeant and another officer in a nearby field, examining the ground alongside the hedgerow. Leo parked the Humber on a grassy layby and waited for Ronnie, who had noticed his arrival and was approaching. He climbed into the passenger seat.

'We're combing the edge of the field in case the culprit threw the murder weapon from a vehicle as he fled the scene. It's a long shot, to be honest. It would be nice to be free from everyday distractions and devote my time exclusively to the case. Take your pal, Mr Troughton, for instance. I had to lift him last night for being tighter than an Orangeman's drum. To say nothing about a report of a bouncing golf ball causing a car to swerve on the shore road near to his house.'

'I don't doubt that the obstreperous Troughton must vex you,' said Leo. 'However, I no longer reside at the Palmery. I should have mentioned to you yesterday: I am now staying in a flat at Ardcaden.'

'Well, mind how you go, and make sure the Brothers Grim don't get you.'

'I beg your pardon?'

'Vincent's brothers came over to Sonna yesterday. There are three of them, and they are fairly scary customers. They've been spotted prowling around. So, if you hear a knock at your door and it's them outside saying they want to pick your brains, don't open up. More likely they'll want to splatter your brains with half a yard of gas piping. I just hope we can identify the perpetrator before they do.'

'I've spoken with Davie Heron, and I believe him and his wife to be innocent of any involvement in the deaths of Andy Lamb and Vincent.'

'But we know they're some sort of neopagans – what if the killings were ritual sacrifices?'

'I have undertaken some research. It suggests that the curious activity which I filmed three nights ago was merely an old ordinance to appease the demon which legend has it resides in the Cathair.'

'Aye, they told CID that, eventually. Bloody weird, though.'

'The sources I found mentioned only an animal oblation, not a human one. Also, the Herons conducted their sacrifices according to a precise rite and by fire, totally unlike the deaths of Andy and Vincent.'

'What if Andy and Vincent were silenced for discovering the Herons' occult hobby?'

'If they so objected to folk knowing, then why didn't they slay Rab Haddow? He informed me that he first came across the Herons making a burnt offering years ago, and that he has been teasing Davie about it ever since. I've also considered that the real perpetrator could have known about the Herons' odd proclivities, and calculated that killing Vincent near to Inkpot Farm would cast suspicion upon them.'

'We've searched Vincent's house and business premises for clues, but it didn't turn up anything interesting,' said Ronnie. 'His computer and phone records are being analysed, but the data guy's initial scan says there's no suspicious activity, in terms of, for example, threatening emails or text messages or unusual calls. By the way, there were also no inculpatory texts exchanged between Nicky, Norris and Johnathon, but, of course, they might have been being careful and done their plotting via phone calls and/or face to face. All of our suspects have permitted us to search their homes and premises, but we drew a blank. The lab results from the suspects' body swabs, clothing and footwear are back, and there are no traces of Vincent's blood or DNA. But they could have washed themselves and dumped any contaminated clothing. Forensics managed to identify the footprint from the ditch. Those boffins are so clever that they even deducted the brand, which is of a widely available leather-upper, rubber-soled gents' shoe. It didn't match any of the suspects' footwear and is a size or two larger than they wear, but that doesn't necessarily get them off the hook. The perpetrator could have bought a bigger size for the job in order to put us off the scent, then disposed of them. Also, Norris' Land Rover came back clean. There was no trace residue from it having conveyed the murder weapon.'

'I visited the Meiklejohn residence this morning,' said Leo. 'I spoke to Elizabeth and asked her precisely when she confessed about the fact that Andy Lamb had sexually assaulted her. She said that she told her mother, who immediately told her father, on the day I first spoke with her, which was the day *before* Vincent's death. I am therefore convinced of Norris' version of events. He knew the truth prior to Vincent's demise and was actually attempting to make peace with him when he tried to intercept him on the road by the brewery.'

'Perhaps Elizabeth had been coached.'

'No, it was only when I pressed her that she mentioned a detail – waiting for *Coronation Street* to finish before she informed her mother. That television programme is broadcast on Wednesdays, placing the conversation on the eve of the murder. It was too subtle a detail for Elizabeth to confect. What do you know about Dr Morgenthaler?'

'Nothing much. Queer sort, keeps himself to himself. But there's no crime against that. Why do you ask?'

'Troughton saw him speaking with Vincent outside the Co-op on Wednesday morning. Apparently, Morgenthaler appeared to be very cross, as though Vincent had in some way offended him, although he wouldn't have had time to have then sabotaged the brewery.'

'What's your point, Leo?'

'I found it striking that someone as reclusive as he just happened to be in Kilmichael at the time of the murder, in full view, and it's almost as though he was undertaking activities which would timestamp his alibi, even purchasing some knitwear from a drapery at the height of summer.'

'That all seems a bit thin. Is there anything else you want to discuss?'

'I was shot at last night.'

'Excuse me?'

Leo related his fearful experience.

'Why the hell didn't you dial 999 straight away?' demanded Ronnie exasperatedly.

'The shooter would have been long gone by the time you boys arrived. I tried to get hold of you this morning to report it.'

'I wonder if the Comiskey brothers were responsible.

Those guys are quite heavy hitters in Glasgow – they'd definitely have access to firearms.'

'But why would they target me? I had been attesting Vincent's innocence.'

'They needn't have known that. They might just have associated you with *The Repository's* investigation and suspected that you were in on the murder in some way.'

'No. Vincent told me that he spoke to at least one of his brothers on the telephone every night. He'd have updated them as to the position I had taken.'

'Let's take a look at where this shooting incident occurred. You lead on and I'll follow in the cruiser.'

The men parked in Ardcaden and walked back out along the road, then scaled a rusted metal fence and approached the heap of plastic-bound animal feed from where the shot had been fired. They surveyed the sod; there were off-road vehicle tyre tracks and footprints, but nothing else of note.

'Shotguns and many hunting rifles don't eject their cartridges,' commented Ronnie. 'Either that, or the shooter could have picked it up. Let's have a word with the farmer.'

They drove to the steading, which was at Melford, but nobody was around apart from a labourer, who stated that the farmer and his family were shopping in Kilmichael. The man claimed to know nothing about the gunshot.

De Mortuis Nil Nisi Bonum

RONNIE was concerned for Leo's safety, but his recommendation that he go home to Glasgow was rebuffed, as were his subsequent suggestions that he stay in the police cell at Kilmichael for his own protection, or at least return to the Palmery to be with Troughton. He therefore urged Leo to be vigilant that night, advising that he ensure his door and windows were properly locked, and promising to schedule a patrol car to periodically survey the village and surrounding countryside.

'And if you think something's up, for Christ's sake ring me right away,' he concluded, before departing in the police cruiser.

Leo drove back to Ardcaden, where he nipped into the post office and bought three locally reared beef sausages and a bottle of Sonna-brand raspberryade. Upon his return to the flat he felt overcome by lassitude, and therefore peeled off his shoes and went to bed for a nap. He dozed for an hour and a half, then rose and boiled some potatoes, fried the beef links, heated half a tin of beans and buttered two slices of plain bread. After he had consumed this banquet, he made a pot of tea and ate the remainder of his Bakewell tart. He then pulled on his tweed jacket and raincoat, and went for a stroll along the seafront, using a red telephone box to call his mother rather than risking the capriciousness of the local mobile signal. He walked past terraces of holiday apartments, the Saint Caden's Hotel and a row of red sandstone villas and out of the village. He sat on a varnished wooden bench to meditate upon the case as he observed the black and ruby shore, the teal sea and the ashen sky which broke into occasional territories of cold, polished aqua. A freighter loomed into view having despatched her cargo at Port Glasgow, unfeasibly colossal for this narrow strip of firth. The temperature was unseasonably low, and although the wireless had stated that the weather system was not expected to set in, the conditions were like an overture to the coming autumn. Leo dreaded that hinterland of late August and early September, that sole period of the year when it wasn't really any season at all: 'Harvest', he had christened it. The cloud suddenly drew its shoulders against the last bluish redoubts. The freighter's wash was now crashing upon the shore in great grey waves. She slipped towards the sound beneath the louring sky, her bridge taller than the headland. The rain came on, and Leo stood and began retracing his steps. It was Saturday night, and he noted the welcoming glow of the public bar at the hotel, but he couldn't be bothered going in. Once back at the flat he considered texting Amy, perhaps to suggest going for drinks in Kilmichael, but he resisted the temptation. However, she soon happened to text him, and he was dismayed at how his heart leapt when he saw her name on the phone's screen, although she was merely requesting a lift to church in the morning.

Leo felt a little on edge sitting in the flat alone after the previous night's drama. On a few occasions he found himself peering out of the back window but he didn't see the weird light again. For solace, he lit a fire and tucked himself alongside it in a creaky armchair with a bottle of Scotch and a dog-eared version of Rudyard Kipling's *Complete Stalky & Co.* he had scrounged from the apartment's rickety book trolley, which was mostly inhabited by thriller novels and dated editions of *Reader's Digest*.

It was after midnight when he thought he heard a noise from the rear of the property. He went into the kitchen and flicked the light switch, the naked electric bulb buzzing rudely to life but illuminating nothing untoward. He returned to his cosy berth, found a classical station on the wireless and set the volume at a subdued level. He then gazed into the fire, an occupation that often drew him into a melancholic study. It was in its prime, the wood blazing cheerfully and the anthracitic heart in full glow, the busy little drama of combustion as though imparting some allegorical narrative, some secret to life's meaning. Outside a curlew issued its haunting call through air which was heavy with rain and salt and coal smoke and wet leaves and damp soil. And all the while the water lapped the shore and the big old hill sat silently, emitting its strange, eternal vibration.

Leo drifted off to sleep and eventually entered the realm of mad dreams, which soon mutated into a brief vision, just an image of a black symbol on a white background: a long band with a barb on each terminal and a short bar intersecting its midpoint. He came to abruptly, the radio signal fizzing valiantly through the heavy weather, the fire low now, crackling quietly in the grate. He turned off the wireless, picked up his crocodile leather-bound notebook and sketched the symbol. He then switched off the table lamp so that the only light in the room was from the dying fire. He sat and listened to the rain for a minute, and then resolved to visit the lavatory and go to bed.

He rose with a groan, and as he approached the door a broad shadow loomed towards him and he felt a strong hand grab his neck. He was wheeled round and slammed against the wall with tremendous force. The assailant now used both of his hands to pin Leo's neck and he instinctively stood on his tiptoes, struggling to inhale and trying in vain to prise the iron grip from his throat. For a few terrified seconds all he could hear was the interloper's angry hyperventilation. He had alcohol on his breath and his clothing was slick with water.

'Take your ugly bastard barbecued hands off of mine, and I'll let you breathe.'

Leo recognised the voice of Johnathon Lamb, and obeyed. The vice lessened marginally, just enough to permit him to speak.

'What do you want?'

'You to stop spreading shite about our Andrew.'

'I know it must be painful for you, but I merely deduced the truth.'

'Wrong – you convinced Elizabeth Meiklejohn that it was my brother who raped her. You could make that halfwit believe in unicorns if you put your mind to it. You've got Norris fooled too – he rang me. And, without a shred of evidence you've persuaded Nicky Barrett that Comiskey definitely didn't kill Andrew.'

'You lost your elder sibling, therefore you will always have my sympathy. But you are going to go home before you get into trouble.'

'Trouble? You gonnae hurt me? I could tear you limb from limb.'

'I do not doubt it. However, you are going to leave this abode now, so that I will not be forced to report this incident to the police.'

'I'll kill you first!' hissed Johnathon.

'Like you did Vincent?'

'No, someone beat me to it.'

'Who?'

'No idea. But it wasn't me. I didn't know for certain that

he'd done in our Andrew.'

'Then you are not going to start being a killer now.'

'How do you know I'd be starting out? I was in Iraq, in the battle for Basra. Then we got it tight when we were stationed at Dogwood.'

'It is not the same thing. You were serving your country, not murdering a man in cold blood.'

Leo felt one hand remove itself from his neck and then heard a flick-knife blade being engaged. He could see its dull metallic lustre out of the corner of his eye. 'I'll have your liver out!'

'No, Johnathon. Because if you do, you will cross a line into a place that you can never come back from. I once took a man's life, but I managed to keep it together because I had acted in self-defence and because he was so despicable.' Leo heard the flick knife's action again as the blade was withdrawn, and breathed a slight sigh of relief. 'Last night you missed me, which is fortunate for both of us.'

Johnathon now released Leo. 'What the fuck are you talking about?'

'Was it you with the light last night?'

'Aye. There's no law against it.'

'Shooting at a man? I think you'll find there is a law against that.'

'I wasn't shooting at you – I didn't even see you. If I'd been aiming at you, I wouldn't have missed. It was hares I was firing at. I was out lamping. If you don't believe me, ask the farmer at Melford whose land I was on and who was with me as lamp man. Better still, pop by my place and I'll give you a plate of hare stew, just to prove the point.'

The tension in the room seemed to diminish a further degree.

'Were you at one point shining a light from the hillside out back?'

'Of course not. It's all wooded – lamping's done on flat, open ground. Now shut your hole and listen up good: do not sully my brother's beloved memory again.'

With that, Johnathon stormed off, slamming the front door behind him and leaving Leo rubbing his neck and wondering what on earth the light he had seen last night on the tree-cloaked lower slopes of the Cathair had actually been.

The Ogre's House

It took Leo a good deal of time to drop off to sleep due to the trauma inflicted by his night caller. He woke to the trill of his travel alarm and because of the unreliability of the water heater he had to endure a cold bath, which at least served to invigorate him. As he filled the kettle for his shave, he noticed that the kitchen window had been expertly forced, evidently the means by which Johnathon had gained entry. Leo performed a rudimentary repair, then shaved, dressed and set off in the Humber, his spirits lifted by the return of the fine weather and the prospect of seeing Amy.

The sands at Herrick Bay were white-gold against the sparkling aquamarine, the fields and hillsides and tree foliage impossibly green. Finches chirruped in the branches of the sycamores at Fagr Vágr. Leo admired the lushness of Amy's sloping lawn, above which were palm trees, roses, buddleia, fuchsia, hydrangea – with pale-blue and pink-violet lacecap flowers and bright pink and purple mop heads, and then mixed woodland. She was looking out for him from the sunroom, then she emerged and walked elegantly down the path, dressed in a knee-length dark-blue sleeveless dress, carrying a little handbag and wearing Jackie O sunglasses and a patterned silk scarf.

'Have you been sleeping okay?' enquired Amy after they

had driven off. 'I hope you don't mind my saying, but you look a little rough around the edges.'

Leo indeed felt washed out and ugly with tiredness in comparison with Amy's easy beauty, her scarf billowing in the breeze which flowed through the opened windows of the car. He glared at the melted purplish skin of his hands accusingly, hating himself for their unsightliness.

'I am fine, thank you. Let's just say I had a disturbed night.'

'Did something happen?'

'Do you know Johnathon Lamb, Andy's brother?'

'Not really.'

'Well, he paid me a nocturnal visit with a flick knife.'

'That's awful!'

'Don't worry, he didn't use it. He just wanted to put the frighteners on me, keep me quiet,' said Leo as he unconsciously touched his neck.

Amy noticed a contusion there. 'Leo, he hurt you! I take it you've informed the police?'

'No. He is rather a disagreeable fellow, but now that he has discharged his spleen, I am confident he will not molest me again. And I have no pressing desire to ruin his life.'

'What got into him?'

'He had been made aware of my deduction that it was Andy who had violated Elizabeth, and not Vincent.'

Amy considered this grimly for a few moments, then said: 'Did he break into your flat?'

'Yes. He forced a back window.'

'So, he has committed housebreaking, manhandled you and threatened you – all criminal offences. It might well have been him who killed Vincent Comiskey. You *must* report it.'

'If he did slay Vincent, then let him stand trial for the greater crime. But I am now convinced that he is innocent of it.'

'Why?'

'Because last night he denied it, and I believed him. Also, he tried to steel himself to stab me, but he didn't have the stomach for murder.'

'Nonetheless, it was unwise of you to move to Ardcaden Bay after what has happened at the south end,' said Amy as she folded her arms and stared glumly at the passing countryside.

'Troughton and I didn't exactly hit it off.'

'But you'd have been welcome to stay at Fagr Vágr.' There followed an awkward silence. 'I mean, it's just me living there – there is plenty of room.'

'That is most kind,' said Leo gently. 'However, I also felt I needed to be in the south end for the purposes of my investigations.'

A couple of times during Mass, Leo glanced around the church to see if he could locate Troughton, but he evidently hadn't attended. No doubt he was wallowing in some pit of post-inebriation despair. At least Leo would avoid any histrionic entreaties that he return to the Palmery.

'Would you like to stay for lunch?' enquired Amy before she disembarked from the Humber after Leo had driven her back to Herrick Bay. 'It's such a lovely day. We could sit out.'

'No, thank you, Amy. I'd better get on.'

'Oh, I see. Well, thanks for the lift.'

With that, she got out and walked towards the house.

Leo headed to the murder scene, hoping that the police presence there had been stood down in order that he might inspect it properly. He motored down the west road, occasionally glancing to his right to take in the jagged blue mountain range of Erran. Racing yachts peppered the gorgeously blue expanse of the Sound of

Sonna. The countryside which the Lagg Road intersected looked particularly resplendent in the sunshine, not least the magnificent rock formations which characterised its coast. Only a few retreating clouds and a slight surface haze evidenced the previous night's dreichness. Even the cattle in the pastures looked contented.

When he arrived at his destination, Leo was satisfied to note that there was no longer a sentry on duty. The gate through which the trough had been dragged was still ajar, and he swung the Humber through it and a little way up the track there. He yanked the handbrake up, turned off the engine, got out and regarded the scene. The branches of an apple tree framed the spectacular view down to the sound, the humpy land dotted with squat hawthorns and flowering gorse bushes. The undergrowth hummed with insects and a buzzard circled lazily overhead. Leo walked down to the road and began surveying the vicinity, trying to put himself in the mind of the killer, trying to scope out escape routes and contingency plans. With his foot, he meditatively poked the undergrowth which bowered the drainage ditch in which it seemed the murderer had concealed himself. What if the villain had been required to have lain in wait for a protracted period – would the ditch have been too inhospitable an environment for any mortal? Leo again observed the surrounding landscape. For comfort and indeed for a better view of the road, the killer may well have chosen atop the craggy little drumlin that overlooked the scene as his initial vantage. Then, after Vincent had passed by on his way to making his beer delivery at Crochadh House, he could have quickly descended, opened the gate, hauled out the trough and then prostrated himself in the ditch, awaiting his quarry's return.

Leo walked back up the track, fetching his detective's kit from the Humber as he passed it, and found an easy way to scale the rough hillock from its rear. He had a sense of the summer flora beginning to brown and wither, and noted early fruit on the bramble. There was scrub to the immediate south, which merged into a little broad-leafed wood, beyond which was Inkpot Farm. The surface of the drumlin itself was largely naked rock, sometimes clothed with sun-frazzled moss or scruffy turf. Leo estimated that it would be virtually impossible to lift a footprint from this, even for modern forensic geniuses. He tried to visualise where the killer would have placed himself and then scoured the ground. Soon he noticed something jammed between a stratum of turf and the rock: a little cylinder. He withdrew his tweezers and plucked the item from its berth. It was a white cigarette butt. He raised it to his nose and found the stump of tobacco to be fresh-smelling, and the filter quite free of the ravages of prolonged exposure. The manufacturer's stamp was perfectly intact: 'FERNANDO'.

'I've never heard of a ciggy-smoking demon,' muttered Leo.

He found several more butts, extracted them all and placed them in an evidence bag. He wasn't familiar with this brand of cigarette; it was foreign, probably, and he wished to identify it. Unfortunately, the library in Kilmichael would be closed because it was Sunday, and Leo didn't trust the local mobile signal for what could be an obscure internet search. He withdrew his phone and called Fordyce on speed dial. Thankfully his friend picked up straight away, and the connection was strong enough for Leo to explain his requirement.

'As it happens, old stick, I believe we possess a reference book in the family library which could be just the thing: an encyclopaedia of the world's tobacco products. It was probably purchased by my late Great Uncle Hugo, a hoarder of obscure publications.' Fordyce continued chatting merrily as he marched through the palatial chambers of Biggnarbriggs Hall, his ancestral pile in Kirkcudbrightshire. Eventually, Leo heard him mutter to himself as he sought out the tome, and then make a small exclamation of triumph. He then heard pages being flicked. 'Ah, here we are: Fernando cigarettes. An upmarket brand produced by Castedo Tobaccos Ltd., Montevideo. Company founded in 1880. Fernandos are sold only in South America, chiefly Uruguay, Paraguay, southern Brazil and northern Argentina.'

Fordyce's words felt like a eureka moment, because Leo was struck by how the cigarettes' provenance chimed with what Rab Haddow had said about Dr Morgenthaler receiving post from South America. He thanked his friend for his help and sat on the drumlin to gather his thoughts. Several people had described Morgenthaler to Leo as excessively private, odd or mysterious. Vincent had told Leo that Crochadh House gave him 'the creeps', and Troughton had witnessed the doctor being angry after conversing with Vincent. Was it possible that Morgenthaler had some secret he wanted maintained, and that Vincent had stumbled across it and had to be silenced? Leo also pondered how all of the mysterious deaths, and that of Gus Blessing, had occurred after Morgenthaler's arrival on Sonna. Obviously one reason that Morgenthaler was a person of interest was that he was a regular customer of Vincent's, and the brewer was scheduled to, and made, a delivery to his property on the day of his death. Morgenthaler obviously would have known Vincent's planned whereabouts on that fatal morning. The doctor would also be familiar with the lie of the local land, and therefore where best to stage the attack – somewhere far enough away from his own abode to avoid attracting suspicion. Also, if he happened to know about the Herons' weird ceremonies, he might have chosen Inkpot Farm in the hope that suspicion might fall upon the local oddballs. However, Morgenthaler had certainly been in Kilmichael at the time of the murder, yet it had already occurred to Leo as singular that someone as reclusive as him had just happened to be in town that day, and doing things that would render his alibi unimpeachable. Leo remembered being struck by the amount of beer Morgenthaler consumed, taking possession of a firkin of German-style pilsner every week. He did a quick calculation: a firkin is nine gallons, and there are eight pints in a gallon. Therefore, that was seventy-two pints a week – surely too much for one thin old man to get through. Could a cigarette-smoking, lager-swilling ally have carried out the crime on his behalf? And did this shadowy individual still reside at the remote Crochadh House?

Leo gazed down towards the sea. He wondered if the hypothetical murderer's flight to Crochadh could have been covered by the shoreline's geology, not least the looming volcanic headland of Oganach, the most dramatic of the rock features in the area. He decided to find out. Then take a look at the house itself.

Leo paused at the Humber, stowed the evidence bag in the glove compartment, and put his detective's kit and his aluminium water flask into his knapsack, which he slung over his shoulders. He placed his bushman hat on his head and hung his binoculars round his neck, leaving his jacket in the car due to the intense heat. It was hard to countenance that only last night Leo had lit a fire to keep warm, so temperamental was this maritime climate. He crossed the road, scaled a wire fence and set off across a lumpy field, noting that an intersecting drystane dyke would have screened one side of the progress of a crouching man. He was soon among the tight confines of some rising land that was studded with gorse and hawthorn and which descended to the sandy inlet of Oganach Bay. The next leg, towards the rock formation, was across open ground, but probably too far from the road for a passing motorist to notice a person there, and, furthermore, the trees by Inkpot Farm obscured its line of sight. Leo reached the towering basalt columns, gazing upwards from the turf and feeling as though he had just been deposited on the set of a classic episode of *Doctor Who*. He then explored the shore, curious to see if it was passable. It was, but only by negotiating slabs of black magma and clambering precariously over sierras of bleached rock stained by ancient lichens. Purple cranesbill and bladder campion flourished here, and Leo spotted devil's bit and harebell growing higher up. Beyond Oganach he reached a derelict boat house, after which he chose an easy, grassy route amply hidden from view by furze-clad banks above the foreshore. As he neared Crochadh House, Leo realised that he had indeed just traversed a perfect escape route. He became aware of the sound of an engine, and picked his way up the bank, avoiding the prickly furze. Using his binoculars, he viewed Dr Morgenthaler's metallic-blue Audi 100 C1 sedan drive up the private track from his abode towards the end of the Lagg Road. Leo considered how serendipitous the doctor's absence was as he made his final approach.

It was an edifice of angular roofs, lofty, grey-finished gables and tall chimneys. It was set behind the granite-belted arrowhead of Hangman's Hill, and nestled within the terminus of a river of woodland which flowed down from the higher ground. Perhaps there had been a time under a previous occupancy when Crochadh House did not frown so and did not seem so forbidding. A time when family life invigorated its now quieted recesses, when many of its windows were not blinded by ugly, narrow shutters, when the paintwork was fresh and cheerfully defiant of the shadow cast by the melancholy hill and the sombre woods, whose branches were then less invasive and concealing. A time when the waterwheel chattered merrily and was not choked by briar and rampant grasses, and when children played upon the turf which stretched to the flowering gorse and then the intricate shore and then the shimmering sound.

Leo crept over the gravel apron of the property and into the porch. He tried the door but it was locked. He withdrew his detective's kit, selected a skeleton key and began tampering like an expert cat burglar. The movement in Leo's hands was somewhat restricted due to the damage inflicted by the house fire in his youth, but dogged practice had made him adept at this task. The lock soon gave, and Leo sneaked inside. The hallway was in better trim than the exterior, a place of perfect order and clean white walls which was furnished and ornamented in an austere but by no means tasteless manner. Leo checked the grand rooms to either flank but found nothing of interest. He returned to the hall. A deep red strip of Axminister carpet led to a heavy sideboard at the foot of the stairs. Upon it was sat a bust of Xenephon, with a utility bill envelope addressed to 'Dr Julius Morgenthaler' clamped beneath it. Leo realised that until this moment he hadn't been aware of the doctor's forename. Something else caught his eye on the sideboard: a wooden figure of a Dark Ages warrior bearing a sword and a shield. Upon the shield was carved in low relief precisely the same symbol which Leo had encountered in his vision of the previous night. His wonder at this discovery was interrupted by a bump from above. He froze, a chill rushing up his back, and gazed up the stairway. He then began his ascent.

Leo explored the upper rooms in turn, cringing at every creak of a treacherous floorboard and dreading what lay behind each door he pushed open. These rooms were gloomy and Leo had to take a pencil torch from his detective's kit in order to properly review their scant contents. He reached one with unshuttered windows which was presumably Morgenthaler's bedchamber, a fastidiously neat space virtually unadorned by any personal touch or artistic decoration. There then came another bump, emanating from directly above where Leo was standing. He stole out of the room and found a further flight of stairs. Murmuring a prayer, he climbed upwards, and found himself facing a strong oaken door secured by a hasp and padlock. He made short work of it with a skeleton key and heaved. The door opened with a foreboding yawn. He could see only a little portion of bare boards and brickwork. A deep voice from further inside began uttering: '*For want of a nail the shoe was lost. For want of a shoe the horse was lost ...*'

Leo gulped and stepped forwards and around a dividing wall to take in the main cavity of the attic. At the far end, an ogre was sitting on a grubby mat. As he recited the proverb, he intently fingered some species of puzzle, which incorporated a length of string to which was attached little wooden rings and balls.

'*For want of a horse the knight was lost. For want of a knight the battle was lost –*'

The creature noticed Leo.

'Halloa! Ich heiße Tristan Morgenthaler. Wie heißen Sie?'

'Moran. Leo Moran.'

'Wie geht es Ihnen?'

'Ich spreche kein Deutsch.'

'De onde você é? Você é um médico?'

'Em inglês, por favor.'

'Where are you from, Leo Moran?'

'Glasgow. I am an investigator.'

The man digested this for a few moments, then said, 'I saw you. From my window. My brother says I mustn't go near the window, but I get bored, so sometimes I look out. The beer man saw me looking out, and my brother got very angry with me. Now he says he is going to shorten my chain so that I can't get near to the window any more.'

His diction and accent were unusual: Teutonic consonants with a Latin lilt. And, of course, his first attempts at communication had been in German and then Portuguese.

'Did you kill the beer man?'

'*For want of a battle the realm was lost. And all for the want of a horseshoe nail.*'

His broad face was impossible to age, his skull entirely bald and his body thick and powerful. Leo reckoned he would measure at least six and a half feet when standing in his stockinged soles. He was wearing grey trousers and an off-white vest which exposed his mighty arms. A strong leather harness bound his waist and shoulders. It was attached to a heavy chain which was fastened to an iron ring on the wall. Leo ensured he kept a distance from the man in excess of the chain's length. The chamber was well illuminated by the sunlight that streamed in through the barred windows and picked out motes of dust which hovered in the stuffy atmosphere. Apart from the man's puzzle, sleeping mat, rough blanket and pillow, there was a portable toilet, a chair, a basin, a water ewer, a beer firkin, a tankard and a cup. Leo had a sense of a person held against his will for years.

'Why are you chained up like an animal?'

'I have a ... condition. I get restless. Agitated.'

'Do you ever get outside?'

'Seldom. And only when I have been very good and calm, and only ever at night. Then I go a-roaming. A-roaming I do go. Ha – perhaps you think me an imbecile? A monster? I was once clever – a gentleman of letters, a scholar fluent in many tongues. But then I lost my reason and he was worried that I would blab so he tried to *fix* me,' he said as he tapped a scar on his head. 'But still I remained a blabbermouth. Blabbertey-blabbertey-blabber. That is why he keeps me up here. In case I blab about what he did.'

'What did he do, Tristan?'

'He served the Angel of Death!' said the man, a manic light appearing in his small eyes.

'Do you mean the demon piper who is said to dwell in the hill? Or do you mean Death himself? Did your brother kill or have people killed, such as the beer man three days ago?'

'*For want of a nail the shoe was lost ...*'

'What about Andy Lamb, the boy who died at Glen Colm many years past?'

'*For want of a shoe the horse was lost ...*'

Leo heard the sound of tyres tearing across the gravel outside. He peered out of a window and saw Morgenthaler's classic Audi pull up. The doctor, who was wearing a brown safari suit, got out and Leo took in his gaunt visage. His long nose and prominent chin were the only features redolent of his brother. He tilted his head slightly, as though to sample the air, and the sun caught his spectacles to make the lenses two eyeless discs of pure light. Morgenthaler went out of sight for a few moments and returned with a wheelbarrow. With great effort he unloaded a sack of potatoes from the boot of his car, and pushed the laden barrow round the side of the house, presumably towards a rear kitchen door. Leo decided to take his chance and made a break for it. He trod as softly as he could down the two flights of stairs. When he reached the hall, he heard the doctor approaching through the house and looked around frantically for a place to hide, at the last moment pinning himself against the wall beside a tall mahogany linen cupboard to his left and praying that Morgenthaler didn't proceed in his direction. After a few desperate seconds he breathed a sigh of relief as he heard the doctor start to ascend the stairs. He crept towards the front door, opened it silently and then ran out, out, out, into the light, into the sweet Sonna air. He intuited he should head south – this would be the opposite direction in which the householder would expect him to flee, and also if he went up the track towards the Lagg Road he would be in the open, vulnerable to being run over by the Audi or cut down by gunfire. If he took the circuitous route by which he had arrived, he could easily be headed off before he reached the Humber. For, assuming Morgenthaler had been going upstairs to check on his sibling, the visit of an interloper would be immediately evidenced by the opened padlock, and presumably the brother's testimony. Perhaps the ogre would even be let off the leash and commanded to chase Leo like a bloodhound.

Beyond the trees the terrain funnelled to a gate, and Leo's fire-damaged hands complained as he vaulted it. The land then sloped downwards in a broad sward, and he was glad to be out of the eyeline of Crochadh House. He realised he had entered the smallest, westernmost glen of the south end which he had previously noticed on his OS map. It was enclosed to his left by Hangman's Hill, and to his right by a modest summit called Barr Buidhe, on the other side of which was Grog Head. It was a lonely, rough, grassy valley fringed with the yellow and deep green of gorse. Leo forded a wide, red-bedded burn and the ground swept upwards again; beyond its crest was a fine view of the cliffs of Little Cunrae and the perfect-blue firth on which a tanker was heading out towards the Irish Sea. He left the glen and picked up a thin path above the ragged coastline. As he beat his hasty retreat beneath the unforgiving sun, Leo encountered not another soul – no farmer or rambler to cheer or aid him, only the song of the meadow pipits and the flight of a wheatear, which fluttered from a post as though merely to show off its beautiful zebra tail feathers. From on high, a hovering kestrel regarded the absconding man's plight with sympathy as it effortlessly mastered the thermals. At one point, two roe deer noisily broke cover and Leo clutched his heart, fearing it would fail. He soon reached the foot of the next glen where he had to stop to catch his breath. He was sweating profusely, and he slugged greedily from his water flask and then tried to telephone Ronnie MacKellar, but there was insufficient signal strength down here to connect the call. He gazed through the gap in the ridge which enclosed this second glen's extremity, and for a moment he considered cutting through it in order to make a beeline for the Humber. But in truth he simply wanted to be as far away from Crochadh House as possible, and he decided instead to push on towards the lighthouse and then round to Ardcaden and civilisation. He was by now too exhausted to run, and so negotiated the bleak promontories of Glencolm Bay at a rapid walking pace, then crossed the boulder field by the lighthouse, regularly glancing over his shoulder to see if he was being pursued. Leo progressed northwards, and soon neared the cave he had noticed when he had traversed this route in the opposite direction ten days ago. Suddenly a hulking figure emerged from its entrance, looming over him as it barred his path.

'It's all right – I'm not going to hurt you,' said Johnathon as he watched Leo almost shed his skin in fright. He was wearing motorcycle trousers and a washed-out T-shirt bearing the logo of the rock band Rush. His face was grazed in places and bruises were coming up.

'What are you doing down here?' enquired Leo between hyperventilations.

'I like this place. It's kind of desolate, but in a good way. It calms me down. I come here sometimes to think about Andrew. Last night, after I ... visited you, I couldn't sleep. What you and Norris had said about what Andrew had done to Elizabeth kept preying on my mind. So I went to Norris' place first thing this morning. I asked to speak with her. I had to know, for sure.'

'And?'

'I believed her.'

The man sat down on a large rock and withdrew a packet of cigarettes, offering one to Leo.

'Thank you,' he said as he accepted one. 'Usually I don't partake, but I am feeling a tad stressed.'

'You should try out my day so far – it's not exactly been a picnic,' said Johnathon as he lit the fags. 'It's a hell of a thing, realising that your life's hero wasn't all he was cracked up to be. Do you really think Vincent Comiskey was innocent of doing in my brother all those years ago?'

'Yes, Johnathon, I do.'

'The cops grilled me like a sardine after Vincent's murder, and they aren't going to leave me alone. But I didn't do it.'

'I believe you, Johnathon. What happened to your face?'

'Vincent's brothers must have been watching me. Outside the Meiklejohns they came at me as I went to mount my bike. I fought back but I took a few punches. They bundled me into the boot of their motor and drove off. After a while we stopped and they dragged me out. I realised we were up on the moors. They kept insisting that it was me who had killed Vincent, and I kept denying it. When they got the pliers out, I just lost it – I got down on my knees and begged them to believe me. Anyway, that seemed to convince them. They left me up there, so I had to walk overland to Kilmichael to fetch my bike.'

'On the subject of your motorcycle, we must put it to use forthwith. I need to get to the police station.'

'You're not going to grass me up for last night, are you?'

'If I was going to do that, I'd have done it by now.'

'I just want to sit here. My world has fallen apart, Leo. My spirit is broken,' said Johnathon as he exhaled a stream of blue smoke.

It was disconcerting and moving to Leo to behold the hardboiled man so conquered. 'Then dare to do something good in the teeth of it. I don't have time to explain. Suffice to say, you'd be serving the cause of justice.'

'For fuck's sake man – a few hours ago I pulled a blade on you, and now you're wanting to ride pillion with me?'

'I believe it providential that we have met here, and we must cooperate with God's mysterious graces. Now, *will* you help me? Consider it penance for last night.'

The bike was parked where the road terminated just south of Ardcaden Bay, at the macadam ellipse where the buses turned. Leo had to endure a hair-raising four hundred yards before Johnathon popped into his cottage to fetch his spare crash helmet. Leo donned the item and clung on for dear life as the ex-soldier reached death-defying speeds on the west road. Leo was thankful to dismount onto terra firma outside the police station in Kilmichael. He faced Johnathon and shook his gauntleted hand.

Leo asked the duty officer if Ronnie MacKellar was available. The man picked up the desk phone and made a brief internal call, and then bade Leo to go through to the room furthest to the rear. He walked up the corridor and noticed the CID men hunched over their laptops in the main office. Through the glass of the next door, he saw Ronnie relaxing with a Styrofoam cup of tea and a Blue Riband. It was a drab, windowless chamber painted in institutional grey, the only decoration a calendar bearing an image of a Caledonian MacBrayne ferry proudly ploughing her way between some Hebridean islands.

'Leo Moran – the very man!' said the sergeant. 'I'm not long after enquiring with the farmer at Melford, upon whose land the shot was fired two nights ago. Apparently, he and Johnathon Lamb were out lamping together. It's a pity you were so imaginative as to think that they were aiming at you, and hence wasted my precious time. Anyway, would you care for a cuppa and a chocolate biscuit?'

'Just a biscuit, if you please,' replied Leo gratefully, realising that he hadn't had any lunch. 'But, if you will excuse the indecorum, I shall consume it on our way to the south end. There's no time to lose – he might try to move him.'

'What are you havering about, man?'

'Forgive me, I am a touch overwrought. Permit me to explain: I have just fled Crochadh House. Dr Morgenthaler keeps his mentally unstable brother there under lock and key. This solves our alibi problem – what if Morgenthaler instructed his brother to kill Vincent?'

'You saw this man?'

'Saw him, spoke with him.'

'Like you did Gus Blessing?'

Leo took a deep breath. 'No, Sergeant, not like that,' he said exasperatedly. 'My encounter with Gus was a waking vision ... it is impossible to explain. The man I found at Crochadh House is as much flesh and blood as you or I.'

'How did you get inside that residence? Are you confessing to an officer of the law that you forced entry to private property?'

'Oh, never mind all that now.'

'Okay, Leo, I shall humour you one last time,' said Ronnie tiredly as he rose to his feet.

'Are you going to inform the CID bods?'

'To be honest with you, I'd like to check it out for myself first.'

As they drove southwards in the cruiser, Leo updated Ronnie on his latest sleuthing and theorising. When he mentioned how Tristan Morgenthaler had spoken in German, Portuguese and English, Ronnie observed mordantly, 'Well, well, we have a multilingual ogre on our hands.'

'It is not so fantastic. I once watched a television documentary about German communities in South America, members of which would obviously require to speak both German and Spanish or Portuguese,' replied Leo. He then concluded: 'I believe Morgenthaler had Vincent killed because he had spotted his brother at the attic window. Vincent must have mentioned it conversationally to Morgenthaler when he bumped into him outside the Co-op in Kilmichael, which is why he was so ill humoured when he passed Troughton.'

'But why be so ashamed of a peculiar relative that you would have someone killed?'

'Because Tristan knows of his brother's sins.'

'Andy Lamb?'

'Tristan said his brother "served the Angel of Death", which could mean he is seduced somehow by the demon piper legend. Or it could just figuratively mean that his brother was directly responsible for people's deaths.'

At Leo's request, Ronnie then activated the cruiser's radio and asked the despatcher to do an online search for the names Julius Morgenthaler and Tristan Morgenthaler.

He painstakingly spelled out the letters using the NATO phonetic alphabet.

'By the way, Leo,' he said after he had finished the call, 'I meant to tell you yesterday – CID spoke with Henry Gaston, who repeated to them what he told you: that he saw Nicky, Norris and Johnathon in the pub together, acting furtively.'

'That may be so, Ronnie, but I firmly believe that those three amigos are innocent of Vincent's murder, every one of them.'

The cruiser swept down the track which led to Crochadh House, the light spangled by the branches of the trees which clothed the final stretch. Leo observed aloud that the blue Audi was gone. The men stepped out of the cruiser and regarded the edifice for a moment, a strange silence having descended as the sun beat down relentlessly. They approached the porch and Ronnie knocked on the front door three times, but nobody answered.

'Now we are faced with a problem of Scots Law, Leo.'

'Which is?'

'That police cannot force entry to a person's residence without proper cause. However, I am responding to a report that someone may be being kept inside against their will. And did you hear a seagull calling just now?'

'No.'

'Neither did I. But to offset any future comeback to my good self, I am going to say that I did hear it, and I am going to deliberately mistake it for a cry for help – which puts me within the realms of legality. Just be aware of how much I am going out on a limb for you here, Leo.'

Ronnie made to put his shoulder to the door, but Leo stopped him and withdrew a skeleton key from his detective's kit and went to work on the lock. It gave, and

Ronnie looked at Leo disapprovingly before pushing the door open and stepping inside.

The pair walked up the hallway, Leo feeling like a Jesuit spy partaking in some perilous Elizabethan plot. When they reached the sideboard, he hissed, 'The carving I mentioned to you in the car, which was visited to me in a vision – it is gone!'

A look of doubt formed on Ronnie's countenance. The men ascended the two flights of stairs and reached the attic level. The strong door was wide open. Leo made the Sign of the Cross and followed Ronnie inside.

There was no sign of Tristan Morgenthaler, and the chamber had been completely cleared of his possessions.

'For pity's sake, Leo,' grumbled Ronnie.

'He was here – I swear it upon all that is holy!' insisted Leo desperately. 'Dr Morgenthaler must have driven his brother off in his car or concealed him somewhere hereabouts, and hidden all of his things. Mark ye – bars upon the windows. Step back outside and you'll see the padlock which I unpicked. The place is a veritable prison! And observe the iron ring on the wall – that is what the man's chain was fastened to.' Ronnie looked deeply unimpressed. 'Inhale deeply, through your nose. What do you detect, Sergeant?'

'Brick and cedarwood beams, Mr Holmes.'

'But beneath that – can't you discern the odour of chemical toilet fluid, human effluent, foodstuffs, cigarette smoke, beer? And look at the stains on the floor. This place is *lived in*, man!'

'That's enough!' snapped Ronnie. 'If you genuinely saw what you said you saw, then why didn't you take a photo of the man as proof?'

'To be honest, it never occurred to me. I was just too taken aback by my discovery of him, then startled by the return of his brother.'

'Do you know what I think? I think you have a pretty vivid imagination, Mr Moran. Either that or you suffer from apparitions or delusions or, for all I know, bleeding LSD flashbacks. And I think that you need to leave this old man and his home well alone from now on. CID have the right suspects in their sights.'

The men left the house and entered the cruiser. The Motorola crackled into life and the despatcher informed that out of the three and a half billion males living on the planet not one online record or profile matched the name of a Julius or a Tristan Morgenthaler.

Ronnie dropped Leo off where he had left his motor car, and waited for him to drive through the farm gate in order that he could ensure that he quit the area. Leo rolled the Humber onto the road and then stopped, got out and handed Ronnie an item.

'These are the South American cigarette butts I mentioned,' said Leo. Ronnie accepted the evidence bag reluctantly. 'If you send them for analysis they will yield the DNA of Vincent's killer.'

'Even if they did, it would be circumstantial evidence. The smoker could just say they had been sunbathing on that drumlin on a date different to that of the murder.'

Leo drove to his flat in Ardcaden Bay, feeling deflated by the anticlimactic nature of his second visit to Crochadh House, and somewhat discomposed by the police sergeant's reaction. The symbol from his vision which he had seen engraved on the wooden statue seemed portentous, and Leo wanted to properly investigate it. He came up with a plan of action. When he had telephoned Fordyce earlier, his friend had happened to mention that he intended to set off tomorrow for a few days of fishing at Loch Dhonn in Argyllshire. His route from Galloway would take him through Glasgow, and perhaps Fordyce would be willing to spend a day there with Leo to help him with his research. Leo wanted to tap into the man's cryptographic mind, and indeed Fordyce might help him view the entire investigation through a wider aperture. Leo had been glad of his friend's input at Loch Dhonn two and a half years ago when he broke a runic cipher during the hunt for the killer of a young nurse by the name of Helen Addison, and he was also invaluable in helping him decode an esoteric symbol during a mystery at Biggnarbriggs the previous summer. Perhaps they would even take advantage of the largest public reference library in Europe, the Mitchell. A visit to Glasgow would also provide Leo with the opportunity to try and connect with Edith Prichard, the widow of the archaeologist who had abandoned his dig at Glen Colm in 1982. Leo walked to the telephone box to put his proposal to Fordyce, who readily agreed to it, and returned to the flat to pack his essentials. He then cooked himself a plain dinner of tinned Irish stew, tinned vegetables and potatoes, washed the dishes and drove to Kilmichael to catch the last ferry to the mainland.

Leo climbed the stairs to the upper deck to take in the view of the evening sun on the firth as the vessel cleaved the calm waters. He noticed three male passengers there who possessed various versions of the lamented Vincent's features. They were big fighting men, and a gold crucifix dangled from the neck of the scariest-looking one, but he didn't look like the merciful type. This fellow was gripping the safety rail and Leo noticed that his knuckles were raw. The Comiskey brothers would doubtless return to Sonna, to try and extract information from the wrong people and mete out their wild justice.

A horrible realisation suddenly descended on Leo.

Troughton hadn't been at Mass that morning. Leo had assumed that he had been suffering from a hangover, but what if he had been paid a visit by these hoods and was caught unawares? After all, he was the proprietor of *The Belmartine Repository* and had reopened the investigations into Andy Lamb's death, a fatality which some had suspected Vincent had been responsible for. The Comiskeys might have mistakenly believed that Troughton had stoked up murderous rage against their brother or even been a party to the crime. Leo now cursed himself for not having returned to the Palmery as soon as he knew that the Comiskey crew were on the island – how could he not have realised the danger? He withdrew his mobile phone and called Troughton, thanking God when he picked up.

'Troughton – I just wondered how you were?'

'Well enough.'

'It's just that I didn't see you at Mass this morning.'

'I overslept. I must confess that I overindulged a tad last night.'

The slight slur in Troughton's voice betrayed that he had already begun imbibing the hair of the dog that had bitten him.

'You haven't been aware of any toughs hanging around?'

'No. Why do you ask?'

'Vincent's three brothers were on Sonna. I saw them surveying Norris' home yesterday and they roughed up Johnathon this morning. Anyway, they are on their way back to Glasgow now. But I'll wager they will return, so stay alert.'

'You are forgetting I have my friends to protect me.'

'What friends?'

'The Smith and Wesson. The Colt .45. I might even rig up the Vickers gun on the balcony. It would give me a grand line of fire over the driveway.'

'For God's sake, Troughton, you can't start shooting the place up – you'll end up dead or in Barlinnie!'

'Be careful, Moran. I might start thinking that you actually give a damn about my wellbeing,' said Troughton, before hanging up.

The Secret of the Weird Rune

LEO was glad to sleep in his own bed after the lumpy affair at Ardcaden Bay. Once he had prepared for the day, he stood within the bow window of his sumptuous West End apartment and gazed down at the pink granite bridge which was bathed in morning sunshine. He telephoned Ronnie MacKellar and was pleasantly surprised that the copper took the call.

'It's the ogre-in-the-attic man,' he said sardonically. 'What is it now, Leo – a ghoul in the cellar? The bogeyman in the lavvy?'

'I travelled back to Glasgow last night. Just to make you aware, the Comiskeys were on the last ferry.'

'We know.'

'Can I level with you? I'm a bit apprehensive they might return and have a go at Troughton, what with him being *The Repository's* proprietor. Or someone else, for that matter.'

'I shouldn't worry – we have taken steps. The staff at both ferry terminals on the mainland have been given strict instructions to alert us immediately if the brothers turn up. They've been given names, photos, number plates. And if the Comiskeys do return to Sonna, we'll put a close tail on them this time.'

Leo, his concern for Troughton having been assuaged, set off in the Humber to visit his mother at the sheltered housing complex where she resided, in order to assuage her concerns regarding his latest adventures. His next port of call was the address of the late archaeologist WG Prichard. It was a magnificent red-stone mansion flat in Dowanhill. He hoped to gain admittance to its doubtless stunning interior, in order that his aesthetic as well as his detective's nosiness might be indulged. Leo walked up the box hedge-lined path and hovered for a moment at the dark-wood and leaded-glass door, trying to figure out what to say into the intercom.

'Can I help you?' came a female English voice from behind him.

Leo turned to see an elderly lady carrying a bulging cotton Waitrose bag.

'I beg your pardon, madam – I am trying to make contact with a Mrs Prichard.'

'I am she,' said the lady a little suspiciously.

'I am sorry to bother you. My name is Leo Moran, I am a private detective, currently employed by a journal on the Isle of Sonna.'

'Are you investigating the murder down there a few days ago? I heard about it on the radio.'

'My inquiries are connected to that case, yes. I believe your late husband conducted a survey on the island in 1982, which was abandoned at short notice. I wonder if you remember anything about that?'

'I certainly do. Will took part in numerous digs, and that was the only one he never completed.'

'What happened?'

'I simply don't know. When he arrived home, earlier than expected, he was a nervous wreck, and he just point-blank refused to discuss the matter with me. Which was unusual because we didn't really have secrets in our marriage. I don't believe he ever gave the university a proper explanation as to why the excavation wasn't concluded.'

'Is there anything else you might recall that could be of relevance?'

'Not really. Only that he became a bit depressed and fretful for a while, unwilling to leave the house. Fortunately, it wasn't term-time so he didn't miss any work. The most curious thing was that he began coming with me to the Episcopal church on Hyndland Road, even though up until then he had been the most nominal of Anglicans. I am certain that his religious revival was linked to whatever happened to him on Sonna. Anyway, he was back to his old self soon enough, but he never gave up on his church attendance and he never returned to that island.'

'Was anyone with him during the survey?'

'No. A PhD student was scheduled to assist him but he'd pulled out sick beforehand with glandular fever or something. Will had to camp out by the dig site at night, alone. I've always been convinced that something spooked or upset him.'

Leo drove through the university and stopped by an Italian delicatessen on Eldon Street to pick up a few items for an easy luncheon with Fordyce. He bought bread, ricotta cheese, tomatoes, basil, garlic and olive oil for a simple bruschetta antipasto, as well as two portions of prawn and baccala cannelloni, several slices of prosciutto and a bottle of good Vernaccia. He then drove up Park Road and along Great Western Road, and hung a right up Kirklee Road and back over the Kelvin to his home in Spring Gardens, the leafy West End looking resplendent in the sunshine.

Leo prepared the dining room, the light streaming through the window and resting upon his bookcase, his William IV mahogany table and his Georgian maple sideboard. He looked out to see Fordyce's antique Rolls-Royce draw up sedately across the road, and jogged excitedly down the stairs to greet his friend at the security door. Fordyce was wearing a white shirt with a pink cravat. The men embraced in the Russian style and carried the luggage up to the apartment. Leo showed Fordyce into the guest bedroom where he had changed the sheets and laid out fresh towels. They then sat down to eat, Leo savouring Fordyce's tender company in the wake of the minefield of Troughton's. He gave a summary of his investigations on Sonna while Fordyce listened in silence, digesting the details. Leo concluded with the subject of the weird symbol from his vision which he had seen in Crochadh House. He placed his sketch of it upon the Irish linen tablecloth. 'Any ideas?' he asked.

Fordyce considered the drawing for a few moments, then said, 'I'm afraid I don't know what it is specifically, old stick. But it looks like some sort of rune.'

At Leo's request, Fordyce had brought a couple of volumes with him from the library at Biggnarbriggs Hall which the pair had consulted during their adventures the previous summer, but they couldn't find a match for the symbol in either of them.

'It seems as though we will have to visit the Mitchell,' said Leo.

'How about a game of chess first, to let these matters percolate within the old grey matter?' suggested Fordyce. 'Then we can head to the library.'

'Capital idea.'

It was too lovely a day to be cooped up inside, so Leo proposed that they walk to a tea house he patronised from time to time which had a garden, and placed his Staunton chess set, his notebook and the sketch into a satchel. A path by the River Kelvin would take them most of the way, and Fordyce was entranced by this route which provided him with new perspectives of the area. It revealed nooks and crannies of heavy stonework and lush vegetation. Cyclists tringed their little bells to warn of their approach as all the while the water flowed gracefully towards the Clyde and the sun winked through the late-summer canopy.

The tea house was an eccentric little establishment near the end of a ramshackle row down a cobbled lane which terminated high above the Kelvin. They took a table which was shaded by an ash tree festooned with colourful ribbons and lanterns. They ordered a pot of Ceylon and some ginger thins. Fordyce asked to see the sketch again and regarded it while Leo set up the board.

'Certain followers of Germanic Neopaganism have adapted ancient runic alphabets,' said Fordyce. 'And the Nazis adopted runes for their own purposes – such as the Algiz rune, to symbolise life.'

Leo opted for a Ruy Lopez opening and the contest lurched into a rapid war of attrition. When they reached the endgame, the board was sparsely populated, Leo with the advantage. He had a bishop and a rook eyeing from afar Fordyce's black fortress – his king and a rook hiding behind a rampart of three pawns in the top-right corner. The stronghold made Leo think of Crochadh House, the king Dr Morgenthaler, the blunt bludgeon of the rook his giant enforcer brother. Leo tried to visualise the chess attack pattern Morphy's Mate and realised that he would have to raid enemy territory boldly in order to break the siege. This would mean risking his rook – perhaps a metaphor for his own destiny in the coming endgame on Sonna, with his bishop initially only operating in a support role – perhaps signifying the role of his allies or the authorities. Hopefully not.

Fordyce broke the silence: 'Old stick, the evidence indeed seems to point to the Morgenthaler brothers being responsible for Vincent Comiskey's death.'

'Agreed.'

'Furthermore, it sounds to me that this Tristan character must have been out roaming the countryside on the fateful night in 1989. He either frightened or drove Andy Lamb over that drop to his death.'

'We must keep an open mind.'

'You are saying that you suspect something else might have befallen young Lamb?'

'I am saying only that we must keep an open mind,' said Leo, before advancing his rook to smash a pawn and send the black king scurrying into the extreme-top corner square. He moved the rook left to take that pawn and face off against its black counterpart; the king returned to G8. Leo moved his rook to again threaten the king from G7 and again the king scuttled to H8. He withdrew his rook from the fray and Fordyce advanced his rook two squares to block Leo's menacing bishop, but it was too late: bishop takes rook, checkmate. Fordyce shook Leo's hand graciously.

At that moment, old Arnstein arrived, accompanied by an even more elderly man who hobbled with the aid of a stick. Leo was endeared by the fact that the two gents were from a generation that still wore neckties de rigueur. Arnstein had his worn chess board folded under his arm, an item familiar to Leo as the stage of many a battle. Leo rose to greet his friend, and the stranger was introduced as Rabbi Cohen. His accent had a European undertone, and he had a ragged grey beard and a face like Methuselah, and seemed to be struggling in the heat. Arnstein was delighted to meet Fordyce, about whom he had heard so much.

'I would ask you gentlemen to join us,' said Leo, 'but we are just leaving.'

The men made small talk, Arnstein informing his companion that Leo was a regular Philip Marlowe. But Rabbi Cohen seemed distracted, staring at the sketch which was still lying upon the table.

'This symbol – why do you have it?' he asked a little abruptly.

'It relates to my latest case – I saw it in the home of two suspects. We are just about to leave for the Mitchell Library to see if we can identify it.'

'I have seen it before,' began the rabbi. 'In Munich, in 1945, just after the Shoah had ended. I will sit down for a moment,' he said as he drew up a chair and the other men followed suit. 'Europe was in chaos, it was as though all humanity was in flux. The roads were crammed with people: victorious Allied soldiers, demobilised German soldiers, men freed from POW camps, liberated foreign labourers, people who had come out of hiding. There were people who had made a dash for the West to avoid living under communist tyranny, and people desperately trying to find any of their kin who might still be alive. And there were people who had survived the concentration camps, in my case latterly a slave-labour sub camp at Dachau. I had no desire to remain in Germany, the country of my birth, the country my father had given his left leg for in 1918 and which then murdered him and all of my other immediate family. I had an uncle who had moved to Britain in 1934 and I managed to gain citizenship through him. Anyway, this symbol – I saw it daubed alongside swastikas on walls in Munich. It is a Nazi symbol.'

'That would chime with what I speculated about it,' chipped in Fordyce. 'That the Nazis were apt to adopt Nordic runes.'

Leo took a few seconds to digest all of this, then said, 'As it happens, my suspects, who are brothers, possess a German surname. They also have foreign accents and one of them spoke German to me. Furthermore, I believe they lived in South America, which is where many Nazi war criminals escaped to using the ratlines, although my men would not be old enough to have been involved in the war.'

'Indeed. Some, like Eichmann, were brought to justice. Many others, most notably Mengele, lived out peaceful lives there,' said Rabbi Cohen. 'They were sheltered by German diaspora in various Latin American countries. Abortive attempts were made to capture Mengele, but he drowned while swimming off the coast of Brazil in 1979.'

While the rabbi was speaking, the colour had drained from Leo's face. 'Mengele,' he gasped. 'Josef Mengele, the infamous Auschwitz physician. He was known as the Angel of Death, wasn't he?'

'Yes.'

'One of my suspects said that his brother "served the Angel of Death".'

'Perhaps he helped him evade justice,' suggested Arnstein. 'Perhaps he himself is a neo-Nazi.'

'Mengele decided the fate of hundreds of thousands of new arrivals at Auschwitz,' said Rabbi Cohen. 'With a blithe wave of his hand he decreed who went into slavery and who went to the gas chambers. It was said he enjoyed the task. Often, he went to the ramp during his time off, for his own amusement or to select subjects for his scientific research. Mengele claimed in his writings that he was simply doing his duty, but that doesn't account for his cruelty. He committed bizarre medical experiments on live subjects, without anaesthetic – he treated those poor souls worse than animals. He had a particularly obscure fixation with twins.'

'The heavens ought to have darkened for his beastliness,' interjected Arnstein mournfully.

'It was Mengele's sheer arrogance that struck those who interacted with him,' continued the rabbi, 'and how much he relished his status at the camp. He was completely drunk on power, which was unfettered – he could do exactly what he pleased to people. He became utterly oblivious to their humanity, but an orchestrated demonisation of a particular group does that to people. Nazism did that to people. Jew hatred does that to people. And Jew hatred is flourishing again, Leo. What we experienced in the camps was so incredible that we were terrified that, should we survive, the world simply wouldn't believe our testimonies. And the number of folk today who refute the death toll or try to reframe what happened or deny that the Shoah even occurred at all, is on the rise.'

'When you are finished up at the library, drop by my shop,' said Arnstein. The old man owned a bookstore which was located not far from the tea house. 'I have some obscure Nazi publications which might illuminate you – although they are not for sale.' He laughed darkly. 'An old Jew with Nazi writings – whatever must you think of me! Yet over the years I came across them and bought them, partly to get them out of circulation, partly in an attempt to get to know my enemy, and partly to try to comprehend what the hell happened to my people, and to the world, back then.'

Leo and Fordyce rose to leave.

'Shalom, rabbi. It was an honour to meet you,' said Leo, shaking the old man's hand.

'It was my pleasure meeting you, Leo. This man you speak of – if he helped Mengele, he broke international law and therefore he must be brought to justice. And remember this: you don't deal with the devil by trying to reason with him. You can't reach out to him or make friends with him. If you are sympathetic to the hateful, they will still hate you. And worse, they will no longer fear you.'

Leo and Fordyce cut through Kelvingrove Park towards the Mitchell. There was a cheerful ambience abroad. Charcoal smoke scrolled from where young people had lit barbecues and boys kicked footballs as they walked home from school. The golden Gothic tower of the university and the Spanish cupolas of the art gallery looked superb in the afternoon light. Yet the men were largely silent as they walked, sobered by their conversation about the greatest crime in human history, and its apparent pertinence to Leo's current case.

'Vincent's murder now makes perfect sense,' said Leo as they passed the Stewart Memorial fountain. 'Dr Morgenthaler would have ordered it because he had discovered the existence of his brother, and therefore felt that his secret – that he aided Mengele and God knows who else – was compromised.'

They entered the library through its magnificent rear façade, which was a remnant of the Saint Andrew's Halls which had burned down in 1962. It was designed by James Sellars, the Greek Ionic fluted columns augmented by stunning sculptures by John and William Mossman.

The men took the lift to the fourth floor and installed themselves at a table by the shelves relevant to the Second World War and Nazism. Fordyce was efficient at perusing the publications, separating the wheat from the chaff at great speed. Within half an hour he had cracked the rune, while browsing a book about Nazi symbolism. The men had to calm themselves lest their enthusiasm disturb the other readers. It was derived from the *Wolfsangel*, a medieval German heraldic device. It was adopted by the Nazi Party, notably as the emblem for *Werwolf*, which was a plan to resist Allied occupation devised by the regime once they had realised that the war was lost. The ill-conceived project was doomed, but certain assassinations and acts of sabotage were carried out in its name.

Leo surmised: 'Therefore, Dr Morgenthaler placed this symbol on display in his home to honour his continuation of the Nazi cause.'

Leo struck the next nugget as he was perusing *The Hunt for the Devil* by one Jonah Goldberg, which documented Mossad and private Nazi hunters' attempts to track down Mengele after the war. In the plates section was a photograph of five men taken in Brazil during the mid-1970s. None of them were Mengele, but according to the key two were former middle-ranking Nazis. They had all lived in a large German ranch in the State of São Paulo in which they were believed to have given Mengele sanctuary for a short period towards the end of 1974. Leo clutched Fordyce's arm as he exclaimed that one of the men was a young Dr Morgenthaler. When his awe had subsided, he pointed out that he had the same pronounced nose, jaw and chin. However, he was named only by a sobriquet, 'Fenrir'. Fordyce whispered that Fenrir was a wolf monster in Norse mythology. The index led them to a brief passage about this shadowy figure, whose identity was not known beyond his codename. Intriguingly, he was believed to be fascinated by Nazi occultism, and conducted equinox festivals for the German expats in the area. This factoid made Leo think of the demon-in-the-hill legend, and he proposed to Fordyce that Morgenthaler might possess some specific interest in it.

An internet search didn't bring up any entries relating to this Fenrir character, so the men turned their attention to the subject of the occult in Nazism. They read about the influence upon the Nazis of Ariosophy, Norse mythology and the teachings of völkisch groups such as the Thule Society. They learned about how the Third Reich claimed that the Germanic tribes were descended from the submerged civilisation of Atlantis. They dipped into SS Reichsführer Heinrich Himmler's creepy obsession with witchcraft and Arthurian legends. They flicked through books such as *The Occult Roots of Nazism* by Nicholas Goodrick-Clarke, *The Morning of the Magicians* by Louis Pauwels and Jacques Bergier, and a couple of volumes by the Austrian pagan Guido von List. Leo held his nose and scanned notorious Catholic-baiter Alfred Rosenberg's 1930 diatribe *The Myth of the Twentieth Century*, which laid out the Nazis' outlandish theories of race mysticism. But the books and another internet search bequeathed nothing that related to the Nazis' interest in a folk phenomenon like that of Sonna's demon piper. They decided to take up old Arnstein's offer of a perusal of his private collection. Before leaving, they photocopied their findings about the symbol and the young Dr Morgenthaler in Brazil.

It was a picturesque building known as a cottage ornée, one of the oldest structures in Hillhead, built the year after Victoria took to the throne. It was an anomaly, a sole survivor of a handful of villas constructed alongside the Kelvin before the nearby warehouses and tenements went up. The rear of the house widened and had an additional two lower floors, and its sagging, tumbledown impression meant it sprawled as though it had developed organically to cling to the land which dipped steeply towards the river. It was surrounded by a narrow jungle of trees and vegetation, and abutted the crumbling gable of a tall, long row of yellow-sandstone tenements. To this gable was fastened a streetlamp housed in an elegant sconce of curved wrought iron. To Leo, the anachronism was somehow emblematic of Arnstein, as though instead of being a mere quirk it had been commissioned by the man, or left extant by the city in honour of the resident's eccentricity. The faded paintwork on the tall wooden gate spelled out 'Arnstein's Trove of Books' in an arching, cursive script. Leo opened it and the men walked up the short path and entered the establishment, Fordyce noting with interest the mezuzah attached to the doorpost. A recording of a piano piece by Nikolai Tcherepnin was playing quietly. Leo knew from countless afternoons spent exploring the shop's inner doors and staircases that it possessed room after room of dusty second-hand books, often stacked high in chaotic piles. There was indeed no apparent order or classification, but the elderly proprietor possessed a mental inventory of the location of every item of stock. Arnstein, who had heard his visitors enter, removed the needle from the Tcherepnin record and emerged from the back shop to greet them. Leo explained about Dr Morgenthaler's interest in Nazi occultism, and the bookseller stated that a couple of the books he possessed were concerned with that very topic. Arnstein eked out his solitary domestic life between the top floor of the building, and, to the rear of the ground level, a kitchenette with an elderly water heater and a gloomy little dining room. He showed the men into the latter chamber and bid they be seated at a polished antique table. He withdrew a bottle of Russian Stolichnaya vodka from a sideboard which had an ornate menorah and a nice framed photograph of Arnstein's late wife upon it, and three cut-crystal shot glasses. He filled them and passed them round, and then toasted his guests' health: '*Vashe zdorovie!*'

The men necked the vodka, and after Arnstein had replenished the glasses he disappeared for a minute or so. He returned carrying a cardboard box which he placed on the table.

'My unholiest of unholies,' said the old man before knocking back his second vodka with a gasp. 'I shall leave you gentlemen to process their vile innards. Feel free to keep anything that might help with your endeavours.'

Leo and Fordyce sifted through the box's contents, many of which were post-war self-publications with poor production values and printed on cheap paper stock, some featuring obscene caricatures of Jews on their covers. They found the two Nazi occult books, one of which was filled with the fevered ramblings of some basement dweller from 1980s Belfast. The other was a bad translation of a 1930s offering by one Ottmar Glauber, entitled: *Bergentrückung and National Revival.* A note inside explained that *Bergentrückung* literally means 'Mountain Rapture', although the term was usually translated into English from the German as 'King in the Mountain'. Leo began skim-reading the book and reciting any passages of interest to Fordyce.

The oddball author expounded his interest in hero-under-mountain myths, which were not uncommon across Europe. Glauber believed that the National Socialist movement could channel the power of these mystical beings by gaining their favour. There was even an invocation spell, which Leo quickly realised had been adapted from Crowley's *Liber Advocabit Oreas*, with certain völkisch claptrap appended to it. The intrepid Herr Glauber had evidently done his research thoroughly, and in a typically crackpot Nazi sub-project had travelled extensively throughout the continent to visit as many of the sites of such legends as possible, including, notably, a lonely hill in the south of the Isle of Sonna in the Firth of Clyde.

'By Jove – we've hit the jackpot!' exclaimed Fordyce.

'Providence has brought us to this bookshop today,' declared Leo.

'What if Morgenthaler had read this book – perhaps in the original German, and so decided to move to Sonna, in order to revere the piper and try to invoke his power?' proposed Fordyce.

'My thoughts exactly,' said Leo.

Glauber detailed certain astronomical occurrences when

the connection with hill spirits was at its strongest. Arnstein came in to refill the men's shot glasses, and Leo took the opportunity to request from him a look at an almanac for the current year. A short time later the old man returned with one and then departed again. After a quick consultation, Leo announced excitedly: 'Fordyce, tomorrow night is one such celestial event – Neptune will be at Opposition, that is to say in perfect line with the sun and the earth.'

'I say, old stick, this Morgenthaler fellow will know that you have discovered his brother,' said Fordyce. 'He will be gunning for you. If you are planning on attending the ceremonial site tomorrow night, then I shall accompany you, bearing a stout staff, in case things turn ugly.'

'There's no need for that, thank you anyway, Fordyce,' said Leo as he tucked Arnstein's book into his satchel. 'Because the first thing I am going to do when I arrive on Sonna tomorrow is to report all of our discoveries to the police. They can take it from there. Now, we can be proud of our efforts today. And as a thank-you for your vital assistance, I am now going to treat you to a few pre-prandial drinkies followed by a spot of supper.'

Apotheosis

LEO stood on the upper deck of the ferry as she plied her merry way towards Kilmichael. It was a beautiful morning, the sky clear but for some peripheral cloud. It had felt good, seeing people he loved: his mother, Fordyce and old Arnstein. After they had completed their research, Leo and Fordyce had imbibed several drinks at the Belle in Great Western Road, then partaken of supper at a place in Queen Margaret Drive – accompanied by a good deal of wine, then enjoyed a nightcap at Leo's flat. Consequently, Leo had a headache, but it could not spoil the sense of satisfaction he felt at cracking the case. From now on, the good people of Sonna would sleep peacefully in their beds, he mused. He rehearsed the presentation of his findings one last time.

After the vessel docked, Leo drove the short distance to the police station, went inside and asked to speak with Ronnie MacKellar. He was again directed to the rear office, where he found the sergeant on the telephone to his superior. He gestured for Leo to take a seat.

'The wanderer returns. What gives, Leo Moran?' said Ronnie after he had replaced the receiver.

'First off, have the Comiskey brothers come back?'

'No.'

'Where are the CID bods? I noticed their office was empty.'

'They're on the mainland today.'

'Are they still fixated on Nicky, Johnathon and Norris as their suspects?'

'Those remain our main lines of inquiry.'

'Then I am about to disabuse you of your notions,' said Leo, a little more grandly than he had intended.

He expatiated on his discoveries in Glasgow, placing them within the context of his theories and his wider investigations on Sonna. At the appropriate moment, he theatrically slammed the photostat of the relevant page from the book about Nazi symbolism upon Ronnie's desk.

'I put it to you, Sergeant, that the symbol carved on the wooden figure in Crochadh House represents Dr Morgenthaler's continuation of the Nazi cause.'

'The statue that wasn't there when I attended?' said Ronnie dryly.

Leo faltered momentarily, then held forth on Ottmar Glauber's *Bergentrückung and National Revival*, which he also placed on the desk. He drew Ronnie's attention to the passages about the Cathair legend, but realised with dread that the policeman's eyes had begun to glaze over. However, there remained his *pièce de résistance*: the photostat of the pages from *The Hunt for the Devil* by Jonah Goldberg. He first began relating Josef Mengele's crimes against humanity and subsequent escape to exile.

'I know who Mengele was – we're not all uneducated bumpkins down here,' interrupted Ronnie testily.

'*Et voilà* – our man Dr Morgenthaler was a member of a German community who aided this beast,' said Leo, as he presented the photograph of the five Nazis taken in Brazil during the mid-1970s.

Ronnie peered at the image for a few seconds, then said: 'Which one is supposed to be Morgenthaler?'

'Why *that* one, of course,' said Leo, pointing out Fenrir.

'It *might* be him, I suppose,' said Ronnie, before picking up the telephone receiver and requesting that the duty officer at the front desk come through.

Ronnie explained Leo's premise to the man, a special constable in his mid-thirties with thinning auburn hair. He examined the picture and then said, 'I'm not so sure it's him.'

'Why of *course* it is he!' insisted Leo pleadingly. 'Hang it all, look at the jawline, the deep eye sockets ... Sergeant, there is a man living on your island who aided and abetted one of the most wicked human beings ever to have walked this earth. Tristan Morgenthaler told me that his brother had "served the Angel of Death", and Vincent was killed because that secret was threatened.'

'Leo, have you any idea how fantastical the words you have just said to me are?' said Ronnie gravely, nodding at the constable to take his leave.

'I am in deadly earnest. According to the Glauber book, tonight is a special cosmic date, when the connection with spirits such as the demon piper are strongest. There's a good chance Morgenthaler will be by the Cathair later, undertaking an incantation. Now I charge you to take action.'

'Oh, what is all this, Leo?' snapped Ronnie. 'Since you arrived on Sonna, I've had you trespass on private property on more than one occasion, have me be accessory to your housebreaking, imagine that you've been shot at, hallucinate about having drinks with a resuscitated Gus Blessing, and come across an ogre and a statue which mysteriously vanished into thin air. And now you want me to believe that a private citizen who lives peacefully in the arse end of nowhere collaborated with the camp doctor at Auschwitz! Do not go near that man's house again, or I will arrest you.'

Leo, speechless, marched out of the station, his mood

fouled. He hadn't anticipated the police taking such a dim view of his rationale. He was consoled that he had at least packed his suitcase with essential items for the eventuality that he was required to remain on Sonna a while longer.

Presently, he heard the iconic four-note phrase from Beethoven's Fifth Symphony's *Allegro con brio* inform him that a text message had arrived. It was from Fordyce: 'All in hand, old stick?'

'Tickety-boo,' he lied in reply, not wishing to perturb his friend with his planned activity for that night. Right now, he needed to see a friendly face.

Leo parked at Fagr Vágr and found Amy in her workshop to the rear of the house. She was wearing overalls and had her hair tied up in a scarf like a wartime armaments factory worker. Leo praised the artistic flourishes she was applying to a racing dinghy. 'I took the liberty of nipping into the bakery in Kilmichael, in case you were in need of luncheon,' he added as he held up a paper bag.

They sat at the garden table, eating the savoury cheese sandwiches Leo had brought as Amy updated him on Nicky Barrett's status.

'He rang me yesterday. Nicky can be a pain in the bum, but I felt sorry for him. The police interrogated him relentlessly after the murder, plus he's petrified that Vincent's brothers are going to take some unjust revenge on him. They've been seen on the island.'

'Yes, I know.'

'Therefore, he has sent his wife away to Erran and he has been living on his yacht, too terrified to step onto dry land. Anyway, he's sailing it round to my mooring later. He's decided to rename it and he wants me to do the paint job. What's new with you, Leo?'

Leo sighed, and then launched into a lengthy monologue

about his latest findings and theories, and about his dismay at Ronnie's rejection of them. He concluded by mentioning the fact that there would occur tonight an astronomical phenomenon which might draw Morgenthaler and, perhaps, his ogreish brother into the open.

'You aren't thinking of wandering around the south end in the middle of the night, are you?' asked Amy. Leo was silent. 'I beg you, Leo, don't. It's not safe. Leave it to the cops.'

'I told you, the police don't buy my ideas.'

'Please don't go, Leo.'

'I'll think about it.'

'You won't think about it – I can tell you are set on going. At least let me accompany you.'

'Out of the question. Listen, Amy, I will be perfectly safe. I shall park above Manach Bay and head inland at dusk. There's a fir grove in which I can conceal myself, which I believe commands a view down Glen Colm, where any ceremony would be held.'

'I know that grove.'

'Nobody will be able to see me, and anyway, there's every chance nothing will unfold. But if it does, I will hopefully be near enough to video any occult high jinks. That would surely pique Ronnie MacKellar's interest.'

Amy gazed at Leo admiringly, then said, 'Do you know what your friend Stephanie told me about you? She said that you are a genteel man, a man of great culture and refinement, and that people are often misled by that, because you actually also possess immense physical courage. She said you have placed yourself in dangerous situations that most men would baulk at, in the cause of doing right.'

'Shucks, kid, you'll make me blush,' said Leo. *Good old Steph*, he thought, but also, he regretted having divulged to Amy his intentions for that night. He had worried her unnecessarily.

Leo drove to Ardcaden Bay, dropping by the post office to buy fresh milk and some sweets. When he entered his rented flat, he had a sense that the landlady had been snooping around during his absence. He had the afternoon to kill, so he did something he hadn't done in years. He walked round to a deserted stretch of beach, disrobed to his underwear and swam in the sea. It was a cathartic and invigorating experience, and on his return home the volatile immerser behaved itself and bequeathed him enough hot water for a comfortable long soak. He took a nap and then cooked a plain dinner of pea and ham soup, followed by a hunk of corned beef served with potatoes and tinned vegetables, and for dessert treacle sponge pudding and custard. After he had done the washing up, he prepared for his nocturnal manoeuvres. He placed a lambswool jersey, his detective's kit, his aluminium water flask and his notebook into his knapsack. He changed into his walking shoes, tweed trousers and tweed sports jacket, and placed his deerstalker on his head. He knelt and prayed that his endeavour would be successful and pass off safely, then departed.

The late evening sky was coral pink, and the strange landscape around the Lagg Road was rendered in a soft warm grey as eternal ranks of breakers rolled in languidly from the sound. Leo sang 'The Battle Hymn of the Republic' as he motored, to stir his courage. He parked on a verge above Manach Bay, scaled a fence and followed the bank of a burn inland. He gave some lumbering cattle a wide berth and had to carefully negotiate a barbed-wire perimeter before he reached the fir grove. The ground trended upwards, the dying sunlight slanting gorgeously to illuminate the fragrant understory. Vincent had been right to describe this as a beautiful place. Leo installed himself before a wire fence at the woods' extremity. Night fell, and he chomped on a Fry's Orange Cream for sustenance as he battled legions of midges. The waning gibbous moon and a diadem of stars lit the countryside quite well. All was perfectly, deceptively at peace.

Leo soon discerned a figure coming down the western hillside carrying a powerful electric lantern and a large bundle, who by his gaunt frame he believed to be Dr Morgenthaler. Leo began videoing the proceedings with his phone. When he reached the floor of the glen, Morgenthaler prepared and lit a small bonfire, and planted some species of standard, perhaps a Nazi banner, in the sod. Leo thought he saw the man give a straight-armed salute before busying himself with his weird rites. The bonfire was not far from where the Herons had held their ritual, and about four hundred yards from Leo's vantage. He realised that his mobile wasn't recording anything other than a nebulous yellow-orange blur. He adjusted the zoom, a tricky task for his fire-damaged hands, but it didn't do much good, and therefore he decided to steal closer to the action, in order to get a better shot. He made the Sign of the Cross, rolled under the wire fence and began creeping forward, crouching in an effort to hug the contours of the terrain. He squatted behind a knoll and began filming again as puffs of sparks billowed from the bonfire. He wondered where Tristan was. Chained up in his attic, most probably.

At that moment, Leo felt himself being seized from behind and pulled backwards into a bearlike hug, his feet losing contact with the ground, his phone and deerstalker falling into some long grass. Tristan's face was alongside Leo's, the stench of his breath and unwashed body rank. The ogre called upon his brother in German, the volume impossibly loud in Leo's ear. Dr Morgenthaler began sidling towards them, carrying his lantern. When he arrived, Leo realised that he was wearing a replica black SS uniform, complete with a death's-head peaked cap.

'I see you've got the jodhpurs on,' said Leo. Dr Morgenthaler was silent and his features seemed to contain no emotion. 'Poor Vincent. You set it up for your brother to kill him, didn't you?'

'I had to. He had seen Tristan,' said Dr Morgenthaler in a scratchy Germanic accent.

'You were terrified your secret would out. That you helped Mengele.'

'Among other great men.'

And suddenly Leo remembered. He remembered the sinister driver on the motorway in the summer of 1973. And he realised it had been this man, Dr Julius Morgenthaler, the man known as Fenrir among his confederates in South America.

'Ask me,' said Dr Morgenthaler.

'Ask you what?'

'You know what.'

Leo gulped. Then spake: 'What was he like?'

'Unrepentant.'

'*For Christ's sake!*' wept Leo.

'The invocation I was just concluding was for the purpose of your destruction. Yet now we have no need of it.'

Leo tried to struggle free but Tristan's hold was like a vice. And so, it ends, he thought as he let his body go limp. Come in number 51, your time is up. Send in the clowns, I have fought the good fight. Time, gentlemen, please. So, what do you do now? You go down like a man, Glasgow-style. You fix your eye on the enemy and say, 'Do it, you bastard.'

'Crush him, Tristan.'

And so it was that the ogre began constricting Leo to death. He cried out in agony and then felt the air begin to shrink in his lungs, his internal organs straining. His ribs began to pop and as he waited to pass out, he recalled some words of the old man Simeon in the temple in the Gospel of Luke: *At last, all powerful Master, you give leave to your servant to go in peace, according to your promise. For my eyes have seen your salvation which you have prepared for all nations.*

Leo's vision faltered and then there was an intense red light and he fancied he glimpsed to the east the sinister silhouette of a crooked figure from a dream, poised on the brow of the glen, regarding him.

Yet during the light, the deadly embrace abated, and then an oar blade swung its glorious parabola as Nicky Barrett saved Leo Moran and himself.

'Move a muscle and you will get some of the same!' barked Nicky at Dr Morgenthaler as he brandished the paddle.

Leo lay catching his breath where he had been dropped to the ground. He gently surveyed his aching sides with his fingers. Once he had composed himself, he addressed Nicky: 'Thank you for rescuing me. You are a hero.'

'I can't say I've been called that before.'

'Such men are not born, they are made,' uttered Leo.

Amy soon arrived with Davie Heron, who stood guard over the Morgenthalers with a shotgun. Tristan lay prone but breathing, blood seeping from where Nicky had struck him on the head. Amy crouched by Leo, anxiously questioning him as to his wellbeing.

He reassured her, and then gestured towards Tristan and added, 'He was crushing me to death. The *strength* of the man, it was almost unnatural.'

'The police are on their way,' she said. 'I'll ring for an ambulance.'

After Amy had made the call, Leo requested that she

retrieve his mobile, his deerstalker and also his knapsack, which he had left at the fir grove.

Between them, Amy and Nicky explained how they had come to arrive on the scene. Amy had been fretting about Leo's plan to visit the south end that night. She had shared her concerns with Nicky, after she finished painting his yacht at her mooring. He said that to put her mind at rest he would take a look down there at nightfall, but Amy insisted that she accompany him. Therefore, they had eaten dinner together at Fagr Vágr, rowed over to the yacht and set off. The sea was calm but they were delayed by a lack of wind and an engine malfunction by Inchmadden. Eventually they got underway again, hugging the coastline and dropping anchor in Manach Bay. They had come ashore in the rubber dinghy, Nicky bringing with him a wooden paddle and a loaded flare gun 'just in case', and also his night vision monocular. They noticed Leo's Humber Hawk parked on the verge, and headed towards the fir grove with dipped torches. Through the trees they could discern the light from the electric lantern and beyond it the bonfire. When they reached the edge of the wood, they used Nicky's monocular to examine the figures they could see standing at the lantern. They felt sure that the one being restrained by the giant was Leo. Nicky instructed Amy to call the police and run down to the road and fetch help from Inkpot Farm. After she had set off, Nicky heard Leo cry out in pain and was worried that he was being murdered. He decided to risk firing a distress flare near to where the giant was standing in order to disorientate him. He then dashed as fast as he could and struck the stunned brute over the head with the paddle. Leo now realised that he had mistaken the eruption of the pyrotechnic for a mystical luminescence.

Eventually flashlights flickered through the trees. It was Ronnie with his female colleague and a male special constable. Nicky conferred with them for a few moments and Ronnie then began handcuffing Dr Morgenthaler.

'What are you arresting me for?' he demanded.

'Attempted murder of our esteemed Mr Moran, for starters.'

'I never touched him.'

'No, but you incited your brother to kill me,' said Leo. 'And what about inciting the murder of Vincent Comiskey?'

'Prove it,' said Dr Morgenthaler.

Leo fiddled with his phone for a few moments. He then turned the volume up to its maximum level and pressed 'play' on the video function. The audio of his entire conversation with the doctor had been picked up.

'There you go,' said Leo. 'And I'm sure the Israelis will be keen to hear about your exploits in South America.'

Farewell, My Lovely

THE following evening, Leo lay in the men's ward of the Albert Infirmary in Kilmichael, a pretty cottage hospital with a pleasant summerhouse shaded by trees. It was across the road from an open expanse of ground and playing fields known as the Meadows.

Leo had suffered three broken ribs and been prescribed painkillers and rest. He found it sore to move and he had slept through breakfast, foregone luncheon and merely picked at some mashed potato at dinner. In the late morning, Leo had requested a visit from the local priest, and had been shriven, blessed and given the Eucharist, in order to ward off any malediction brought by Dr Morgenthaler's ceremony. The men had also recited the Prayer to Saint Michael together, in Latin. Leo's mobile had then been dropped off by CID after they had lifted the video evidence from it. He had endured a tedious interview with the two detectives, who demanded much and bequeathed nothing in the way of information. Leo was circumspect in keeping his more leftfield theories within his breast. The radio had broadcast the fact that two men had been taken into custody in connection with the recent murder on Sonna, and Leo had telephoned his mother, Stephanie, Fordyce and Troughton to reassure them of his relative wellbeing. Troughton had kindly dropped by to take Leo's flat keys, and driven to Ardcaden Bay to fetch his pyjamas, washbag and a couple of books. He had also gifted Leo a half bottle of Scotch when the matron's back was turned.

Ronnie entered the ward.

'Greetings, Sergeant MacKellar! We'll have no need of public self-flagellation or breast beating ... just a spot of grovelling will suffice.'

'You were right and I was wrong. How are you, Leo?'

'Tender but still perfectly formed. How fareth Caliban? I hope you shackled the creature.'

'We handcuffed him and then it took six strong men to stretcher him to a police van. We brought him here for medical attention. When he regained consciousness, he became distressed and started lashing out. The doctor had to administer a chemical cosh. We put a jacket on him and he has been quite incoherent ever since. I'm no shrink, but I doubt we'll get much meaningful testimony out of him. He's being removed from our cell to a secure hospital on the mainland first thing in the morning. His brother will appear in court in Greenock tomorrow. We fully expect him to be remanded in custody. The Comiskey brothers have been informed that we have our men.'

'I actually feel sorry for Tristan. He was kept chained up like an animal and only allowed out occasionally, after dark.'

'Which is doubtless how the old Cathair legend of the piper came to be resurrected. Folk like the Herons must have glimpsed Tristan at night, and thought they had seen the demon of the hill. Dr Morgenthaler has clammed up, but his writings betray him. We searched Crochadh House this morning and discovered a broad false chimney which led from the attic to a secret cellar. Tristan must have climbed down and hidden in it before you and I paid our visit. His belongings were still concealed there, and also Nazi and occult paraphernalia. There was also the wooden figure with the symbol carved on it which you had seen, and a cleaned hatchet which is probably what was used to kill Vincent Comiskey – it has been sent for forensic analysis. Most incriminating is the doctor's draft memoir, which my colleague Marie, who is fluent in German, has spent the day skimming through. She told me that the Morgenthalers' father had been a fanatical SS officer who fled to Brazil after the war and died there in 1968. Dr Morgenthaler and Tristan are only half-brothers, and they were brought up in a German enclave in Brazil. The community aided Nazi fugitives, and worked for a rebirth of the movement. Absurd as it may sound, Dr Morgenthaler fully expected his memoirs to be published, once the Nazis came to world domination. Tristan was originally a sensitive man who appears to have lost his marbles, probably because he came to be horrified by the Nazis and what they had perpetrated. He underwent quack psychosurgery undertaken by his brother – assisted by one Josef Mengele.'

'The sheer *arrogance* of these men!'

'The surgery, and constant medication, was used to try and keep Tristan subdued, in case he gave away the community's secrets.'

'I wonder how responsible Tristan can have been for his actions, and to what extent he was a victim himself, an automaton weaponised to carry out his brother's will.'

'I am sure the courts will be understanding. The fellow needs treatment, not punishment. Dr Morgenthaler had doubts as to the Aryan credentials of his half-sibling's mother, which is possibly why he saw him as something to be used and maltreated. Anyway, the doctor became interested in Nazi occultism, and scoped out the Cathair in the early 1970s as a potential power source and moved there at the beginning of the 1980s. By the way, there was occult junk at the bonfire, including a German-language version of that

Ottmar Glauber book. The man was completely deluded and believed he could invoke the legendary demon piper to strike down people who had offended him or stumbled across his secrets. Indeed, he laid claim to being responsible for all but one of the so-called mysterious deaths you were investigating for *The Belmartine Repository*, and, would you believe, the passing of Gus Blessing, who he suspected was on to his activities. Which is all preposterous as these deaths were either mere accidents, suicide or by natural causes.'

'In your opinion,' muttered Leo enigmatically.

'But grander still, Morgenthaler thought channelling the demon's power could somehow help foment mayhem in the world which would eventually compel Aryans to unite and take control. He is a fantasist and a megalomaniac – a nonentity waiting for a race war that will never come. The National Socialist reawakening he dreamed of in South America fizzled out, so he picked a myth at a suitably isolated locale, moved here, created his own, new reality, and convinced himself of his ability to commune with a supernatural power that does not exist.'

'Do his writings mention Vincent's murder?'

'Yes. Vincent had indeed innocently mentioned to Morgenthaler that he had seen a face at the attic window of Crochadh. The doctor knew he was due to deliver beer to him and intended invoking the piper to smite him when he came by. But when he got to Glen Colm the night before for that purpose the Herons were already there, performing their appeasement ceremony, which Morgenthaler believed would temporarily deaden the demon's powers. He couldn't take the risk of delaying in case Vincent mentioned having seen Tristan to someone. Therefore, he gave his brother, who had been in a relatively stable mental state, strict instructions about how to despatch him. Morgenthaler would use the threat of withholding rations of beer and fags, which his brother is dependent on, to compel loyal behaviour. By the way, the lab took DNA traces from the cigarette ends you found at the drumlin, which we fully expect to match Tristan's. And they have already matched a photo we took of one of a pair of shoes we found in the secret cellar, which is his size, to the footprint found in the ditch at the murder scene – you can bet your life that shoe will yield Tristan's DNA, too. There was also dusty extra-large clothing and gloves there which are to be tested for possible blood spatter. After Tristan told Dr Morgenthaler about your visit to his attic, you were next in line to have the demon's power brought down upon you. I reckon Tristan was sent out on patrol as the doctor undertook the ceremony, so you were captured anyway.'

'You said he laid claim to being responsible for "all but one" of the mysterious deaths.'

'Yes. Oddly, he doesn't link himself to Andy Lamb's demise. He writes that he didn't have anything against the boy and that he didn't invoke the demon to harm him. He puts the death down to the teenagers dabbling with and provoking powers they had no concept of. He also states explicitly that his brother hadn't been let loose that night, which he was glad of as the teenagers might have spotted him roaming around when they came down the Lagg Road for the dare.'

'What do you think happened to Andy?'

'Perhaps Tristan escaped for a night wander without his brother's knowledge, came across Andy and chased or threw him off that scarp. Perhaps what Vincent saw – the secret he was going to share with you before he was murdered – was in fact Tristan.'

'That's all unlikely – Tristan was kept securely chained up.'

'Perhaps Andy simply got disorientated and died

entirely accidentally.'

'No. Something else befell him.'

'I don't think we will ever know for certain the truth of what happened that night, but tomorrow I shall visit Johnathon Lamb and tell him our theories,' said Ronnie as he stood up to leave. 'Look, Leo, I am sorry I was dismissive of your suspicions about Dr Morgenthaler. I feel rotten that you were placed in danger and got hurt.'

'That's perfectly all right. I knew the risks.'

'The next time you come down to Sonna, look me up and I'll buy you a pint.'

'I shall hold you to that, Ronnie.'

That night, Leo dreamed strange, psychotropic dreams, eventually revisiting a forgotten fragment of his childhood holiday on Sonna in 1973. His beloved late father had bought him a kite and they had flown it at the Meadows. It was bright yellow and red, with an image of an astronaut on it. The dream had felt wonderful, as Leo relived the pure joy of playing with his gentle father.

In the morning, Troughton visited and set up an outmoded device to record Leo's testimony for publication. Leo didn't divulge his every finding or theory, but after the tape had been stopped, he concluded: 'Off the record, Troughton, let me say that I believe Vincent did feel some responsibility for what happened that night in 1989. I believe he saw something in the hills that so terrified him that he turned tail and ran for home. I believe he harboured guilt for not at least trying to warn Andy.' Troughton didn't say anything. He was in a morose mood and seemed distracted. 'You know what, Troughton: I think this story might indeed revive *The Belmartine Repository*. Also, you'll be able to syndicate it to the national media and make a pretty penny.'

'Possibly.'

'What's troubling you, Troughton?'

'Only the way I have treated you these last two weeks. My behaviour revived a deep sin, rooted in our distant university days, which I feel I must now get off my chest.'

'Oh really?'

'You see, I loved Maddi. As a matter of fact, she is the only woman I have ever loved. As you know, she finished with me. I never got over it. She has haunted me ever since. Pathetic, isn't it?'

'I had no idea your feelings were so strong,' said Leo, genuinely moved. 'But I fail to see how that is anything to feel guilty about.'

'What I harbour guilt for is the envy I felt when she took up with you. It was hell on earth, Moran, seeing you two together all the time. Seeing what you had together. That was why I was such a spiteful bastard to you back then. That was why I descended into slackness and folly, and only scraped a 2:2.'

'Such emotions are perfectly human.'

'Worse still is the *relief* I felt when you two broke up, after you became ... ill. Oh, Christ, I am so ashamed saying it aloud! Yet, even then, Maddi wouldn't go out with me again. It was obvious how much she favoured you. She truly loved you. She wasn't interested in a narcissistic waster like me, and who can blame her?'

Leo was silent for a moment, then said, 'Perhaps it is time we both got over her, stopped living on our memories.'

'Do you forgive me for my mean-spirited thoughts and unconscionable behaviour, Moran?'

'Right readily.'

'My ultimate rejection by Maddi served to confirm what I already knew about myself at some primal stratum: that I was unworthy of such ecstasies.'

'Why did you believe that?'

'Truly I have no idea. It is as though I was cursed with it, born with it woven into the very fabric of my consciousness like some wretched original sin. And, as if further proof were needed, now in my middle age all I am left with is a rotting pile and its cellar, well stocked with my fine wines, my demons and the ghosts of the past. I have been brooding upon these matters these last few days, and I have come to the realisation that unconsciously I was keen to get you down to Sonna simply to reconnect with that lost era, as though the experience might somehow be cathartic for me – although instead I reverted to being a bully. The mysterious deaths at the south end were the perfect excuse. For you and I are bound by some peculiar brotherhood, denied as we are the affection of the same cherished Guinevere. So, Leo, will you come and visit me, from time to time?'

'Yes, Marcus. I will.'

Presently, Amy came in and Troughton stood, bowed slightly and took his leave.

'I brought you a box of orange creams – I remember you saying that you liked them,' she said as she sat down. She was wearing a floral-print summer dress and looked lovely.

'Much obliged. Just the thing to restore my appetite.'

'How are you feeling, Leo?'

'On the mend. Thank you for accompanying me in the ambulance the other night. Oh, and thank you for helping to save my life.'

'That's all right. I came to see you yesterday, but you were sleeping.'

'They want to keep me in for another night. My friend Fordyce is going to come down tomorrow and drive me back to Glasgow in my car.'

'Well, I shall miss you.' There was an awkward silence. 'It's hard to believe what those awful men at the south end were into. Rumour has it that the big one killed Andy in 1989.'

Leo declined to comment. Amy then described how two days ago, when she had expressed her fears for the safety of Leo's planned nocturnal expedition, Nicky Barrett had become like a new man, suddenly possessed by an unprecedented energy as though a moment of destiny had descended upon him. Leo then held forth on the nature of courage and redemption, but in truth their conversation was unusually stilted. After a while, Amy stood, leaned over and kissed Leo on the cheek. They exchanged goodbyes and she walked to the door. She paused there momentarily, framed by the morning light which gushed through the tall windows, fleetingly daring herself to say something, or daring Leo to say something. Then she raised her head and left, the sound of her clicking heels in the corridor retreating to nothing.

Leo thought of what Nicky had told him about how he used to suffer whenever Janey departed Ardcaden Bay at the end of the summer. But Leo did not grieve for Amy, because he knew that eventually and in ways which were for now veiled and which were so sublime as to be beyond imagining, all is renewed and all is reborn and all will be resurrected and exalted, but in true essence, in perfection and in radiance. Even an obscure holiday moment from the summer of 1973 which flickers in memory's eye the way a child's colourful kite rides the breeze, and, perhaps, even the soul of a person who helped the devil himself evade the justice of men and then lived in a remote, shadowy old house on the Isle of Sonna.

ACKNOWLEDGMENTS

I am forever indebted to Martin Greig, Neil White, Alison Rae, Gary Sutherland, Lídia Puccetti and Anne McGarry.

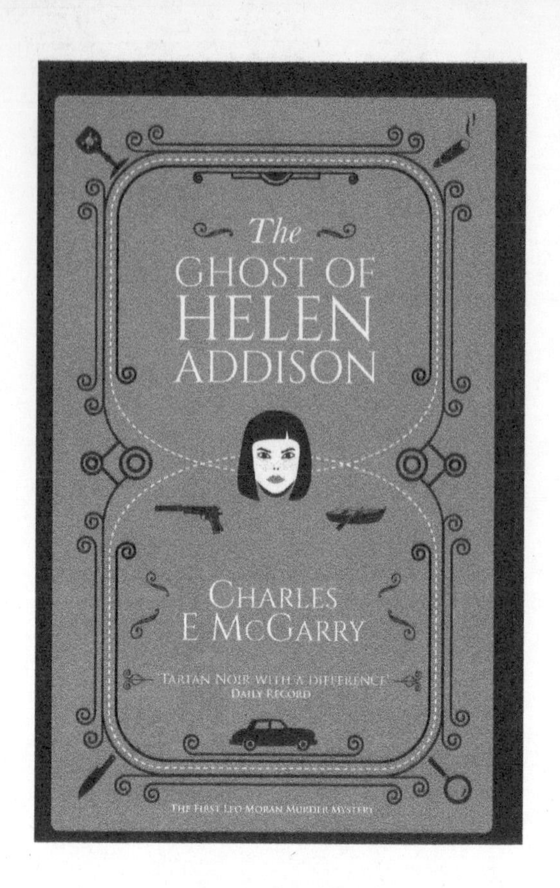

BOOK ONE

Leo Moran – connoisseur, private investigator, seer of visions – sets out from the splendid isolation of his Glasgow apartment to solve the homicide of a young woman at Loch Dhonn in Argyll. He arrives at a brooding, wintry landscape where he encounters a host of coloutful characters, including the spectral murder victim herself. Frustrated by forces of evil summoned up by the killer, Leo fails to make headway, and his pomposity and intemperance test the patience of the police. Close to despair, he must draw on all of his powers to unmask the murderer before he himself becomes the next victim.

BOOK TWO

Haunted by his last case and bereaved by a sudden loss, Leo Moran is invited to spend the summer at Biggnarbriggs Hall, the stately residence of his friend Fordyce Greatorix. He is overjoyed when romance blossoms unexpectedly, but he finds himself plagued by visions after a local girl goes missing, an incident which has chilling echoes of a similar disappearance thirty years previously. As he investigates a host of curious and dubious characters, Leo finds that the very bedrock which surrounds Biggnarbriggs Hall is poisoned by an ancient malevolence that will have its terrible reckoning.

Debut is a podcast series exploring Charles E. McGarry's 14-year journey to the publication of his debut crime novel *The Ghost of Helen Addison*. *Debut: A Crime Writer's Journey from the Bedroom to the Bookshelf* features episodes with two of crimewriting's biggest names, Val McDermid and Chris Brookmyre, and explores what it takes to get a great story into mainstream publishing.

That includes: how Charles ejected out of a well-paid career aged 30 to pursue his ambitions as a writer; how he found a London agent after years of searching, only to lose him in a matter of days; how one rejection note, among dozens of rejection notes, changed everything; and much more.

Neil White, producer of *Debut*, said: 'Charles's is an epic journey which starts with a soul-searching road-trip across Australia and culminates in the publication of his novel. We were captivated by his story and wanted to capture the highs and lows of trying to get published.'

The full six episodes of Debut are available on iTunes, Spotify and all other podcast feeds.

FIND OUT MORE ABOUT THE AUTHOR

www.charlesemcgarry.com

Twitter @CharlesEMcGarry